Peter Canova's novel, The Light of Distant Suns, echoes Edgar Cayce's numerous readings detailing a civilization that surpassed all others before destroying itself. It is an eternal cautionary tale about remaining faithful to the Creative Forces or losing ourselves in selfish pursuits. This compelling book is an incredible weaving of mysticism with high adventure.

—**Kevin J. Todeschi, Executive,**
Director & CEO, the Edgar Cayce Work

A thrilling tour de force of the collective dream we call life. Peter Canova introduces the astounding proposition that we are mind-visitors in the material world, and what we experience in dreams may be glimpses of an underlying reality where our true selves reside.

—**Kelly Sullivan Walden,**
Best Selling Author and Dream Expert

THE FIRST SOULS

Books One and Two of **THE FIRST SOULS TRILOGY—POPE ANNALISA** and **THE THIRTEENTH DISCIPLE**—have won nineteen literary awards including the prestigious Nautilus and Writer's Digest medals. Book One tells the story of a miracle-working African nun who is nearly condemned by the Church as a heretic, yet she actually rises to become pope at the onset of a nuclear conflict between America and Iran. Book two reaches further back in time to relate the tale of the enigmatic Mary Magdalene and the lost feminine mysticism that unleashed the great miracles of the New Testament era.

Each book in the series may be read as a stand-alone, but collectively, the saga of the First Souls is revealed through the critical, formative ages of humanity in the trilogy.

For a fuller comprehension of the First Souls Trilogy, please read **POPE ANNALISA** (popeannalisa.com), and **THE THIRTEENTH DISCIPLE** (thethirteenthdisciple.com) both available through bookstores or on the internet at Amazon and Barnes and Noble in both e-book and paperback form.

THE LIGHT OF DISTANT SUNS

BOOK THREE
OF THE FIRST SOULS TRILOGY

by

PETER CANOVA

Trimountaine Publishing
Palm Beach, Florida

Copy editing by John Paine
Front and rear cover designed by Peter Canova
Interior design by David Moratto
Pope Annalisa model Sheena Williams

ISBN-13: 978-0-9821813-9-3 (hardcover)
ISBN-13: 978-0-9821813-4-8 (paperback)

ACKNOWLEDGMENTS

The author wishes to acknowledge the inspiration from the following sources: the writings of Plato, Rudolph Steiner, the Nag Hammadi Library, and the readings of Edgar Cayce as made available through the Association for Research and Enlightenment (A.R.E).

For more information on the valuable services and information provided by the A.R.E. please refer to the following contact information:

A.R.E
215 67th Street
Virginia Beach, VA 23451
www.edgarcayce.org

THE LIGHT OF DISTANT SUNS

BOOK THREE
OF THE FIRST SOULS TRILOGY

by

PETER CANOVA

Visit **thethirteenthdisciple.com** and **popeannalisa.com**
to learn about the unity between ancient Judeo-Christian
spirituality, quantum physics, and modern depth psychology.

*O*nce I roamed the reaches of the universe in a body of
light. I was all places at all times, for I was filled with the
vision of The One. Now I wander the earth bound in the
form of an animal. Once as spirit I mastered flesh, now flesh
masters me. The memory of my divine origins dims and is replaced
by fables, dreams, and myths. My divine knowledge degenerates into
faith, philosophy, and religion. My mind-power over matter is lost
and is replaced by machines. No longer can I enter and leave the
physical body at will.

Now I die a thousand deaths in the cycle of rebirth. No longer can
I enter the higher realms, for I placed my will before the will of the
Father-Mother God. My vision of the divine has grown dim. Now
I grope my way through the shadow world of matter seeing faintly
as if by the light of distant suns.

—Lament of the First Souls from *The Book of Remembrance*

AUTHOR'S FOREWORD

*"... the educated skepticism of our modern age in the face
of Unseen forces in our midst may not be so much a sign of
our Intellectual advancement as a symptom of our waning
spiritual awareness under the rapid onslaught of materialism."*
—W.H. Church, Story of the Soul

Imagination. How is the human mind capable of envisioning fantastic new things outside the realm of our collective sensory experience? The answer is that *all the things we imagine we have done before*. Imagination is not idle fantasy; it is the subconscious remembrance of things we once achieved in a higher state of being. All art, all scientific advances, and all human innovation pre-exist in our soul memory. *Imagination is the tool we are given to remember our past creations*. It is the grace we're given to lead us out of our ignorance.

If you perceive, as did Joseph Campbell, that myth is not baseless fantasy, then you realize myth echoes the deepest truths about human origins and existence that the rational, conscious mind cannot grasp. Myth chips away at the matrix of material illusions we live under to reveal a higher order beneath, an implicate order as physicist David Bohm called it, a hidden reality that shapes our existence. *The First Souls Trilogy, by this understanding, is a modern myth*, a story that draws forth buried images from the collective unconscious mind. These images indicate that humanity is the tip of the iceberg, the end product of an intelligent power that dwarfs our ability to believe we are an integral part of the force that created the universe.

The First Souls Trilogy is about the soul's descent from the realm of spirit into the material world. If you believe that human beings, at their core, are possessed of an intelligent energy and a mind that exists independently of the physical brain, and if you believe that the ability to think is not a mere random flaring of nerve synapses, then it's a good bet that our essence derives from a transcendent source. This is a story about our connection to and our fall from that source. Our origin lies in a higher, very real plane of existence, one that sages and psychologists say that we strive to return to consciously or unconsciously.

ECHOES OF THE GODS

The seemingly fantastic content of this book may come as a surprise to readers of the first two installments of the saga, Pope Annalisa, and The Thirteenth Disciple. The notion of fallen souls once existing in monstrous forms, lost civilizations of high technical achievement, and a pre-existing psychic world of thought-forms preceding solid matter may seem outlandish to some given the "real world" nature of the settings and characters in the first two books. Let me respectfully try to correct misperceptions about this, for as Pope Annalisa always said, "Nothing in this world is as it seems."

This is a trilogy about the soul's encounter with materiality, and this is the origin story of the initial fall of soul consciousness into the earth plane. Elements of this story have echoes in the "real" world. Mysterious historical records of gods walking the earth and ancient depictions of what clearly seems to be aircraft exist in many diverse ancient cultures across the globe such as Egypt, Sumeria, India, and Greece. The Bible and the holy scriptures of other religions refer to the physical presence of extra-dimensional beings such as Watchers, Nephilim, and fallen angels. Nearly every ancient culture possesses representations of beings who were alternately animal-like or not quite of the human form we know today. Legends of great prehistoric civilizations like Lemuria and Atlantis have persisted for thousands of years supported by circumstantial evidence. Despite the universality and historical echoes of these legends, we call these things myths in the sense of their being fantasies.

MYTH AND FANTASY

Myth, allegory, and parables provide clues about veiled human origins and the hidden nature of reality. Myth is a symbolic representation of the forgotten knowledge, obscured events, unseen forces, and invisible dimensions that created and influence the physical world. *Truths we have forgotten or that our rational minds cannot process end up as myths.*

Jesus recognized this. He used parables to convey high spiritual truths to people whose consciousness was not capable of grasping the raw data. Myth largely draws from the same information pool psychics tap into, the hidden realm where intelligent forces communicate the universal or archetypal thought-forms that have shaped our world. That is really what The First Souls Trilogy is about—the operation of intelligent non-material forces that shape our lives.

QUANTUM REALITIES

Max Planck, the father of modern quantum physics, said, *"Behind the existence of all matter is a conscious and intelligent mind—this mind is the matrix of all matter."* What did he realize that the average person doesn't? The unseen quantum world that gives rise to our 3D experience of reality doesn't operate logically. Inexplicable things happen in Quantum-Land that Einstein described as *"spooky."* The particles that make up our world do not even exist as physical objects at the deepest sub-atomic levels. What does exist is energy waves that can collapse or "pop" into physical particles that form atoms and molecules.

Quantum science knows that energy carries ordering information. For example, the computer I'm using to type these words contains strings of binary numbers (information) electronically (energetically) delivered to produce the word forms you are reading. Matter is also the product of informed energy. Matter derives from energy, as Einstein's $E=mc^2$ tells us. So, energy carries information that "in-forms" matter and that information is guided by intelligence. How so? The information is channeled into distinct atoms, molecules, elements that create the variety of objects we know as the physical world. Organizational diversity is a hallmark of intelligence. Random chance does not reproduce the same forms over and over again. We can say that the Tree of Life looks like this: intelligence> information > energy > physical experience.

This may seem abstract, but this is the underlying reality that science is revealing, and it's the same reality psychics and sages have been describing for millennia. Humanity's origins in higher energy dimensions and the possible existence of great pre-historic civilizations of seemingly god-like beings have a plausible basis in both science and myth. That this seems unbelievable to our minds is a function of how far our consciousness has degenerated. Our logical minds may have grown, but our extra-sensory perception has shrunk in exponential proportion. Einstein said, "*The intuitive mind is a sacred gift and the rational mind is a faithful servant. We have created a society that honors the servant and has forgotten the gift.*"

INNER SPACE

Many unexplained experiences prompt us to look beyond the five senses for explanations. Russian cosmonauts described the appearance of angels in outer space. UFO buffs link life on Earth to extraterrestrial origins along with the footprints supposed aliens have left behind. But more persuasive evidence from quantum physics and ancient mystery teachings point to our *extradimensional* origins, the possibility that life came not from without but from *within*. This means that physical life ultimately originated not from another physical world, but from inner spiritual dimensions of intelligent energy. That our physical dimension derives from and is interpenetrated by other dimensions is gaining wider acceptance in science, as is the role of energy and consciousness. Immaterial consciousness increasingly appears to be the actual "stuff" that creates life and all forms of being. Differing levels of consciousness or energy vibration appear to create and define the different parallel dimensions in which science is so firmly beginning to believe.

WHERE LIES THE TRUTH?

The "first" in First Souls implies origins. The Chronicle of the First Souls is a vehicle to describe the story of human life on earth as a fall into materiality from a higher state of existence. The First Souls Trilogy occurs in reverse order. The initial two books show the trilogy's characters during humanity's historical time period. For instance, Annalisa's triumphant reestablishment of the sacred mysteries as a modern pope redeemed her prior incarnation as Mary Magdalene, who gave her life planting the seeds of enlightenment. *The Light of Distant Suns* completes the cycle of The First Souls. It takes us back to the pre-historic origin of their fall as high beings, who devolved from light to shadow and ultimately back to light. In *The Light of Distant Suns*, we encounter the source world of all souls. We experience worlds beyond this one to find that our true reality lies in other dimensions.

Both science and spiritual mysticism have demonstrated that we live in a matrix of illusion. The physical senses record a mere fraction of the reality spectrum, just as our eyes record visible light but not infrared, ultraviolet, or other frequencies of the light-energy spectrum. The exact truth of our origins may lie somewhere between the literal and the allegorical aspects of this story, but reality is most certainly not what the five senses detect. Our essence is energy, not matter. My hope is that readers will feel or sense their own way to the truth inherent in this modern myth and expand their awareness of what life is really about. Identifying with purely physical consciousness is putting us on the short end of the spectrum of life's possibilities and fullness.

Once people thought the earth was flat, but Magellan saw its shadow on the moon and knew it was round. Just around the corner and beyond the shadowy veil of things yet unknown lie mysteries that are constantly revealed to us. Look through those shadows with the light of your open mind in reading this book, then you too will be a Magellan and not a flatlander.

—**Peter Canova**

TABLE OF CONTENTS

MAP OF KEY EVENTS

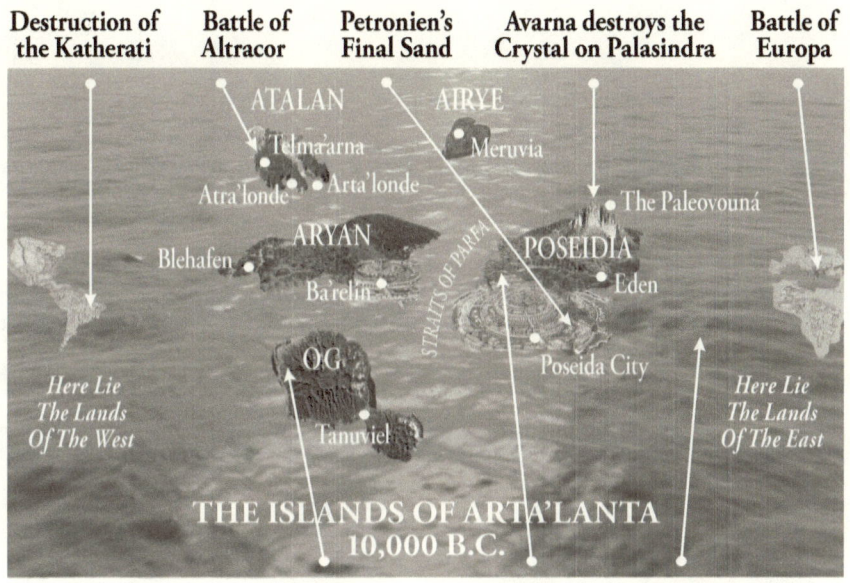

**Destruction of
the Katherati**

**Battle of
Altracor**

**Petronien's
Final Sand**

**Avarna destroys the
Crystal on Palasindra**

**Battle of
Europa**

ATALAN

AIRYE

Telma'arna

Meruvia

Atra'londe

Arta'londe

ARYAN

POSEIDIA

The Paleovouná

Blehafen

STRAITS OF PARÉA

Eden

Barelin

*Here Lie
The Lands
Of The West*

O.G.

Poseida City

*Here Lie
The Lands
Of The East*

Tanuviel

THE ISLANDS OF ARTA'LANTA
10,000 B.C.

**Battle of
Carch'Carai**

**An-Kera
Assassinated**

**Amliea's
Sacrifice**

DRAMATIS PERSONAE

THE FIRST SOULS

Amilius (Ah-*mee*-lee-us)—Sophia's male half. Whereas Sophia brought life to the lower dimensions, the cardinal Aeon Amilius was crucial to bringing order to the material creation. He is the closest of all emanated beings to The One. His Archetype is Order.

Averniel (Ah-*vair*-nee-el)—Archetype of Justice, the impetus toward balance.

Desmoniel (Dez-*moan*-ee-el)—Archetype of Faith, the ability to imagine and instill hope in unseen possibilities.

Petroniel (Peh-*trone*-ee-el)—Archetype of Perseverance, the ability to endure adversity.

Teresiel (Ter-*ee*-see-el)—Archetype of Witness, the faculty of remembrance.

Sophia (So-*fee*-uh)—The Aeon who broke the unity of heaven by plunging her divine energy into Chaos. Her actions subsequently led to the formation of the psychic and material worlds and the rise of the **Archon**. Her archetype is wisdom and knowledge.

THE DARK SOULS

Archon, The (*Are*-con)—Also the **Demiurge,** the Creator God. The quasi-personal force of ego and separation created by the collective aberrant thoughts of souls separated from The One. It radiated from the psychic or soul dimension. Sophia first inadvertently generated this thought-form in chaos when she sought to exert her creative power apart from the Unity.

Dalcoliel (Dahl-*coh*-lee-el)—Archetype of Sloth, ignorance.

Klaiseniel (Kleye-*see*-nee-el)—Archetype of Greed.

Loprestiel (Low-*press*-tee-el)—Archetype of Gluttony, self-indulgence.

Mannemiel (Man-*em*-ee-el)—Archetype of Pride.

Tareviel (Tah-*rev*-ee-el) — Archetype of Lust.
Termadiel (Tare-*mah*-dee-el) — Archetype of Anger.
Valandwiel (Vah-*land*-wee-el) — Archetype of Envy, strife.

THE ARTALANTANS (LANTEANS)

Allied to The Children of the Law of One

Amliea (Ahm-*lee*-ah) — Third Epoch Incarnation of **Sophia**, Princess of the throne of Artalanta, later empress. Called *Tara Amliea Karason*, Empress Amliea of the Golden Hair.

Amilius (Ah-*mee*-lee-us) — "The Unfallen," the guiding hand of Artalanta. Later called Amilius the savior.

Anu (*Ah*-new) — Third Epoch Emperor of Artalanta in the Third Epoch, grew increasingly weak and susceptible to pressure from the Sons of Belial in his later years.

Asel-Sine (*Ah*-sell-seen) — Corrupted Elda-Fera priest of the Second Epoch

Asme (*Ah*-say-me) Princess of the Second Epoch corrupted by Belial, eldest of Tar Esai's daughters, sister to Ouen and Mele

Avarna (Ah-*var*-nah) — Third Epoch Incarnation of **Averniel**, Captain General of the Blackmanes, the imperial guard taking precedence over the military orders.

Ar-Falene (Are-fahl-*ene*) — Third Epoch female general of the Imperial Army.

Braan'dach (*Bran*-dock) — Third Epoch Admiral of the Order of the Dolphin. After reform of the military, Admiral of the Imperial Nautikon.

Damocles (*Dam*-oh-kleez) — Third Epoch incarnation of **Esh Ar'Harden.**

Desamon (*Des*-ah-mun) — Third Epoch Incarnation of **Desmoniel.** A Consular, Prime Pedagogue of the Temples of Learning, Deputy of the Emperor's Governing Council.

Esh Ar'Harden (Esh-are-Hard-en) — Emperor's Prime in the Second Epoch.

Ouen (Ah-*wayne*) — Princess of the Second Epoch, later the **Delphae Oracle**.

Mele (*May*-lee) — Princess of the Second Epoch, advocate of the underclasses.

Petronien (Pet-*rone*-ee-ahn) — Third Epoch Incarnation of **Petroniel**. General of the Order of the After reform of the military, Supreme General of the Imperial Stratia.

Segund (Say-*Goond*) — Third Epoch High Priest of the Elda-Fera.

Terselia (Tare-*say*-lee-ah) — Third Epoch Incarnation of **Teresiel**. Princess, sister of Amliea, and priestess of The Law of One.

Vortegren (*Vor*-tah-gren) — Third Epoch Air Marshall of the Order of the Falcon. After reform of the military, Air Marshall of the Imperial Pneumarta.

Allied to The Sons of Belial

Al-Presta (Ahl-*pray*-stah) — Third Epoch Incarnation of **Loprestiel**. Renegade Priest.

An-Klesen (Ahn-*clay*-sen) — Third Epoch Incarnation of **Klaiseniel**. Commander of the Order of the Ferret.

Belial (Bah-*lie*-el) — Second Epoch incarnation of **Mannemiel.**

Dal-Golia (Dahl-*go*-lee-ah) — Third Epoch Incarnation of **Dalcoliel**. Governor General of Og.

Ra-Mennarial (Rah-men-*ahr*-ree-ahl) — Third Epoch Incarnation of **Mannemiel. P**rince of Aryan, Descendant of **Belial**.

Ter-Madaz (Tare-*mah*-dez) — Third Epoch Incarnation of **Termadiel**. General of the Order of the Jackal.

Ta-Revi (Tah-*ray*-vee) — Third Epoch Incarnation of **Tareviel**. Governor General of Atalan.

Val-Andwar (Vahl-*and*-war) — Third Epoch Incarnation of **Valandwiel**. Commander of the Order of the Bull.

Neutral

Anu (*Ah*-new) — Second Epoch Emperor.

Varandiel (Vahr-*an*-dee-el) — Third Epoch Commander of the Order of the Wolf

Telerian (Tell-*air*-ee-en) — Third Epoch Commander of the Order of the Serpent. After reform of the military, General of the Imperium.

GEOGRAPHY

During the First Epoch, Artalanta was a single, large continent. By the Second Epoch, the land had broken into five islands.

Poseidia (Pa-*sigh*-dee-ah) — The largest island, seat of the emperor and the Children of the Law of One. The capital city of **Poseidia** was the largest of all cities, a magnificent port of concentric rings of canals and beautiful buildings. Párnathal, the highest mountain of Artalanta, was said to be home to the fabled race of the old gods, the White Brotherhood. The Great Crystal Touai Stone was kept on Poseidia.

Aryan (*Ah*-ree-un) — The second largest island, foremost in technical and scientific achievements, but the central base for the Sons of Belial and, therefore, aggressive and warlike. The Aryans condone slavery and conquest of outlying lands.

Atalan (*Aht*-ah-lahn) — Another Belial stronghold, home of the twin harbors of Arta'londe and Atra'londe. The people were prosperous and rapacious seafaring merchants venturing as far as the Lands of the East and the Lands of the West.

Og (Awg) — A large inhospitable island of rugged people surrounded on most sides by sheer cliffs. It is the source of most raw materials that feed the Lantean social and war machines.

Airyre (*Eye*-er) — A beautiful, idyllic heart-shaped island possessing rich soils and an ideal climate that makes it the breadbasket of Artalanta.

GOVERNMENT AND MILITARY

Emperor (Tar) or Empress (Tara) — The supreme Lantean authority

Consularion (Con-sue-*lahr*-ee-on)) — The Governing Council of Artalanta. It consisted of ten Consulars, two from each of the islands.

Gerousia (Gay-roo-*see*-uh) — the junior branch of the Cosularion consisting of one hundred Gerousai. The Gerousia was proportionately based on population. Its members could debate, vote, and recommend in a non-binding advisory capacity. Final decisions and enactment of laws was the prerogative of the Consularion subject to approval by the emperor.

Governors General — Responsible for civil and military affairs for each island

MILITARY ORDERS

The military orders of the Stratia evolved around 20,000 BC. At first, they were militias created to combat beasts and other dangers that made incursions into the land, but later, under the influence of the Sons of Belial, they became offensive weapons used against others both within Artalanta and against peoples in the Eastern and Western lands. Each island housed a military order except for the naval and air forces that were stationed solely on the two most influential islands, Poseidia and Aryan. The Order of the Ferret, the army engineering unit, however, was based on Aryan alone. The Blackmanes and the Order of the Lion on Poseidia took precedence over the other military orders and their officers were technically superior.

The required use of animal masks for the military orders was a carryover from earlier epochs. The practice became such an obsession that for military personnel to appear in public without their Wolf head or Jackal head masks was a form of personal trauma like being publicly naked and a cause for disciplinary action. The exception to wearing masks were the Blackmanes and the military orders stationed in Poseidia where the influence of the Children of the Law of One remained strong. After the defeat of the Aryan-Atalani invasion of Og, all orders but the Blackmanes were abolished and incorporated into a single imperial army.

BLACKMANES — The emperor's personal guard. In theory, they took precedence over all the other military orders, but this status was one of many things challenged by the Sons of Belial.

STRATIA (Strah-*tee*-ah) (ARMY) — Lion (Poseidia); Jackal (Aryan); Ferret (Aryan); Wolf (Og); Serpent (Airye); Bull (Atalan);

NAUTIKON (*Not*-a-con) (NAVY) — Dolphin (Poseidia); Shark (Aryan)

PNEUMARTA (New-*mart*-ah) (AIRFORCE) — Falcon (Poseidia); Hawk (Aryan)

SCIENTIFIC — Elda-Fera (El-dah-fair-*ah*) (Poseidia); Tekna-Fera (Aryan)

PRIESTHOOD — Elda-Fera (Poseidia); Fire Cult (Aryan)

CHRONOLOGIA
From The Book of Remembrance

12,000,000 — **First root-race**, soul expressed as incorporeal thought-form projections about the land of Mu. Soul possession of animals, pollution of soul consciousness, hybrid monstrosities of legend.

10,500,000 — Council of the souls led by the First Souls of the Amilius/Sophia grouping to discuss the problem of soul involvement in matter.

10,000,000 — **Second root-race**, solidified thought-form bodies developed in Mu into which souls projected, often polluted by contact with animal consciousness.

1,000,000–800,000 — Early humanoid development in Mu, second root-race light bodies densify, animal mixtures still present.

500,000 — Mu inundated by water, life forms scattered.

400,000–300,000 — Mu reinhabited, advances to primitive state.

250,000 — Second catastrophe in Mu by fire.

210,000 — Souls incarnate in second root-race androgynous, bodies having both sexes in one, but the feminine dominates this age. Early Lantean culture emerges from souls as spiritual thought-form projections entering into humanoid forms becoming ever denser.

106,000 — The Children of One and the Sons of Darkness incarnate as **Third root-race** godling-beings, first as thought-forms, then as bodies with a third eye. They began to separate into male and female humanoids under Amilius (the Logos) with the consent of The One. Soulless thought-projected things or automatons were mind-created by the godlings, first as servants then as sex objects. As Sons of God they became dense and corrupted by materiality. They take the Daughters of Men (earlier root-races). The offspring were the Naphaalim giants and other mutations that taxed the earth. Family as opposed to community units first appeared. First usage of the Touai Crystal to communicate with the Source to replace lost innate soul abilities.

70,000—**Fourth root-race (Adamic)**, the first race evolved from both earth and spirit. Adamic humans appear simultaneously in five places on earth as five races and slowly begin to evolve. The most advanced was the red race of Artalanta, who inherited third root-race technology. Godlike powers gradually vanished along with the abuses that came with it. Usage of sub-crystals to power mechanical devices.

55,000—Male age arises. Ascent of warrior culture, Belials, and Emperor Esai. Crystals first used as weapons. Human sacrifice instituted.

50,000—Final submergence of Mu.

50,722—The date of the Great Congress regarding the animal incursions. First Lantean destruction.

28,000–22,006—Second Lantean destruction. Artalanta becomes five islands. Adamics survive, third root-race ends. The chaotic mixing of root-races terminates with most new souls incarnating in the new Adamic body form.

10,700—Final destruction and sinking of Artalanta. Lantean diaspora.

10,390—Completion of the Great Pyramid in Egypt by the priests Ra-Ta and Hermes using Lantean technology.

TYER ANGARACH
(TWILIGHT OF THE GODS)
Poseidia, Artalanta
The Third Epoch, circa 10,700 BC

"But afterwards there occurred violent earthquakes and floods; and in a single day and night of misfortune all your warlike men in a body sank into the earth, and the island ... in like manner disappeared in the depths of the sea."
—Plato, The Timaeus

First, the flames ignited. Then came the roaring of men's voices in the distance followed by compression gunfire. Next, the clanging of swords sounded as the battle drew nearer the citadel. The enemy was beginning to cross from the mainland to the first of Poseidia's concentric island rings.

The two sisters, Amliea and Terselia, the last empress and princess of great Artalanta, stood on a terrace of the imperial palace atop the citadel mount in the center of the three-ringed harbor. The wind was hot with smoke and cinders bearing their country's doom to their nostrils. They looked at one another and nodded, their figures framed against the blur of a haze-choked sky.

They would not await a passive fate in the citadel. Each of them bore a separate burden, a separate task that would affect the future of life on earth. With one hundred Blackmane imperial guards, they began the trek down to the lower city where the fighting would become heavy. They came to a main boulevard where the people were fleeing to and fro in panic. Amliea positioned herself in the center of the street. Like an island, the current of humanity flowed around her until she removed her headpiece, her golden hair spilling across her shoulders. People froze seeing the rare yellow locks for which she was famous.

"The Empress!" they shouted. "The Empress Amliea Karason herself is here!" The crush slowed and halted as the people gathered around her, many going to their knees.

Amliea said to Terselia in a low voice, "Make haste now to the appointed place. The Elda-Fera have transferred the sacred manuscripts from Pelion, but you hold *The Book of Remembrance*. It must survive. Humanity must know why we fell or forever be slaves to the world of illusion that ensnared us."

Terselia refused to leave. The danger of Amliea dying or falling into the hands of the Belial rebels was too great. She was too easy to identify with her golden hair, and the Belials would love to capture her.

"Obey me in this," Amliea said. "Mennarial and his ilk shall never touch me again. What you carry is too important for the world to come. I command you to leave, and I will meet you at our appointed destination. My fate is to save my people and that destiny awaits me elsewhere, not in this doomed land."

After Terselia left, Amliea considered her words for the assembled crowd. How could she tell them? Great Artalanta, Lord of the World, Home of the Descended Gods, had fallen by its own hand, fated to extinction never to rise on this earth again. Tears rolled down her cheeks as she saw her adoring people. Her soul was heavy with the knowledge that she had been instrumental in their destruction.

"People of Poseida, I do not ask you to stay and fight but take to the seas and live! Soon our land will be destroyed. No sorting shall be made. Friend and foe alike shall perish. Flee and find what boats you can while General Petronien still holds the mouth of the harbor open. Able-bodied men, stay with me and my guard to protect the passage of the women and children."

The enemy soon reached them. Swords sounded on shields, compression guns echoed in the air, and growls of pain and desperation permeated the final stand of the imperial household. Then a deafening sound caused the fighting to stop. All the combatants went to their knees. Far off, clouds of debris rose over Mount Palasindra and when it cleared, the top of the mountain was gone. Moments later the land shook in violent spasms and structures began to fall like stacked tiles.

As Amliea saw a building coming down on top of her, she instinctively raised her hands, clenched her teeth, and resolved not to die before she atoned for the destruction she helped create. Dying now would be the easy way out, and surely God would not let her of all people go that easily.

THE PRIMARY DIMENSIONS OF EXISTENCE

To understand life on earth, you must understand the life that existed before earth, for life must proceed from life and consciousness from consciousness, not from other-than-life or other-than-consciousness.

In the beginning, only The One existed. The very act of creation was God projecting conscious *parts of Itself* into other dimensions of existence. The spirit dimension was the home of spirit mind-energies remaining faithful to the Will of The One. But spirits using the creative mind-power for their own ends became souls and dwelt apart in the psychic dimension. Souls that projected into bodily incarnations to pursue their own creations became human.

It was in Artalanta on earth that spirit first began evolving physical forms in the days when the material world was young and souls were closer to the unseen reality from which they came They forgot their origins and so began to believe their own power was responsible for the material creation when in truth they interfered with what The One's mind had already created. The false idea that the creation arose from the souls' collective forces produced a quasi-real thought form, a pseudo-god called the Archon. This psychic power based on error became a force in opposition to God and it kept souls from the higher realms bound to the illusions of the material world.

— *From the Innumerata of The Book of Remembrance*

PROLOGUE
WINDOW ON A LOST AGE
Washington, DC
A.D. 2039

*"Far more exists to life than what you see above the waterline.
Our present reality is built upon a magic long forgotten of
people and places that moved this world forward to the
ultimate rendezvous with its Source."*

—Pope Annalisa

"Are you really asking us to believe fallen spirits or angels wrote this book ten thousand years ago in a lost civilization here on earth? Why present this to us?" Congressman Joseph Faller asked. "Airships, ray guns, alien races—is this what the Vatican is pushing these days?"

"Please, Congressman," Chief of Staff Clare Early said. "The president has impaneled us to hear Bishop de Verneaux explain the sealed material Pope Valentinus sent us last month. We're here to listen, not judge at this point though I must say … well, I'm not sure what to say."

On this crisp day with the dying leaves of summer changing into autumn hues, two senators, two congressmen, and the president's chief of staff sat at a conference table in a nondescript meeting room off of the Senate chambers on Capitol Hill.

They faced one of the Catholic Church's most prominent bishops, Catherine Luce de Verneaux. The late middle-aged bishop wore a red zucchetto skullcap on her head and a black simar with the amaranth-red piping and buttons indicative of her episcopal station. She surmised some of them were still unaccustomed to seeing a female in the bishop's vestments of post-Annalisa Church reforms.

"Well now, Joe," Senator La Shonda Conyers addressed Congressman Faller in a pleasing southern drawl, "I came from a church-going Southern Baptist family, and maybe I'm a tad more receptive to angels, so I'm already feeling some of your cold water flowing down my spine." This drew snickers from the others. "A lot of unbelievable things are happening in our lifetime. People said Pope Annalisa performed miracles. No one believed it back then yet she saved our world. Bishop de Verneaux is one of the most respected religious scholars on earth, so why don't we just listen with open ears before judging?"

The bishop sat on one side of the table by herself facing some of America's most powerful people. "Thank you, Senator," she said with a modest French accent, "and thank all of you for your valuable time. Seven years ago, shortly before her death, Pope Annalisa predicted the existence of gospels written by Mary Magdalene hidden in southern France. The Vatican assembled a team of the world's most reputable scholars. They indeed found the gospels. Those texts presented a different picture of the nature of early Christianity, indeed a different picture of reality itself."

"Why the seven-year delay in revealing this?" Congresswoman Giulia Seretti asked.

"Two reasons," de Verneaux replied. "During those seven years, a wide array of experts studied and proved the gospels' validity beyond a doubt before going public. We also had security reasons. The original group of seven discovery scholars was attacked by a shadowy cabal determined to destroy the gospels. A number of people were killed and the seven scholars barely survived."

Clare Early spoke when several people expressed surprise. "Our intelligence confirmed this," she told them, "though I'm not sure why the incident wasn't made public."

"The Vatican had good reasons. It was connected to the murder of the billionaire Felix King that you all read about in the press," de Verneaux replied. "The information in these texts has powerful enemies, but I will not digress. What you have received to date is just an outline. I will leave you annotated copies of the full texts today. By way of disclosure, we have similar meetings planned with the governments of other great nations such as Russia and China."

De Verneaux glanced out a window to see leaves falling to the ground, reminding her how old beliefs must fall to make way for new realizations. *Now for the difficult part,* she thought.

"I present you with two documents today—the *Gospel of Mary Magdalene* and a far more ancient text called *The Book of Remembrance.* Information within these texts strips away the cocoon of what we hold to be reality. They reveal the existence of other dimensions and other forms of intelligent beings."

"That's an awfully bold statement," Senator Clay McLaren said.

De Verneaux smiled. "So was the fact that solid matter is made of invisible moving particles called atoms. Why does every culture from ancient times contain numerous references to spirits and heavenly dimensions? Hopeful thinking reflecting our aspirations perhaps? If so, why were such beings not universally good or friendly? These gospels are verified as authentic as can be, and they provide conclusive proof that higher beings still walk among us."

McLaren fidgeted in his chair. "Are you really serious?"

"I am," de Verneaux replied. "The texts describe beings referred to as the First Souls, cardinal spirits who had much to do with the formation of the material world. You will see incontrovertible evidence in these texts that Pope Annalisa was one of these reincarnated First Souls as well as our current pope Valentinus. The souls of these beings incarnate at formative junctures over the ages. Pope Annalisa predicted the content and location of the Magdalene gospels because *she wrote them as Mary Magdalene.*"

The room descended into a stunned silence with several frowns and sidebar conferences. "You do realize how insane this sounds, that this stretches the borders of credulity," Faller said.

"I understand, sir," de Verneaux replied, "but within the verified two-thousand-year-old texts lie direct named references to the current incarnations of these beings among other proofs." She studied the faces of her audience. Some appeared skeptical, some offended, and others intrigued.

"After the discovery but before the announcement of the Magdalene gospels' existence, another book surfaced, an even more ancient text called *The Book of Remembrance.* It was a gift from Tibetan monks to

Pope Valentinus. It was originally written in a forgotten language but it had a Greek translation."

"What is its significance?" Clare Early asked.

"It is the oldest record of human experience on earth miraculously coming down from pre-history," de Verneaux replied.

"A written document from pre-history? Isn't that an oxymoron?" Faller asked.

"Hopefully you will read it and find out for yourself," de Verneaux replied. "It was too old to date accurately and written with materials that cannot be identified. It is a full-fledged record not only of the earliest human history but of *pre-human* experience. It was held in a monastery for innumerable ages waiting to be revealed '*at the right time,*'—the monks' term, not mine. This book was mentioned in the Magdalene gospels, in fact, it played a central role in those gospels."

The room broke into a shocked buzzing of voices. "Say what?" Conyers exclaimed. "The Magdalene gospels are two thousand years old and they mention this older book? Am I getting that right?"

"Yes. Mary Magdalene's gospels describe sections of Remembrance in detail; that is how we know it refers to the same book the monks possessed," de Verneaux said. "Furthermore, in a kind of mirror image reference, the authors of *The Book of Remembrance*, said to be the First Souls themselves, predicted their reincarnations as figures in the Magdalene gospels including Magdalene and Jesus himself. In other words, both texts together cross-reference the reincarnated lives of the same souls, souls walking the earth even in our own time."

The room fell into dead silence as the people looked around to see each other's reactions. "Okay, okay," Faller said. "This is a bit much to swallow. But let's say we verify everything you've told us. Why are you bringing this to us and to other major governments?"

"And if this is true, why is all this knowledge only appearing now?" Conyers said.

De Verneaux folded her hands and placed them on the table "Ah, my compliments to you, Senator Conyers. That *is* the real question but let me answer both of you. Buddhists have a tradition called *terma*. This is the belief that sacred knowledge is hidden by sages throughout the ages to be revealed at crucial times needed to save humanity from self-destruction or to move it forward in evolution. Prior to Pope Annalisa, hatred and division on this planet had peaked between East and West, liberal and conservative, globalist and nationalist, Christian and Muslim. We narrowly averted a nuclear holocaust between America and Iran."

"We will ever owe Annalisa a debt of gratitude for changing the world's direction," Conyers said.

"But we must learn our lesson to consolidate Annalisa's sacrifices." De Verneaux took a sip of water, folded her hands, and resumed explaining. "The grand story in Remembrance chronicles the fall of spirit into matter and its evolution in human form. It reveals our origins not as creations of God but as *fallen parts of the Godhead Itself* who became trapped in the material world. Our spiritual ancestors built the greatest civilization earth has known, but they descended into wars of dominion and destroyed themselves."

She paused and looked each of them in the eye. "This is a cautionary tale for modern humanity, for we, each of us in this room, are spirits in essence. Quite recently, we nearly repeated the catastrophes of old because our faults, as the texts remind us, stem from entrapment in a matrix of illusions, the limitations of our physical senses to discern the true nature of reality."

"What on earth does that mean?" Faller asked folding his arms across his chest.

The bishop inhaled a deep breath. Explaining the unexplainable was key to her mission. "Just as unseen subatomic particles shape our physical world, so do unseen spiritual and psychic forces shape our human destinies," the bishop replied. "As long as we remain unconscious of them we are doomed to repeat our errors. The Gnostic gospel of Thomas said, *'If you bring forth what is within you, what you bring forth will save you. If you do not bring forth what is within you, what you do not bring forth will destroy you.'* The original purpose of Christianity before it was corrupted was to awaken consciousness to the matrix of sensory illusions and the realization of a higher order with which we may connect."

After a ponderous silence, Clare Early said, "This is a lot to absorb. How could I describe such fantastic things to the president without sounding absurd?"

"You will ask yourself, is this information real or is it all fable? I am not going to answer that question; you have to answer it yourself," de Verneaux said. "The logical evidence is plain in the books, but my advice is to let the imagery the texts create in your minds be your guide to higher truth. Trust your intuition, not just your logic. Logic is based on the senses; we are dealing with realms beyond the senses."

"Assuming you believe in intuition," Congressman Faller said.

Senator Conyers snickered. "Oh, Joe, there you go again. I do recall something Albert Einstein once said. 'The intuitive mind is a sacred gift and the rational mind is a faithful servant. We have created a society that honors the servant and has forgotten the gift.' Now he faced unseen, seemingly illogical puzzles and he intuited his way to brilliant answers. Good enough for Einstein, good enough for me."

"The age of miracles is returning to guide us at this crossroads in human existence," de Verneaux said. "You are leaders. Like Moses, your duty is to lead people forward to a better land, not let them sink into the idolatry of old ways worshiping the 'golden calf' of falsehoods that have been destroying us."

"As grand as your analogy sounds, Bishop, I'm hard-pressed to think of anyone here as Moses," Senator McLaren said.

De Verneaux smiled. "We are much more than we think, sir, and the role we play in the creation is far more exalted than what we have come to believe about ourselves."

She placed a hand on her heart in a gentle, circular motion. "If you allow your intuition to come forth and see the light of day, what you bring forth will truly save you as Thomas told us two thousand years ago, for the people and events you will encounter are really an allegory of ourselves and our world. Whether or not your mind believes these texts, your heart will tell you that their story is *our* story."

The bishop stood indicating she was going to leave, and she addressed Clare Early. "You were wondering what to tell your president. Look into your own heart for the answer, and you just might find yourself telling the president that the recovery of these in texts in our age is no coincidence. You may even conclude as I did that we might be on the verge of witnessing our evolution from Homo sapiens to Homo superior. Let us hope so anyway. Good day to you all."

BOOK ONE
WINDS OF WAR

THE SECOND EPOCH

ISLAND EMPIRE OF ARTALANTA
SECOND EPOCH, 22,000 B.C.

CHAPTER I
The Imperial Palace, Ruach Minas, Artalanta
The Second Epoch, 22,006 BC

*He will suddenly appear and gain
control of the kingdom by treachery.*
—Daniel 11:21

T he sun rose in radiant ochre over an earth that was no longer new, but not yet old. The great spires of the emperor's palace at Ruach Minas pierced the skies, one of many structures rising like the flight of winged birds to greet the waxing ball of fire that cast its light over the waking land.

Over 170,000 years since the descent of the First Souls, the face of the earth had indeed transformed in ways incomprehensible to the mind of man such as man understands the world today. Gone were the crude round huts in the days after the fledgling creatures came out from their hovels in the earth. Great temples dotted the landscape built with giant stones placed with gravity-defying precision by the mind-power of the descended souls. Airships flew overhead, the first of which were dirigibles of gas-filled animal skins, but later came faster vehicles powered by the Touai Stone, the Great Crystal source that would be both the blessing and bane of great Artalanta.

Esh Ar'Haden, Primary of the Emperor Esai, walked into the throne room dwarfed by the height and breadth of the emperor's reception hall. He was accompanied by Asal-Sine, First Priest-Scientist of the Elda-Fera. The approach to the throne was wide enough to fit one hundred horses side by side, and it was lined with gigantic columns of gold and marble inlaid with polished jewels.

Massive statues of a warrior and a philosopher-priest flanked the emperor's throne, which was situated under the great shield and book of wisdom clasped in the mammoth hands of the stone figures.

The emperor, Esai, addressed the men even before they halted to bow. "Ah, Esh Ar'Haden, exemplary work. You managed to cajole the High Priest down from his aerie on Pelion."

Mount Pelion was one of the three peaks that formed the sacred mountain range collectively referred to as Paleovouná. Pelion housed the Temple of Light, the keep of the Elda-Fera. The Touai Stone, the Great Crystal that powered all Lantean technology, was kept on nearby Palasindra under the strict supervision of the Elda-Fera priesthood. Párnathal was uninhabited and said to be the abode of great spirits. None were allowed to venture there, and strange anomalies had befallen the few over the ages who had attempted to penetrate its mysteries.

"Pressure grows from Belial and his followers to use the Crystal's power against the invading beasts," Esai said. "Tell me if this is possible, for the aerial bombardments have not stemmed the tide."

Asal-Sine glanced briefly at Esh Ar'Haden whose face betrayed no emotion in its rigid iron stare. "Possible, perhaps, but wise, no," the priest replied. "We have only used the power of the Crystal for peaceful purposes, to heal, and to commune with the higher realms. To use it as a weapon of destruction could bring unforeseen consequences."

"How so?" the emperor asked fingering the round dragon medallion draped around his neck.

"We have never used the Crystal as you propose. It would require recalibration We have no way to gauge the proper frequency needed to complete the task. If it generates excessive power, it could disrupt the earth's equilibrium. The Elda-Fera could not condone its use in this manner."

"I see. Leave me that I may confer with my Prime."

On the priest's way out a lithe figure with luxurious black hair and reddish-bronze skin approached.

"Asal-Sine, how good to see you."

"Princess Asme," he replied with a slight bow.

"We see little of you here," she said, touching a hand to his shoulder, feeling it stiffen. "Such an important man. The one who could halt the invasion of the wild animals. You would not want to see me mauled by saber tooths, would you? I hope we would see you here more often. Our last meeting together was memorable, no?" Her honeyed voice trailed off with heavy-lidded eyes and a coy smile.

"Y-yes, thank you, Princess. We must not mention such things here. I must be off now." Asme looked at him walking down the hall as he departed to the waiting aircar that would transport him back to the heights of Pelion. His remote predecessors could have traveled the heights by their own mental volition, but the spirits' power of mind over matter had so declined that even the Children of the Law of One had resorted to technological devices to replace those mind-abilities lost in the mists of time.

Back in the throne room, Esai consulted with Esh Ar'Haden. "I was hoping the priest could be more definite about the use of the Crystal for I am inclined to accommodate the Belials," Esai said. "But if the Elda-Fera refuse to cooperate, I cannon force them. Let Belial and his sons focus their rage on them."

Esh Ar'Haden stood silent for a moment. "As you wish, my lord."

"Is that all?" No opinions?" Esai asked.

"It is the logical course. We will search for another way to rid ourselves of the beasts." With those terse words, he was excused. Esh Ar'Haden exited through a side entrance of the great hall. He walked by countless empty rooms until he rounded a corner and halted. "Princess Ouen."

Ouen was the second of Tar Esai's' three daughters. She was not as statuesque as her older sister Asme, nor did she have the rare golden-haired beauty of her younger sister Mele, but by Esh Ar'Haden's estimation, she should have been seated on the throne. Her vision was keen and her heart was pure as was that of Mele, but Ouen's intelligence was far-reaching and her connection to The One was unwavering in an imperial court that had been corrupted by the Belials.

"Esh Ar'Haden, I was seeking you. May we talk in private?"

They entered an empty room along the endless corridor and sat opposite one another at an ornately carved onyx table illuminated to translucence by power lamps "How may I be of service, Princess?"

"I know the nature of your meeting just now. Tell me, did Father give in to the Belials?"

"Princess, you know I am the emperor's Prime. I cannot —"

"Stop. You know who I am Esh Ar'Haden. You know my heart; you know you can trust me, and I know I can trust you."

"How do you know that, Princess? The palace crawls with spies and traitors these days."

The princess nodded, lips pursed as if deciding what to say. "Let me tell you something. One day when I was a young girl, I snuck out to take a walk in the night air. By the light of a half-moon, I saw a figure. He looked to be in deep contemplation. I watched him for some time. Then in the blink of an eye, he disappeared. He did not walk away or hide behind a bush. He disappeared, vanished into thin air."

"Moonlit eyes can play tricks, my princess."

"No, Esh Ar'Haden, it was you, and my eyes were strong and clear. You are a Fade, and I've kept your secret all these years. You are of the early generation, uncorrupted, dating back to the First Souls. Are you in communion with them? Are they still in-body? Where did they go? We have great need for them."

Esh Ar'Haden's head drew back. "Why are you asking these things now?"

Ouen sighed. "My father tries to resist Belial, but he is weak. We are at a fateful crossroads, I sense it. I have many questions. Understanding the past, how we arrived where we are, answering these questions can help me determine what I can do, how I can use my position to change things."

Esh Ar'Haden studied the young woman's face. "I see. But something else troubles you."

Ouen bowed her head avoiding his eyes as she spoke. "Belial and his sons are betraying the Law of The One. For generations the emperors were the bulwark against their evil and debaucheries, but now ..."

"Yes, Princess?"

She raised her eyes to his. "I believe my sister, Asme, is influencing my father. She has gone over to Belial. I believe they are plotting to usurp the throne."

CHAPTER II
Ruach Minas, Artalanta
The Second Epoch, 22,006 BC

*a young girl or person with those
who were given to debauchery.*
—Edgar Cacye reading 1968-2

"Amazing, Father. Seducing an androgyne princess and sharing her with us. Amazing!"

Belial and his sons Ba'al and Be'elsebaab stood in an anteroom outside Princess Asme's chambers while she prepared herself in her countryside villa, not far from the outskirts of the city. Belial's fierce, blue eyes glowed with self-satisfaction or perhaps lust at what was soon to come as he addressed his sons.

"Remember this," Belial said, "sex is not merely a means to pleasure. It is a tool, a powerful tool because it manipulates primal instincts. Androgynes are particularly susceptible. They can reproduce by propagation within themselves, but reproduction is not sex nor are the sensations as satisfying as sex."

"They call sex unnatural," Ba'al said.

"Pah! The sensations of the body are natural to the flesh, and they are in the flesh" Belial said. "It is they who cling to unnatural thoughts. We created this world, but they live by ideal abstractions believing in unseen worlds and the powers of some mythical god beyond. They fight against nature and it makes them weak because nature always prevails. Sex, my sons, is a tool we will use to gain power, to break down the artificial barriers created by the Children of The One and achieve our desires."

The princess called, and the men entered her bedchambers. She stood in a sheer robe of thin gossamer fabric beneath a skylight that boldly accentuated her form. Tall, full-breasted, with a narrow waist and generous hips, Belial's sons had long lusted after the haughty royal beauty, one of the untouchables. As they gaped at her near-naked shape, they dreamed of how they would use her body to satisfy the urges that pounded and churned in their blood.

"So," Asme said. "The sons of Belial. Come then and let us see how the colts compare to the stallion." With no further bidding, the three men advanced, bodies tensed in heated anticipation.

Princess Mele of the golden hair finished her day in the fields trying to ease the labor of the drones or the "things" as the Belial faction called them. The Lanteans were a red race with dark hair. Mele's golden hair and bronzed skin made her stand out in what should have been an appreciation for unusual beauty, but she and her sister Ouen had largely become outcasts from the court for their support of the drones and the working classes. Such was the measure of the Belial faction's growing influence.

Rather than return to the palace, Mele decided to visit Asme at her sister's nearby villa. The door was open and she entered. Immediately she heard moaning sounds issuing from the bedchamber on the far wing of the villa. Alarmed that Asme might be in trouble, she made her way toward the noise. The door to the chamber was partially open. When she peeked inside, she bit her lip and her bronze skin blanched.

Her older sister was naked, face down on the edge of the bed. One man was taking her from behind and the upper half of her body was entwined between two other men. She recognized them — Belial and his sons. Her hand clamped over her mouth to prevent her stomach contents from rising. She turned and ran with no care for stealth knocking against a vase before running out the door. Asme and Belial ran out of the room at the shattering noise. Looking through the open door, they saw a fleeing figure. The color of golden hair glinting in the sun left them no doubts.

THE LIGHT OF DISTANT SUNS

"Mele!" Asme said. "She saw us."

"Then we must accelerate our plans," Belial said. "The priest is the key to circumvent the emperor. And do something about that troublesome sister of yours ... now!"

CHAPTER III
The Imperial Palace, Ruach Minas, Artalanta
The Second Epoch, 22,006 BC

"You are not of this world."
—John 3:12

"**M**ele told me everything this morning," Ouen proclaimed to Esh Ar'Haden. "Asme, my own sister lost to evil. We are a flawed race, the Children and Belials. How did such divisions happen among us?"

"You ask much, Princess, with little time," Esh Ar'Haden said. "Your protection is paramount now. As we speak, Belial and Asme would have you and Mele killed for what you know."

"I do not need protection. I despair. I need answers. I will not move until you give them to me. Is anything in this world worth saving? What are we? How did evil become so powerful?"

Esh Ar'Haden looked out a window toward the Temple of The One that dominated the Citadel hill of the center city with its huge semi-circular columns of onyx, topaz, and beryl. Around this temple, the lives of the Children of The One revolved, and those lives were in great peril.

Esh Ar'Haden clenched his fists, caught between his need to preserve the girl and his need to instruct her. The time of the black cloud was upon them, but she was right. She had an important role to play in the fate of this sorrowful world, and she needed to understand it, though danger loomed at their door.

"The evil among us was inevitable. In truth, we were not meant to be here," Esh Ar'Haden said.

"Why?" Ouen asked.

He sighed. "It began with Sophia, the first spirit to fall from heaven." He hesitated then put a hand to his forehead, and when he turned to face her, a third eye was visible above the bridge of his nose. He touched a hand to her forehead and likewise, the eye of the androgynes appeared on her. He communicated to her telepathically in words and images as he revealed mysteries lost in the veil of ages.

<< Sophia was the first spirit to fall from heaven, and she became the First Soul to pursue her desire to create. That is what a soul is — a spirit pursuing its own ends rather than God's plan for creation. She fell into a new dimension created by her own thought, the psychic dimension. Others followed. From there they became aware of the material world, a denser state The One was coalescing below them. They began to interfere and move their consciousness into it. The first wave of souls were mere thought-form energy projections, but the second wave pushed their soul essence into their own thought-forms. Their ghostly projections acquired mass from the earth vibration. The dreamers had imagined themselves into the solid world and became lost in their own dream projections, believing themselves to be physical beings. >>

"Princess, Time flows against us," he told her, reverting to speech. "We — "

"You shall not tell me a half-story," she said. "Partial knowledge is worse than none. Continue."

Esh Ar'Haden bit his lip, gave an anxious look at the window, and continued transferring his thoughts.

<< Some souls projected monstrous humanoid-animal hybrid images mimicking earth's animal life; others imagined more purely humanoid forms. The animal consciousness of bodily survival in the now solidified creatures became dominant. All earthbound souls became brutish physical creatures, forgetting their higher origins. They were called Terrestrials in the sacred annals. >>

<< What of the First Souls then? I cannot believe they were such creatures. >>

<< The First Souls — Amilius, Sophia, Teresiel, Averniel, Petroniel, Desmoniel — and the others who followed them were different. They

entered into the earth not as projected thought-forms, but in ethereal light bodies retaining their higher consciousness, *in* the world but not *of* it. They had come to rescue the first wave of fallen Terrestrial souls. They came in their full androgynous essence with their souls intact. They used many means to rid the monstrous hybrid souls of their animal appendages and coax them into more human-like forms as first envisioned in the Mind of The One. But the evolution of the body was merely a stepping stone to reawaken the consciousness of God within the confused souls. >>

"If we have little time, you must get to it, Esh Ar'Haden. What was the origin of evil in this world? That is what I must know," she verbally demanded, interrupting his thought stream.

He rushed out his thoughts in a torrent, expecting assassins to arrive at any time.

<< Many of the new souls took on the advanced bodies of the current day as their etheric bodies accumulated mass and became more physical. They were called Celestials. Only Sophia, Amilius, and others of their soul-grouping retained their ethereal forms. The lost souls' consciousness had moved so far into the earth plane that they worshipped the more recently incarnated spirits as gods. Indeed, for a while the Celestials bridged mind and matter with resulting powers that would seem miraculous. The First Souls thought this misplaced worship dangerous. Seven others though, led by Mannemiel, fell prey to the ego force of the Archon and gloried in the adulation. These were Termadiel, Loprestiel, Valandwiel, Dalcoliel, Tareviel, and Klaiseniel. These seven became the Sons of Darkness, portals for evil on earth. >>

"Ah," Ouen exclaimed aloud. "The forerunners, the mind-fathers of the Belials. I see."

"Do you see?" Esh Ar'Haden said. "Then know this quickly, Princess, for I am sensing danger about you and your sister Mele. It was the misuse of The One's gift of free will that started with Sophia, the First Soul herself. She was not evil, only flawed, but others went to extremes. They used earth as a playground for their power to gratify themselves harming themselves and others in the process. Their free will allowed them to sink to depths of abuse unimaginable in the higher realms."

The mental images Esh Ar'Haden conveyed caused Ouen's knees to buckle. The realization of earth as a hellish shadow world of misbegotten god-dreams pounded at her like a great hammer on her heart.

"An abortion of the gods, indeed," Esh Ar'Haden said, reading her mind. "And it did not end there."

<< Renegade Celestials shamefully misused their soul power to create drones, thought-form projections used as slaves, some pleasing to the eye but all soulless. This was against the natural order. Only by propagating souls through the proper channels laid down by The One can an actual soul or true life come into being. The "drone things" projected by the ego-driven spirits were created by them, not by God. These soulless automatons formed the laboring class and were abused as sex objects even to this day.

The Sons of Darkness began to physically copulate with their own drones and with the humanoid Terrestrials of the first-wave souls. This unholy union resulted in all manner of genotypes. The offspring became giants in the earth or they had more normalized forms, but in all cases, they were dull and brutish. The Belials, over time, lost the power to project thought-forms that the Children of the Law of One retained. The Belials often cajoled naive Children of The One to create new forms for them to use. >>

Esh Ar'Haden's head suddenly shook. He clasped his hand over Ouen's. His third eye snapped shut. "Tell me right now, Ouen, where is your sister? Quickly!" She was alarmed by his tone.

"At our country estate at Eden." Before she could question him, he vanished in an instant.

When Esh Ar'Haden appeared out of thin air in the imperial country estate, Mele was backed into a corner of the room. The two men advancing toward her turned to face him, knives in hand, shocked at his appearance. Bolts of energy shot from his fingers and both men went down. He grabbed the startled golden-haired princess' arm and they exited the place that would have been her tomb.

When the two sisters were together, Esh Ar'Haden said, "You are both leaving Artalanta tonight or you will die here. Even now the agents of Belial and Asme seek you."

"We shall not flee like scared dogs," Ouen said. "And what of the First Souls? You have not said."

Esh Ar'Haden took her by the shoulders and bored into her eyes. "No time, Princess. Nothing can prevent the destruction to come, but I showed you the source of this world's evil. Now you understand. You have a role in earth's salvation and it shall not be in this doomed land. I have left instructions for you to follow in exile. You wish to know about the First Souls? Your destiny lies with them. Now go!"

CHAPTER IV
The Imperial Palace, Ruach Minas, Artalanta
The Second Epoch, 22,006 BC

When the time of dissolution arrives, the
first power of darkness will come upon you.
—The Dialogue of the Savior, a Gnostic Gospel

In one of the many deserted rooms of the imperial palace, two figures were heaving in a heated embrace. Her robes drawn up and back against the wall, Asme reveled in the sensations the Children of The One foolishly denied themselves.

Belial groaned with his final thrusts, his pale blue eyes piercing her soul. He drew in a deep breath and spoke into Asme's ear. "What of your meddlesome sisters?"

Asme ran her hands down her robe smoothing the folds. "Gone, fled I believe. But I have my father under guard, even from seeing them."

"Still, we must move swiftly with them still loose. Will the priest do as you instructed?" he asked stroking her flank.

Her body shivered. "He knows quite well what the news of molesting a princess would do to his position. I reminded him with recorded images of the act. I have my father's proxy for today's vote. With Asel-Sine verifying that the use of the Crystal is safe, achieving our goal is ensured."

Belial placed a hand on her breast and squeezed it. "You have learned well the ways of seduction. After we eliminate the beasts, we will see you named heir to the throne. With Asel-Sine compromised, we will control the Crystal and use it to control this entire world," he said with a sweep of his arms.

"The Crystal that powers all Lantean technology," Asme mused. "Indeed, we will have the power of life and death over the earth itself."

The meeting of the emperor's Privy Advisory Council convened, some thirty people in the room including Esh Ar'Haden. The members sat at a semi-circular table of carved exotic wood in a high-ceilinged chamber with murals depicting scenes from Artalanta's seafaring culture. Statues of dolphins breaching ocean waters and flying winged horses framed the central meeting area.

Asme announced that the emperor would not attend but she would sit in proxy to make all decisions. This drew murmurs. "Is this true, Esh Ar'Haden?" one of the members asked.

"As the princess says," he replied stone-faced.

"We take up the matter of the beastly invasions," Asme said. "Saber-tooth tigers, dire wolves, and larger animals are ravaging the countryside killing stock and farmers alike. Measures taken so far have failed to cure the problem. A far-reaching weapon of greater power is required. We have asked the Elda-Fera to study the use of the Touai Stone, our greatest energy source, as a means to end this scourge."

Asel-Sine, eyes cast down to the table, made a terse statement, "We have recalculated. We now believe we can safely recalibrate the Great Crystal for the purpose mentioned here."

A debate ensued. The discussion centered on the historic precedent the action would create, as well as the potential for future misuse of the Crystal. Several times members asked Asel-Sine about the reversal from his original position.

"As I said, we have recalculated many times," he replied. "Besides, many of these beasts lurk and breed in lairs in the earth. The rays of the Crystal are the only means we have to penetrate subterranean depths and destroy the animals where they live."

Asme approved the measure over the protests of several council members. Their opinions were advisory only. All she needed to act was agreement by the Elda-Fera to make the required modifications, and now she had it from the High Priest. She instructed Asel-Sine to make immediate preparations.

With the meeting adjourned, a number of council members sought out Esh Ar'Haden. He told them, "What is done is done lest we face outright civil war. You have thirty days to relocate your families from Artalanta. The land will rise in a catastrophic reaction, I have sensed it. You will lose what you have now, but you will live to rebuild the culture of The One, hopefully, stronger than before. Go, and be mindful of the lessons from this experience."

Days later, the skies grew dim. The sun faded to a sickly red, choked in the ash and embers of the dying earth. The first of the upheavals that signaled the doom of Artalanta had already begun. The Crystal, now called the Firestone by the Belials, had penetrated too deeply into the earth's core triggering eruptions of giant gas pockets and molten matter that moved the underlying tectonic plates. The giant earthquakes, volcanic eruptions, and tsunamis that first engulfed the western portion of the continent with horrific loss of life soon became pandemic. The earth's violence continued over several months until proud Artalanta was broken and brought to dust by the very forces of nature they sought to control.

CHAPTER V
Mount Párnathal, Artalanta
The Second Epoch, 22,006 BC

... for he put aside the world which is perishing.
—Treatise on the Resurrection, a Gnostic Gospel

The First Souls looked down upon the fate that befell Artalanta from Párnathal, the highest peak of the trimountaine Paleovouná range where they had dwelt for ages in their ethereal bodies. For eons, they remained between worlds attempting to influence the course of events on earth. They had failed, and now a fateful choice lay before them.

The heights of the Paleovouná remained untouched by the cataclysm below. Beneath Párnathal lay the Temple of Light on Mount Pelion and the Touai Stone Crystal on Mount Palasindra with its retractable domed roof. The power source for Lantean technology had become its bringer of doom.

"Esh Ar'Haden has passed beyond the veil," Desmoniel said. "He remained in bodily form evacuating The Children of the One."

"He was a great soul," Averniel said. "He sacrificed himself to save others while we remain here."

"Had you entered into physical bodies, you could not have prevented this," Amilius said. "You could not force the embodied souls to change their course; you cannot violate their free will."

"No," Petroniel said, "but perhaps we could have influenced them to a different path."

"When we first held council to aid the lost terrestrial souls," Amilius said, "some wanted to leave the Terrestrials to their own illusions.

Others feared succumbing to the temptations that imprisoned the first generation of lost souls. They were correct. We made great progress, but the world of matter has proved too strong for souls to exist in a spiritual state. Even the Celestials fell back into the evil of their own material desires."

"What would be done then?" Terselia asked.

"How may we correct our error?" Petroniel asked. "A way to atone must exist."

They well knew the problem lay in a fundamental paradox of the spirit. After all, they were the first to assert their wills before the Will of The One and depart from the consciousness of the Whole. The material universe projected by The One was a mind-stream they were supposed to help shape and guide. They were not supposed to immerse themselves in it and change its course. They were not to interpose their own thought essence into it, floating along to be carried away by their own dreams.

They violated the Will of The One no matter how innocent their initial intentions. Alone among them, Amilius, Sophia's other half, remained in a form untouched by the stain of the fall and so he was the bearer of harsh tidings.

"I have communed with The One," Amilius said. "The earthbound souls are too drunk with power or forgetfulness to overcome the amnesia that imprisons them on this plane. They become denser with time. The current beings on earth are stained by the nature of the fall, which came from the psychic plane of the soul, not from the realm of spirit. The earth cannot be purified by you as you are now."

"What then is the way out for the lost souls?" Averniel asked. "Is there even a way for *us* to return?"

And Amilius put before them the grave choice upon which their fate and that of the entire material world would be decided. The current physical forms occupied by the various incarnated soul waves were either too brutish or too corrupted by godlike power. In such besotted states, they would never rise again. A new physical vessel had to be evolved, one more limited in power and more aware of its own mortality yet with the capacity to hold spirit consciousness. In this state of balance, embodied souls might strive to uncover the source of their suffering and so awaken from their dream state to their true being.

"This new being must be born of both earth and spirit," Amilius said.

They would work over time to evolve the body of a hominid creature natural to the earth, influencing and modifying its glandular centers with their spiritual energies from the Telian T'Meso, the mental energy dimension closest to the materialized world. When the process was complete, the new body would serve as a vehicle over many ages for reincarnated souls bound to the earth plane to learn and escape the Great Illusion.

"Only you can lead these new *Adamic* earthbound souls back," Amilius said. "But you must enter the same physical bodies they occupy under the cycle of birth and death."

He could feel them recoil at the idea of assuming dense bodies. "You can withdraw back to the psychic plane. It is not too late. You may re-ascend and leave the earth's souls lost in the spider web of their dream matrix. But the Archon's influence on both planes will grow because of the souls fallen into captivity on earth, and you may not return to the heavenly Pleroma."

Sophia responded first. "My path is clear. I have the most for which to atone."

"My beloved, my companion, my other half," Amilius said. "Beware. You most of all shall be tempted and tested and face the greatest challenges incarnated on earth."

The price of salvation for all fallen beings required the First Souls to fully enter the world. They had to correct the error in creation they had begun so long ago when they first broke the Unity of the heaven and entered lower dimensions of existence. To this course they committed. They would seal their fate to the destiny of the earth and its people in ages of sorrow and suffering.

The First and Second epochs of Artalanta ended in destruction. And it came to pass during the reign of the emperor Anu in the Third Epoch that history would repeat itself. This is the doom of the creature called man, a blind spirit roaming a simulated world of its own making in an amnesiac fog. The weight of the material world proved stronger than its spirit consciousness. The souls trapped in flesh forgot that reality is a state of mind, and materiality is a constructed belief, a mind-spell that turns creators into their creations, puppet masters into puppets, souls into bodies.

When you grasp the truth that Universal Consciousness is a Mind-Energy that limits Itself to push into lower forms of experience, then you will understand how the myriad parts of God came to dwell in physical form.

A thought is a thing and it has force. Once conceived, it gains power from the energies of the minds that contemplate it and believe in it. The One conceived the *possibility of contradiction*, so the thought of opposition existed from the beginning. In the spirit world, it exists only in potential and it is called Authades, the Pleaser of Itself, the power devoted solely to its own gratification. In the lower planes, it actualizes as the Archon, the force compelling souls to think and act with no respect for others but only unto themselves in opposition to the Law of The One.

Now the people of Artalanta would cleave more than ever to opposing beliefs--those who kept the remembrance of spirit and The One in their hearts and those who replaced the thought of The One with their man-made images and false gods allowing them to run rampant over the earth in rapacious conquest and enslavement of others.

To all generations to come who read this, to those who think our words are mere lore or removed from reality, remember the fate of proud Artalanta, for failure to overcome this insidious power drove it into the depths of the sea.

— *The Book of Degrees, Temple of Knowledge, Artalanta*

THE THIRD EPOCH

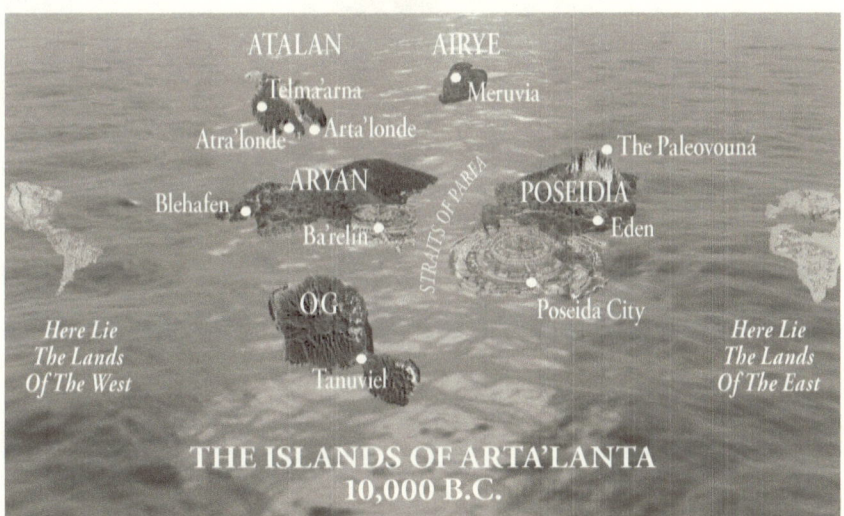

ATALAN
Telma'arna
Atra'londe • Arta'londe
AIRYE
Meruvia

ARYAN
Blehafen
Ba'relin

STRAITS OF BAREA

The Paleovouná

POSEIDIA
Eden

O.G.
Tanuviel

Poseida City

Here Lie
The Lands
Of The West

Here Lie
The Lands
Of The East

THE ISLANDS OF ARTA'LANTA
10,000 B.C.

**ISLAND EMPIRE OF ARTALANTA
THIRD EPOCH, 10,700 BC**

CHAPTER VI
Poseidia Island
The Third Epoch, circa 10,700 BC

And they were condemned to be killed.
—On the Origen of the World, a Gnostic Gospel

The beginning of the suicidal war that would destroy a large part of the earth and send a magnificent civilization into the mists of legend could be traced to one fateful day. The air wing bearing Consular An-Kera of Airye landed at the airfield of Poseidia, the capital city of Poseidia and all Artalanta.

The original single continent of Artalanta had broken apart some twelve thousand years ago. Five islands remained—Poseidia, Aryan, Atalan, Og, and Aiyre.

Intrusions of the ocean penetrated Poseidia's low southern plain. These formed irregular fingers of land culminating in a large lake half a league inland from the coast. Here the land was excavated and filled to become the mighty port capital of Poseidia with its ringed harbor.

Poseidia's land mass graded upward to the north to form the highest peaks on Artalanta, the Paleovouná or the "ancient mountains," sometimes called the Trimountaine for its three distinct peaks of Párnathal, Pelion, and Palasindra. These had survived the destruction of the first two epochs.

To the southwest lay the harsher island of Og, its plain lands broken by rocky hills and tree-covered vales leading to a forbidding coastline of massive cliffs forming a wall against the ocean on three sides.

North of Og lay the fertile island of Aryan with its beautiful rolling valleys and uplands. Blessed with fine soil, green grasses, and gentle forests, Aryan possessed an abundance of earth's raw elements. Atalan, the seafarers' island of great twin harbors, and Airye, the fertile land, were the two smaller islands.

From the airfield, the consular entered a traditional horse-drawn carriage that would transport him along the Celestial Way from the mainland to the Hall of the Consularion on Poseidia's citadel mount occupying the central landmass of the port's concentric island rings. Hover cars were available but most forms of air travel were restricted to the military and chief government officials. Originally, the law was meant to prevent the chaos of private air vehicles clogging the skies over the islands. In later times it remained owing to the tensions between the Children of the Law of One and the Sons of Belial so that neither side could employ excessive aerial technology against the other.

Thanks to the Laws of Amilius and the Children of The One, the great technology of Artalanta was largely limited to peaceful uses. Mechanical transportation and telecommunication devices were in use by the civilian population on the Lantean islands but strictly prohibited in foreign lands lest the technology should turn to aggressive use against less advanced cultures or fall into their hands.

The Nautikon and Pneumarta, the naval and air forces, existed strictly for defensive purposes. Artalanta was forbidden to outsiders, and no external power had ever attacked them owing to their technological superiority. The Nautikon and Pneumarta formed a virtual shield against foreign visitation, peaceful or otherwise. Advanced weaponry was stored in Poseidia under the strict control of the Elda-Fera, the scientific priesthood, in case of dire emergencies but was never issued for other uses.

The Lantean armed forces were restricted to employing gas compression guns along with weaponry comparable to that of the non-Lantean peoples in the lands of the West and East. This was meant to curb any impulse to overwhelm and destroy less developed societies. These controls were often circumvented by the warlike Aryans who illegally staged periodic raids on foreign lands to add to their slave pool. Slavery was a major point of division among the Belial and the Law of One factions. Now Aryan was pushing the slavery issue again, the reason An-Kera was on his way to the Consularion for a crucial vote.

An-Kera wore a silver torc about his neck with the consular insignia of his station. His high-collared red cape formed a crescent around his lower face that ended just below the ears. His satin tunic was embroidered with patterns signifying his origin from Airye. He gazed over the rolling green countryside of farms and villages typical of the geography that lay between Poseidia's port on the south and the sacred mountains of the Paleovouná to the north.

An-Kera felt the sense of ordered grandness that permeated Artalanta's main island, and they had not even reached the approaches of incomparable Poseidia with its magnificent waterways, massive statuary, and the many sacred pyramidal temples designed to capture the intelligent light of the sun.

His favorite sight was the approach to the port city's outskirts along the Golden Mean with its row of statues, one hundred feet in height, one side depicting warriors, the other philosophers. Figures of similar scale existed on Aryan but minus the philosophers. Poseidia's artistic representations emphasized respect for balance in all things; Aryan's art reflected their obsession with one thing—power. It was Aryan's quest for power that had brought him to Poseidia today.

An-Kera looked out the carriage window and saw the gigantic figures along the Golden Mean in the distance. His mind raced with anticipation at what he expected to be the most dangerous and confrontational meeting of the Consularion in memory.

At one point the carriage slowed, then came to a halt. "What is it?" An-Kera called out to the driver.

"Sorry, Consular. Transport wagon dropped a load of lumber ahead of us. The road is completely blocked. Let me see how long they will be."

An-Kera heard the driver climb down from the carriage. As he waited, a glint caught his eye. Off to his right along the tree line, a man appeared to be pointing something like a large diamond in his direction. Momentarily confused, he stared at the figure, but recognition soon dawned on him and his heart nearly jolted out of his chest. He knew what the man was holding. He had seen such objects in the guarded weapons vaults of the Elda-Fera, forbidden remnants created in the early Third Epoch. But how could this be and who was this man to have such a weapon?

It was the last question ever to run through his mind. One brilliant flash and the carriage vaporized into sparkling shards in the afternoon breeze bearing An-Kera's molecules away in the wind.

CHAPTER VII
Poseidia, the Consularion
The Third Epoch, circa 10,750 BC

they plot wrath with craft.
—Pistis Sophia, a Gnostic Gospel

Captains General Avarna and Petronien rode the funnel tube uphill from lower Poseidia to the citadel, where they made their way toward the Consularion. The great assembly hall was part of the government complex surrounding the Imperial Palace. The streets of the upper town were made of gleaming polished alabaster adorned by magnificent squares and gardens watched over by modestly scaled golden statues. The typically huge Lantean public artworks were not allowed to dwarf the environs of the imperial complex, a sentiment of pride that struck many as more Aryan than Poseidian.

The two military leaders had been summoned by Desamon, Deputy Consular and Prime Pedagogue of the Temples of Learning. The three men met periodically, but rarely all together and never by formal summons. The ceremonial guards greeted them with the customary salute of one arm clapped open-palmed over the heart, then raised forward. The thirty-foot high metal inlaid doors opened at the touch of a guard's remotely held device. The men walked up to Desamon's office above the main assembly hall.

Entering Desamon's office, the two were surprised to see Segund, High Priest of the Elda-Fera, Keeper of the Portals. This indicated something truly must be amiss. The Elda-Fera rarely came down from their Temple of Light Pyramid on Mount Pelion, one of the three peaks of the Paleovouná. They were charged with the keeping of the Touai Stone on Palasindra, the great crystal that powered all Lantean devices. The mystical priest-scientists of the Elda-Fera, also known as the White Brotherhood, were able to maintain communication with other dimensions beyond space and time. The carefully guarded upper reaches of Pelion and Palasindra were off-limits to all but the Elda-Fera. Even the emperor asked permission to access the area, though this was more of a formality, a show of respect as opposed to a requirement.

The bald-pated Segund wore a white mantle with red embroidered lapels open at the chest, vaulted epaulets on the shoulders, and a white tunic with a round gold-embroidered collar. Desamon wore the simple multi-colored robe of the Pedagogue, the primary minister in the Lantean educational system, rather than his consular attire. Desamon was one of the most influential men of the empire with his conjoining roles of Pedagogue, Deputy Consular, and a primary advisor to the emperor.

Avarna took off the dark-plumed helmet signifying his position as a Blackmane, the emperor's bodyguard. Petronien followed suit. "You summoned us, Consular?" Petronien said.

"Yes," Desamon said, "for a meeting I had hoped would never happen. Consular An-Kera has been assassinated."

"Murdered?" Petronien said. "How?"

"That is the most disturbing part," Desamon replied. "It appears he was vaporized by an energy ray." The two soldiers looked at each other with grim faces. "Some farmers saw a flash of light and heard the muffled explosion signature of a striking energy weapon. The driver was found dead, stabbed on the road, and evidence of the carriage was outlined on the ground. The security forces have cordoned off the site."

"But how is that possible?" Avarna asked. "All energy weapons are stored under the Elda-Fera's keeping on Pelion. To create new ones would require a modified frequency of the Touai Stone to operate the weapon's internal power crystal. No one can get near the Great Crystal that unless ..."

"No, Captain-General, no one has modified the Crystal," Segund said in a low monotone, calm as the waters of Poseidia's inner harbor. "Such an action would register. We would know."

"How then?" Petronien asked.

The priest folded his hands together and rested them on his chest. "The sub-crystal of the weapon itself could theoretically be modified, but only for the briefest of times, and then it would implode without attunement to the Touai Stone." The Children mostly referred to the

Crystal by its ancient name. The term "Firestone" used by the Belials had come into use in the Second Epoch during the reign of Tar Esai, when the Great Crystal was disastrously weaponized for use against the giant marauding beasts of that age.

"But who has such capabilities?" Avarna asked.

"That answer," Desamon said, "will follow if we find out who killed An-Kera and why. I have a good idea about that, and if I am correct, we may be in the opening stages of a civil war."

Desamon bade them sit around a table to continue the discussion. "You know that the Aryans and Belials are trying to pass a historic law in the Consularion tomorrow to allow slavery on Airye."

Slavery, an ancient practice of the Belials, had survived into the Third Epoch as a prime point of contention between the Belials and the ruling Children of The One. The issue was increasingly polarizing Artalanta. The slaves were descendants of drone mind-projections from earlier epochs when Lanteans of the Third Root-Race possessed the power to generate material beings. The slave ranks had swelled with human captives from foreign lands raided by Aryan and the Belials for cheap labor.

"The Belials argue that it makes perfect sense for the island to have slaves work the fields since Airye is the breadbasket of the Empire," Desamon said. "But besides the great evil of slavery in the eyes of The One, grave social and political consequences will ensue if we allow this."

"Yes," Petronien said. "With Atalan already in their camp, the Aryans and the Sons of Belial would control three of the five islands, not to mention the food supply for Airye we depend on."

Desamon nodded. "Their ultimate aim is to isolate Poseidia, then gain control of the Touai Stone."

"That," said the normally quiet Segund, "would be a disaster, not only for Artalanta but for the world. The Sons of Belial and the Tekna-Fera will want to alter its uses for offensive purposes. They forget the disaster that happened the last time the Crystal was weaponized."

"But how could that come to pass?" Petronien asked. "The Consularion would not support this and certainly the emperor would not agree."

Desamon sighed. "Do not be so sure, Petronien. Last month, Consular

Tel-Ra of Og transitioned to the higher realms. Upon the death of an elected consular, the governor general has the right to fill the vacancy with an appointee. Governor Dal-Golia of Og is aligned with the Belials, though the people and military orders of Og are neutral or support the Imperium. The views of Dal-Golia's new appointee, Onzayre, are not yet public. He has been too quiet. I suspect he will vote for the slavery proposal."

"The Belials will likely kill Consular Tolraden of Og by Dal-Golia's command," Petronien said.

"I have already taken measures to conceal and extricate him," Desamon replied.

"What about Airye itself?" Avarna asked, his platinum armor catching the light of a nearby glow lamp.

"Though the population, in general, does not support the proposal, the large landholders do," Desamon replied. "They are greedy and short-sighted. But whereas An-Kera detested the idea, the remaining consular, Tel-Karna, favors the landowners and by extension the measure."

The men sat a moment looking at the huge wall mural showing the five islands. Avarna stood and pointed at the map. "By my count, the Aryan-Atalani bloc would have four votes plus one each from Airye and Og, if your suspicions are correct. Poseidia and the remaining consulars from Og and Airye make only four. The slavery law would pass the Consularion. Can the Gerousia have any influence?"

"They would probably vote to reject the measure, but the Consularion is not obligated to take their advice," Desamon replied.

"Then why not delay the vote until An-Kera's seat is filled? Governor Viskanderen of Aiyre will never appoint a Belial. That would create a tie vote and tie votes do not leave the chamber," Avarna said.

"Correct," Desamon replied, "But such a delaying motion itself requires a vote. They have the current majority, and it will not pass. My friends, I am quite certain how this came about. Furthermore, I am quite certain who is behind An-Kera's murder, and we must stop him. If I am correct, not only is Artalanta in danger, but the entire world may be headed for suffering unknown since the Second Epoch."

CHAPTER VIII
Poseidia
The Third Epoch, circa 10,750 BC

He who will plot evil against
another, he is the first ...
— The Sentences of Sextus, a Gnostic Gospel

Desamon pointed to the map of Aryan on his office wall. "When Dal-Golia filled the vacancy on Og, Ra-Mennarial of Aryan saw his opportunity to shift the balance of power. He needed just one more vote, or the absence of one opposing vote, to push his agenda through the Consularion."

Ra-Mennarial was the Prince of Aryan, said to be a descendant of Belial himself, and the only person to carry a royal title in all of Artalanta apart from the royal family of Poseidia.

"So Mennarial had An-Kera assassinated," Avarna said.

"Likely so," Desamon said. "How they produced an energy weapon, short-lived as it may be, I do not know. But, I do know why they used it. Mennarial was hoping to leave no evidence, so fingers could point at him. Fortunately, the farmers arrived before they could remove the driver's body and the winds could blow away the carriage's remnants."

During Mennarial's governance, Aryan had become more aggressive and belligerent than ever. He sent out periodic raiding parties to obtain slaves from outlying lands. The training levels of his military orders had become alarming, though nominally they were under command of the Poseidian orders. Poseidian technology was superior in the sense that it could still employ the spiritual energies from the earlier epochs through the Touai Stone, the Great Crystal. Aryan technology, however, was the most advanced in the empire in mechanical proficiency through the technological objects it created with the crystal energies.

"I agree with Avarna that neither Viskanderen nor Telerian would tolerate slavery on Airye," Desamon said referring to the governor general of Airye and the commander of the Order of the Serpent based there. "Viskanderen still adheres to the Law of The One, and Telerian, though neutral, obeys the commands of the governor. But if the law passes and the emperor approves it, they will have no choice."

Avarna stiffened upright in his chair. "What? I did not take this too seriously until now thinking the emperor would veto the measure, yet you say he would allow this to become the law of the land? He would be signing a death warrant for the Children of The One. Surely he knows this is just the first step to an Aryan takeover."

Desamon pursed his lips. His head inclined toward the table, but his eyes rolled upward in an admonishing stare. "This is not to leave this room. Tar Anu, the emperor, may soon pass on to the higher realms. He is not mentally competent; he has not been for some time. He is reaching the end of his span."

People's lives in Artalanta during the Second Epoch could endure for thousands of years, for the early soul incarnations had more control over the flesh. As human consciousness came to identify more with perishable bodies than spirit essence, the power to regenerate deteriorated along with life spans. The Third Epoch Lanteans had reincarnated in fully human "Adamic" bodies that had evolved later. They experienced abbreviated birth and death cycles though still living between one hundred fifty to four hundred years.

The wise among them knew this shorter lifespan to be a grace of The One. The human evolutionary cycle required time to rise up again in consciousness. Death allowed more frequent crossing of the dimensions between incarnations to evolve soul memories. This learning after death increased the potential for souls to awaken and realize their separation from The Whole. Otherwise, souls would stay forever lost in their own dream world on earth indulging in their limited dream creations.

Anu, the emperor, was nearing his fourth century. Children of The One maintained a stronger soul link to the higher worlds and attunement to the life-giving Great Crystal. This afforded them greater health, knowledge, and prosperity.

The Sons of Belial denied the existence of God and were prone to shorter lives. The resentful Belials foolishly believed the Children of The One hoarded some secret to longevity. This was another source of friction between them. The Belials did not believe that it was the Children's faith and connection to The One through the Crystal that prolonged their life energies.

Desamon paced the room, looking nervous given his normally stoic demeanor. "The emperor is sorely affected by the pressures of the Belials and worries constantly about war," he said. "In his state, no certainty exists as to what he would do to maintain the peace."

"Hah, any peace with the Sons of Belial is a false peace," Petronien said. He looked at Segund, the priest. "Can you not use the power of the Crystal to rejuvenate him?"

Segund replied in his even monotone. "We have been doing so for the past hundred years, but our connection to the higher realms has weakened since the Third Epoch. Our powers to use the Great Crystal for such purposes has lessened to a great degree."

As their own internal abilities to linger in physical bodies waned, the Lanteans found a way to channel life-increasing cosmic energies through the Touai Stone. In the Third Epoch, the level of a person's spiritual consciousness would attune with the activities of the Crystal to prolong life, but as time passed the strength of this connection was waning with most people, and life spans were accordingly shorter.

"Control of the Great Crystal's power is the real prize sought by the Sons of Belial," Avarna said. "They do not live as long as we do and they think they will become immortal again with its use. The fools do not realize that their own lack of consciousness will render the effort useless."

"Why were we not told of the emperor's condition before?" Petronien asked.

Desamon sighed. "The two of you are amongst the most respected and important figures in the Empire, but Mennarial has his spies. The fewer who knew the better. Only Segund, I, and the emperor's daughters knew."

"What now then?" Petronien asked. "Just how ill is the emperor? What will he do?"

Desamon walked to a window with a view toward the imperial palace. "I cannot tell you for certain. We have announced that the emperor will attend the Consularion to render his decision in light of the importance of the event. I am worried how he will react to the provocations of the Aryans and the Belials and the pressure they will exert. He desperately wants peace, and they want to control Artalanta and the Great Crystal to gain dominion over the entire world."

"Then war is coming," Petronien said, fist clenched, his expression looking more sad than angry.

Avarna had drawn a fist to his mouth in a pensive posture. "The Children are not so disposed to war as are the Belials. We know what killing does to the soul. It draws us further into the earth away from the Source. We have been a defensive army, not an army of aggression."

Desamon walked over and placed a hand on his shoulder. "Your sentiments are well put, General, and you have solved your own dilemma. It is intention that counts. If you fight to defend and preserve, it is a very different vibration than to assail and destroy. If you fight for the love of what is good and not from hatred or greed, you do not harm your soul's progression."

"Still, death and destruction release passions leading to the dark side," Avarna replied.

"That is a choice each individual must make and guard against within the confines of his own heart," Desamon replied. "But we were not put here to be the sacrificial lambs. We have a right to defend ourselves and others against the evil that comes. For now, let us see what we can do to forestall the day of reckoning in the political arena."

"Only the emperor can stop this," Petronien said. "What will you do about him?"

Desamon smiled. "Why, that is clear. I must change his mind by any means necessary."

CHAPTER IX
Poseidia, Artalanta
The Third Epoch, circa 10,750 BC

The contemptible spirit has grown stronger
in such people while they were going astray.
—The Apocryphon of John, a Gnostic Gospel

Avarna sat in the imperial gardens reflecting on the events Desamon had just related. *Mennarial.* He should not have been surprised. Avarna closed his eyes. His presence in these gardens recalled memories of growing up together with Mennarial as adolescents in imperial court along with Amliea and Terselia ...

Petronien whacked him on the side with the flat of his blade. Avarna cursed under his breath. Emperor Anu's commander-at-arms was training his two prize students, Avarna and Ar-Falene, an orphan girl from Aryan. Ar-Falene was attractive but less given to things feminine than eager to learn the arts of war, an impulse that seemed fueled by some personal rage.

Ar-Falene had come from a family of Aryan Belial followers, as did Mennarial, but she displayed only animosity for the Belials and the Aryans. She had eyes for Avarna and he for her, though much of that in admiration of her martial skills. All he knew about her was that she had an older sister whom Mennarial's father, the ruler of Aryan, had sent to work in the household of Ta-Revi, now governor of Atalan. The mock duels between Ar-Falene and Mennarial became so heated that Petronien ceased pairing them up.

Both Avarna and Ar-Falene loved Petronien, whom they knew to be blunt and headstrong, but he advised them about more things than warfare. "I will tell you I am not the most brilliant of men, say like

Desamon, but I am focused and I stick with anything I do. You will see others drop away when things get difficult, but no one ever won a battle by quitting. No matter what the odds, never give up. The way becomes clear for those who persevere."

Mennarial was fairly proficient at arms, but he had other interests such as the exotically beautiful golden-haired Amliea. Avarna suspected a political marriage for peace in the offing. They often roamed the grounds hand-in-hand, yet Avarna thought their relationship odd. What struck him was that Amliea was not taken aback by Mennarial's self-centered aggression, an attitude common amongst the Belials.

During a conversation they were all having about their futures, Amliea said to Mennarial, "You seek to subdue everything that exists. I seek to create things that do not exist." No one understood the cryptic comment except, perhaps, Mennarial. Terselia detested him, and she told Avarna that Ameliea's fascination with him was "dark," and made her uneasy.

A drone servant, one of the mind-projected class of beings from the olden days, dropped a glass of wine on the garden terrace as he was serving it. Mennarial kicked him down a flight of short stairs. Amliea was silent, but Terselia protested. Avarna grabbed Mennarial and shoved him to the head of the stairs.

"Do you think you would like it if I threw you down there?"

Mennarial pushed him away. "You would take me to task over one of these soulless things? Fool. You see your purpose in life as the champion of justice? Or are you merely trying to impress Terselia?"

That remark hit a chord. He was infatuated with Terselia, the quiet, dark-haired beauty so unlike her sister. Amliea was a rash and compulsive whereas Terselia was a reflective student of events, always making notes in her journals, always observing and analyzing people and circumstances. Avarna knew Terselia liked him, but Emperor Anu, a practical man, frowned upon any serious involvement his daughter should have with him. Pro-slavers had destroyed his father's business. Though high-born and respected at court, his family had no money or political power, and Anu was saving Terselia for a more strategic alliance.

Under the emperor's eye, other than a few awkward kisses, the relationship could never go anywhere, much to Avarna's frustration. Avarna's destitute father told the boy to redeem their misfortune by leading a life of helping others gain the justice his family had lost. His best option had been to devote himself to training for a top military command. He had little training with women, and he tried to forget Terselia.

"The other races in the primitive lands should be under our dominion," Mennarial said. "People like the whites, browns, and blacks would benefit from our influence, and we can use their labor."

"Superior technology does not make us superior humans," Amliea replied.

"Of course it does," Mennarial said. "Technology is the very indication of our superiority. It makes us gods compared to them. They even think of us as gods, so far is our advancement."

"Being godlike is measured by the awareness of our souls, not our technology," Amliea replied.

Mennarial snorted. "Oh, come, Amliea. Still spouting that nonsense about some benevolent god. You speak with two minds. You have mistrust for commoners and you love your royal pampering, admit it. It is plain as day that the only power in this world is nature and the force we humans bend it to."

"You and the other Belials should spend more time in the temples and with the Elda-Fera," Terselia said. 'That would open your eyes to higher dimensions and a different understanding of the world. Instead, you and your Tekna-Fera spend all your time developing new gadgets."

"The gadgets that allow us to fly while others walk, to traverse beneath the waters while others float upon the top, and to store energies in crystals," Mennarial retorted.

"And just where do you think those energies arise from?" Amliea asked. "Yes, some energies come from the earth, but the finer energies that created everything come from a higher dimension of mind and I can tell you personally those are the very energies of creation."

"What do you mean by that?" Mennarial asked.

Amliea did not respond looking as if she had said more than she wanted, but Terselia spoke up. "The drones you abuse were mind-created by the old Lanteans. How do you Belials account for that?"

"We have our own innate mind powers," Mennarial said. "Granted, many of those arts have been lost, but that power is from our collective minds, not some mythical god-being."

"Then that collective mind would include the so-called inferior races, would it not?" Avarna said.

Mennarial grew frustrated and ended the conversation as worthless drivel typical of the naïve Children of The One.

Despite his behavior, Amliea seemed to return Mennarial's attention until something strange occurred. Her father suddenly dismissed Mennarial from the court and sent him out to the wilds of the Inland Sea "to better learn to be a leader," or so they were told. Avarna admired Mennarial's force of will and lack of inhibition, but he treated most people as objects for his amusement to use or abuse. He and Avarna held an uneasy friendship at best, so Avarna was not too upset by his absence. Amliea though became sullen and remote from the day he left. Avarna would not have thought her so taken by him.

Some months after Mennarial's departure, Amliea withdrew from view without much explanation. They had assumed she was upset about Mennarial's leaving, but it was not the first time she had gone absent from the court under mysterious circumstances. On another occasion before Mennarial's exile, Segund, High Priest of the Elda-Fera, had taken her to Mount Pelion for some sort of spiritual training which no one understood, not even Terselia, and Amliea would speak to no one about it upon her return. Mennarial, however, said he knew the reason, but to everyone's annoyance he left them dangling with his secret knowledge, a typical Mennarial ploy to lord it over others.

On Mennarial's parting, Petronien's comment to Avarna was, "Mark that one. He is trouble in the making. Sword practice is one thing but one day you may be fighting him for real stakes."

Avarna sat in the garden, thinking how prophetic Petronien's comment had been back then and how blind he had been not to see it coming. Since the time of his youth, the Children had outlawed slavery on the three islands. They still used the drones for labor but as voluntary wards cared for by the state. On Aryan and Atalan, the slave problem had grown worse swelled by human captives illegally taken from the outlying lands.

Of the many divisions between the Children and the Belials, the slavery issue inflamed the most passions. It was no surprise that it was now the primary cause of what appeared to be certain civil war.

CHAPTER X
Poseidia, Artalanta
The Third Epoch, circa 10,750 BC

... because of the rejection which happened to him ...
—The Apocalypse of Peter, a Gnostic Gospel

varna donned his chest plate then hefted a few swords until he found one to his liking. He turned to face Ar-Falene, a lithe, attractive woman with dark hair and exotic brown eyes opposite him in the courtyard. Her bare arms were well defined and her body athletic as one would expect of a warrior.

"We have not sparred for a long time. Why now?" she asked.

He moved closer to her. "Events are happening rapidly. We may soon be at war. I can think of no one better to get me prepared."

She smiled. "I agree. You went into the Blackmanes and me to the Stratia. You are a glorified house guard and I soldier," she taunted.

"Yet we take precedence over the Stratia," he said. "Brains as well as brawn, would you not say?"

"What I say," she countered, "is that it is a good thing I am in the Order of the Lion or I would be wearing a beast mask. Instead, you get to see if practicing with a beautiful woman will distract you while I beat you," and with that, she launched an overhead attack which he parried then ducked to the side.

"What makes you think I find you beautiful?" he said while they circled each other.

"Your eyes, for one thing," and she lunged at him with a series of thrusts and slashes, all of which he countered. "Not bad," she said. "You have remembered Petronien's lessons. Rather womanly using wooden swords, though."

"I do not want to hurt you after Petronien invested so much in your career," he quipped.

And so, they dueled for the better part of an hour in the courtyard of the Blackmane barracks, neither able to break through with a winning stroke, each trading barbs about the other's ability. At one point, both their swords met in midair. Avarna grabbed the end of his own sword and slid it down the shaft of hers. He wedged a foot behind her as he pressed his sword against her for leverage and tripped her to the ground landing on top of her.

"After all that good swordplay, you go down with a stupid trick like that?" he said.

"What makes you think I did not desire this position?" she said and she reached around the nape of his neck and drew him down in a passionate kiss that he returned with equal feeling ... for a moment. She searched his eyes as he backed off from her.

They stood and she turned from him dusting herself off and unstrapping her arm guards. "It is the princess, no?" she said with her back still turned.

He clasped her shoulders and rested his forehead on the back of her head with a sigh inhaling the fragrance of her hair, surprisingly sweet for such a daunting woman. "You know how I feel about you. I would give my life for you but ..."

"But you have a history," she said, "a bond with her since childhood, a dream you are chasing because the emperor will not condone your relationship."

She never turned to face him but spoke over her shoulder with her head tilted to the side. "Star-crossed love, so romantic, the stuff of poetry, the source of dramas. Even a woman like me knows it well and I can tell you something from personal experience."

"What?'" he asked, his mouth tightened into a constricted circle.

"It is the path of sorrow and the journey of fools," and never looking back, she walked away leaving him standing alone in the empty courtyard.

CHAPTER XI
Poseidia, Artalanta
The Third Epoch, circa 10,750 BC

*For the knowledge of the things which are ordained
is truly the healing of the passions of the matter.*
—Asclepius, a Gnostic Gospel

T he woman thrashed around in a glass chamber, growling and periodically pounding on the wall. Two women stood in the room outside observing her

"See the two large magnets on either side of the chamber," Amliea said to Terselia. "That is one of three elements I will use in an attempt to heal her."

"I never knew Alarien to be like this," Terselia said. "What became of her? Is it possession?"

"Possibly," Amliea said, "but I think otherwise. We know from the annals that in their headlong rush into matter, early souls entangled themselves in the animal kingdom taking on their energies and even hybrid humanoid-animal forms. We still have sightings of such creatures in the remote outlands."

"Most people think them a matter of legend," Terselia said placing her face nearer the glass to observe.

"No legend," Amliea replied. "The Elda-Fera have visual records of these creatures stored in rare crystal images surviving from the earlier epochs. I have seen them. They performed surgery back then among other means to rid them of animal appendages and characteristics. Some cases, like Alarien, may be suffering from vestigial memories, psychic throwbacks to a time when they had incarnated in less than human forms."

The woman lunged at Terselia who was looking at her on the other side of the glass. She clawed at the surface as if to tear her like an animal would. Terselia stepped back, startled by the feral ferocity of her actions. She turned to her sister "What can you do for her?"

"Let us see," Amliea said as she pulled a switch. The entire room and the glass cage became bathed in blue light. "This color aids the healing process. Our bodies are just solidified frequencies of energy. I am going to attune my mind-vibration to these," and she pointed to a bank of cylindrical crystals. "The vibrations will be amplified to pick up resonant energy from the magnets. The magnets help to establish the correct polarity that her energy frequency needs, for she is clearly imbalanced. Watch."

Amliea pulled the crystals up from their casings in what appeared to be a particular order then closed her eyes and began touching them as if playing a musical instrument. Her hands played over the crystal array as if by memory. Sometime later, a low humming started, and the large circular magnets embedded in the wall displayed faint coronas of energy.

Within an hour, Alarien's writhing body froze stiff as if someone had encased her in ice. She remained this way for a long time until Amliea opened her eyes and withdrew contact from the crystals. At that moment Alarien's rigid form slumped to the ground as if an unseen force had just released her from its grip. Terselia entered the glass enclosure and knelt by the woman.

"Alarien? Alarien?"

Alarien blinked and looked up. "Terselia? What am I doing here? Why am I in this glass cage?"

"You were unwell," Terselia replied. "Amliea helped you. How do you feel?"

The woman looked around the room. "I am perplexed, but I feel fine."

Amliea smiled. "You are indeed fine. My men will escort you home. I will come and explain to you later."

When they were alone, Terselia said, "Can anyone do what you just did?"

Amliea pursed her lips. "I do not know. I do not think so. I have practiced and I have an abil—" She cut her explanation short as if catching her words.

"Is this what the Elda-Fera taught you when they took you as a child?"

Amliea's mouth tightened. "The Elda-Fera," she said in a voice tinged with bitterness. "They do not teach so much as they correct like father does. Men are all the same."

"What do you mean?"

Amliea began shutting down all the devices in the room. "I want to speak no more of it," she said, "but you came to see me about other matters."

"Yes," Terselia said. "Sit with me a while." They stepped outside to another room less austere and more stately looking with sumptuous furnishings and wall murals.

"Desamon would speak to you," Terselia said. "You know what is happening, what will soon take place in the Consularion?"

"I do," Amliea replied.

"Father is old and weak," Terselia said. "Desamon fears he will give into the Belials and allow the slavery measure on Aiyre to pass."

"That is Father's decision and what if he does? I do not condone slavery, but is it worth a war if he stops them?"

"Amliea! Why do you talk like that? That would go against everything we stand for."

Amliea sighed. "So, what would Desamon have me do?"

Terselia related Desamon's plan. "Remember, you are next in line for the throne, and you can be sure Mennarial is behind this. Do you wish him to replace our rule?"

Amliea's demeanor changed at this comment. "Mennarial, that bastard? No, of course not."

"You were always creative, but Father stifles you, and so you must go about your interests in secret," Terselia said. "Apparently, I just stumbled across one of them today," and she pointed to the glass cage. "We face an immediate crisis. Father is senile and he will soon make his transition, so you must focus now on earthier matters. If you want to express your creativity, what better way than to sit upon the throne?"

"And you will write the histories of everything I do as empress," Amliea said. "Will you be kind?"

Terselia looked her in the eye. "I think the better question is will you be?"

CHAPTER XII
Poseidia, The Consularion
The Third Epoch, circa 10,750 BC

... so that I might thwart their aim
which the one revealed by her appoints.
—Trimorphic Protennoia, a Gnostic Gospel

The Great Hall of the Consularion was filled to capacity. The ceilings of the immense chamber were one hundred feet high inlaid with gold and onyx. The walls were gleaming polished alabaster. Massive columns of white marble interspersed the rows of upper balconies arrayed in a crescent shape looking down on the floor below.

The lower floor held seats for the hundred gerousai carved from exotic woods. In the front and facing them was the raised dais for the Consularion with ten elaborately carved chairs bearing seatbacks ten feet high. These were in the form of a broken semi-circle with a single throne-like chair in the center rising above all the other seats in the chamber. This vacant seat reserved for the emperor was made of gold and silver with inlaid jewels.

Every gerousai and consular was present with no absences. The gallery was full. Ra-Mennarial himself attended sitting next to Ta-Revi, the licentious governor general of Atalan well known for his debaucheries. Captain General Avarna stood with several Blackmane Guards around the vacant bejeweled emperor's seat, though normally the emperor did not attend Consularion sessions. He rather rendered his verdict on proposed laws afterward.

The Gerousia, after a lengthy and heated debate, had just rejected the proposal to allow slavery on Airye by a vote of sixty-two to thirty-eight. The Belials had argued that the drones were soulless, had no rights, and performed labor citizens were unwilling to do. The Children countered with the argument that all sentient life had rights and no one understood The One's plan for evolution of a particular species.

The Gerousia then referred the matter to the Consularion. A motion by the sole consular from Airye to postpone the vote until Airye's vacant seat could be filled was rejected by a five-four vote. Debate ensued for several hours with rising passions on both sides. People ignored numerous calls to order, and the Blackmanes had to step in several times to maintain peace when physical altercations threatened.

But when the vote was taken, pandemonium broke loose when the measure passed. Cries of outrage issued from both the floor and gallery. Several fights ensued and, in the melee, some people were pushed to their deaths from the gallery heights striking the floor below. Had weapons been allowed in the chamber, more people would certainly have died. As it was, Avarna deployed the armed Blackmanes in force to restore order.

Outnumbering the observers four to one, the Blackmanes eventually got matters in hand. As deputy consular, Desamon stood and addressed the assembly. "We would normally clear the chamber under such shameful circumstances. What have we come to when death pervades these very halls? Keep your seats, however. This matter is of such import we will have an immediate disposition from the imperial throne. The assembly sat down amidst a great buzz of surprised voices. Those voices rose to a crescendo moments later when a figure walked out from behind the raised throne chair and took a seat.

The female who sat on the chair was a celestial beauty with flaxen-gold hair rarely seen among Lanteans, who were a dark-haired red race with slight mixtures of the white and brown races that had filtered into the racial pool from the outlying lands. Her calm demeanor contrasted to the palpable tension in the chamber clearly indicating one not alien to the ways of command.

A consular from Aryan spoke. "I do not understand. We welcome the Princess Amliea, but she sits in the position reserved solely for the emperor. How is this so?"

Desamon stood and addressed the chamber. "The emperor has gone to the Paleovouná on a spiritual pilgrimage to seek higher guidance in these turbulent times. He is not to be interrupted."

"This is absurd," the Aryan consular said. "She cannot make decisions for the emperor. He displays no confidence in this mere girl and would never accord her any authority."

Desamon held up a document in his raised hand for all to see. "Hold your tongue and sit, sir. This is a writ of proxy signed and sealed by the emperor himself. It grants Princess Amliea temporary authority to render all decisions pursuant to matters of law. This is an established precedent and a prerogative of emperors, not that they need the consent of this body to exercise such a right."

The consular from Atalan said, "This is not legal, and her decisions cannot be binding."

"The princess speaks with the voice of the emperor," Desamon said. "Would you care to be on record refuting the emperor's authority? That might have a negative effect on your career, no?" The consular remained silent. "Now I suggest we hear the princess," and he yielded the floor to her.

Amliea stood in front of her raised seat. She paused to take measure of the audience, then she spoke. "Slavery is an abomination in the eyes of The One and all who engage in it should be ashamed. Whether from the outlying lands, whether one of the soulless projections of past makings, whether one of the hybrid beasts harboring our unfortunate kindred souls, slavery corrodes our very essence and separates us from The One."

"There is no God," a voice from the gallery shouted.

Amliea's eyes glared in sharp focus in the man's direction. "And that denial of the truth causes you to justify any action, satisfy any selfish desire at the expense of others. You harm your brothers and sisters because you no longer understand that we are all connected in the Unity. You recognize no consequences, but I tell you there are consequences. If you were not blind, you would see that the very universe ultimately rises against evil. The very earth rises against it.

"Why is our civilization today divided into five separated islands instead of the single great continent we once were? Because the earth rose up groaning against the evil men do. The earth is alive. It knows good from bad. It tolerates only so many insults before it reacts. I warn you, stay on this path and it will react again, only this will be the last time for Artalanta. We reject the proposal in question. Furthermore, never bring one like it before this body again. For the sake of peace, we tolerate slavery in parts of this empire as a practice handed down at the end of the Second Epoch. But any more attempts to expand it may result in the abolition of this evil altogether."

The assembly erupted in cheers, some even weeping at the eloquent and unexpected decisiveness of the princess's words. Avarna had kept the Blackmanes on the floor, so the Belials were unable to cause more trouble. Several of his guards escorted the Amliea out the back of the chamber, but not before he saw her look directly at Mennarial whose neutral expression must have been exhausting to maintain given the rage he felt at being thwarted. Avarna remembered Mennarial's budding temper when they were impressionable youths cavorting with Amliea in the imperial gardens. Avarna sought out Desamon and Petronien after they had cleared the hall.

"That was a masterstroke, Desamon," Petronien declared. "How did you get the emperor to agree?"

"I did not lie. I did convince the emperor to pray on a spiritual retreat to the Paleovouná. I told him that if the answers did not come to him, they would come *through* him to the princess. He was relieved at this. I know his daughters Amliea and Terselia. They are good souls. I did not realize Amliea could speak with such passion and eloquence, however. That helped."

"It certainly did," Petronien said. "We escaped the storm."

Desamon put a hand to his chin. "For now perhaps, but I cannot help feeling we have accelerated the conflict. Mennarial will react, and soon. He was certain he would win, and his followers feel entitled to power. Sirs, prepare your armies for action, while I try to work through our intelligence network. The hour may soon be coming when we must descend into a conflict that will reshape the earth, for better or worse."

CHAPTER XIII
Poseidia, The Imperial Palace
The Third Epoch, circa 10,750 BC

And behold, then, now I charge you
with the murders you committed.
—The Apocalypse of Paul, a Gnostic Gospel

The princesses Amliea and Terselia stood in the Tower of the Moon speaking and taking in the brisk night air. "Father is failing fast, Amliea, even with your healing abilities and the power of the Crystal," Terselia said.

"He should have adopted a son," Amliea said. "We are a disappointment to him, especially me."

"He was easier with me," Terselia said. "You are next in line and not the son he wanted, so you bore the brunt of his frustration. But I do not believe he comprehends the gravity of events now transpiring in the empire. I think you must soon replace him for the good of Artalanta."

"And for your good too," Amliea said, her gaze fixed on the starry night sky. "I would not prevent you marrying Avarna, who, fool that you are, you may lose to Ar-Falene one day. She is a formidable woman."

"It may be too late for Avarna," Terselia said. "The empire is disintegrating, war seems inevitable, and love is a peacetime luxury for people in our position. The Temple of Wisdom on Aryan broke with our sister temples. They renamed it the Temple of the Fire. Rumors are that Al-Presta and Assha, the high priest and priestess, have instituted fire worship and human sacrifice of slaves."

News of the temple's subversion broke Amliea's contemplation on the evening sky. The moonlight caught flecks of her reddish skin and rare golden hair. Terselia had the more common dark hair of the

Lanteans. Because of Amliea's coloring, some whispered that the emperor's line may have been mixed with white slaves, a rumor meant to insult because many red-raced Lanteans looked down on the black, white, yellow, and brown peoples of the outlying lands.

Such a mixing was unlikely but possible because the Children of The One delineated people by their hearts and minds, not their race. In any case, the scrupulously maintained hereditary records yielded no such past liaisons, and most held Amliea to be exotically beautiful.

"Father, senile or not, will never step down until he is dead," Amliea said, "But human sacrifice is a greater evil than slavery. It makes us worse than animals and sinks the human soul to depths I cannot even fathom. When I assume the throne, I will end it."

"Amliea, I have smelled the charnel stench of battlefields in my dreams," Terselia said. "The wheat will be sorted from the chaff and soon. Yes, think long and hard on what you will do, sister. I am afraid the empire you shall inherit will pit Lantean against Lantean. I bid you good night."

After a time of contemplating her sister's warning, Amliea retired to her chamber below the tower. She hesitated before entering the chamber — a strange place to sleep — but she heeded Captain General Avarna's warnings. Foolish as it seemed, Avarna had her safety in mind so she did as he instructed.

In the early hours of the morning, two whooshing sounds permeated the corridor of the hall below the stairs to Amliea's chamber. The guards posted at the door went down with arrows expertly shot into in their throats. Two figures in black opened the door and crept up the stairs with great stealth. Pausing for their eyes to adjust to the dim light, they spied the bed. Knives drawn, they approached. On signal, they began stabbing in unison — but into soft feathers rather than a firm body.

The perplexed assassins looked around the room for their intended victim but found no one. They ascended the stairs to the Tower of the Moon, but again, no trace. Running down the stairs, they exited the corridor, only to find armored men coming at them from both directions. They retreated up the stairs using the narrow passageway to fight off the guards, but they soon were pushed back into the room.

Realizing their position was hopeless, they ran back up to the tower from the bedroom where the guards cornered them. The Blackmane officer told them to lay down their weapons, but instead, they turned and leaped off the balcony to a crunching death far below.

When Avarna arrived, his officer inquired as to the princesses' whereabouts. Avarna gave no answer asking for a report instead. He then asked the guards to leave. "You may come out now, Amliea," he said standing close to a wall to the right of the bed. The wall section swung open, and Amliea emerged.

"I heard sounds of a struggle and stayed quiet as you instructed," she said. "What happened?"

"Two men came to kill you in your sleep," he replied.

The princess absorbed the news. "And to think," she said in a low voice, "I thought having me sleep in this secret chamber was foolish and excessive."

"And yet you heeded me or, more likely, heeded your intuition."

"Both, actually," Amliea replied. "But who?"

The assassins? We need to recover the bodies," Avarna said. "Probably warrior slaves promised freedom. They failed, so only death or torture remained. I know someone who would use slaves to such ends."

Amliea shook her head. "The boy we grew up with here around the gardens and battlements of this citadel. Oh, Mennarial! I cannot believe he would do this to me."

"He is not the Mennarial of our youth, Amliea. He left court abruptly with no notice and disappeared from Artalanta for a long time," Avarna said. "He came back Ra-Mennarial of Aryan, committed to Lantean domination of the world. His Belials are behind every move to undermine the Law of One. He has proclaimed no God exists and he worships blind force to rule men. You stand in his way."

A panting guard came running up the stairs and headed straight for Avarna. "Sir," he said blurting out his words and interrupting their conversation, "Deputy Desamon and Captain General Petronien require your presence. Aryan and Atalan have invaded Og."

CHAPTER XIV
Poseidia, The Imperial Palace
The Third Epoch, circa 10,750 BC

*Protect yourself, lest you be delivered
into the hands of your enemies.*
—The Teachings of Silvanus, a Gnostic Gospel

"What news from Og?" Avarna asked immediately upon entering Desamon's office at the Consularion.

Desamon and Petronien stood around a table upon which lay a three-dimensional map of the five Lantean islands. With them were Vortegren, Air Marshall of the Order of the Falcon, and Braan'dach, Admiral of the Order of the Dolphin.

"Dal-Golia has purged the Order of the Wolf on Og of any officers sympathetic to The One or even neutrals like Varandiel. He has appointed new pro-Belial officers." Petronien said.

"Only the emperor or you as overall commander of the armed forces have the authority to approve such an action," Avarna said. "Mennarial now uses force to gain what he could not do legally."

"I sent an order for Dal-Golia to stand down," Petronien said. "He ignored it. Varandiel rallied those loyal to him, and fighting broke out between the factions. Varandiel was getting the upper hand and had Tanuviel surrounded. Out of nowhere, a fleet of subsurface ships appeared."

"Let me guess," Avarna said. "The Sharks, and they probably spewed out Jackal troops." He referred to the naval Order of the Sharks and the army Order of the Jackals, both based on Aryan and under Mennariel's control. The animal references to the military orders came from the helmet masks they wore, a relic from evil times of the Second Epoch that had stuck for all but the orders based on Poseidia.

"Exactly," Petronien said. "The Jackals broke the siege of Tanuviel. They combined with the forces loyal to Dal-Golia and scattered Varandiel's troops. We estimate about forty percent of Og's forces now follow Dal-Golia, not counting the Jackal invaders."

"And how many men did the Jackals field?" Avarna asked.

"Perhaps thirty-five to forty thousand," Desamon said.

"So they left two-thirds of their forces plus the Orders of the Hawk and Sharks to guard Aryan in case we attack them," Avarna said. "Aryan's defenses are formidable. That reduces our options."

Just then the princesses Amliea and Terselia entered the room. Terselia's and Avarna's eyes instantly locked on each other, and Avarna smiled at her in a way he hoped was not too noticeable. The sisters had some similarities but more differences. Both were beautiful with the reddish skin of the Lantean race, but Amliea had rare pale hair while Terselia had the raven hair typical of most Lanteans.

Amliea's personality was given more to extremes while Terselia was consistent in her moods and behavior. Amliea was adept at healing using magnets and other means in service to others, but she was also overly infatuated with the pomp and circumstance of the imperial court. It seemed she had a desire to experience all things, but often in a rash, even reckless way. Terselia became a priestess whose interests lay in recording histories and events for people present and future. Whereas Amliea reveled in the accumulation of experience, knowledge, and wisdom for herself, Terselia's passion was revealing the value of experience, knowledge, and wisdom to others.

"I did not have time to tell you in light of this new crisis," Avarna said. "We just stopped an assassination attempt on Amliea."

"What?" Petronien exclaimed. "How?"

"The assassins were men of the brown race from the West," Avarna said. "But most assuredly they were slaves forced by Mennarial to do the deed under penalty of torture and death."

"To think you all grew up together," Petronien said, shaking his head.

"The Sons of Belial and Children of The One have always grown up together and lived side by side," Desamon said. "After all, the difference is a mindset of beliefs, of soul orientations, not a racial or physical divide. It is only in the past two centuries the divisions became so hardened into political factions. Many people are of neither side, just helpless pawns of greater powers. Still, I understand Mennarial's action against the princess is shocking given their past relationship. It shows how far into the darkness he has fallen to achieve his aims."

"You do not know the half of it," Terselia said. "I hesitated to tell you until I could substantiate it, but a former priestess of the Temple of Wisdom told me the Aryans have converted the temple, now called the Temple of Fire. They have started human sacrifices of slaves and captives to the Archon and Belial."

"The Archon!" Desamon said. "They resurrected that cult from the Second Epoch? This is truly disturbing. They are reintroducing an old cult of evil. This is what I have feared. He is distorting religion to turn the populace into an army of fanatics to serve his thirst for conquest."

"The war we have feared is upon us," Avarna said. "We must rally the Children and all decent Lanteans to forsake their natural pacifism and counter this threat."

"As you said, Avarna, war will draw us closer into the earth," Desamon said. "We will end up more like the people we fight."

"What would you do, Consular?" Amliea said. "Flee to other lands, pursued like wild game? Even if we were free of the Belials, others like them will always rise from the ground like locusts."

"I propose we defeat them and bring order back to the world," Desamon replied. "But I do not harbor the illusion that the world or any of us will be the same, even if we prevail."

"Why Og?" Petronien said. "They have some of the fiercest troops in the empire. Why not attack Airye and control the food supply? That's what they were trying to do anyway with the vote at the Consularion."

"Aryan is the most industrialized island," Avarna said. "Og is the richest island in raw materials. And Mennarial wouldn't try to starve us because we could cut off his access to the Crystal power. That would slow Aryan's production capacity."

"Not so easily done without hurting ourselves," Desamon said. "The Touai Stone emits power over a radius, not a channel. We could reduce the range and weaken it, but that would affect everyone including our allies in Og and Airye. It would be a measure of last resort."

"How have they secured the island?" Avarna asked.

"The Sharks have ringed Og with warships, maybe thirty percent of their fleet," Braan'dach said. "The rest are guarding Aryan in the Straits of Parfa. But they supplemented the cordon around Og with lightly armed merchant vessels from Atalan. Not the best in a fight, but effective support for spotting a naval attack and assisting the warships if it came to a battle."

"Vortegren?"

"Oh, the skies are full of reconnaissance aircraft," the air commander said. "If we come, they'll know it soon enough."

"They have the island tightly sewn up then," Desamon said. "We would have to commit a significant part of our forces that would leave Airye and us vulnerable to a combined attack by Aryan and Atalan. Remember, the Atalani forces are as yet uncommitted. Their orders stand in full readiness."

"Poseidia is too powerful to assault," Avarna said. "By attacking and controlling Og first, they tip the scales with some of the best warriors in the empire. They will be bent on eliminating Varandiel and the troops loyal to him to consolidate the island. Varandiel has always been neutral but he is now fighting the rebels. We need to help him quickly."

"But how?" Desamon asked.

Avarna directed their attention to the map of Og, which was almost two separate islands save for the narrow neck of land connecting them wherein lay the capital city of Tanuviel. The larger northern section was more rugged and mountainous, the southern section flatter with arable land.

"The people of the Oggian highlands are fierce and loyal to the Children of The One," Avarna said. "Dal-Golia derives his support from the agrarian south, which would like slave labor in their fields. The northerners won't like the idea of starvation dangling over their heads when Dal-Golia surely uses that as a tool to control them, and the north is the key. They are fierce. We need to supply them and get them to join with Varandiel. Warships will not do, but if Braan'dach's subsurface vessels can transport me there with a load of weapons, I can help organize a resistance."

They deliberated this idea and Braan'dach said, "I can likely get you there undetected, but what then? Are you just going to roam the countryside toting cases of weapons, looking for an army?"

"Unlike the military orders composed of native island troops, the Blackmanes' ranks are made up of soldiers from all islands," Avarna said. "I personally selected many soldiers from northern Og for their temperament and fighting abilities. Land me with a hundred Oggian Blackmanes near a point where the woodlands meet the sea. We will store the weapons in the forest until my men find us an army of their kin."

The group adopted the idea as their only feasible military option. "We need to work on all fronts," Desamon said. "The Belials think us weak pacifists. We can keep them off guard by trying to negotiate. I will call a meeting of the Consularion. I won't be surprised if Mennarial offers to leave Og in exchange for introducing slavery on Airye."

"And the emperor?" Vortegren asked.

"Leave my father to me," Amliea responded. "Desamon and I will handle the political end. And I'm hoping Mennarial himself comes to the meeting. In fact, I intend to demand it. I want to see his face."

So events went into motion that would change the course of the world. The repercussions from this day would be deep and profound, with unborn generations to come having their lives shaped by the waves of cause and effect that would radiate outward from this moment forward.

CHAPTER XV
Ba'relin, Aryan
The Third Epoch, circa 10,750 BC

they acted according to the creation of the archons ...
many works of wrath, anger, envy, malice, hatred, slander,
contempt and war, lying and evil counsels, sorrows and pleasures,
basenesses and defilements, falsehoods and diseases,
evil judgments that they decree according to their desires.
— The Concept of Our Great Power, a Gnostic gospel

N o king or emperor dwelt in Aryan, only a prince, so the seven men met in the prince's palace. In scale and size, it approached the emperor's palace in Poseidia, the product of decades of Aryan pretensions now finally coming to a head. The ceiling of the grand hall of the court stood one hundred feet high. The adjacent living quarters were smaller in size though no less impressive in opulence. The men sat around a long rectangular piece of solid carved onyx with a tabletop of inlaid diamonds.

"You should call this the imperial palace," Tar-Revi said as he fondled a serving girl's bare breast.

All the female servants in the palace were naked or half-naked. They were thankful Ta-Revi was not a more frequent visitor. Fair-looking as he was, he was lascivious in the extreme. He could not keep his hands off the women. One woman told the others how she had been taken by him on a table on a previous visit in the very same room while the prince and the other men went about conducting their business. But fortunately for the woman now being manhandled, this would not be a similar occasion.

"Ta-Revi, no time for that now," Mennarial said. "We have a war to prosecute, and you feel compelled to grope the servants. It makes one question your judgment."

"Atalan and I are ready," Ta-Revi replied. "I got our ships to Og with haste, did I not?"

"Speaking of Og, how goes it there?" Val-Andwar asked.

"Remove your mask when you speak to me," Mennarial told him.

The room froze in deathly silence. The Lanteans orders were obsessive about their masks, insane in the view of non-Lanteans. Over the centuries the masks had become part of the individual soldiers' military persona. Removing a mask was similar to being naked, but this was Mennarial's meeting, and these men needed to know who was in charge. Mennarial sized up three powerful commanders of the military orders—Ter-Madaz of the Jackals, Val-Andwar of the Bulls, and An-Klesen of the Ferrets.

Val-Andwar, in particular, was an envious bastard, always eyeing Mennarial's position with scheming intent. Mennarial looked at Ter-Madaz for a reaction. He was the most volatile of the lot with an angry, mercurial temper. He had his fists clenched, and Mennarial could picture his teeth grinding beneath his Jackal head mask. An-Klesen was the first to comply. He was more practical, being of a greedy mercenary temperament and looking to somehow line his pockets from the pending war. The others eventually followed suit looking uncomfortable with their helmet masks sitting in their laps.

Dal-Golia reported on the events at Og. "We have Varandiel on the run. He has fled to the north, hiding out in the mountains. Tanuviel is secure."

"Nothing is secure until you get rid of Varandiel," Mennarial said. "I know the Oggians in the north resent the Aryan and Atalani presence, so you need to get him before he can rally those highland savages."

"What can we expect from Poseidia?" Al-Presta asked.

Mennarial looked at the renegade priest, amused by the fat man's pious pretensions. He was about as holy as one of Ta-Revi's orgy sluts. Still, his consolidation of the new fire cult of the Archon was an important part of building a fanatical corps of true believers like

Assha, the female priestess of the new Aryan Temple. Mennarial made a mental note to visit Assha soon.

"Poseidia," Mennarial said. "You need to look at who makes the decisions there now. It seems the emperor is senile, so the real powers are Desamon, Avarna, Petronien, and now Amliea whom, apparently, they intend to install soon as empress. Petronien is slow, steady, and conservative. Desamon is a semi-mystic. He is the most faithful servant of The One, for all that foolishness means anything."

"You grew up with Avarna and Amliea in Poseidia," An-Klesen said. "What of them?"

"Yes, my father and the emperor thought to bring Aryan and Poseidia closer in that manner," Mennarial said. He sighed and rolled his eyes upward in reminiscence. "Avarna is a self-righteous fool who jumps at what he sees as any injustice, but he is bold and competent nonetheless. You can count on his hard stance toward us. Amliea is … unpredictable. She has a wild streak in her. She wants to grab this world and do something with it in a way that makes me think she could be one of us, but some impulse still binds her to the Children of The One. She could somehow be the key to all this if she comes over, but we will see how fate plays this out."

"Well, the Consularion has called an extraordinary meeting," Ta-Revi said. "If that is the extent of Poseidia's response to our invasion of Og, we should have a smooth path."

"Og is militarily untouchable now, but Amliea issued a personal summons for you," Val-Andwar said. "Sounds like a big wrist slap is coming," and the others laughed.

"You all think this humorous?" Mennarial said. "Do not underestimate our opposition. We handed Avarna a cause and he will exert his righteous anger. And we will all appear at the Consularion together."

"What?" Ter-Madaz said. "Go to Poseidia? Why? What if they arrest us?"

Mennarial ran his finger around the rim of a jeweled goblet on the table. "We will attend to flaunt whatever decisions they make, and they will not arrest us. We will be immune as part of our registered consular entourages."

"A technicality and we are at war," Ter-Madaz said.

"Neither the emperor nor the Consularion has yet declared war," Mennarial replied. "You still do not understand the mind of the Children. They will honor technicalities while we show our resolve."

"What if Poseidia and the Elda-Fera turn the Firestone into the weapon you want, then use it against us?" Dal-Golia asked. "That would end our ambitions in the blink of an eye. Is this all worth that?"

"Worth it?" Mennarial said in a contemptuous voice. "Lazy, insouciant bastard. Makes me wonder why we installed you in Og. Listen to me. At the heart of existence lies cold, darkness, and abandon. Life has no meaning except what we make of it. You are either master or victim—power determines which. Might and will are the only real forces that exist, the sole impulses that move the world forward."

Mennarial pointed at the enormous wall tapestries depicting his ancestors' conquest of foreign lands. "If you are on the wrong side of the sword, you are a slave to the desire of others, but if you understand power and have the will to use it, the world is yours. If any afterlife exists, then surely it will honor those who rose over others, not the sheep we use to achieve our aims. The Children are sheep weakened by their moral code honoring a non-existent god. They will never convert the Firestone for offensive uses."

"But what do you hope to gain by going there?" Ter-Madaz asked.

Mennarial smiled, drank a draught of wine from his goblet and said, "I hope to renew old acquaintances and test a theory." That cryptic statement ended the meeting.

Upon the conclusion of the conference, Mennarial summoned the priestess Assha to his chambers. "How goes the business of religion these days?" he asked the tall, slender woman in the sheer robe.

"We are gradually introducing the fire-worship of the Archon into Atalan," she replied. "Al-Presta's zeal is more effective than I had originally thought."

"Excellent," he said motioning her over to the bed upon which he reclined. As she sat next to him he said, "What we worship is a force, the force that moves this universe. That is the force of the Archon, and you are personalizing it in a way the people can grasp. That force is fear, obedience, and power, but also pleasure without restraint or consequence." He seized her, tore off her robe, and plunged himself into her moaning body time and time again. All the while he thrust into her, he thought of Amliea.

And that thought was not a fantasy as he used Asha's surrogate body. It was a memory of something past.

CHAPTER XVI
The Consularion, Poseidia
The Third Epoch, circa 10,750 BC

Now perhaps he will be deceived.

—On the Origin of the World, a Gnostic Gospel

Desamon greeted Mennarial in a crowd entering the Great Hall of the Consularion. "Ra-Mennarial," he said, taking him by the arm. "I am curious. I see Consular Tolraden of Og here and in good health."

"He is a consular and this is a meeting of the Consularion. Is there something remarkable about that?" Mennarial replied, his icy blue eyes narrowed.

Desamon folded his hands together and smiled. "Only that he made it here alive. Being the sole consular from Og who does not support an invasion of his island is not the most secure position one can be in, you agree? It might be in the interests of some to see him removed … one way or the other."

Mennarial's lips curled into an off-center sneer. "A person who would think that way would be a fool, considering it would have no effect on whatever the Consularion will vote today."

"True. As it stands, the Consularion will have a tie vote and not enough to condemn and censure those responsible for invading Og," Desamon said.

"A tie vote only because the emperor and Governor Viskanderen replaced Consular Tel-Karna of Airye, an outrage we would never accept on Aryan," Mennarial said.

"If I did not know better, I would think I was, in fact, speaking to the emperor," Desamon replied.

Mennarial merely smiled at the jibe.

Desamon placed a finger on the side of his temple. "Well, I suppose slipping out of Og at night with a personal aircraft at low altitudes after hiding for a week helped Tolraden's life span too. In any case, he will remain here for the foreseeable future as a guest of the court."

"How gracious of you," Mennarial replied, "but tell that to Dal-Golia. It is his concern, not mine."

Desamon studied the man in silence. "Ra-Mennarial, you think this world the only reality because you are blind to the worlds that existed prior. Your physical senses lie about reality. They conceal the single true force that created everything and prompts us toward love and the equality of all."

"Eloquently stated and patently absurd," Mennarial replied. "This world demands survival, and surviving means dominating. Survival is the mountain humans struggle to gain. I want Artalanta to be at the mountaintop. Is that not the highest form of love?"

Desamon sighed. "You are blinded by your pride. This world may be shaped by fire or by love, but even evil, in the end, dances to the music of The One. The fire you bring upon the world will forge the noble human qualities in your enemies to a hard edge. You are awakening a sleeping tiger. All you are doing is leavening the bread of life with needless suffering, the price of which your own soul will pay."

"Thank you for the lesson in philosophical abstractions, Deputy Consular, but today is a day when practical matters shall be decided," Mennarial said. With that, he stormed through the massive doors of the consular chambers and took his seat among the rebel cohorts he had forced to attend. Ter-Madaz was seething, Dal-Golia looked nervous, and the rest looked impatient.

The assembly was called to order. The Gerousia were seated on the lower floor, but they would have no say on this day. The matter at hand was for the Consularion whose ten members were seated on the upper dais in a semi-circular array. The emperor's chair in the center was vacant, but tables were placed at the opening of the semi-circle facing the consulars for those who would testify.

The first surprise came when the assembly steward invoked the sequester rule by decree of the emperor. This sent a flurry of murmurs through the chamber not the least of which came from Mennarial's group. Mennarial had to restrain Ter-Madaz from rising and shouting out his displeasure.

The sequestering applied to the entire Gerousia and Consularion as well as to any named witnesses or testifiers, which included Mennarial and his six cohorts. For the duration of the proceedings, they would be incommunicado and confined to guarded quarters in and around the citadel complex.

Mennarial gained recognition from the Consular chair, and he stood to speak in a loud voice. "The sequester rule has not been used in memory. This is most unusual."

"So is an invasion of one island by others," Tolraden of Og exclaimed to the applause of many.

"Your so-called invasion was a friendly request for aid by Og's legally constituted governor general," Mennarial replied. "Do not divert the issue. Is this a ruse to place the affected parties under arrest?"

"Not at all," Desamon replied. "The affected parties include the entire Gerousia and Consularion, myself included. Everyone, and I stress *everyone*, will be released upon the conclusion of the proceedings."

"That is a matter of record, then," Mennarial stated.

"Of course," Desamon replied, and Mennarial took his seat.

"What are they up to?" Ta-Revi asked. "They surely want to try and condemn you, Mennarial."

"If not all of us," Dal-Golia said." I do not like this, being out of touch while Varandiel still roams Og, not to mention what retaliation they may be planning against Aryan and Atalan."

"Calm down, all of you," Mennarial said. "They dare not attack Aryan or Atalan. Even with Airye on their side, they do not possess the forces to land, let alone occupy the islands, and we have Og sewn up tight. This is probably their weak attempt at intimidation, to do psychologically what they cannot do militarily. We will make our case when the time comes and show them the strength of our will. They will have to compromise sooner or later, and compromise is the first step to capitulation."

Mennarial confided in no one that his true purpose in coming to Poseidia transcended these useless proceedings. His focused his thoughts on how to effectuate his real goal, something that would end this impasse in his favor.

CHAPTER XVII
The Highlands of Og
The Third Epoch — circa 10,750 BC

... he who has come from the depth.
—The Gospel of Truth, a Gnostic Gospel

In the twilight of early morning, three submersible boats sank back into the depths of the rough sea along the inhospitable coast of northern Og. Avarna looked down from the cliffs above at the beach as the men off-loaded the weapons caches. They had landed in one of the few locations where ravines, long ago run dry, cut into the sheer cliff walls affording passage to the forested highlands above.

Hours later when all of the ninety-two men had gained the heights, the Blackmanes planned their next moves in the midst of a grove surrounded by a dense forest of tall trees.

"Well, we made it here undetected," Avarna said. "So far, so good. Now, Tairon, this is your country. Show our objective to everyone."

The soldier pulled out a map that indicated a village named Andovar some forty miles inland. All of the Blackmanes were Oggians with friends or relatives in highland villages, but Avarna liked several things about Andovar. It housed a good cross section of Wolfshead veterans, including Tairon's uncle, and a strong segment of men of combat age, all of whom, Tairon assured him, would be hostile to the Aryan/Atalani incursion and willing to fight. What they needed were organization, guidance, and arms.

"Ten of us will go to Andovar. The rest of you will stay and guard the weapons," Avarna said. "The Highlanders should be friendly, but we might run into hostile troops loyal to Dal-Golia on patrol. I imagine he, Ter-Madaz, and Mennarial are keeping their eyes on the highlands."

Avarna and his men set off. Their trek took them through dense forests, over hills and vales amid broken, rocky terrain, and they forded several rushing rivers. Avarna personally rescued Tairon who was nearly carried away in a torrent. "Damn it, Tairon," he said as they washed up downstream, spitting out water, "of all the people I cannot afford to lose. How in The One's name would it look for me to haul your bloated body to your uncle while asking for his help?"

Tairon smiled. "Uncle would be mad at *me*, not you, for dying with the fishes, no sword in hand."

The man was dead serious. *Surely a land that breeds the people we will need*, Avarna thought.

Avarna's troops camped for the night at the foot of some hills. In the early hours of the morning, still shaded by dark skies, Avarna woke from a hand shaking his shoulder. "General," the man said, "the woods around us are crawling with Wolfsheads."

"Dal-Golia's men?" Avarna asked.

The soldier nodded. "A few Jackal officers are among them."

"Patrols to make sure the highlands stay quiet," Avarna said. "How many?"

"Hard to say sir, but at least one hundred."

The thumping sounds of air-compression weapons broke the morning silence. "Damn it," Avarna said. "They must have spotted one of the sentries." Avarna had the men retreat toward the hills, where they stood a better chance on the high grounds, but they ran into a group of Wolfsheads.

"They have flanked us, cut us off from the hills!" a soldier said.

"Over there," Avarna said. "Take cover among those large boulders." The huge rock outcroppings made for secure cover. Avarna rallied his seven remaining men and with concentrated fire, they beat off the attackers.

"We are trapped here," Tairon said. "Looks like I will not see my uncle on this trip after all."

"We can hold out for a while," Avarna said addressing his men. "They have to come at us through those rocks, so it reduces their numerical advantage, but as we run low on ammunition, they will break through. I instructed the men back on the coast to send out another patrol tomorrow to contact the Highlanders. If we fail, let us hope they succeed. In the meantime, make every shot count. After that, it is down to swords. We haven't had real sword practice for a while, so here is your chance, men."

They beat off two more attacks in the early morning hours. Avarna took the opportunity of a moment's lull to catch some sleep until shouting outside woke him. He found Tairon. "Another attack?"

"Not sure," Tairon said. "They started coming at us, but then we heard shots and shouting and they turned away. I think I heard highland accents out there. We might be getting help."

Avarna had his men advance closer to the front. The Wolfsheads were being attacked from the rear and driven back toward Avarna's position. "Hit with all you've got, men! This is our chance," he shouted.

The Wolfsheads were now caught in a deadly crossfire and their numbers were dropping fast. Their return fire dwindled and Avarna heard pleads of surrender. The shooting soon stopped. Avarna walked out with his men to see about thirty soldiers in Wolfshead helmets, hands raised in the air, encircled by men Avarna assumed to be local Highlanders.

A tall man with a full beard walked toward them. "So, you were the ones they were after, eh? Who—?"

"Uncle Dai-Ter!" Tairon shouted.

"Tairon? Is that you?" the bearded man replied. "How in the five islands did you get here?"

As the Highlanders rounded up the prisoners, Avarna, Tairon, and Dai-Ter sat on a boulder exchanging information. "The surrounding villages heard compression weapon fire in the early morning and alerted us," Dai-Ter said. "We know the Wolfsheads loyal to Dal-Golia have been roaming around trying to intimidate the highlands, so we put three hundred men together and came upon this group."

"Help unlooked for is a gift of The One," Avarna said. "As it happens, we were on our way to see you." He explained the course of events to Dai-Ter, since Og had been under virtual quarantine since the Aryan invasion. "Where is Varandiel now?" he asked the Highlander.

"Holding up on Carch'Carai about eighty miles north," Dai-Ter replied. "He is surrounded by maybe seventy thousand troops, Wolfsheads and Jackals. They will starve him out before long."

"How does the north stand?" Avarna asked boring straight into the man's eyes.

Dai-Ter met his gaze unblinking. "The Highlands have no love for the puppet Dal-Golia or the Aryan invaders. The people here are followers of The One or they affiliate with neither party but they know when they are being abused. The Highlands will fight to a man. The problem is we have few compression weapons, mostly swords and pikes. Otherwise, we would already have aided Varandiel."

Avarna smiled. "I am fortunately in a position to repay you for rescuing us. We have twenty thousand small weapons and a number of cannons hidden on the coast northwest of here."

Dai-Ter raised an eyebrow. "Well now, that is very useful. Give me those weapons and in a few days I can field twenty thousand men ready to fight."

"Good. We have many problems yet and a short time to prepare," Avarna said. "Every day we wait, the enemy grows stronger."

CHAPTER XVIII
The Highlands of Og
The Third Epoch, circa 10,750 BC

It is this one who attacked and
cast down every haughty tyrant?
—The Teachings of Silvanus, a Gnostic Gospel

varna had days to accomplish what needed a year—build a functioning army. The men of northern Og were willing and brave but not trained or organized. Avarna built a corps of officers around his Oggian Blackmanes and veteran highland Wolfsheads like Dai-Ter. Avarna's Poseidian background did not count against him while resentment toward the Aryan Jackals ran high. This helped a great deal.

"We cannot meet the Wolfsheads and Jackals in open battle with untrained troops," Avarna told his officers sitting on logs and rocks in the forest clearing. "So we need to move fast. The longer we stay here, the more likely the Aryans are to find us. And Varandiel's men will be hungry. We need to link up with them while they can still fight."

Avarna walked around the circle of men as he spoke. *They will outnumber us in any case, and our forces are separated. It is essential we coordinate an attack with Varandiel's army, but the mountains and the Belials' jamming prevents communication. We must reach them somehow.*

"Impossible," Dai-Ter said. "The enemy is camped on the plains to the south of Carch'Carai waiting to starve out Varandiel. The other mountainsides are impassable, which is why Varandiel is boxed in."

"Sir," one man called out. "I grew up under the shadow of Carch'Carai.

There is a way to ascend the north face, at least in small numbers. We called it the Horsemen's Pass when we were boys. More than a few of us saw the centaur creatures we went looking for along that trail in the high mountains."

"Pah, legends," another soldier said.

"No, I saw them with my own eyes," the younger man said.

"What is your name?" Avarna asked.

"Ereden, sir."

"And you say you can get me up that mountain?"

Ereden smiled. "Are you scared of heights, sir?"

Avarna set off with Ereden. In his final coordination with his officers, he told them Mennarial and the enemy leaders were tied up in Poseidia, unable to communicate with Og. Their chain of command was at its weakest, but only for a short time. This was Og's best and only chance. If victorious, the road to Tanuviel was wide open, as nearly all the rebel troops were committed to destroying Varandiel. This battle had to be won at all costs to restore rightful rule to Og and save Artalanta from prolonged civil war. If successful, Avarna would find Varandiel, bring him in on the plan, and coordinate an attack.

Avarna and Ereden traveled north by horse. Hawk air patrols did not concern them. Two men riding horses was not unusual. It was enemy ground contact they had to avoid. They rode the better part of the day but made good time because they were able to exchange mounts in friendly villages along the way.

They reached their destination when Ereden said, "There it is, the Horsemen's Path." He pointed to what looked like a narrow gouge in the mountainside. The path was a waterfall that had carved its route down the mountainside ages ago, then ran dry. At some points, it ran horizontally; at others it was vertical. When Ereden remarked about heights, he was not joking.

"How could you have seen centaurs here?" Avarna asked. "Such creatures could not pass this terrain."

"Not here," Ereden said. "Higher up it plateaus out before it makes this vertical drop. It is up there they dwell. Most people do not believe me, though."

"I do not doubt you. I have read the annals about early souls in the earth who mixed with or imitated animal forms. We still have some among us who display vestiges of the old animal heritage. Those unfortunates are part of the underclass like the drones. Many of our temples were founded for the purpose of untangling and purifying those beings."

"I cannot imagine what it would be like to possess an animal's body," Ereden said.

"The ones who mixed with existing animal bodies eventually went insane," Avarna said. "Others projected their own imitative animal forms, then entered them. If we encounter the centaurs, hope they are of that breed. In either case though, the pollution of animal consciousness retarded their souls."

Reaching the plateau Ereden described took longer than expected. Avarna expressed his concern. "The weakness of our plan lies in timing and coordination. If we take too long to get to Varandiel, they may detect your uncle's troops. It is all over if they engage the Highlanders separately."

On level ground, they ran to pick up the pace. "How much longer?" Avarna asked stopping to rest.

"At least a day," Ereden replied.

"Too long, too late," Avarna said breathing heavily.

"The lower pass deteriorated since I was a boy," Ereden said. "The climb took longer than I thought."

The two men slowed then drew their weapons when they heard a distinct crackling of brush in the distance. Avarna made out forms in the dusky twilight coming toward them. "Wild horses," he said.

"No," Ereden said, placing a restraining arm against Avarna, pinning his compression rifle against his chest.

As the figures drew closer, Avarna sucked in a deep breath. Before him walked the creatures of the annals, the legendary half-horse, half-human centaurs. They ringed the two men in a still silence for many tense moments. "Easy," Ereden said. "The lore always said the horsemen avoid humans. But I never heard of them attacking anyone."

One of their number stepped forward. He had the body of a horse and the upper torso appeared not exactly human, but humanoid. The creatures had pointed ears and a sharp, upturned nose that looked like it belonged to some other animal Avarna could not bring to mind. Otherwise, all upper appendages and features looked relatively human.

To their astonishment, the creature addressed them in broken older Lantean. "Men fight below. Now many come to mountain. Why?"

"They are fighting a war," Avarna said.

"War? Why fight?" the creature asked.

Avarna gathered his thoughts to explain. "We lived in peace until some people attacked us. They want power, money, slaves. We fight to be free."

"Slaves?" the creature said, pawing hooves against the ground as if agitated. "Who these people called?"

"They are called the Sons of Belial."

"Belial!" the creature roared. The entire herd reared up on their hind legs emitting a terrible inhuman sound akin to a collective wailing that made the two men wince and tighten their grip on their weapons.

"You fight these Belial?" the creature asked, and Avarna nodded. "Belial evil god, kill many ancestors," the creature said. "Men on mountain Belial?"

"No, they fight the Belial too," Avarna replied. "They are friends and we must get to them for help."

The creature nodded his head toward Avarna in a gesture to single him out. "You different. We feel you from far. You old like ancestors. You name?"

"My name is Avarna. I am a Lantean from Poseidia Island come to fight the Belials."

The creatures murmured in conference, then the spokesman said, "Lanta. Once land was bigger in days of ancestors, then break. We hear Poseidia dream memory."

They must be referring to the Second Epoch when Artalanta was still a single continent, Avarna thought. He doubted they possessed written records, but it would be incredible if his references came from oral traditions handed down over tens of thousands of years. The creature said something that shocked him.

"Lantas. Ouen, Mele, help ancestors. You of Ouen Lanta?"

Avarna recognized the names Ouen and Mele from the annals in the Hall of Records, part of his temple studies. They were princesses from the Second Epoch who championed the underclasses and vanished during the Great Destruction. They somehow lived on in the memories of these creatures.

"Yes," Avarna replied. "We are of their line, the Children of The One."

"The One," the creature mused in repetition. "You fight on mountain?"

"No," Avarna replied, shaking his head with emphasis. "We fight to keep Belials off the mountain. I come to lead the men down to the plains below and fight the Belials."

The creatures conferred amongst each other, then their spokesman said, "You different human. We feel you from far, from memory of ancestors' time, we help you," and in a puzzling gesture, the creatures genuflected toward Avarna with their upper torsos.

Avarna had no idea why they considered him special. What mattered was that he and Ereden found themselves riding the backs of these creatures toward Varandiel's encampment. Avarna conversed with them as they rode. He verified that they had no written language or records. It seemed they possessed a primitive soul memory that connected them to elder days in a very different way from human memory. They dwelt in both past and present as if historic events lived inside them in present time. Dreams made them eyewitnesses to bygone events as if the threads of past timelines ran through their minds, connecting them to the days of their ancestors. How Desamon would love to meet them!

They cut their time to Varandiel's camp by two-thirds, thanks to switching creatures when one got tired. They dismounted and thanked the creatures just short of the encampment so as not to raise needless problems or questions with Varandiel's troops about their new allies.

Upon seeing the two men enter his camp, Varandiel exclaimed, "Avarna, how in the five islands did you get through the rebels' lines? Are they that lax?"

"We came up the backside with the help of some natives," Avarna said, "and now let us kick some Jackal hides and get you off this mountain so you can fill your gut with wine once again in Tanuviel."

CHAPTER XIX
Og, the Plains of Carch'Carai
The Third Epoch, circa 10,750 BC

... we shall receive the crown of victory ...
— The Interpretation of Knowledge, a Gnostic Gospel

The commanders of the Wolfshead and Jackal orders sat in their tent speculating on how long it would take to starve out Varandiel, when a breathless aide burst in. "Commanders, our supply trains have been attacked. They are burning as we speak!"

"What! Who?" shouted Entor through his Jackal helm. Entor was commanding the expedition against Varandiel in Ter-Madaz's absence. He looked at the Wolfshead order's leader, Taak-Ar, who was Dal-Golia's replacement for Varandiel.

"They appear to be local Highlanders, sir," the soldier said.

"But we have a thousand well-armed men guarding the supply columns," Entor said. "How could a group of highland woodsmen break through them?"

"They appear to be well-armed too, sir, and they vastly outnumber our defenders," the soldier said.

"Damn it, Taak-Ar, why were we not warned they could mount such an attack?" Entor asked.

"We knew they were seething," Taak-Ar said, "but they had no arms, nothing more than swords, no means to attack."

"Well they do now," Entor said as they stepped outside the tent to witness a thick column of smoke to the south. He said to his aide, "Taak-Ar, get fifteen thousand of your Wolfsheads from the third and fourth companies to that supply column immediately or we will be as hungry and weaponless as Varandiel's army in short order."

Varandiel's army had filtered into the lower mountain pass and foothills, ready to pour down into the plains on a moment's notice. They were eager to break the siege, and the adrenaline of impending freedom quelled their hunger.

Avarna sat high above on a boulder outcropping, overlooking the plain with his eye scope. The plain formed a semi-circle beginning at the foothills of the mountain and ran several miles deep before ending in thick forests.

"There, look to the south," Avarna said. "Smoke. Our men must have fired the supply column. They never expected any resistance to their rear. Looks like it is drawing off a large number of troops as we hoped. Now we wait for Dai-Ter's cannons, then we are off."

Tairon, Dai-Ter, and other group leaders waited in the forest to the northwest of the plain looking out from the tree line. "Looks like our men did a good job on the supply train. They drew off a good number of troops and then melted back into the forest to keep them busy. Now is the time, Uncle."

They ordered the air cannon brought out from concealment. "Now listen up," Dai-Ter said. "Aim high and well because we will be attacking beneath your fire to reach them before they can set their artillery against us. Cease firing when you can no longer maintain safe trajectories. We don't want our asses blown up by our own men, see?"

The highland troops were ordered into their skirmish line, and they took off at a trot. The cannoneers fired immensely to allow the infantry time to close the gap. On their way to victory or death the loud Highland cry of "For Og, Artalanta, and The One" reverberated across the field.

Confusion reigned in the camp of the Aryan-backed rebels. "These are not Poseidian Lions or any other military order attacking. They are damned Oggian Highland irregulars. How in the name of the seven shades did they get so well equipped?" Entor shouted. "Bring the cannon around quickly!"

"Look," Taak-Ar said, pointing north. "Varandiel's men charging down off the mountains! They are almost upon us. They must have come down and hidden in the passes."

"Unbelievable," Entor said. "This was a well-coordinated attack, but how? How could Varandiel know the exact moment of the Highland attack? We jammed air frequencies and communications don't work in the mountains anyway."

Key to Avarna's battle plan was having Varandiel's more disciplined troops enter the fray first. This would enable the Highlanders to close on the enemy ranks before they got into set firing lines of cannon or rifles that would decimate the Highlanders' charge. Once they engaged, the rebel compression guns would yield to swords, and the Highlanders were deadly with blades at close quarters.

Helping Varandiel's attack were the fifteen thousand enemy troops siphoned off to chase five thousand Highlanders to the south. This substantially reduced the numerical advantage of the Jackals and Dal-Golia's forces. Varandiel's cavalry went straight for the enemy artillery before they could fire on the rushing Highland army. The Highlanders were able to close in unscathed, fighting with a zeal unmatched by the Aryans and Dal-Golia's half-hearted Oggian troops, who now had to fight their own countrymen face to face.

As Varandiel's men and the Highland army flanked the rebels and gained the upper hand, the Oggian Wolfsheads began to throw down their arms, taking a knee with hands clasped behind their heads in surrender. The allied troops concentrated on the Jackals, who fought on as the Jackals began killing any Oggian allies trying to surrender.

Two hours later, the battle was over. The combined forces of Varandiel and the Highlanders had lost twelve percent of their forces, but the enemy had suffered massive losses, including all of the Jackal forces. Thirty thousand of the estimated thirty-five thousand Aryan occupiers on Og were dead. The remainder were garrisoned in Tanuviel.

"I'm sending my army to roll up the remaining troops fighting our Highlanders in the woods," Varandiel said. "Should not be difficult. They are my former men, and after this they might just quit if I offer them amnesty. Avarna, that was a brilliant plan of yours."

Avarna shook his head. "It was the worst. Too many moving parts hastily improvised. Using so many untrained troops, not getting detected before we engaged—too many small things could have gone wrong and we would be eating dust on this plain instead of them. Only by the grace of The One did we prevail."

"Rubbish," Varandiel said. "You knew they were undermanned to the south because they never expected organized resistance, and you knew damn well the Highlanders' ferocity in close quarters would be unmatched defending their homes against foreign invaders. Of course, luck was involved. It is in every battle, but you calculate the risks, create your best plan, and let roll the dice. You did what any good commander would do and you won."

Avarna looked across the plain through the smoke and dust at the heaps of dead bodies fallen like so much harvested wheat. He tried to reconcile what his soul knew to be right against what he had been forced to do. He remembered Desamon's words: "*War will draw us closer to the earth. Neither the world nor any of us will ever be the same, even if we prevail.*"

Varandiel's voice broke his melancholy reflections. "What next?"

"Gather up the Jackal armor and have the men exchange it for ours," Avarna replied, "then we march into Tanuviel to be welcomed as the victorious Aryan army."

Varandiel smiled. "I like that idea. Yes, I really like that idea," and he rode off to prepare the men for an attack on the capital.

CHAPTER XX
Poseidia The Consularion
The Third Epoch, circa 10,750 BC

... they condemned its ruler.
—Zostrianos, a Gnostic Gospel

Ra-Mennarial was at the end of the little patience he had, Ter-Madaz was angry to the point of outburst, and even the normally phlegmatic Dal-Golia was uneasy and agitated. Going into the second week of the consular conclave, something was clearly wrong. Nothing of any substance had happened.

They took testimony from Petronien as to how Aryan, Atalan, and Og had defied direct military orders to stand down. They heard the testimony from various legal experts about how many oaths and laws the aggressors had violated. They called on the rebel leaders—Mennarial, Ter-Madaz, Ta-Revi, and Dal-Golia—to testify and limited them to answering questions but not making statements.

Mennarial protested. He intended to use the assembly as a way to propagandize Aryan's position and influence wavering members of the Gerousia and the public. Desamon promised him that he and the others would be allowed to make their statements at the appropriate time. Several other things nagged Mennarial at the back of his mind. Avarna was absent from the outset at his usual position leading the Blackmanes guarding the assembly. Then too, the emperor Avarna was supposed to protect never took the center chair, nor was Amliea present as his proxy.

Most peculiar was that Desamon and his backers had made no effort to formally denounce or censure the rebels, which would have been the cue for Mennarial to make his own dramatic condemnation of the empire's status quo. "I think they are stalling," he told his cohorts, "but why? What does postponing the inevitable censure gain them?"

"Say what you need to say then let us leave," Ter-Madaz said. "Let us see if they have the stomach to enforce the conclave."

Mennarial stood and interrupted a consular who was babbling on about some nonsense. Desamon called him out of order, but Mennarial continued his monologue denouncing the pacifist government, and declaring an empire is no empire that does not expand its territory by force. He proclaimed it the right and the destiny of Artalanta to dominate the inferior races saying they would be better off serving the civilized Lanteans rather than living in the chaos of their own squalor. The Blackmanes moved to forcibly seat him, but Desamon waved them off. Mennarial eventually ended his tirade.

"What you have just declared, sir is treason," Desamon said in a firm voice. "The only reason I do not have you and your co-conspirators arrested is that you are here under consular immunity, and we still honor our laws. I am sure your presence here counted on that. Since you stand condemned by your own mouth, I order you out of the conclave where we will take up a motion to censure you, sanction you, and declare war on all who support your rebellious cause."

"What took you so long?" Mennarial shot back. "Was this not your purpose from the beginning? I spit on your motions. This will be not be settled by bureaucrats in hallowed halls but on the field of battle."

"Indeed," Desamon said in a calm voice with a cryptic smile that only added to Mennarial's unease.

The Blackmanes rounded up Mennarial's group including the rebel consulars and escorted them through the mammoth doors out of the Great Hall. "I told you they would never arrest us," Mennarial proclaimed with pride in his own judgment. But no sooner had he spoken than a clamoring group of envoys from Aryan, Atalan, and Og flocked around them.

"Quiet, you fools. One at a time and he gestured to one of the Aryans. "Bad tidings from Og, my Prince. Our combined armies were destroyed in northern Og by Varandiel and an army of Oggian Highlanders."

It took several minutes for the shock to set in as the herald explained how the battle unfolded. "Highlanders with compression weapons and air cannon?" Ter-Madaz said. "Impossible. How would they come by such arms?"

"It gets worse," the envoy said. "Varandiel's army dressed in the armor of the dead Jackals and marched into Tanuviel. By the time our garrison recognized the ruse it was too late. The city fell to surprise and superior numbers. They destroyed a large number of Atalani and Shark ships. The remaining vessels fled the port but were destroyed or captured by a Dolphin fleet lying in wait before they could gain the Straits of Parfa."

"How many of my Jackals survived?" Ter-Madaz asked.

"Virtually none," the envoy said.

"One-third of our army gone," Ter-Madaz muttered in disbelief.

"And who knows how much of our fleet," Ta-Revi added.

"This whole conclave was a ruse, a way to keep us out of communication," Mennarial said. "Somehow, they managed to smuggle weapons into Og, but weapons do not win battles alone, especially with a bunch of highland animal herders. I wondered why Desamon looked so smug when I said matters would be decided on the fields of battle."

"What do we do now?" Dal-Golia said.

"We go back to Aryan as soon as possible and discuss our options," Mennarial said. "You all leave now. I must stay a while longer to speak with someone."

"Do not stay too long, or you may not get out of here at all," Al-Presta said. "I hope it is important."

"It is," Mennarial said, and he walked off in the direction of the Imperial Palace.

CHAPTER XXI
Poseidia The Imperial Palace
The Third Epoch, circa 10,750 BC

... seduce and violate her in order to pollute her.
— The Gospel of Philip, a Gnostic Gospel

T o Mennarial's surprise, Princess Amliea allowed him an audience. After thoroughly searching him with half a dozen armed guards in calling distance, they led him into an empty room with a long rectangular table. Banners of vivid colors hung on the wall. The Great Seal of Artalanta was displayed on the ceiling, a serpent devouring its own tail encircling a pyramid enclosing the sun, the symbol of The One. Mennarial had ordered all such symbols removed from Aryan and replaced with a flaming lion's head, the symbol of the Archon, whom their new Fire Cult worshiped as the creative force of the world.

After waiting for over an hour, Amliea appeared on the opposite side of the room from where the impatient Mennarial was pacing. "Sit," she said.

Mennarial began to advance, icy blue eyes fixed upon her. "There," she said, gesturing to the seat at the head of the long table opposite her. He paused, unaccustomed to being ordered. Lips pressed tightly together, he made an amused half-smile and took his place.

"Rather childish to keep me waiting. Quite formal after such a long time, no? Not happy to see me?"

"What is it you want?" she replied.

Mennarial clasped his hands together, placing his forearms on the table as he leaned toward her to reduce the long distance between them. "I remember when we were younger, you had a talent, an ability, a throwback to the legends of the elder epochs … interesting things."

Amliea slammed her hand on the table. "You are a hair's breath from my guards removing you."

Mennarial held his hands up in mock defense. "Come now, it was your father who forbade you and punished you. I always lauded you for this. That is the trouble with you Children. So judgmental, so narrow-minded. We are all flawed, and human flaws cause dissension. You could be the mother of a newer, better race. I may have a way to peace, a way to save our empire with your help."

"Ah," she said. "You choose to talk of peace now *after* the recent events on Og? You seemed more eager to attack than talk before this."

Mennarial smiled and nodded his head. "I commend you. I do not know how you did it yet, but Og was a brilliant stroke. Certainly, that is why I am here in part. But I would have come for this meeting in any case, though perhaps with a bit more gravitas behind me."

Amliea sneered, unable to contain her disdain. "Gravitas? Leverage, you mean."

"Pah," Mennarial snorted. "Be that as it may, think back, Amliea. We had a relationship once."

"A relationship? Yes, we were young, we were friends, and you raped me!" She stood up, pounding her fists on the table. "Have you forgotten the reason they sent you packing from Poseidia? Only your father's pledge of renewed loyalty, his forced restitution to poorer citizens, and your exile to the lands of the Inland Sea prevented a war that you now brought upon us regardless."

Now Mennarial's hands slapped on the table, his mouth twisted in contempt. "The Inland Sea. Yes. I learned just how superior we are to the white and black primitives who would be better off laboring for us here than wallowing in their own rude cultures. But rape? Do not be absurd. You wanted me too."

"You took me against my will! Humans do not copulate in the manner of animals."

"But we do, and you wanted it as much as I did," Mennarial replied. "The days of the androgynes, if they even existed, are long gone and we were just expressing our feelings."

"It is intention that distinguishes us from animals when two people come together," Amliea said. "There are intentions to love or to lust, to give or to seize. Your intention was quite clear."

"Intention determining the quality of sex? Pah! More drivel from the Children," Mennarial said. He stood and approached her at the other end of the table. "You chain yourselves to the notion of a god who does not exist, a god of codes and restrictions, of things that stifle life's possibilities."

"We keep the balance by remembering the real world and our true origin in the spirit," Amliea said.

"And how has that worked for you?" Mennarial said. "A god does exist, but not yours. It manifests as a force you do not comprehend. It is a natural force we created that requires us to dominate or perish."

"Nature? You believe we created life?" Amliea said. "Only fools believe spirit came into being from the body. How can visible bodies give rise to invisible spirits? Matter is dumb, spirit is intelligence. How then does intelligent life arise from dumb matter? Spirit energy created matter, not the other way around."

"Amliea, I know you, Mennarial said. "You recite things you do not believe. How were the drones created? By a god? No, by beings of flesh and blood. Ah, I see by your face I hit a nerve. And you know how far above common people we are despite all the hand-wringing of the Children. *The Children,*" he spat the term. "Aptly named, for they are as naïve to the world as newborn lambs meant to be sheared. We have predators and prey, and we can choose which to be. You are no one's prey."

"You think of other lands and people as your natural-born slaves, but you know the story of the race of Adamas," Amliea said. "Humans appeared simultaneously at five locations and in different races around the earth, but only we in Artalanta had the advantage of the technology handed down by the old race."

"So what?" Mennarial shot back. "So our red race had an advantage in knowledge. That is not what makes us superior. But this is all immaterial. I come with a vision for creating superior humans and creating true equality for all. You could be the mother of a new race, but you let some stupid notion that I raped you get in the way. You half-heartedly resisted something you wanted. After all, you could have chosen someone like Avarna instead if that had been your true desire."

"Avarna and Terselia have had eyes only for each other since our youth, but you used youthful attraction to take what you wanted by force," Amliea said. "Why have you come, Mennarial? What peace do you propose? What is this talk of superior humans?"

He came close to her, and for a long time whispered in her ear. Her eyes grew ever wider.

"Impossible," she said, moving away from him.

"If you accept," he said, suddenly embracing her, "you will achieve what the Adamic creation failed to do and restore the intent of The One. You will save all souls on this plane, and if we were to wed under such conditions we could create a paradise on earth, unify the empire, and bring peace."

Her body momentarily went limp in his arms. He kissed her neck with a satisfied smile she could not see, but that quickly vanished when he felt the point of a knife at his throat. He backed off.

"So you want to bring back the peace that you broke?" she said, brandishing the blade that she had concealed in her hand. "When you of all people speak of The One I am wary, and I do not believe you can do what you told me. Trying to assassinate me sealed the nature of our relationship forever."

Mennarial appeared perplexed. "Assassinate you? Someone tried to kill you? I ordered no such thing. What would that gain me when Terselia would just replace you as heir, and she despises me more than you do. Look to your own sister. Perhaps she covets the throne."

Before he could further protest or deny, she raised a hand to silence him. "Here is the peace you will get. You will reduce the Order of the Jackal to half its current strength. If you do not, the combined forces of Og, Airye, and Poseidia will lay siege to Ba'relin. As we speak, the Dolphin fleet is blockading Atalan, so expect no help from the Order of the Bull. I would replace you, but I know you would sacrifice every living soul on Aryan to preserve your position. I will allow you to retain your some of your status, but Ta-Revi on Atalan and Dal-Golia on Og will step down and I will appoint new governors."

"Is that all?" he asked, staring at her across the length of the long table separating them.

"No," Amliea replied. "You no longer bear the title of prince. You were a pretender anyway."

"My title derives from the time of the Ten Kings before imperial rule," Mennarial objected.

"And I say your ancestors fabricated it," Amliea replied. "You will cease aggression against foreign lands and your slave trade is ended. The slaves you have now will gradually be freed over a period of time so that you may replace the vacuum created in the economies of Aryan and Atalan. We are going to reform the Stratia. The military orders will be integrated rather than using island-based militia troops. This way, the Orders will not owe loyalty to their own islands but to the empire as a whole."

"I suppose you think this is generous," Mennarial said.

"Oh, but it is," Amliea replied. "I would arrest you right now, but others prevailed on me not to break our immunity laws."

"Ah, old Desamon? So ethical" Mennarial said with derision. "Avarna too, perhaps? By the way, where is Avarna? He has been curiously absent from your sham assembly."

"Never mind Avarna," Amliea said. "And rest assured, the assembly is no sham. After you leave, I will assume the center seat, override the deadlock in the Consularion, and implement everything I have just told you. We are still investigating the murder of Consular An-Kera and the attempt on my life. Should that lead to your door, you will hear from me again."

"Do not forget I offered you a path to lasting peace," Mennarial said standing up. "Just because you have the upper hand now cannot erase the fact that the Belials living throughout the empire will never change their worldview. I offer you a new beginning, a new race, no more Children, no more Belials. I know you seek the knowledge of creation, but the spiritual path of the Children is a sham. A different, more powerful way exists within you, and together we may achieve it."

"Yes, with you fanning the flames," Amliea said, "and peace to you means utter domination."

Mennarial smiled. "Say what you will. I felt your breathing grow heavier when I whispered in your ear.

If my words had not reached you, that knife would not have been at my throat. Just think on my words."

After Mennarial walked out of the room, Amliea buried her face in her hands and wept out her anger and betrayal. Mennarial had haunted her dreams for years, for truly he had been the most compelling man she had ever known. Now he had come to her knowing the desire of her heart and offering her the path to it, yet he was a man who resorted to murder to achieve his aims, the demon who had molested her.

But what disturbed Amliea the most was realizing that she had not fully excised the demon.

CHAPTER XXII
The Imperial Palace, Poseidia
The Third Epoch, circa 10,750 BC

*Sophia, being an Aeon, thought
a thought from within herself.*
—The Apocryphon of John, a Gnostic Gospel

Emperor Anu had passed into the other realms, and Amliea was immediately declared empress. A few months later, after securing complete victory on Og, Avarna approached Terselia on the terrace of the imperial palace. The raven-haired princess had her eyes closed and head tilted upward, clearly enjoying the sun's rays on her skin.

"Who approaches?" she asked.

"I thought I was quiet," Avarna said.

Still looking skyward with eyes shut, Terselia said, "Feeling the sun's rays makes me aware of the light and air energies around us. Your movement created ripples and I felt them. So, General, how nice to have a visit from the hero of Carch'carai."

"Being rather formal, are you not? In fact, you summoned me, remember?" She turned to look at him. He moved in close and took her wrist in his hand. "Things are different. Your father is gone."

"What difference?" she said. "You made no effort all this time and you always had Ar-Falene."

"Your father was emperor. He forbade a close relationship. What would you have me do?"

"Find a way. You obeyed like a soldier when you should have acted like a man."

"Easy for you to say, Princess. I *am* a soldier."

"So predictable, so captive to your codes," she said. "Do you ever go by your heart? I will tell you what I think."

Avarna shrugged.

"I know your family lost everything," Terselia said. "They tell me your father was a good man who helped others. Poverty should not be the reward for good people. I think much of the reason you joined the army and rose so rapidly was your desire to set right the wrongs you perceive in this world as if to serve justice for your family, to right the scales for their undeserved fortunes."

Avarna did not respond but his pursed lips indicated his discomfort at her words.

"I am sorry for what happened to you," Terselia said. "To have and lose is more difficult than never having in the first place. But you cannot right all the world's wrongs."

"Where are you going with this lecture?" Avarna asked.

"Men like you avoid their feelings. They bury themselves in their causes at the expense of their personal happiness," Terselia said. "I am here, this is now, and I have waited. I want a man, not a hero or an icon to be gazed at from afar."

"And yet war was upon us," Avarna said. "I fought for all of us. What would you have me do?"

Amliea then joined them on the terrace. "Are you two quarreling? I suppose suppressing feelings for so long can do that. She is mad about lost time and some neglect, Avarna. Perhaps a bit of jealousy too, Ar-Falene and so on. But why do you think she resisted marriage all these years? You may be a war hero, but you grasp precious little about women. I am empress now. I command you both to pursue a relationship. And I will order Ar-Falene not to kill either of you. I would have to execute her and we need her."

"Ar-Falene and I did not —"

"Spare me the details," Amliea said, and a moment later she burst out laughing, soon joined by Avarna and Terselia. "We can go back to just being friends now and enjoy this beautiful day," she said. "Now, Terselia, why did you want to see us?"

Terselia took a piece of paper from her robe and handed to Amliea who read it aloud:

"She is the first fallen, savior and destroyer, life and death.
By her the world shall perish, by her may it yet be reborn.

"What is this?" Amliea asked.

Terselia shrugged. "I found it in my chambers. I questioned the servants. No one knew anything of it."

"Someone placed it there, and our rooms are supposed to be secured at all times," Amliea said.

"The guards saw no one enter or leave," Terselia said.

Amliea squeezed her lips together as if she were readying to curse. "What were your guards doing, Avarna? We must summon Desamon for this."

When Desamon arrived at the palace they brought him to the anteroom of Terselia's chambers, a large sitting room with a massive stone fireplace. Amliea handed him the paper as they all sat at the table in front of the fire. Desamon studied the note and asked them a few questions.

"My sister found this in her bedroom, a place that should be more secure than anywhere in the palace," Amliea said in a voice dripping with annoyance.

"Your thoughts?" Terselia asked.

Desamon folded his hands on the table and tilted his head as he spoke. "The message is esoteric," he replied. "I will consult with Segund, but I have an idea. The 'first fallen' is a term linked to Sophia, the First Soul, the spirit of God's wisdom. Sophia was the first Aeon—high spiritual being—to break the unity of heaven when she plunged her consciousness into unformed chaos."

"We know of the First Souls, just not the details of their story," Terselia said. "But chaos, you say?"

Desamon took a deep breath as if the explanation would be a task. "What I tell you now is from the most sacred annals in the PelionTemple that only adepts for the priesthood can study."

"How are you aware then?" Avarna asked

Desamon smiled. "I have my ways. The high esoteric texts spoke of a crisis in heaven—an identity crisis, you might call it. God has both a hidden and manifest aspect. The spirits were only aware of being part of the manifest nature of The One. Many, like Sophia, burned to know the ultimate hidden Source of Creation, which is to say, to know the essence of God Itself. But no being can know that without losing its individuality and being absorbed into the Whole, so Sophia entered Chaos seeking the answer."

"Why Chaos?" Terselia asked. "Chaos is confusion and darkness." She looked at Amliea. Was she imagining it or was her sister already looking very uncomfortable about the conversation?

Desamon shook his head. "You misunderstand, Princess. "Chaos was neither light nor dark but gray. The perfect realm is static and unchanging. Chaos was the dimension of dynamic potential left unordered by The One, a virgin dimension where The One would allow random-chance possibilities to occur."

"Chaos, First Souls? Why leave messages alluding to esoteric things like that?" Amliea asked.

Desamon backed up to give them a more complete picture. Spirits are truly individual parts of God Itself, he explained, so how could something part of the Whole become distinct from the Whole? The parts had to experience creation from a limited consciousness. This gave them the illusion of individuality, but also precluded them from complete awareness of The One. Sophia, personifying the Wisdom of God, naturally sought to solve this paradox before all others.

"Quite the cosmic puzzle," Avarna remarked. "She wanted to fully know both herself and God."

"Indeed," Desamon said. "And it gets more complex."

"This is going far afield," Amliea said sounding like she was about to terminate the conversation.

"They asked about the meaning of 'first fallen,' and I am telling you what I think it means," Desamon said. "If it alludes to Sophia, we need to recall details of her legend to grasp the message's meaning."

Individuality, Desamon went on to explain, was not only a matter of consciousness but will. A spirit could choose to stay aligned with the Will of The One in a fixed dimension, but then it would not be a true individual. A soul, by contrast, is a spirit exercising its free will to accumulate individual experience apart from the experience of the Unity by pursuing its own desires in a lower dimension.

Since The One exits in a static, unchanging, infinite state, individual experience could only occur in a different, lower, finite state. Chaos contained the potential of possibilities that could become realities. Sophia's divine energy activated those random seeds of potential, which actualized as new dimensions of being, the lower psychic and material planes where individuality could express itself. But where did the quest for individual desire end? At the extreme, it produced evil self-gratification at the expense of others.

"That is why they taught us about multiple layers of realities that are mind-constructs?" Avarna asked.

Desamon nodded. "In the higher realms, thoughts are things that express as realities or states of being."

"What of the part about a savior and destroyer mentioned in the note?" Terselia asked.

Desamon shrugged. "My best guess again goes back to Sophia. She played a large part in creating this world and she watches over it as a kind of savior, but she destroyed a higher, unified order to do it."

Amliea's impatience finally broke. She carried on about the discussion being an abstract waste of time with so many other pressing practical matters at hand. Desamon asked if she had any insight to offer.

The corners of her lips tightened and Amliea snapped, "How would I know anything?" The sky outside seemed to darken just then along with her mood. "This angers me, this uselesss arcana. How did this note come to be in my sister's private quarters and who put it there? Avarna, your Blackmanes are in charge of palace security. The attempt on my life and now this tells me you are not doing your job."

"It would seem so. Apologies, Empress. I will see to it immediately."

Amliea made an abrupt exit.

"Her lack of interest in this note's meaning is most odd," Terselia remarked.

Avarna shook his head. "Stranger to me is that she seemed to take something about this personally."

"One thing I do not understand," Terselia said, changing subjects. "If Sophia embodied The One's wisdom, how is it she did something so unwise?"

Desamon leaned back in his chair and smiled. "Wisdom can only grow by experience, not knowledge. To know is to be aware, to experience is to understand. If I tell you fire burns, you become aware, but if I place your hand in the fire you truly understand. Sophia believed that in the potential of Chaos she could create as God creates. By that action, she sought to discover the path to the hidden aspect of God. But that is impossible and she unwittingly threw creation out of balance."

"Amliea was right about one thing. We need to find who placed this note and how they did it," Avarna said. Then he noticed Desamon's expression "What is wrong?" he asked the older man.

Desamon sighed. "I may not fully understand the meaning of this message, but I feel this may be a legitimate warning that bears real tidings of doom. I hope it is the work of a deluded individual but I doubt it. Anyone who could gain access to your room is likely no mad person but quite intelligent and possibly close by. I need a list of palace personnel that can get by the guards to service your room."

"We also have to consider whether whoever placed this message is connected to the attempt on Amliea's life."

Desamon sighed. "Yes. It appears someone or some group has penetrated our inner circle. Very troublesome indeed."

Avarna and Terselia left hand in hand. "I'm doubling the guard throughout the palace," he said on the way out. Once in the corridor, he kissed her, but her reaction was lukewarm.

"Just when you and I seem to find each other, this note makes me wonder if our moments of peace will be interrupted by some shadow lurking around us," she said.

"Someone is trying to break our morale," Avarna replied. "I hear it in your voice. Do not let that happen. This is either a new threat or the Belials have found a way to penetrate our inner sanctum. Either way, I will get to the bottom of this."

CHAPTER XXIII
The Imperial Palace, Poseidia
The Third Epoch, circa 10,750 BC

*Mind wished to create something by
means of the word of the invisible spirit.*
—The Apocryphon of John, a Gnostic Gospel

mliea looked at herself in a mirror. Her golden hair was so rare among the dark-haired, red-skinned Lanteans. Could it be true some white-skin had snuck its way into the royal bloodline long ago? No matter. She did not hold the other races to be intrinsically inferior as did the Belials.

It was a sign of her uniqueness, the uniqueness others tried to stifle all her life. But no longer. She had tried to put it all aside, her cravings and feelings. *Damn that Mennarial.* She remembered why he was the only man in life who ever interested her. He was the only one who gave her the freedom and understood what she wanted, the only one who encouraged her to fulfill her desires.

But she was no fool. The man was a beast, albeit with a fair face and haunting eyes, yet a viper nonetheless. She had had no relations with a man since Mennarial. How could she? The one person she trusted had betrayed her in the vilest way possible, treating her like one of his casual brothel wenches. It was not the touch of a man she craved any longer, and certainly not Mennarial's.

No, the lust he had unleashed in her was a different desire, a need to achieve and create what no one else could, to use her unique gift, the power of the legendary three-eyed Celestials to bring life in into being, better life. If the annals were correct, the Higher Power had evolved the Adamic race to supplant the Celestials, who had abused their power. But she was different from all the others, an Adamic with the ability of the three-eyed Celestials to mind-project realities.

Why could she not create a new form for souls with the temperance and intelligence of the Adamics and the higher abilities of the old Celestials, a being that would be moderate and benevolent with its power? No more Belials, no more Children, just one race with the ability to achieve the consciousness of The One.

And so, as she had done in her youth, she took to her special room in the palace and reopened a closed chapter in her life. She became more reclusive and self-absorbed but was careful to be present just enough not to raise questions. She was the empress, but if they knew they would not understand. If they discovered what she was doing, it might create a rebellion within her own inner circle.

Just short of raising eyebrows, she would sit as often as she could for as long as she could alone in her meditative state. Using her mind like a magnifying glass concentrating sunlight, she focused on the consistent thought of an image perfect in body and awareness. She saw herself talking to her new creation, nurturing it and watching it grow in power and wisdom. She knew that hoping for a thing leads nowhere. The inner power only responded to visions of end results, not wishful thinking. The power must be imagined to one's desired conclusion, not begged or pleaded or pulled along the way.

Yet, try as she did, she still did not reach the point she had achieved as a young girl and this frustrated her. She knew she had to cast aside such feelings, for frustration led to doubt and doubt was the mind-killer. She needed a belief so firm that the end result was a foregone conclusion waiting to manifest. Anything short of this mindset would spell failure. But this was easier said than done. She had been so chastised and conditioned by the backward thinkers around her that regaining the mental state of her unquenchable youth was elusive.

All she could produce after months of effort was a ghostlike flicker of something that could have been a trick of her mind as well as a reality in her eyes.

"Damn their restrictions, the narrow-minded fools. I am the empress!" she cried in an involuntary shout. She, and only she, had the god-bestowed power to bring beings to life and in doing so did this not bring her closer to the mystery of The One? She might change not only the course of the world but also gain knowledge about what no one else comprehended, the nature of the Ultimate Source, and they had filled her head with mind blocks and prohibitions.

It would take nearly every waking hour to get where she needed to be, but she had an empire to run, and she grew increasingly aware of time as an enemy to her ambition. Mennarial had told her the Tekna-Fera had a way to enhance her inner capability and that might be the quicker solution to her problem, but it only posed another problem. Everything with Mennarial and the Belials was a negotiation. Despite the fact that he had opened the door, she could not run to him like an eager puppy looking for its bone. She was no longer an innocent, naïve girl. This was a power game. Mennarial had to seek her, but he was not approaching her anymore and this was troubling.

Somehow, some way, she would get what she needed from Mennarial, but with no immediate ideas at hand, she tried to still her mind and get back to her task. So, the solitary empress sat motionless in her sparse room and dreamed of things forbidden to dream about.

CHAPTER XXIV
Poseidia, Artalanta
The Third Epoch, circa 10,750 BC

Has such a woman not utterly defiled herself.
—The Exegesis on the Soul, a Gnostic Gospel

The royal procession walked toward the Temple of Music as thousands of cheering people lined the stairway leading upward to the magnificently columned structure. Terselia waved, though the empress kept her eyes down, seeming anxious to proceed. They passed through the loggia and entered the building.

Besides the dozen Blackmane imperial guards, Petronien and Ar-Falene accompanied them. Amliea claimed they were due for some culture after spending so much time on affairs of war. Tonight, they would hear a composition by Ba'arth-Van, one of the empire's most gifted composers.

They entered the Great Hall of Harmony, built of marble and gold. They proceeded up to the balcony and looked down upon the audience clapping for them until it was time for the performance to start. The orchestra stood ready faintly tuning their wind and string instruments. The crystal section was notable with its celestial sound, and the bright scarlet robes of the chorale lent a colorful backdrop to the ensemble.

Ba'arth-Van appeared on the stage, bowed, and the assembly grew quiet as he began his work. The composition started low and tenderly with light rhythmical string play becoming gradually more pronounced. The wind instruments then came in imparting a sense of slowly rising power. The crystals and the chorale entered together and the composition absolutely soared as they sang an ode to The One.

Amliea shed tears as the music reached a crescendo, and she

clutched her sister's hands. "Only God could inspire a human to such a creation. Oh, sister, to create is to know God. That is what I desire most. This man shall have a medal from me. So sublimely beautiful. Look, at that section over there. Even the Belials are moved. That is what a beautiful creation can do. Bring us together. *Maybe Mennarial is right*," she said in a low breath.

"What did you say?" Terselia asked. "I cannot hear you above the music."

"Have Ba'arth-Van come to court. I would honor him," she replied, and Terselia nodded.

The royal entourage left the building. Ameliea, Terselia, and Petronien were flanked on either side by the Blackmanes as they descended the stairway leading down from the temple.

"What did you think of the performance?" Amliea asked Ar-Falene and Petronien.

"It was … moving," Ar-Falene said, as if uncomfortable expressing an opinion.

"Good that we can express ourselves without swords," Petronien said patting the hilt of his weapon.

"Bravo, Petronien," Terselia exclaimed. "Would that I could hear such sentiments from Avarna."

Even as the words issued from Terselia's mouth, loud fighting broke out to the left of their procession. The entourage stopped as some of the Blackmanes stepped over to investigate. The men appearing to fight amongst themselves wheeled on them with hidden knives and swords, taking many of the Blackmanes down. The remaining bodyguards rushed to engage the attackers, leaving only two men to guard the empress when from the right side ten more attackers emerged. The two Blackmanes took down four attackers before falling themselves. Outnumbered and with the royal lives in grave danger, Petronien and Ar-Falene drew their swords to confront the six remaining assassins.

Ar-Falene and Petronien shielded Amliea. Terselia had been cut off farther up the stairs and Petronien feared for her, but the assassins seemed intent on Amliea. Outnumbered three to one, Ar-Falene moved like a whirlwind as she and Petronien were all that stood between the killers and the empress. Ar-Falene ducked under the swipe of one attacker as Petronien followed up with a thrust to his chest then she moved forward, parried, and slashed a second man.

Petronien threw a knife that took one on-rusher in the throat. Ar-Falene cleverly drew two of the men up the stairs away from Amliea leaving one for Petronien to handle. They had to follow her or be flanked. She had the uphill advantage. She parried an overhand swipe and sent one man sprawling down the stairs with a kick to the mid-section. She made a fierce downhill assault on the remaining man, using the force of gravity to back him down. She dispatched him in a few moments with greater sword skill.

She looked down to see that Petronien had killed his attacker and was standing over the man she had kicked down the stairs. She ran down to his side.

Petronien held a blade to the man's throat. "Who are you? Who sent you?" he demanded.

"Sh- she will destroy all of us," he sputtered pointing toward Amliea. Then he bit down on something, convulsed, and went limp.

"Poison! The shadow take him," Petronien said. "You will get nothing more from this one."

Amliea called a meeting to reconstruct the events of the attempted assassination and seek some answers. They met at the Consularion, where Desamon chaired the gathering.

"Thank The One you chose to expose Petronien and Ar-Falene to a little culture," Avarna said. "If not for them, you would not be here now. This is the second attempt on your life."

"Yes," Petronien said. "We should arrest Mennarial immediately."

"We have no evidence yet that he was behind it," Desamon said. "We will stir things to no avail."

"I do not believe it was Mennarial," Amliea said, raising a few eyebrows. "He had nothing to gain by doing this now. If he were in a position of strength I might agree, but we defeated him and revenge would do him no good. His thinking is more long-range."

"The assassin said you would destroy us all. Do you have any idea what he meant?" Desamon asked Amliea.

"Of course not," Amliea replied, averting her eyes as she spoke. "These people are insane."

Avarna pointed out that the dead men once again were of the brown race from the western lands and they all bore scars on the back of their necks. Able to go no further pending more investigation, they adjourned, though not before Amliea requested a word with Ar-Falene.

"I know your feelings for Avarna. I am sorry he has chosen my sister, but understand they had a bond from youth suppressed by my father."

"Avarna is not my main passion in life," Ar-Falene said in a toneless voice.

"What then?" Amliea asked.

"Revenge. Revenge on the Belials and the house of Ta-Revi in particular," she replied.

"Why do you hate them so much?" Amliea asked.

"You would have to be a slave to understand," Ar-Falene said. I escaped, but the degenerate Ta-Revi abused my sister in the vilest ways possible until my sister was no more." She declared this with an eerie calmness that must have concealed a volcanic animosity.

"I see," Amliea said. "I am sorry. Well, for now, I am promoting you to Petronien's second in command, and from what I hear, you will soon be a general. We will need good leaders. I am increasing the military presence on Aryan and Atalan to monitor the Belials and make sure they have no means to make war again."

"That of itself will make them even more hostile and dangerous," Ar-Falene said.

"Exactly," Amliea said. "That is why we need good military leaders. I am not letting this apparent peace fool me. Twice now someone has tried to kill me. The empire is still at war, only for now that war has gone underground. I must seek a new solution to humanity's problem."

Ar-Falene had no idea what Amliea meant by that remark, but if it meant eradicating the Belials then this was the empress they needed for the times.

CHAPTER XXV
Poseidia, The Consularion
The Third Epoch, circa 10,750 BC

Where did the words of deception, which all
the powers have failed to discover, come from?
—The Apocalypse of Adam, a Gnostic Gospel

C aptain Philonter of the Poseidia City Security Force strode briskly through the halls of the Consularion to Deputy Consular Desamon's office, papers tucked under his arm. The few times he had been here, he noted the contrast between the grand opulence of the Consularion compared to Desamon's sparse office. That said something about the man to Philonter's mind.

The secretary admitted him. Desamon sat on a fur-trimmed leather-backed chair in front of a simple blond wood table, all framed against a large window facing the imperial palace.

Philonter approached holding a file in his extended hand. "Consular, the initial report on the investigation you ordered last week."

Desamon leaned forward and took the file. He flicked through the contents. "Tell me the short version," said. "Anything of note?"

"Yes, sir. Two things," Philonter replied. "All the men bore scars at the base of their necks. They were excision scars, as if something had been removed. As you wisely requested, we compared findings on the body examinations to the records of the previous two assassins."

"And?" Desamon asked.

"They paid little attention to it years ago, but examination records at that time indicate they found scars similar to those of our recent group of corpses," Philonter said.

Desamon's eyes narrowed and his head made a slight nod. "I see. What is the second matter?"

"Sir, the clothes of our would-be assassins all contained traces of a certain pollen from flora found almost exclusively in the vicinity of Plytheron."

"Plytheron? Some distance from here," Desamon said. "So they were either in Plytheron or their clothes came from there."

"It would seem so, sir."

The men conversed for some time. Desamon sighed and leaned back in his chair. "The assassins must have had some common identifying mark removed. Only cults or secret organizations brand such symbols into the flesh. What organization would want the empress dead?"

Philonter shrugged. "My best guess? The Aryans or some group of Belials angry at all the restrictions after Carch'Carai. Could be disgruntled Belial ex-military avenging the empress's breaking up of the old beast orders."

Desamon leaned on his desk with crossed arms, his fingers tapping against his forearm in thought. "Possible, but I doubt it. For one thing, the Belials would never use brown people—or blacks or whites for that matter. They think other races inferior and unreliable. Certainly, they would not trust something as serious as killing an empress to them."

"I would put nothing past Mennarial," Philonter said.

Desamon nodded. "I agree with you. He will do anything in pursuit of his interests, but he has no profit or interest in killing the empress, not even for simple revenge. He's in a weak position with too much to lose and too little to gain. No, this is something more hidden, subtler, and perhaps even more sinister than Mennarial and his ilk."

"What are your thoughts?" Philonter asked.

He rose from this desk and walked to the great window overlooking the imperial palace. He clasped his hands behind his back and stared outside for some time. Philonter waited in silence to hear his next thoughts. Desamon eventually turned to face him.

"We have naturally looked to Aryan," Desamon said. "Perhaps we should be looking closer to home."

"How close to home?" Philonter asked.

"Even as close as the imperial palace," Desamon said. "Avarna will help you."

"Will that include Princess Terselia?"

Desamon raised an eyebrow.

"It would not be the first time in history imperials plotted against one another," Philonter said. "She is next in line for the throne."

"No one is above suspicion, Philonter, but I have no reason to focus on the princess at this time," Desamon said. "Alert your men about people bearing neck scars. I will have Avarna get the Blackmanes to inspect all palace personnel for such marks. As for Plytheron, it may have been a passing point for the assassins or it may be more deeply involved. Begin infiltrating the village with men over a period of months so as not to arouse suspicion of the locals. No uniforms, and include some biologists to see if they can further pinpoint the source of the pollen."

Once Philonter was gone, Desamon continued rolling information over in his mind. A hidden organization that managed to infiltrate Poseidia with the avowed purpose of killing Amliea, indeed believing her to be the destroyer of the world. He checked all records with his security forces, but no information existed pointing to any such organization within the five islands.

And Terselia? Anything was possible, but if he began to go down that road it could just as well be Avarna. He refused to let panic or paranoia rule his decisions. Yet how deep and how close did this conspiracy run? Past threats had come from relatively known or identifiable quantities. But now something more deceptive and mysterious was going on.

He had past success in discovering hidden information from visible enemies, but now he had to discover a hidden enemy with no discernable information, a difficult task made more complicated and pressing with Amliea's life at stake.

CHAPTER XXVI
Poseidia, The Imperial Palace
The Third Epoch, circa 10,750 BC

Seven appeared in chaos.
— On the Origin of the World, a Gnostic Gospel

Avarna knocked on the door of the princess's bedroom and Terselia answered. He stepped forward, pulled her to his chest with a passionate flexing of his muscles, and kissed her. She did not resist, but she did not reciprocate either.

"What is wrong?" he asked.

"I am sorry, come sit with me on the balcony," she said. "I know you have something to show me, but I too have matters I must discuss with you."

The skies were clear, but a bit of chill breeze blew in as they sat on the carved marble chairs. Avarna tried probing her expression for a hint of what was bothering her.

"I hope this is not more about why I did not disobey your father years ago. I—"

"No," Terselia said. "I was being angry and selfish, two bad traits I do not normally display. I was more disappointed at all the lost moments. I knew we were meant for each other, and I thought you felt the same. I did not understand your restraint, but I do now. No, that is all past."

"What then?" he asked.

She leaned back and clasped her knee. "How long have you known Ar-Falene?"

"A long while," he replied. "You know that we trained under Petronien together. Why?"

"Just curious," she said. "What do you know of her?"

"What you know. Her parents died, and she was kicked around some high-ranking Belial households as a menial. She hates them."

"Oh, does she now?" Terselia said.

"What path are you traveling with this?" he asked.

"She is the highest-ranking Aryan in the imperial upper echelon, and her rise coincides with the attempts on my sister."

"You think her involved with the assassination attempts?" Avarna asked.

Terselia shrugged.

Avarna took a deep breath. He looked away for a moment, then he turned to her. "In no way would Ar-Falene betray her military oath to the throne. She is an Aryan, not a Belial. There is a difference."

"Not much," Terselia said. "I saw the two of you sword sparring the other day. Were you lovers?"

"This is old ground. Why do you ask again?" he shot back.

"Because I see the way she looks at you even in mock combat. A woman sees such things."

"I prefer to think it is admiration for my swordplay," Avarna quipped. In a more serious tone, he said, "Yes, we had feelings for one another, her more so, but we were not lovers. And you had much to do with me holding back. The hope of you at least. Can you see *that* as a woman?"

She leaned over and kissed him. "I was just being cautious after speaking with Desamon. I did not mean to offend you. Now, what was it you wanted to show me?"

Avarna took a paper from his pocket and handed it to her.

Awaken and stand forth in the time of the seven.

"What is this?" Terselia asked.

"I found it in my barracks room," Avarna replied. "I hoped perhaps you or Desamon might understand it."

"I have no idea," Terselia said, "but who would place it there?

"I hope someone can answer that too," he said. "We need to take this to Desamon."

They did make Desamon aware of the note, and later that day they met in his office. They first discussed how the note came to be placed in Avarna's room at the Blackmane barracks between the palace and the Consularion, but as with the previous message, no explanation was obvious. Avarna told them rotations of soldiers passes through the barracks all day. Though it would not be impossible to gain entry to his locked chambers, it would be very difficult to do so unnoticed. They then discussed the note's contents.

"I took it to the Elda-Fera, for I could find no reference or significance to 'the seven' other than some arcane symbologies that made no sense," Desamon said. "The Elda-Fera did come up with something in the annals, but again I am uncertain it makes any sense."

"What was it?" Terselia asked.

"Again, it relates back to the story of the First Souls," he said. "When they descended to earth with their followers to rescue the earlier lost soul incarnations, they were worshipped as gods by the Terrestrials. The First Souls themselves rejected this glorification, but seven of the Celestials, as they were called, rejoiced in the adulation and became corrupted by power. They were sometimes referred to as the Sons of Darkness because it was said that evil entered the world through them."

They pondered over the issue a while but still could make no sense of how legendary beings of the misty past could have anything to do with them or why anyone would think to resurrect their memory in surreptitious messages.

Then Avarna snapped his fingers. "The current leaders of the Belials number seven, do they not? Mennarial, Ter-Madaz. Ta-Revi, An-Klesen, Dal-Golia, Val-Andwar, and Al-Presta — the Sons of Belial. Sounds similar to the Sons of Darkness in both name and meaning, does it not?"

"Indeed it does," Desamon said. "We may be grasping at straws, but if what you say is true, it has several implications. It could mean another future conflict with the Belials despite our victory."

"You said several implications. What else?" Terselia asked.

"Well," Desamon said, "someone is either insane or predicting the future. And since these messages seem to be warning us, that someone appears to be a friend, not a foe."

"Unless that someone is trying to sow fear and confusion among us," Terselia said.

"But how is this messenger or whatever it is so easily penetrating our security, and why does he or she simply not come forth and state outright what they know?" Avarna asked.

"For whatever reason, it seems someone is nudging us toward some revelation, not pushing us all at once," Desamon said.

Avarna and Terselia left Desamon's office as confused as ever. "If the purpose of these messages is to create anxiety, it has succeeded with me," Terselia said. "I believe there is something to them. I have a foreboding feeling. Stay with me tonight. I would not be apart from you. We lost too many years, and I am afraid things may happen that will cause us to lose more."

"May The One make it not so," Avarna said, but there was no conviction in his voice. For a man not normally bothered by vague feelings, he too, like Terselia and Desamon, was plagued with a growing sense of unease.

CHAPTER XXVII
Plytheron, Poseidia
The Third Epoch, circa 10,750 BC

... she conceives evil.
—Authoritative Teaching, a Gnostic Gospel

T he woman arranged jars on the shelf of her farmhouse. She turned and told the girl, "Never touch these or you will die, is that clear?"

The girl nodded. Not more than sixteen years old and newly arrived, she was adjusting to her surroundings. "How long have you lived here among the apostates?" she asked.

The older woman gave her a stern look. "Too long, and never use that word here. I will give you away. Tell me who you are and from where you come."

The girl stood erect. "My name is Varnelia, Mistress. I come from Comys on Atalan. My parents died, and you are my nearest relative."

"Good. At least you learned that correctly," the woman said. "You are a Lantean. Never mention apostates and no more Mistress. I am your aunt."

"Yes, Mis—I mean Aunt. But I do not understand. Most of the people in our country are brown-skinned, yet these people look like us and have different features from those in our land. Are these our people or are the ones back home our people?"

The women sighed. The girl's question was natural, but the answer was complicated. "Many years ago our ancestors came from this land and settled in the West among the brown people. Many took wives or husbands among the native people, though some maintained our pure

Lantean line. But these are not your people just because they look like you. You will have a longer life from your Lantean blood, but your people are those of your birth country."

"Like the brown men who hid here recently."

'Yes, like them, but they were fools. You will succeed where they failed. You are a pureblood."

"Are you going to teach me swordplay or to be a markswoman?" the girl asked.

The woman gave a sardonic smile. "Oh, no, my dear. You are far too refined for that. You are going to learn a valuable trade that will put you much in demand. In the next decades, I will instruct you in the fine art of cooking."

"Cooking?" the girl asked, looking out the window at the staked herb garden in the cleared area around the immediate cottage.

The woman pointed at a wall lined with all manner of pots and pans. "People are more easily conquered by knife and fork than sword and bow," she said. "Even the high houses will one day seek your talents. Consider yourself fortunate, more fortunate than the fools who passed through here. But your first lessons will consist of becoming a normal Lantean."

The girl shrugged. The priests had sent her across the sea to obey all instructions of the mistress. The mistress was in a good mood today, but the welts on her back attested to her previous infractions. She was learning it was better to heed the priest's advice than to ask the mistress too many questions.

After all, she was to be here a long time before they would send her to do whatever they had in mind.

CHAPTER XXVIII
Poseidia, The Imperial Palace
The Third Epoch, circa 10,750 BC

the schemes of the Adversary are not few,
and (that) the tricks which he has are varied ...
—The Teachings of Silvanus, a Gnostic Gospel

mliea was meeting with some engineers about new road construction on Aiyre when they turned toward the metallic sound of walking armor. Petronien approached with half a dozen soldiers. "General, what is this about?' Amliea asked.

"News from Aryan," Petronien said. "An assassination attempt on Ra-Mennarial in Ba'relin."

"What?" Amliea said. "Is he alive?"

"Wounded but alive," Petronien said. "The Belials will blame us. They will see it as retaliation for the attempt on you that many believe Mennarial was behind. We are already seeing large, angry demonstrations in Aryan and Atalan."

Amliea called her ministers and military together to discuss what facts were known, what to expect, and what possible courses of action to take. After the discussion, Amliea announced her decision. It silenced the room for a brief moment before the outcry of a dozen shocked voices.

"You cannot go to Aryan alone!" Desamon said. "First the humiliation of their defeat and now the Belial leader nearly killed. Civil unrest is sweeping the islands. Feeling against the Imperium is at a peak. For all we know, we still may have Belial agents here on Poseidia waiting for another chance to kill you let alone you going to them unprotected."

"I am empress of all Artalanta, not just Poseidia, and the Belials need to know it," Amliea said. "To hide now encourages suspicion. To make an appearance would calm the waters not stir them. We need to be respected not suspected. It is my opinion Mennarial was not behind the attempt on me, and this attack on him seems to validate that."

Her mind jumped to the thought that if it was not Mennarial, who was it? Her own people? They were not like her. They never had been. They could never understand the burdens of an empress, never understand what she was trying to do for them. They did not know her. They thought she was aloof and she had to be. Who else could achieve what she was attempting, touching The One Itself?

But did they suspect? If they did they might try to kill her for knowing she had the power, for doing forbidden things of which they could only dream. The low always tried to bring down the high, but what she was doing was for their good, was it not?

And so, these images ripped through her mind like random peels of lightning disrupting the peace and tranquility of the heavens until someone spoke and broke her out of her thought stream.

Though she believed everything she had said about Mennarial's innocence, Amliea would not let the opportunity pass to see if Mennarial would make good on his previous offer. Yes, she had matters of state to address, but this was the opening she had sought. By going to Aryan, she could put several matters to rest, most importantly her personal project.

"Empress, you cannot assume Mennarial did not stage the assassination," Desamon said. "The sympathy would serve his interests and cloud the recent attack on you. Do not put anything past him."

Amliea nodded, not really hearing him, for her mind was not fixed on politics but on another agenda closer to her heart.

CHAPTER XXIX
Aryan, Artalanta
The Third Epoch, circa 10,750 BC

... seducing her with a gift.
—The Exegesis of the Soul, a Gnostic Gospel

T he air car landed in the courtyard of the Prince's Palace in Ba'relin and a lone hooded occupant emerged to be greeted by Ra-Mennarial himself, his arm folded within a sling from his wound. They immediately walked inside, where Mennarial received his guest in a private room. In typical Aryan fashion, the room was adorned with militaristic trappings—warrior statues along the walls, tapestries with battle scenes, and maps of subservient nations. The grand windows were ten feet high, adorned by curtains of equal height.

The hood came off now they were alone, and Amliea's golden locks tumbled down her shoulders. "My physicians said you were fortunate. You will regain the use of your arm. How are you recovering?"

Mennarial wiggled his arm. "If not for my security detail covering me against another shot, it might have been far worse," he said.

"Walking along the streets of Ba'relin, no less," Amliea said. "Risky, perhaps, in these times, no?"

"Not usually," Mennarial said. "My people love me."

Amliea made a slight tilt of her head "Apparently, not all of them."

Mennarial made a puzzled face.

"Whoever shot you. Oh, and Ar-Falene, just to name a few," Amliea said.

"You new general? What has she got to do ... ah, I remember. She was in my household as a girl before I sent her and her sister to Ta-Revi in Atalan. No, I think one of your Children, more likely."

"Doubtful any Children of The One would resort to such methods," Amliea said.

"Oggian Highlanders looking for revenge would," Mennarial said. "Not all of you are pacifists."

"Yes, I suppose Avarna proved that point at Carch'Carai," Amliea said. "Well, you reap what you sow. We have been unable to find leads on your shooter."

"How hard are you trying?" Mennarial said fixing icy blue eyes on her.

"Your local people are working with the imperial investigation team," Amliea said. "Ask them. But so far no clues."

Mennarial sighed. "Who wants to provoke civil war? That is a question to ask. Anyway, it is time. Are you ready?"

Amliea nodded and he led her over to a balcony on the other side of the palace facing the Plaza of the Kings, where a large throng of people waited below. They had erected a transparent shield to protect her. Mennarial remarked that nothing was left to chance for her protection.

"I guarantee your safety and no wars will be started here on my watch," Mennarial declared as Amliea stepped onto the balcony to a largely silent audience with scattered faint cheers.

"People of Artalanta, we come here today as one people and one empire," Amliea said in a loud, firm voice. "Both I and Governor Mennarial" —she did not use the title "prince" as Mennarial liked to refer to himself —"were recently attacked, and an attack on one of us is an attack on all." A slightly warmer applause from the crowd. "Some out there seek to divide us, seek to reopen closed wounds, and if we allow that to happen, we give power to them."

Amliea spoke for several minutes longer, and the response by the masses at the end was considerably warmer than at first, ending with Mennarial holding up his good arm with Amliea's in a gesture of unity.

Once back inside, Mennarial said, "Well done. You are a natural leader." He offered her some wine, which she rejected. "Afraid I will poison you?" he asked as they sat down at a small table.

"I need all my wits around you," Amliea replied. "Besides, Aryan wines taste like the sap of a kilu tree. It reflects your general lack of refinement."

Mennarial snickered. "Is that becoming of an empress to insult her host? I had hoped for some small talk to get reacquainted, to warm you up a bit."

"Do you really think the empress came here to banter with you? Have you something of importance to discuss?"

Mennarial closed his eyes and smiled. "I am thinking back to when we were young and what attracted me to you. It was not so much your beauty, believe it or not."

"What, then?"

Mennarial twirled his golden wine goblet on the table, one of the numerous trappings of the fabulous wealth evident in the palace. "You Children of The One believe in this god figure, but when I look into the face of this world I see a void, a black hole of nothingness without purpose except for the purpose we give it, the purpose we create. You say your god is in all of us and we reflect his light, yet you call me evil. How do you account for that contradiction, that foolish attachment to a comforting lie?"

"We cloud our lives with false beliefs. Each of us makes our own dirt with which we cover our innate divinity," Amliea said.

"Pah, delusions for the weak-minded," Mennarial retorted.

"You are a like a dusty mirror lying in a shed, Mennarial. But taken out, cleaned off, and exposed to the sun, you would shine. You would display the brilliance you were meant to reveal, reflecting the purpose of The One on this earth. Cleanse yourself and you would glow."

"Stop that nonsense, and listen to me," Mennarial said. "I told you once that *we* created this world, not any god, but our power lies beneath our consciousness—except in you. You are the chosen one, the epitome of the collective power in all of us."

Amliea bit her lip, looking at him without saying a word.

"Of all the people I have ever known, the creative power burns most strongly in you. I know why they sent you to Pelion. I know they tried to stifle that power."

Amliea's eyes went wide, and she sucked in a deep breath.

"And I know something else," Mennarial said. "They failed. You still have the power and the desire. You, the Empress of Artalanta, the only human who retains the gift of the mythical three-eyed Celestials.

This is what drew me to you and caused me to make a grievous youthful mistake for which I humbly ask your forgiveness. Can you forgive me for what I did because I did — I do — love you." He placed his hand upon hers.

Amliea retracted her hand at his touch. Her face reddened, and she turned her head away seeking anything nearby upon which to fix her attention. She started to speak but no words issued from her quivering mouth. After some time, she was able to talk.

"You tried to have me killed. Is that how you express love?"

Mennarial shot up from his chair. "I tell you again; I had nothing to do with that. You know it or you would not be here. I would never harm you. What would that gain me? Have I not just explained that I value you more than anyone?"

"Why now, Mennarial? Why after all this time? What do you want from me?"

He knelt, rested his forearms on her legs, and held her hands. "I want what you want. To create a new world better than the one we live in, a world no longer on the brink of conflict."

He sounded so sincere. She looked around at statues of men with jutting jaws and spears in hand, swords hanging upon walls, and battered shields that had seen someone die an inglorious death. All such memories of violent death were now elevated to anonymous glory in this prince's palace, and so she was reminded of with whom she was dealing. She stood, breaking his embrace. She walked over to a window and stared outside trying to regain her equilibrium.

Mennarial came up behind her and held her by the shoulders. "You alone have the power to mind-project beings into the world. The old drones created by the androgynous Celestials were soulless and dull-witted. The Tekna-Fera now have a method to enhance newly created drones with human material."

"To what end?" Amliea asked, still looking outward.

"You know our people need labor," Mennarial said. "Few are willing to work the fields and factories, so we keep the drones as slave workers. Yes, they are maltreated as inferior because they are inferior and they do not breed. Their life spans are long, but they are dwindling so they become fewer."

"Better to let them dwindle in peace," Amliea said.

"And that aggravates our problem," Mennarial said. "If we had a new intelligent race of drones, perhaps even with souls, we would integrate them as paid labor, not as slaves but as a new working class."

"You would do that?" Amliea said.

"Of course," he replied. "The increased productivity because of their intelligence would balance the economics of lost slave labor. We could even make them citizens. Labor shortages and the need to raid foreign lands for slaves would cease. The slavery issue would be removed as a point of contention, bringing peace and prosperity to Artalanta. You can do this by exercising your power to create that which they should never have tried to stifle in you. My Tekna-Fera can greatly enhance your chance of success."

Amliea's mouth wrinkled. She wrung her hands, and Mennarial heard her breathing grow heavy. "I—I cannot—" She spun about and looked Mennarial in the eye. "I must leave now."

"As you will," he said. "But I give you the chance to do what you were born to do. He bowed, took her around the waist, and kissed her hand. "Think on this. You will see the truth in my words."

She hesitated a long while and said, "I will think on it."

As Amliea left the room, a hand pulled back one of the great curtains by the ten-foot-high windows and a figure emerged. "She clearly softened. Perhaps you were right after all," the man said. "Your staged misfortune may turn out fortunate for us after all," he said with a smirk. "You had to go to quite an extreme though to get her to come."

"You do not know her like do," Mennarial said with a satisfied half-smile to Ter-Madaz. "She was *looking* for an excuse to come."

CHAPTER XXX
Poseidia, The Imperial Palace
The Third Epoch, circa 10,750 BC

Mind wished to create something ...
—The Hypostasis of the Archons, a Gnostic Gospel

mliea was pleased with herself as she stood on the ocean-facing balcony of the imperial palace. The sky nearly matched the sea in its crisp azure blue, its vault adorned with wisps of foamy white clouds breaking up the otherwise infinite singularity of the heavens. The cries of seabirds in the breeze carried to her ears.

Mennarial had opened the door and she had not accepted. She had not shown eagerness or weakness. He would pursue her again, this she was sure of, and when the time was right, she would accept his help on her terms.

A drone servant approached her with a goblet of wine. She had specifically asked for the drone, not a human. She took the wine and studied the creature. "How are you called?" she asked.

Eyes down, the drone took overlong to respond but finally said, "T-Telmar,"

Amliea cupped its chin in her hand and tilted its head upward to see her sympathetic smile. "Telmar, what do you feel?"

Again a pause, then "Hungry."

"I will see you are well fed. But I mean, what do you feel about humans?" Amliea asked.

"Some good, some bad," it responded. "Treated good here."

"I am happy to hear that, Telmar. I will tell you a secret. Neither your kind nor humans are enough to fulfill our destiny to unite with

The One again. We need a new race, a portion of both to make things better."

The bewildered creature merely bowed and walked away. Soon after, Avarna and Desamon reported to her. They told her they had made little progress in solving the mystery of the messages. Desamon mentioned the lead they were pursuing in Plytheron, and that he had sent a team of spies to gather information about the source of the assassins. To their surprise, she was in a good mood, almost euphoric one might say.

A chevron formation of white birds flew directly overhead, but then a large shadow blanketed the ground in ominous, wavy ripples. A giant black predator appeared in view, spiky angles of head, beak, and wing looking like a massive claw ready to puncture anything in its path. Amliea summoned a messenger.

"Alert the Falcon command," she said. "We have an Atladactyl. Have the Pneumarta shoot it down."

"They are on their way, Empress," the man said. "It was reported from the eastern side of the island."

"An ill portent. Was anyone injured?" Desamon asked, and the man reported only livestock killed.

"Rare beasts arising from the past to cause destruction in the present," Avarna said. "I cannot help but think the failure to remove Ra-Mennarial will come back to haunt our future as well."

"Removing him will cost many lives," Amliea said. "Let nothing darken this beautiful day. Defanging the snake is as good as killing him."

"Some snakes grow new fangs," Avarna said, sighing into the wind. "I think him one of those.

BOOK TWO

A DREAM OF DARKNESS, A DREAM OF LIGHT

CHAPTER XXXI
Poseidia, the Imperial Palace
The Third Epoch, circa 10,700 BC

For I foretell it to those who have a heart.
—The Paraphrase of Shem, a Gnostic Gospel

The citadel atop Poseidia's central mount afforded a panoramic view of the ringed harbor and the vast sea beyond. Against the salty breeze and azure sky, with clothes fluttering in the wind and standing on a high rampart overlooking the ocean, two figures were locked in the passionate embrace of youth, for even at the age of eighty, people who can live over two hundred and fifty years are still youthful.

"What is wrong?" Avarna asked when Terselia abruptly pulled from his kiss. She thanked herself that she had resisted her father's attempt to marry her off to some island governor. With him gone she had declared her feelings to Avarna, who came out of his military shell and returned her emotions.

Terselia sighed. "Amliea. In the fifty years past since Father died and she assumed the throne, she has been changing. In the past ten years, the change is more pronounced."

Avarna turned to stare at the sea. "I know. Others have noticed too."

"She seems like two people," Terselia said. "She studied with the Elda-Fera and became a proficient healer with crystals and magnetics. I witnessed her purify the body of a friend who appeared possessed. But it seems she is growing ever more introverted with her conjurings. She is phasing out slavery, but she is developing a contempt for commoners. She is discontented and mistrustful of people, particularly men. She holds grudges, imagines people are acting against her. She even asked if I ever thought to replace her."

"Really? Is it that bad? But then I see the way she treats Desamon," Avarna said. "Petronien and I discussed her behavior with Desamon but he was as puzzled as we are. We can talk more with him when he arrives. Do you know why he wanted to meet today?" Avarna asked, but even as he spoke Desamon approached striding toward them with purpose. Petronien was with him, and when they neared, he held a paper out. Avarna took it. It read:

The Time of Sorrows nears. Fear not the enemy's sword and spear; beware the enemy's mind and idea.

"This was on my desk this morning at the Consularion," Desamon said. "Our security is stringent, and no one in the offices would write this," Desamon sighed. "For this discussion, we should remove inside and sit with your permission, Princess."

Terselia nodded, and they retired to a receiving room, where they sat around a long table.

"The Belials are making a resurgence on Aryan and Atalan, holding massive rallies and paramilitary marches against the abolition of slavery and the curtailing of drone labor," Desamon began telling them. "And as you know, Mennarial has revived the cult of the Archon. But our problem is far larger than just Mennarial. I have just studied statistics from the Elda-Fera derived from their readings of the Touai Stone. The connection of average people to The One is waning. That is why the Belials are growing in number and the Children are not."

"What is the reason?" Petronien asked.

"More people are succumbing to the illusions of this world," Desamon said. "The annals and the ancient wisdom remind us of what we have forgotten. We live in a simulation. This world is not real, at least our presence here is not. People fall into the fixation of what they detect with their physical senses. God's presence becomes remote in their lives. We face a rising tide of materialism despite our past victory over the Belials. We won the battle, but we are losing the war for the awakening of earth's souls."

"I see you are upset," Avarna said. "Sit for a moment."

Desamon nodded and sat, calming his agitation. "The Belials accept the world for what it seems, for whatever their senses detect, and they take that for reality," Desamon said.

Petronien knocked on the table. "It does all seem real, no?"

"Oh, the material world is real enough. Water, mountains, animals —they were all here first," Desamon said. "What is not real is *us* being here."

"I suppose that is true from a soul perspective, as they taught us," Petronien said.

"Think of it this way," Desamon said. "Animals come to an equilibrium with their environment. Only humans destroy it. Why are we different among all species? Because our essence is non-material. We do not belong here. We are alien beings to this world. We do not have the instincts to be in rhythm with it. The material world was meant to be a dimension apart from higher energies. We used our divine mind power to project the thought of ourselves here. We are intruders in a place where we were not meant to be. We interfered. We warped The One's intention for the material creation."

A silence ensued as they considered Desamon's statements. "Even if all you say is true," Terselia said, "how does this bear on our immediate situation with the Belials?"

"The note," Desamon said. "*The enemy's idea*, see? As time goes on, humans increasingly identify with this simulated dream world and not our true state as souls residing in a higher plane. The idea is that the material world is the final reality. So, deluded spirits use this world as a playground to satisfy their own selfish desires until the playground becomes a hell. Divorced from the goodness of The One, selfishness gives rise to all manner of power-seeking evil. Does that not sum up the essence of the Belials?"

Avarna leaned forward, elbow resting on the table and said, "They replace God with themselves, and bending the earth to their will is their 'divine' act of creation. Is that what you are saying?"

Terselia's vision fixed on a wall tapestry depicting the legendary ten kings of the First Epoch, when Artalanta was a single land. "What you describe," she said, "is more an eternal nightmare than a dream.

How do people break out of this simulation or, for that matter, come to know it truly even exists?"

"Speaking with the Elda-Fera, I am convinced The One would not allow us to be perpetually lost in illusion in these lower planes," Desamon said. "A way out, a safety valve, must exist and so too a key to finding it. I believe we must find a way to enter the higher planes for the answer while still embodied."

Terselia showed intense interest in this last statement, and she probed Desamon with a series of questions. He ended his explanation with a disconcerting warning that the Belials were the symptom and not the cause of the problems they faced, but the symptom was spreading rapidly.

"Think on the progression of our history in the annals," he said. "The early Lanteans were said to have moved objects with their minds to build cities. They communicated telepathically. They did not need air vehicles; they could fly on their own, for their bodies still responded to their mind-energy."

"All things we now do by machines because we became ever denser terrestrial creatures," Terselia said.

"Yes, that is the path of the Belials, and we are all on it to some extent," Desamon said. "The world outside Artalanta is younger and more primitive, and we grow blinder as we grow more technological. As our mass consciousness diminishes, we will misuse that technology against weaker people. Look how the Belials agitate to expand slavery. Imagine if they gain control of the government and the Touai Stone."

"What of the first part of the note?" Petronien asked. "*The Time of Sorrows nears?*"

"You know the legendary prophecy of *Tyer Angarach*, the Twilight of the Gods, the end of the world?" Desamon said. "Another name for it is the Time of Sorrows. This message and the one Terselia found years ago, point to some impending cataclysm. This is no idle warning. The earth's etheric field reacts to the vibrations of our collective unconscious. The Elda-Fera have detected deep disturbances in the field."

"Do you have any thoughts or guidance for us?" Avarna asked.

"The ancient wisdom hints at an evolutionary cycle for souls on earth that implies hitting a bottom before rising up," Desamon said.

"Tyer Angarach may be that bottom, and if it is fast upon us, our true task beyond these wars is to find the path back upward."

The information was sobering, for it meant their previous military victory was only the stemming of a dark and rising tide. The Belials would wax as the Children of The One waned; the light would gradually recede before the shadow. Their best hope was something they could barely define and might not even exist, the key to the doorway of an unknown higher reality—could anything be more elusive?

CHAPTER XXXII
Ba'relin, Aryan
The Third Epoch, circa 10,700 BC

by the evil power which is called "the serpent"
... the evil order begins to do evil.
—The Tripartite Tractate, a Gnostic Gospel

Ter-Madaz pulled the curtain aside and glanced down over the balcony of the Palace of the King at the throngs of people packed into the streets below. He noticed how his paramilitaries stood out in their smart black leather uniforms displaying the lion-headed serpent insignia of the Archon on their arms.

With a self-satisfied smile, he turned to face Mennarial and the others. "My AA troops look good out there," he declared. The AA stood for *Archontes Artalantas*, rulers of Artalanta, the presumptuous name by which they had come to be known.

Mennarial was about to address the mass rally from the balcony. His lackeys and the paramilitaries were whipping up the crowd with chants of "Hail Mennarial," and "The Archon wills it." Mennarial and his cohorts had converted all the temples on Aryan and Atalan to the fire-worship of the Archon, which to them was the force of nature expressed as the drive to dominate and exert control over inferior lands and peoples. The dark side of nature was their god, and accordingly, they had instituted human sacrifice in the Temple of Fire, in a complete perversion of the former Temple of Wisdom.

The Palace of the King, so named for one of the former ten kings of whom Mennarial claimed improbable lineage, was a magnificent structure of gleaming white marble, alabaster, and onyx. Its highly articulated façade featured domes, spires of all shapes and sizes, loggias, and numerous columns carved in a variety of patterns with ornate capstones. The back side of the palace rose out of the waters of Ba'relin Harbor, itself part of the Straits of Parfa that separated Aryan and Poseidia. The rectangular, column-lined Temple of Fire with its winged cornice and intricate friezes rose above the palace on the Ta'an I Hayt mount and was the primary focal point of the city. The palace entrance faced an enormous plaza now filled with people waiting for Ra-Mennarial to make his entrance on the balcony five stories above.

"I see Petronien and plenty of Imperial troops out there to keeping an eye on things," Val-Andwar said, peeking out the window. "They probably outnumber your paramilitary boys."

Ter-Madaz scowled. "I made those 'boys.' What have you done lately, you envious bastard?"

"Besides watching you play with your toy soldiers?"

Termadus balled his fist and made a move until Mennarial shouted, "Sit, you idiots, and shut up."

"We will need those paramilitaries as officers for our new army," Al-Presta said. "Through force of arms we will spread our religion to other lands."

"Fuck your pseudo-religion," An-Klesen said. "It is the spoils of other lands I want to spread ... on the doorstep of my palace."

The others snickered, but Mennarial raised a hand. "Don't let your greed blind you to the fact that religion is an effective tool to keep the masses under control."

Al-Presta puffed up at the statement, but Dal-Golia said, "All well and good, but can we get on with it? I am losing attention."

"Because you have none, you lazy dog," Mennarial said with a frown. "Open the doors and curtains," he ordered, gesturing with a sweep of his arm. "It is time to address our subjects."

Dal-Golia went out first to speak, for despite his phlegmatic ways he was a brilliant orator. His task was to whip the mob into a frenzy for Mennarial, and this he did well. The mob emitted a great roar as Mennarial stepped onto the balcony. He paused to absorb the adulation, looking resplendent in his polished bronze cuirass, black tunic, and black cape emblazoned with the golden insignia of the Archon.

"Fifty years ago, we struggled to preserve our way of life," he declared, commencing his speech. "Defrauded by traitors at the Consularion, the will of the people was thwarted. They disbanded our military orders and abolished slavery to the detriment of our economy. We, the people of Aryan and Atalan and all throughout the Empire of Artalanta who share our beliefs, have had enough!"

Large roar from the crowd.

"The Children of The One perpetuate this myth about descent from a Supreme Source to justify their rule as if ordained and sanctioned from a god above. We of the Belial faction know that lie for what it is—a mere justification for their rule, a tool for the imposition of their moral views, and a corral to pen up our aspirations like so much livestock. Even worse, what secret do they keep to prolong their lives beyond ours? This is a high crime for which they must pay."

Grumbles of discontent from the mob.

"I promise you a new day is on the horizon when we will cast aside the shackles of our humiliation. Look with pride upon our AA troops. They are here to defend you from that likely day when the imperial army occupiers turn on their own people."

Jeers, fist waving, and even some refuse thrown at the Imperial troops on the perimeter of the crowd. Petronien addressed his commanders. "Make sure your men hold the line. No retaliation. They want nothing more than to provoke us."

"You were not born to perform menial labor and till the soil," Mennarial shouted. "That is the work of drones and slave labor. You were destined to rule the earth by your might and technology, but no, the Law of One says that is bad. You were born to achieve mastery, but no, the Law of One says you are equal to the drones and inferior races. Well, there are no more temples of The One on Aryan. We now worship nature and the force that expresses through nature, the power of the Archon that whispers to us, 'arise, arise, and claim what is rightfully yours.'"

As Mennarial backed off the balcony with a defiant shake of his fist, the mob broke into a frenzy, making the Aryan salute en masse and beginning to sing:

O' Aryan, Aryan when will you rise
To make all the Lanteans free?
The day soon will dawn
When the world is mine
The earth will belong to me.

Back inside the palace, the others congratulated Mennarial on his performance just as Ta-Revi came through the door. 'Where have you been?" Mennarial asked.

"I was occupied."

"Yes, occupied with two of the serving girls," Val-Andwar said.

"Never mind that," Ta-Revi replied. "Petronien was on my heels coming here with thirty Imperials."

"He would not dare arrest us and provoke war," Ter-Madaz said.

No sooner had he spoken those words than a guard opened the door and ran up to Mennarial. "My prince, Captain General Petronien demands entry."

"Let him —" Mennarial's order was cut short as Petronien burst into the room with his troops.

Ter-Madaz growled, "By what authority do you come marching in here like you own the palace?"

"Shut up, Ter-Madaz, or I'll punch that scowling face in," Petronien said. "Mennarial, you and the Belials are skirting sedition. Are you trying to provoke civil war? I am disbanding your paramilitaries."

Mennarial sneered. "Oh, I doubt that, Petronien. When you think it through, that will cause the very civil war that you fear."

"And what do you intend to fight with, sticks and stones?" Petronien asked. "We monitor all your factory production. I warn you now to cease this agitation or pay the consequences."

After Petronien left, Mennarial said, "Petronien is irrelevant and his threats are hollow. Like all the Children, he is indecisive, hemmed in by his own moral fences. We will unleash our secret plan before any of them can act, and then they will fall before the new world order."

CHAPTER XXXIII
Poseidia, The Imperial Palace
The Third Epoch, circa 10,700 BC

For their delight is deception.
—The Apocryphon of John, a Gnostic gospel

mliea, Avarna, and Terselia awaited Desamon in the imperial receiving room. Petronien had come with another note from an unknown source he found in his room at the Stratia barracks:

From dark earth the Archon rises.
An end and a beginning as six lights above shine forth.

"Soldiers are present there all day and night," Petronien said. "No one could have gained entry without being seen. Whoever is leaving these messages must be an extraordinary being."

In the distance, the massive copper-plated doors swung open, and Desamon embarked on the long walk from the entry to the dais where the others waited. Accompanying him were two Blackmane guards and a disheveled man. Something unexpected was happening. Discussing the latest message Avarna had found would have to wait.

As they made the trek along the glowing white marble floor Terselia said, "Ridiculous. One practically needs transport to get from one end of this room to the other. Why did they have to make everything here so gargantuan?"

Amliea shot a puzzled look at her. "Why, to impress, of course."

As Desamon's party approached them, they could see the man with him was of the white race. "I realize this is unexpected," Desamon said, "but this man is a mariner from the Inland Sea bearing incredible news. The Nautikon picked him up after a storm pushed him into the forbidden zone."

Artalanta was cordoned off from the outside world, more for protection of the foreign lands than from any concern of outside aggression. By avoiding contact with foreign lands, they obviated the temptation to use the vastly superior Lantean technology against inferior forces. Besides, the island empire was self-sufficient. It needed nothing from outside to flourish. The man's presence was indeed puzzling.

"His people call themselves Achaeans from a land on the north Inland Sea called Hellas," Desamon said. "Normally, we would have simply sent him back from where he came, but our friend here had a strange tale to tell." He nudged the man.

The man cleared his throat and bowed. "My name is Damocles. Thank you for not killing me."

"We do not kill needlessly here," Amliea said.

"Begging your pardon, Empress, but things seem otherwise."

"What do you mean by this?" Amliea asked.

"Some months back, your armies landed on our continent we call Europa. They started near the straits, the Great Pillars that lead into the Mediterraneo."

Amliea shot a quizzical glance at Desamon.

"Their name for the Inland Sea," he explained.

"They are working their way east, conquering all before them, taking treasure and captives at every point along the way," Damocles said. "They have not yet reached my land, Hellas, or my city, Athena."

"And these invaders are Lanteans, you say?" Petronien asked.

"They wear your armor, use your weapons, and look like you," Damocles said, "in a manner of speaking."

"What is your meaning?" Avarna asked.

Damocles paused to think. "Many of them, the bulk of them seem ... different. Rather dull-witted so to speak. Some who fought and survived against them said that the officers and their subordinates seemed to direct the slower-witted ones, though they fight well enough and with abandon."

"Drones," Petronien said. "It sounds as if he speaks of drones, but drones are not capable of combat."

They questioned the man for hours then had him taken away in order to confer among themselves.

"What do you make of this?" Terselia asked.

Amliea gave Desamon a stern look. "You are supposed to anticipate things like this. How could all this happen under our noses?"

"Let us not make premature judgments before we are sure what has happened," Avarna said. "The ability to materialize drone thought-forms was lost with the Old Race in the Second Epoch," Avarna said. "If any demonstrated that ability today, they would come under the control of the Elda-Fera."

"Legends say Fades still exist," Desamon mused. "They might do it too."

"Fades on Aryan?" Terselia asked. "If they exist would they not be beyond reach in the Paleovouná? And how does one produce so many drones in only fifty years?"

"Fades aside, we never knew the extent to which the ability lies dormant within common people," Desamon said.

"And you saw fit not to mention any of this?" Amliea asked in an accusatory voice.

"I had Aryan scoured several times by a special force," Desamon said. "We found nothing to substantiate the rumor of mass drone creation."

"If this is true," Amliea said, her blond hair framing her angry frown, "how could they transport an entire army to the Inland Sea without detection by the Home Watch?"

"I can think of several ways, and none of them bode well," Petronien said. "Submersibles could have made it undetected, or even aircraft. We do not watch the skies since no nation but Artalanta has such technology. But in any case, bribery, collusion, and treason must be involved for such an operation to go unnoticed. Remember, we could not purge all Belials from the Stratia and the Pneumarta."

"If what the Achaean says is true, the unbelievable has happened," Avarna said. "Mennarial has been nearly invisible and he must be behind this, but how could they thought-project such a huge number of drones and ones with intelligence enough to execute military orders? It took millennia to raise the mental levels of the earlier drones."

"We should have dealt with Mennarial when we had the chance," Petronien said.

"Are you questioning my decisions now?" Amliea snapped, seeming to pale at the news.

"My questions right now they have to do with whether any of this is true," Petronien said, looking her in the eye. Avarna smiled. Petronien was a persevering bulldog even when crossing an empress. "We need intelligence. I will lead a small force to the Inland Sea to assess the situation."

"Should you not bring a larger army, Petronien?" Terselia asked.

"No," Amliea said. "We cannot commit a large force based on the word of an errant sailor. Petronien needs to assess the size, strength, and disposition of the invading troops."

"Exactly," Petronien said. "But now that I think of it ..."

"I know your thoughts," Avarna said. "What if this is a diversion? Sending too many troops to the Inland Sea would leave us more vulnerable here. If somehow the Belials created a drone army, the forces at the Inland Sea may be a fraction of the hostiles. Then again, this Achaean could be a spy. Petronien, you are needed here as commanding general of the Stratia. I will go east to survey the problem."

"Desamon," Amliea said, "produce some helpful information and redeem yourself."

The room went silent, and people exchanged glances. Desamon did not merit the insult, but Amliea's hands trembled and she seemed unsteady. The others sensed this was not the time to confront her. Later that day, the entire government and armed forces met in council. They formed strategies and assigned tasks. Movement of troops for deployment within Artalanta would soon happen on an unprecedented scale pending information from the Inland Sea.

No one wanted to believe the news that had come to Poseidia, but they had felt a shadow stirring for some time, and part of that shadow was their empress, whose behavior was becoming ever more erratic.

CHAPTER XXXIV
Plytheron, Poseidia
The Third Epoch, circa 10,700 BC

... their fruit is deadly poison and their promise is death.
—The Apocryphon of John, a Gnostic Gospel

T he windy night shook the rafters of the small cottage on a farm that produced few crops because it served a purpose darker and more sinister than feeding the masses.

Two women, one younger, one older, stood before a gas-fired hearth inhaling the aromas of cooking food. The older woman took a spoon and dipped it into the kettle. She closed her eyes, savoring the smell, then slowly sipped. The younger woman looked on, face tight with contracted nerves.

The older woman smiled, and the younger one's expression relaxed. "Ah, excellent. Such skill will secure you the opening in the imperial kitchen soon."

"How do you know a position will come open?" the younger woman asked.

The older woman's eyes drew together. "By now you should know not to ask such questions. I said a position will be available soon. Just concentrate on the exotic dishes and no others will compare to you. You are pretty and have a pleasant look. They like your kind in dull kitchens. More direct attacks have failed, and they are now on guard against such assaults. You represent our best chance of eliminating the cursed one who will bring the world to ruin."

She then led the younger woman in prayer before a makeshift table altar. On the table was a metal symbol of an infinite loop the size of a man's forearm. The older woman uttered some invocations, then handed the young woman a vial.

"Guard this well. Upon it depends the survival of this world. May the Infinite be with you in your task. Now keep practicing your art and await your appointed time."

CHAPTER XXXV
Poseidia, The Imperial Palace
The Third Epoch, circa 10,700 BC

But those who live above the world
cannot fade. They are eternal.
—The Gospel of Philip, a Gnostic Gospel

T he day's news sent Amliea into her room, trying to hide her agitation. She sat in front of a mirror *Mass drone creation, an army. Cannot be. Not mine, no!* she fretted, wringing her hands. She stared into the mirror in a state of dark confusion, the numbness of a disturbed mind in denial experiencing a waking nightmare. Hypnagogic images flowed and formed, halting her conscious thoughts, taking over her mind. The mirror formed a different image, herself as a young girl, and she sat numb and watching...

Amliea sits in the west tower in her childhood playroom, adolescent things strewn around in discarded disdain. A solitary chair in a darkened room. Beads of concentrated sweat blanket her forehead. Eighty weeks daily without fail for hours. The familiar fixed image is gaining focus in her mind, settling in her inner vision. Ah, at last! A holographic shape. It is forming, slowly externalizing in the space in front of her! The transparent outline of a humanoid form.

It flickers, struggling to acquire mass, to achieve solidity. Her first success. She intensifies her concentration. The ghostly projection labors to materialize.

Two men burst through the door. She recalls everything

they say — *We caught her before it was too late* — *Foolish girl, you have no idea of the forces you play with* — and her materialization sputters and vanishes with her broken concentration.

She whimpers like a wounded animal as her father slaps her repeatedly until Segund stops him. *You will leave the palace and go with Segund to Mount Pelion, where he will instruct you, he growls.* Kind Segund wipes the tears from her shocked eyes.

A full year passes in the Temple of Light teaching her what she did wrong. History lessons, instructions in the use of spiritual forces. Segund is kind but firm as he steers her. "Projection of beings has dire consequences." He leads her into a room with a high ceiling and a huge blue glass globe in the center. He motions her to sit in a chair.

"What is this?"

"The globe will translate the words and thoughts filtered through my mind into images as I speak to you."

"What use is that when you can speak to me directly?"

"Images are more powerful than words."

A dark room. A bluish light from a globe that emits a pulsating hum. Her head lolls down limply. A voice over the humming. Spoken, projected? She cannot tell.

<< You possess an extremely rare ancient power to materialize thought-forms. >>

<< Is that why my father strikes me? Is that a bad thing? >>

<< We shall see, >> the disembodied voice responds.

She remembers the globe. Inside it images form, images of things past.

<< Many thousands of years ago, souls descended upon the earth, fascinated by the animal life forms roaming the face of the planet. Using their powers, they projected their essence into the animal forms, mixing with them, mutating them. >>

Within the globe is a young, twilight earth. Herds of nomadic beasts wander the land. Balls of light fall from the sky. Animals are struck. They show visible alterations in their demeanors. More lights descend into plants and oceans. Points of sentient energy bombard the world, a torrent of higher beings never meant to be loosed upon the material creation. Soul minds project all manner of thought-forms across the face of the earth. The history of spirit in flesh flashes across Amliea's mind.

Souls begin projecting thought-forms just like she tried to do. But then ... they push their spirit essence into their own projections like filling empty buckets with water! They inject themselves into their own dream creations! They fill their thought-forms with their own souls, something she would never think to do.

She sees Old Lanteans, the three-eyed androgyne humanoids. The embodied three-eyed god-beings are mind-projecting new thought-forms into existence.

The voice sounds over the increasingly rapid humming of the globe. << It was one thing for souls to project into their own thought-forms and become solid bodies. But to materialize other thought-forms is a most egregious sin in the eyes of The One. Only The One can emanate souls, so the projected mind-offspring of the three-eyed race were sentient but soulless drones abused by their creators for sex and labor. >>

Drones. The globe shows her how the creation of such beings caused division, dissension, and the idea of inequality among the now earthbound souls who misused their creative powers. Amliea's fists clench.

<< The creation and abuse of the drones contributed to the corruption of the higher race. This is why the higher souls, in keeping with The Law of The One, caused the Adamic humans of our age to lose the ability to mind-project such creations. >>

Amliea recalls a year of conditioning, then leaving Mount Pelion pretending to be duly chastised yet defiantly thinking that projecting new beings did not have to be bad. She could still create something superior, something no one could exploit.

Her mind churns—her father beating her, Mennarial raping her, throwing herself into healing and energy manipulations avoiding her real passion and the memories of men crushing her dreams, again Mennarial, damn Mennarial, coaxing her urge to create new life. And her old desire reemerges. It seizes her passion and energies. She creates what only she could create, the fateful action that will affect all life on earth.

She broke contact with the mirror and snapped out of her memories, but her mind could tolerate only a moment of present reality as a single thought struck her — *what have I done?* — And she began to scream.

Terselia came running into the bedroom. She dismissed the Blackmane guards standing inside. "Amliea, what is it? The guards heard you cry out."

Amliea did not respond. She only stared outward with a blank face.

When Desamon and the physicians arrived, Terselia told them how she found her sister. Amliea remained in the same catatonic state as the Elda-Fera priest-physicians examined her.

"She is sound in body," one of them told Terselia. "She has withdrawn into her mind. Some trauma might have caused it, some deeply emotional event she cannot face. Do you know what that would be?"

Terselia dismissed everyone in the room but Desamon, telling them not to speak a word of this incident or she would have them severely punished.

"Could the news of war in the Inland Sea have done this to her?" Desamon asked.

"I doubt it," Terselia said. "The signs if this have been building for a while, I think, although no other cause seems proximate to her breakdown. I just do not know. What can we do?"

"Perhaps send her to Pelion, where the Elda-Fera can perform more tests?" Desamon said.

"Not at this time," Terselia. "She must stay here. "We are in a war that will determine the future of the empire. It cannot be known the empress has gone insane or we may have a coup on our hands as well."

"Or you assume the throne," Desamon said.

And validate my sister's paranoia, she thought. "That will never happen while my sister lives," she said. But between attempted assassinations and Amliea's condition, she hoped that day was not looming.

CHAPTER XXXVI
Hellas, the Inland Sea
The Third Epoch, circa 10,700 BC

... let us make our entire flight before we are imprisoned
perforce, and taken down to the bosom of the underworld.
—Trimorphic Protennoia, a Gnostic Gospel

"Flight like the birds? How is this possible? Only the gods can do this," Damocles said when he and Avarna had set out by airship to the Inland Sea.

"Artalanta, last stronghold of the gods," Avarna mused. *How to explain humanity's true story to an awestruck seaman on his first flight?* He was about to all say souls were once gods. Instead, he told him, "We are men, no different from you. The gods just lingered longer in Artalanta before passing from the earth."

Avarna's group, including twenty of his best Blackmanes, surveyed western Europa from air and ground, and indeed they saw evidence of conquest and destruction. The vanquished locals described land armies and aircraft raining death from above. The invaders had forced men of fighting age into their army under threat of harming their families. They also looked to be erecting factories and shipbuilding facilities in port areas. The hostile forces were making their way east toward Damocles' homeland. Their description of the invaders verified what Damocles had told them.

"What are these things that attack us, these drones I heard you speak of?" Damocles asked.

"You would not understand," Avarna replied.

"We may not have your weapons and we may be white, but we are not stupid," the fair-haired Achaean said.

"Then how did you stumble onto our forbidden zone in wartime? The boundaries are well known to all foreign mariners."

Damocles grunted. "We were in neutral waters when we ran across some of your strange sea craft. Like great fish, they breached out of the depths, just like that," he said, snapping his fingers.

That confirmed that they used submersibles, Avarna thought.

"They began to shoot weapons at us that flew through the air like javelins at close range. Tore our ship apart," Damocles said. "I escaped in a rowboat with two injured friends. They died. The current took me west. I had no power against it. At least it was in the opposite direction your shark boats were headed. Now then, about the drones?"

Avarna sighed, once again struggling with how to explain the unbelievable to one whose racial memories were so obliterated. "Your people, I believe, tell stories of gods and heroes, no?"

"They do," Damocles said.

"Those stories come from human minds, which make characters borne out of nothing. Think of the characters as mind-projections, you understand? But those gods and heroes take on a kind of life of their own, do they not?"

"I suppose so," Damocles replied.

"Well," Avarna said, "when the first souls, gods as you called them, entered the earth they had the ability to materialize thoughts or mind-forms. They called them 'things' because they had no soul."

"They lived but had no soul?"

"Only The One can create souls," Avarna said. "They have animal life force and a rough level of intelligence but no souls."

"Did the Naphaalim giants come from them?" Damocles asked.

"No," Avarna said. "A group of souls called Celestials, the Sons of God, once mingled with lower soul forms, called the Daughters of Men, long ago. The Naphaalim were said to have been their offspring. Naphaalim in the old tongue. But they were long ago destroyed."

"Not so, but is it these drones who invade our lands?" Damocles asked.

"It seems so," Avarna replied, ignoring the comments about the Naphaalim, "but their numbers and the descriptions we are hearing are disturbing."

"How so?" Damocles asked.

"The ability to project thought-forms was mostly lost ages ago," Avarna said. "It has also been against the law to project mind-forms for millennia. If any possessed this ability, they would come under the control of our priesthood. The remaining drones on Artalanta today are semi-intelligent unskilled labor, but these invaders seem like a more superior variety of drone projections. Who caused this or how they perpetrated this abomination is a mystery we must quickly root out."

An hour late as they flew east, the pilot spotted three aircraft on the horizon headed in the opposite direction. "That cannot be our Pneumarta. It has to be the Belials."

"Have they seen us yet?" Avarna asked.

"No indication so far," the pilot said. "I am pulling up to cloud cover. That may be a scouting party. Looks like they are heading back to their base because they just converged into formation from all directions."

A few minutes into their ascent, a series of metallic thuds impacted the airship, which sent it into a sudden lurch. Avarna looked at the cockpit and saw the pilot's bloody head lolled off to one side. He moved the body aside and took the controls heading back to the cloud cover.

"A hostile aircraft has struck us with gunfire," Avarna shouted. "Our ship is damaged. We have to climb to lose him." More metallic clangs as projectiles struck the craft. "We are going down," Avarna shouted to the men as he struggled with the faltering craft. "He is going to strafe us on the descent. Find a place to strap yourselves in. He will be on our tail. I will open the rear bay; he will not expect that. Wait until he closes range and concentrates your compression rifles on the cockpit."

Avarna descended into a steep dive, rolling his aircraft to elude the strafing. The enemy pilot closed for the kill. Avarna opened the rear bay, and the soldiers commenced fire. The surprised pilot loosed rounds into the opened door, killing several men but the withering return fire found the cockpit. The hostile airship veered off out of control and plummeted toward the ground.

"He will not be reporting us to his base, but we are in for a rough landing," Avarna said.

As they neared to the ground, Damocles said, "That looks like Evvia, a large island opposite my city. Look to the left. That is Athena in the distance."

"Then Evvia best have some even ground because that is where we are landing."

"Evvia! The Naphaalim dwell there. The gods help us," Damocles said. "It is an evil, desolate place."

Naphaalim? The man was making no sense. Avarna could not tell if the fear on Damocles' face was from their freefall or the place in which they hoped to land intact, but he had no time to ask what he meant as the ground loomed larger in rapid motion.

CHAPTER XXXVII
Poseidia, The Imperial Palace
The Third Epoch, circa 10,700 BC

Your mind is deranged on account of the
burning that is in you, and sweet to you are
the poison and the blows of your enemies!
—The Book of Thomas the Contender, a Gnostic Gospel

The winded Blackmane guard tracked Terselia down in the south side of the palace, facing the Consularion. "Princess, come quickly! A disturbance in the Empress's quarters," he rasped.

Terselia entered her sister's bedroom to find Amliea sitting in her bed looking calm and perhaps more alert that she had in weeks. Several Blackmanes surrounded a trembling servant girl whose pleading, fearful eyes immediately locked on to Terselia's.

"Oh, highness, please," the girl implored. "It was a fade, a great, bright, white fade and I—"

"Stop!" Terselia said with her hand raised palm out. "Calm down and start from the beginning."

The girl explained that she had come to serve Amliea her usual mid-day meal. She walked in with the tray. She saw a tall, glowing, semi-transparent figure stood between Amliea and the dressing area. It moved toward her and knocked the food tray from her hands. She could not describe its features. It looked more like a human outline of light than a physical body.

Terselia looked around the ornately appointed room, touching pictures and shaking wall tapestries but saw nothing unusual until she looked by the dressing area. A note leaned against the base of the mirror on the polished onyx table top. She picked it up and read it with a raised eyebrow.

She folded the paper and tucked it into her robe. "You say he attacked you?" Terselia asked the girl.

The girl hesitated as if trying to recollect. "I — it did not seem it was me he wanted. He went straight for the tray and struck it from my hands. After that, he vanished into thin air."

She went to the bed and sat next to her sister. "Amliea, was someone here?"

Amliea nodded.

"Did he try to hurt you?"

"Oh, no," she replied. "I quite believe he wants to help me in Telian T'Meso."

"What?" Terselia asked. "Did you recognize him?"

Amliea just sat quietly. She said one word — *Sophia* — then said she wanted to rest. It was the most and clearest she had spoken in a week, so Terselia did not press her. She had another thought in mind.

Terselia walked over to the spilled food on the stone floor and knelt by it. She asked them to fetch her some gloves. She donned them, then picked at the food, sniffing it. "Get the Elda-Fera here," she ordered a guard.

Several hours later, an Elda-Fera priest declared to her, "Your instincts were accurate, Princess. The food contains a poison found only in the lands of the Far West."

Terselia immediately went to the kitchen with the priest and a dozen Blackmanes. The aroma of cooking food, the pots and pans on stoves and walls, and some twenty servants and cooks busy going about their work presented a bustling picture of the imperial kitchen. Terselia gathered all the staff in a line in front of the giant stone cooking ovens.

"Any of you who handled the empress's mid-day meal step forward."

Five women and two men stepped out. Terselia walked back and forth looking them up and down seeing which ones might look nervous, but they all did. "Who was the last to handle the food?" Terselia asked.

A middle-aged woman stepped forward. "I believe I was, Princess."

"Alderetha, I have known you a long time," Terselia said. "Did you notice anything unusual?"

"No Princess," the woman replied. "I did place the meal on the plates ... but now I recall I handed them to her to put on the tray." She pointed to a younger woman still standing in the group that remained in place.

"You girl, why did you not step forward as I ordered?" Terselia asked.

The girl broke and ran, but the Blackmanes had all escape avenues cut off. She put up a stiff fight but then made a gagging sound and went limp during the struggle. The soldiers told Terselia she was dead and assured her they had nothing to do with it.

"No doubt the same poison she tried to use on my sister," Terselia said. "Who was this girl and how did she come here?"

"She applied for the position from Comys on Atalan after Mistress Sertinela died suddenly," the Master of the Kitchen told her. "She surpassed everyone in the cooking arts, especially in the exotic cuisine of the western lands."

"We will have more questions for all of you," Terselia announced to the staff, "and I would learn how this girl was checked upon to work here." She turned to the Elda-Fera priest. "Take the body to Mount Pelion for examination. Desamon and I will meet with Segund. Too many questions have arisen this day, and I will root out this shadow that dares to threaten the imperial throne itself."

CHAPTER XXXVIII
The island of Evvia, the Inland Sea
The Third Epoch, circa 10,700 BC

There were giants in the earth in those days; and also after that,
when the sons of God came in unto the daughters of men.
—Genesis 6:4

Avarna and his surviving fourteen men had marched eight hours west toward the gulf separating Evvia from mainland Hellas when they saw a bright shimmer of reflected sunlight in the distance.

"Be careful," Damocles said. "They may use this to lure their prey."

"Who?" Avarna asked. "Your Naphaalim? Still, we will be cautious."

The land itself felt alien, denuded, and dying, as if some predators had stripped it of all semblance of life. "General," one Blackmane said, "have you ever seen anything like this? If not for the rocks and boulders, not a single shelter is to be had. Something feels wrong about this island."

Avarna looked at Damocles, who shuddered and put his head down. As they crossed the hilly, arid terrain they saw the source of the glinting light was a downed aircraft.

"The plane we shot down," Avarna said. "They crashed just before us."

They approached guns raised. "Looks like two pilots, both dead, sir," a soldier noted.

Avarna searched the cockpit. "Ah!" he exclaimed holding a device in hand. "A backup portable wave carrier for emergencies. It will be useful. Looks like the power crystal is not damaged. It should work."

"Sir, come see this," one of the soldiers said, and he handed Avarna a field glass. In the distance, three figures approached. "Too far to tell, but something seems off about them."

Avarna agreed, but the distance and lack of contrasting objects for scale threw off the perspective.

"We must leave now!" Damocles warned. "They come."

Avarna frowned then pointed saying, "We will hide among those large boulders. I want to see these people, whoever they are."

"No!" Damocles pleaded. "They will eat us alive, kill us first if we are fortunate."

"Take shelter now. We have adequate numbers and weaponry to handle three men," Avarna replied.

"Not men," Damocles mumbled.

The figures drew closer. Their shuffling feet among the rocks and dirt sounded out of proportion to the noise any three men could make. The reason soon became apparent. The gnarly-haired, unkempt gargoyles clothed in skin loincloths were at least fourteen feet in height with dull, brutish, vacant faces. They approached the unfamiliar aircraft with caution. They grew bolder, finally realizing it would not attack them. They looked into the air wing, and upon seeing the dead pilots they went into a frenzy.

They fought, clawing at the bodies like wolves in a death battle for food, all the while tearing off pieces of flesh and devouring them. Many of the soldiers looked away in disgust. Avarna motioned them to stillness. He gripped the shoulder of the Damocles, who oddly stood firm despite that for him, the scene had to be a whispered nightmare story from childhood come true.

The creatures finished their gory feeding and fell into a stupor, punctuated by sickening intermittent belching. Avarna led his group away along the backside of the boulder formation putting several miles' distance between them and the dreadful creatures. By the moonlight, they came upon hills of boulder formations and spotted a cave. They worked their way in with extreme care making sure no occupants had preceded them. They decided to put up with the rank smell since they could not risk sleeping in the open, but none of them could sleep. They sat in a circle, trying to make sense of what they had witnessed. They lit no fires for fear of being seen.

"I owe you an apology," Avarna said to Damocles by the light of a very dim glow lamp. "It is not that I doubted the histories about the Naphaalim, I just did not think any still existed. I should have known better after encountering the centaurs on Og. Remnants of ages past still lurk among us. Tell us your lore about these creatures."

Damocles sucked in a deep breath and hesitated, probably not wanting to revive memories of the ghoulish scene, but then he spoke. "Legends say that ages ago this land was once fertile. At some point, these giants appeared. We do not know from where they came. They were parasites, a burden on life from the beginning. At first, they devoured the plants and wildlife. When they depleted that, they began to prey on humans. The land, stripped of life began to die. Eventually, they began to devour themselves so the story goes, which is likely why they are not more numerous."

"Then why are any of them left at all?" a soldier asked.

Damocles shrugged. "Sailors of old with the courage to approach the near shores of this forbidden island claimed to see in them in the waters. Apparently, they learned to fish."

"That makes sense as the only attainable food supply," a soldier said. "But as we were crashing I saw the mainland you dwell upon. It seemed but twenty or thirty leagues away. Why have these creatures not sailed or swam across seeking new prey?"

"The waters in the straits are treacherous, even for creatures of their stature," Damocles said. "They would drown. Nonetheless, we have a series of forts on the opposite shore to propel any intrusions."

"And I can tell you another reason why they do not sail over," Avarna said. "Have you seen any trees for lumber? And did you any sign of intelligence on their faces? The concept of building and sailing is beyond them. Now," he pointed at two of the men, "go out and stand guard. We will rotate on two-hour shifts to get sleep then make for the coast tomorrow."

What he did not mention in order to avoid lowering morale, was the dilemma he had touched upon earlier. How, on an island devoid of trees, could they find enough wood to build rafts to float across the channel? But that was a river he would ford when he came upon it, and he fell to sleep exhausted.

Sometime in early next morning, loud screaming and rumbling jolted the men in the cave awake. "We are being attacked!" Avarna shouted. "Grab your weapons and follow me."

CHAPTER XXXIX
The island of Evvia, the Inland Sea
The Third Epoch, circa 10,700 BC

... that you might escape (in safety) to the One who is yours.
—Allogenes, a Gnostic Gospel

The situation outside the cave was as bad as it sounded. A Naphaalim, at least fourteen feet in height, was holding the body of a sentry with one arm. He had broken the soldier into grotesque sections like a twig. The brute was tossing the corpse aside and advancing on the second guard when Avarna and the others arrived from the cave. He yelled to divert the monster's attention.

"Fire your compression rifles at his head," he shouted. "Aim for the eyes. If we cannot kill it, blind it."

The men started to shoot. The giant raised its hands to its face as if protecting against a swarm of insects. It roared and staggered backward, groping its way up the rocky slope above the cave.

"It did not go down, but it is not seeing too well from the looks of it," a soldier said.

The creature bellowed loudly in what sounded to be words or some attempt to communicate. "The thing is calling for help," Avarna said. "We need to get out now!"

The men ran as fast as they could, pausing periodically to catch their breath then running again. At some point, they stopped to regroup and get their bearings at the bottom of a stony hillock.

"What happened back there, Torden?" Avarna asked the surviving sentry.

"In the morning dusk, we heard falling rocks from the hill above the cave," the man said. "Next thing the creature is on us and grabs Ex-Tal. Broke him in half like a child with a stick."

Avarna shook his head. "Damocles, any idea how far we are from the coast?"

The Achaean shrugged. "Evvia is long but not wide. As far as we have come and as long as we head west, I should think a few hours more."

Three hours later they crested a hill and the men cheered. The afternoon sun shimmered on the stretch of azure blue water that lay before them. "Which way do the prevalent currents flow in that strait?" Avarna asked Damocles, who told him from north to south.

"We make for that headland to the south, then," Avarna said.

"Why there?" one of the men asked.

"Did you think a boat would be waiting to ferry you to the other side?" Avarna asked. We need wood for rafts. That promontory lying south is like a bent arm extending into the sea. It will act as a catch basin for the flotsam and jetsam found on all coastlines."

Sure enough, when they arrived, the windward north face at the base of the promontory was lined with driftwood. The men waded in, gathering wood, then bringing it to shore, where they began to bind it together with rope from their packs. Not long after, the sentry Avarna had placed on some high ground with the field glass cried out. "General, they are coming!"

Avarna scrambled up the hill and took the spyglass. "Light of the Crystal, they may not be smart, but they have an animal's instinct for tracking. Ten of them. They will soon be on us, and we do not have enough rafts completed." They ran down the hill and conferred with the others.

"Three men with me," Avarna said. "We will take our position in the high rock formations and intercept them inland to divert them away from the shore while the rest of you work. See if you can complete another raft, then take as much loose wood as you can and bundle it. That way you can assemble more rafts out in the water. When you hear us shouting, launch off."

Avarna chose a small ridge with a steep incline to make their stand.

"This is a good place," he said. See how those large boulders cluster near the edge? We can roll those down on them, and the back side of the hill is negotiable so we can escape."

As the giants approached, the men shouted and threw rocks at them. The creatures grunted and began to climb the ridge. The men put their backs to the boulders and toppled them over. This triggered a slide that caused the Naphaalim to trip and made it hard to avoid the larger rocks. Three of them were struck and badly injured—one looked dead—but no more boulders remained.

"Use your guns," Avarna said. "We may not be able to kill them but we might slow them down or injure them. Aim for the heads." It soon became apparent the fire was annoying them and giving them pause, but it would not stop them. "Let them advance closer and concentrate fire on them one at a time," Avarna said.

This tactic worked better. Two of the creatures dropped, apparently dead from strikes to the head. Two others turned and ran, but the remaining three charged on as the men ran out of ammunition.

They retreated to the backside of the ridge and began to make their way down narrow spaces between the boulders covering the hillside. The Naphaalim, demonstrating surprising agility and using their size, skipped along the top of the boulders. Two of them jumped down onto the path ahead of them as the other one came up from behind.

"They have cut us off," Avarna said. "Get inside the spaces under these boulders."

Fortunately, the boulder formations offered numerous crawl spaces under boulder piles big enough for men their size but not for the giants. Avarna crawled into one hole, the other three scattered elsewhere. Avarna picked a bad hole. It was not deep. The Naphaalim could not enter, but they could reach in and do damage. The One was with him, however. The meter on his compression rifle registered remaining rounds. He pointed it at the mouth of the hole and drew out his long knife to rest it at his side.

Not long after he heard grunts. A huge arm reached into the hole like a giant snake feeling its way around. Avarna stabbed it with his knife, and the creature withdrew it howling in pain. "Show me your handsome face, creature, do not be shy. You are a legend, after all, and legends should be dead."

He heard snorting, and sometime later a shadow cast across the front of the hole. The Naphaalim's face appeared a distance back, the knife jab apparently reminding it not to get too close for inspection. It was humanoid in appearance, or maybe hominid was more accurate. It had a wide nose and protruding brows above deep-set eyes. It seemed to smile or sneer showing sharp, crooked teeth as if it was enjoying the challenge of its hunt, but then again it might just be thinking of the rare potential feast within its reach. Avarna kept talking to keep the giant's head in position.

It worked. The creature grunted and continued to stare at him with curiosity. Avarna kept the gun close to the ground in front of him, afraid to aim it and scare the thing off. He had no rounds to spare, and estimating the trajectory from an awkward position was tricky, but the moment came and he pulled the trigger. The bullets caught the giant square between the eyes. It whimpered as its face went slack and its eyes dropped shut. Soon the sounds of large footsteps approached. He assumed it was the other two Naphaalim. He saw large hands pull the dead body from view. He was out of projectiles.

He braced himself with his knife waiting for angry probing hands to grab him. None came. It sounded instead as if they were leaving. He waited for a time, then he called out to his men. It seemed all had survived by crawling for cover. "Now we run for the beach," Avarna said.

They did just that eventually working their way out of the boulders onto open ground. But as soon as they were out in the open, the two Naphaalim emerged from behind the boulder cover to their left.

"Run!" Averna shouted. "Split up. You three stay together. I will take care of the one that follows me."

They took off in different directions toward the shore, and the two Naphaalim separated to chase them. Avarna came to a high bluff above the beach and shouted down for the men to launch. The giant closed on him with its longer strides. Avarna took a breath and jumped over the bluff grabbing on to roots to break his fall. He slid and tumbled his way onto the beach, coming up with a limp. The giant followed suit and landed less injured. Avarna stood but twenty feet from the angry Naphaalim.

He picked up some rocks and cast them at the ogre, but it merely brushed them off as it advanced on him. Avarna tried to dodge from side to side, but his injured leg hampered him. He picked up the largest, most jagged rock he could hold, and he charged the Naphaalim. It took the thing by surprise, likely because it never feared an attack from anything it had encountered before. Avoiding its grasp, he slammed the rock into the thing's knee. It howled in pain, and as it clasped its leg Avarna moved in instead of instinctually backing off and hammered its arm. But this time the enraged hulk caught him with a reflexive swipe of its arm and sent him reeling to the ground.

It limped toward him with rage in its eyes, reached down with its good arm, and hauled him into the air. It bared its teeth and opened its mouth with a sickening exhalation of fetid breath. The thing intended to bite him to death! But then it sucked air in with a gasp, dropped Avarna, and turned, sinking to its knees. A makeshift spear protruded from its back. In front of it and backing away was Damocles.

The Naphaalim reached around with a roar and snapped the spear. It started to rise from its knees. Avarna regained his jagged rock. He moved with all the momentum he could muster, leaping at the monster, and smashing the rock into its head before it could rise. It slumped down again, and he continued pummeling it as Damocles came up and joined him with a rock of his own.

"From spirits to cannibals," Avarna choked the words out. "This is what happens when gods fall."

Damocles said, "I hid, knowing you would need help." Avarna gave a weak nod back.

Avarna's other soldiers soon appeared. "Why two of you? Where is the other Naphaalim?" he asked.

"We fought the beast on the high cliffs," one them said. "We maneuvered him over the cliff to his death, but he took Tarx'tel with him."

Avarna put a hand on his shoulder. "You did well. Now let us depart this accursed land."

The men rafting offshore returned. They finished their work and cast off again. "With our remaining water and rations plus some calm weather, we should make the other side," Avarna said. Later that night, he told Damocles, "If all the Achaeans are as worthy as you, we just might win this war."

"You came to help us, so I helped you," Damocles said. "Something tells me you are special, as if you were born to this task. I saved you because I believe you are the only one who can save my people."

"If only I were as sure that I could save mine," Avarna said as they drifted off into the night.

CHAPTER XL
Mount Pelion, Poseidia
The Third Epoch, circa 10,700 BC

Understand that you have come into being from three races:
from the earth, from the formed, and from the created.
—The Teachings of Silvanus, a Gnostic Gospel

Desamon and Terselia gazed down at the land below from the Elda-Fera's keep on Mount Pelion, adjacent to the great dome that housed the Touai Stone on Palasindra. The Great Crystal's power seemed palpable in such close proximity. Segund, the High Priest of the Elda-Fera and Keeper of the Portals, soon joined them.

"We have much to talk about," Terselia said. "A number of mysteries whose threads have woven together like a tight ball of yarn. Perhaps today we can begin to unwind it. The appearance of this elusive light figure has given us a tangible thread with which we might begin to undo the knot."

"Have you found anything, Segund?" Desamon asked. "We are in desperate need of information."

"We have found several things. Where to begin?"

Terselia put the note found in Amliea's room on the desk. "Begin here first," she said.

If you would defeat the Archon, defeat the shadow within.

"Who was the assassin, and what of the apparition in the room that left this message?" Terselia asked.

The shaven-haired priest had them sit at a table of transparent material that looked like glass but of a much lighter substance. The chairs too were transparent, furniture that would be seen nowhere else in the world but Artalanta.

"Your servant claimed whatever was in the room was essentially light in a human outline," Segund said, and he produced a drawing. This is what we believe the earliest ethereal soul bodies would have appeared like. It seems the closest match to the description."

"Would this be a fade?" Terselia asked. "I mean, the way it vanished."

"If it was ethereal, technically no," Segund replied. "Fades were solid bodies of the early second or third root races. Ethereals preceded them. Ethereals were essentially thought-form bodies, the very first soul appearances on earth. You said she called the entity Telian T'Meso?"

"She said two things. That and the name 'Sophia,'" Terselia replied.

"Curious," Segund said. "Telian T'Meso is not a person but a place, a place not in the physical world. It was said to be the mental plane nearest to the material dimension from which the souls projected themselves into materiality. And you know from your temple studies that Sophia was the first soul to break the unity of heaven leading to the creation of the lower planes of existence."

"Yet," Desamon said, "both Amliea and the servant referred to it as a male presence. Moreover, whatever it was seemed to know the food was poisoned, and it moved to protect Amliea, so we know it is friendly. But who or what could do that?"

Since it now seemed evident this being was the source of the mysterious messages, they decided to reexamine them to see what answers they might now yield. They assembled the messages on the table for scrutiny.

Hand cupping his chin, Segund studied the writings. "I must reveal something to you that we have known for a long time but only now may have significance."

Desamon sat silent for a moment, then said, "Explain."

Segund stood to speak to them, his white robe with scarlet trim on the sleeves and collar denoting his status as high priest.

"You are aware the Elda-Fera perform certain tests on all Lantean infants at birth," he said. "The ostensible reason is to determine the health of the child, but another dimension exists to it that we reveal to no one."

"You Elda-Fera have many secrets," Terselia said.

"We have our reasons," Segund replied. "Physical bodies contain a code that determines many characteristics of a person. We call this code *genitas*, and the individual components of the code are *genera*. Markers are a particular sequence of genera. Certain common markers appear in a minuscule fraction of the population."

"How minuscule?" Desamon asked.

"Five people."

"Who are they?" Terselia asked.

"The two of you, Avarna, Petronien, and Empress Amliea."

Desamon and Terselia looked at one another.

"How is this so?" Terselia asked

Segund told them of guarded sacred lore describing how The One, through the medium of Amilius and the First Souls, perfected the current human Adamic body in Poseidia in the area of Eden and in four other locations around the world, corresponding to the red, white, black, yellow, and brown races.

"The Crystal hummed in the background as Segund spoke. "The consensus theory is that some early Adamic humans may have mixed with the surviving remnants of the old androgyne race."

The discussion turned to the possible effects of possessing genera from the old root race. The Elda-Fera could offer only theories, since so few people possessed the genera markers and nothing remarkable had emerged until, perhaps, now. Segund pointed out that the markers could indicate latent abilities such as the capacity to fade or to project thought-forms, a power, traditions indicated, that the Source desired to breed out of existence to stop souls from misusing their abilities in the physical world.

"But how does this help us decipher the messages?" Terselia asked.

Segund paused with a deep breath then sat. "Tar Anu has passed beyond the veil. I may now tell you this. Your sister, Tara Amliea Karason, is the only known human able to materialize thought-forms."

Terselia pushed back in her chair wide-eyed and silence seized the room.

"Another note of interest," Segund said.

"What more can you possibly have?" Terselia asked in a tremulous voice.

"You seek answers, I provide facts of possible relevance," Segund said. "All of you were born in the month of Artanael under the ascendency of Arcturus, a sign of great upheaval and change. The seven Belial leaders of the last rebellion — Mennarial, Ter-Madaz, Ta-Revi and the others — were also born in the same month under the sign of Arcturus, and we have cataloged only one other anomalous series of human genera markers. It belonged to them."

"Different from ours?" Terselia asked

"Quite," Segund said.

"And you have no idea what it means," Terselia said.

"Not with certainty," Segund said.

"Then what do you surmise?" Terselia asked.

Segund sighed. "You are asking me for theories? Very well," he said. "It is almost as if you were born to oppose one another."

Desamon did not react to the shocking statement. Something more shocking had caught his eye as he stood with hands splayed on the table, studying the assembled messages. After a minute he began to rearrange their order like moving around pieces of a puzzle. When he finally stopped shuffling the notes, his jaw dropped and she looked at Terselia.

"What?" she said.

"I pray I am wrong about what I am seeing here," he replied. "Because if I am right what I am seeing is unbelievable."

CHAPTER XLI
Aryan, the Underground City
The Third Epoch, circa 10,700 BC

The Revelation of the Mysteries hidden in silence.
—The Apocryphon of John, a Gnostic Gospel

"What a discovery this was! A marvel how it survived largely intact from the First Epoch," An-Klesen proclaimed, extending his arm around to indicate the vast, cavernous sight before them.

Indeed, it was a staggering view the four other men surveyed, an expansive city hewn from the bowels of the earth with streets, massive statuary, and buildings of all sizes. Thousands of people labored therein like a colony of bee drones beneath a dark sky of rock and ore punctuated by columns of basalt that exceeded in scale the more refined structures of the cities above the earth.

The subterranean city echoed with the pounding and grinding of implements of war being forged with the energy of a palpable malice, the clanging of armored men shuffling about with blank expressions. To a sane person, this picture of encircling underground darkness punctuated by fires leaping up to light the gloom would be a materialization of hell. But to the gathered men it was a source of comfort and power. In their hearts they took solace in the dark, where they could lay their plans in secret. The darkness nourished and protected them from prying eyes that would interfere with their desires and blunt the will they wished to exert unfettered by the restrictions of the stifling Law of One.

"The restoration took over two decades," An-Klesen proclaimed with pride. "It had substantial damage from the old cataclysm ...

though it has been functioning well enough for some years," he added in deference to Mennarial.

"My ancestors discovered this. We kept it a strict secret within our family, and now I make good use of it," Mennarial said, addressing his top henchmen. "Your improvements were well done, An-Klesen."

"Who built all this and why?" Dal-Golia asked.

"The city was called An'ga-Bande. We found inscriptions on some of the walls," Al-Presta said. "Some were so old that we could not decipher the language — early proto-Lantean or possibly Murian — but later writing in old Lantean indicates it was built at a time when the council of ten kings ruled the land. They were worried about some destruction coming from above."

'What does that mean?" Ta-Revi asked.

"Unclear," Al-Presta said. "We do know that large animals were a great problem then, and they may have fled underground to avoid the beastly depredations. At some point in history, this place was abandoned, lost, and forgotten until Mennarial's grandsire rediscovered it."

"That this city was on Aryan soil is no accident," Mennarial said. "The force of the Archon led my ancestors here. The Law of the One is a ruse to justify the rule of our enemies through benevolent lies. Any thinking person can see that the law of nature prevails on this earth as the power of the strong to exert their will. What we have created in this stronghold will lead to our complete domination of the world and the achievement of our desires. What is your dream, Al-Presta?"

"To be the prophet of the Archon's cult, to bring his word to the masses," the renegade priest replied.

"Dal-Golia?"

"I do not need to dominate the world, just have complete control over my own part of it and live in easy luxury. Let others conquer the earth. I will be content with my portion."

Lazy fool, Mennarial thought, but at least he was not as envious of Mennarial's right to supreme authority as Val-Andwar who was leading the attack on Europa with Ter-Madaz. "And you, An-Klesen?"

"I don't care about ruling; I care about wealth, wealth beyond measure," he replied.

"Well, my noble friends, my ambitions are more pointed," Ta-Revi declared. "Of course, some of what each of you has said are things I too wish, but I also want to rape every high-born woman in Poseidia, including the empress herself."

The others snickered. The handsome rake was known to go through numerous women regularly, some willingly, some not, and some truth probably lurked behind his absurd statement.

"So, An-Klesen," Ta-Revi said, "tell us how things stand here."

"The city is divided into four quarters," he replied. "The human officers and soldiers occupy one section, the Tekna-Fera another, and my Ferrets, uh, my engineers, are centered in their part of the city."

An-Klesen caught himself. The Imperium had absorbed the Order of the Ferrets into the Poseidian-controlled military during the purge. His men were deserters or retired. "The drones comprise the last sector," he said in conclusion.

"Drone numbers?" Dal-Golia asked.

"One hundred twenty thousand. Thirty thousand are out conquering Europa," An-Klesen replied.

"Formidable," Ta-Revi said with a whistle.

"Bred in the past fifty years," Mennarial said, "and you can thank that empress you want to rape for the template we used with the able enhancements of the Tekna-Fera. Their intelligence level is higher than that of the old drones. No generals among them, but they take orders well enough."

"Are you ready to unleash the rest of them?" Dal-Golia asked.

"No need yet," Mennarial said. "So far the government has committed no troops to the Inland Sea, allowing us an optimum strike. The slaves and weapons we will bring back from the East will further swell our ranks and put Poseidia in a vise."

"The Stratia deserters hiding all over the islands can divert their attention for a while," Ta-Revi said. "I think a little dose of sabotage and terror to dishearten the civilian population is in order."

Mennarial smiled, blue eyes icy-sharp and eager. "Make it happen, then."

CHAPTER XLII
Mount Pelion, Poseidia
The Third Epoch, circa 10,700 BC

... save me also from all their mighty threats.
—<u>Pistis Sophia, a Gnostic Gospel</u>

P etronien joined Terselia and Desamon as they sat in the keep of the Elda-Fera. They had been meeting all day with Segund and still had much more ground to cover, but now they listened to Desamon's insight into the riddle of the messages.

"I see things I would not have understood before Segund's information, before the incident with your sister and the being in her room. I see things that are dire," he replied as he laid the notes out in order.

The time of sorrows nears. Fear not the enemy's sword and spear; beware the enemy's mind and idea.

Stand forth in the time of the seven. Awaken in the between.

She is the first fallen, savior and destroyer, life and death. By her the world shall perish, by her may it yet be reborn.

If you would defeat the Archon, defeat the shadow within.

From dark earth the Archon rises. An end and a beginning as six lights above shine forth.

"The time of sorrows, Tyer Angarach, is upon us," Desamon said. "The enemy uses the Archon cult like a psychic virus to focus people on the lie of this world, not on the truth beyond. Someone is urging us to oppose the seven leaders of the Belials. That seems clear following Segund's astrological interpretation. The 'in between' must be the Telian T'Meso that Amliea was speaking of, and finding it will open our eyes, telling us how to proceed. That is our safety valve, our way out of the blindness imposed by the simulation. It is the way to defeat the shadow within."

Segund remarked that the statements had a ring of truth to them. Desamon felt one of the messages was specifically about Amliea.

"Amliea uttered the name of Sophia after her encounter," Desamon said. "Why? As I said before, the 'first fallen' in the message is a reference to the fallen Aeon Sophia. Somehow Amliea is being likened to Sophia. If Amliea had something to do with the appearance of these new drones, then this makes sense. Like Sophia, she would be the first to fall into an illusion, a great lie. Sophia's error distorted the creation. Amliea's error has distorted the world order, putting the earth in grave danger. But, like the legends of Sophia, it also seems to say she has a role to play in saving the world."

Terselia drank a deep draught of wine then said, "You put much on my sister, Desamon. These are but guesses after all."

Segund defended Desamon's reasoning saying they were not guesses but reasonable interpretations that seemed both logically based on the facts and intuitively correct.

"The message about defeating the Archon or the shadow within is certainly Amliea's greatest challenge now, is it not?" Desamon asked. "She has withdrawn from some shadowy thing she cannot face."

"Perhaps," Terselia said.

"What of the Archon arising from the earth and the six figures?" Petronien asked.

Desamon shook his head. "No idea."

"The First Souls are six in number," Segund said. This caused the room to go silent.

"Are you saying the First Souls have returned somehow?" Petronien asked. "Where are they, then?"

Segund merely shrugged. "It says six lights above in contrast to the Archon rising from the earth."

"Above where?" Terselia asked. "Other questions remain unanswered apart from these messages such as what the Elda-Fera have found out about the dead poisoner."

Segund's mouth tightened, and that did not comport with his normal taciturn demeanor. "The would-be assassin woman was approximately sixty-years old of pure Lantean ancestry," he said, and he produced a paper with a symbol on it. "She bore this small tattoo at the base of the neck beneath her hair.

"The Elda-Fea are familiar with the mark. It represents the Infinite, the preferred symbol for The One used by a renegade cult relegated to near fable. It started many hundreds of years ago when a group of priests broke with Pelion and set sail for the West."

"What was their problem?" Terselia asked.

"They were fanatical purists. They even called themselves the Katherati, the Pure Ones. Among other things, they criticized us for co-existing with the Belials whom they said should be eradicated or expelled. That was impractical and against our beliefs, so they left to live apart and practice on their own."

"What became of them?" Terselia asked.

"They settled in the lands of the West among the brown race and began making converts to the Law of One, but not as we practice," Segund said. "They were militant. They trained the native people to fight and resist the Lantean incursions. The Order of the Bull was dispatched from Atalan to subdue them."

"Did they succeed?" Desamon asked.

"The accounts claimed the fighting was fierce," Segund said. "The Bulls eventually prevailed and drove them into the jungles and mountains. All contact with them ceased long ago. We thought them extinct."

"Why would an obscure, far-removed cult want to kill Amliea?" Desamon asked.

"I cannot answer that," Segund said. "They had their own practices and some say even their own sacred texts handed down by a controversial priest they held as a prophet. He claimed to have received engraved golden plates on Párnathal written by the First Souls."

"That sounds like a fable," Desamon said.

Terselia stood from the transparent table and walked over to a window looking over the mountains deep in thought. "Two assassination attempts by people of the brown race to the West, but now by a Lantean. This vanished cult may have a longer reach than we think. I would learn what these Katherati know and end their assaults."

"How would you find a long-lost cult that may not still exist?" Desamon asked.

"Why, by traveling to the West, how else?"

Desamon, Segund, and Petronien looked at one another, and Desamon spoke. "Is this really the time for your absence? War has broken out in the Inland Sea, we face a threat from the Belials, and your sister is incapacitated. You may even have to assume the throne."

Terselia took Desamon aside. "Under no circumstances will I take the throne. I have always sensed that Amliea has a destiny to fulfill as empress, something she was born to do. Neither power nor duty will tempt me to reign over this land. Find a way to bring her back, and do not mention this again."

Terselia turned around and spoke to the others.

"My sister is incapacitated, and it appears these Katherati may know something about it or even have something to do with it. This threat is as serious as any of the others we face. Amliea is not just my sister but the rightful empress of Artalanta. We cannot sit passively waiting for another attack. I will end this."

Avarna off to war in the Inland Sea, Petronien to deal with the Aryan threat, and now Terselia seeking a phantom cult trying to kill her sister — many grave matters were impacting them all at once like several storm fronts converging. It raised the question if a single hand were behind all the turmoil.

"A single hand or blind fate to be played out, it matters not," Terselia said. "We must pursue the individual threads to see where they lead. Amliea seems somewhat better since the mysterious visitation in her room. Desamon, I want you to remain here as acting regent, propping her up until my return."

Desamon argued against her leaving. He asked where she would even begin her search, as the lands to the West were vast. Terselia noted that Segund's records indicated the settlement on the coast from which the cult was driven inland. It still existed as a Lantean trading port. She would start there by questioning the locals for information. Petronien told her that Atalani seafarers were the bulk of the port's population, not the most reliable lot in the world. Desamon pleaded with her to hold off until they could gather better information. Terselia agreed but told him she would not wait long.

Petronien, who had been silent for most of the discussion, said, "Segund is supposed to have new information for me."

"I do," the priest replied. "The tracing of thought patterns."

"Explain," Petronien said.

Segund began speaking about Consciousness as the force that creates and sustains the material universe, how it ebbs and flows and reshapes the shores of the world for good or ill. It separates men from one another, the good from the evil, the creators from the destroyers, and it leaves is footprints.

The practical Petronien had no idea what he was talking about, but Desamon understood.

"He speaks of tracking thoughts and feelings," Desamon said. "But how?"

"Emotion is a thought attached to a feeling," Segund replied. "Emotions are strong thought energies that carry signatures. These energies span material and non-material dimensions, registering themselves on the skeins of time and the universal energy field."

"Please, something I can understand and use," Petronien insisted.

Segund sighed, not accustomed to being rushed. "The character of thoughts, particularly ones backed by strong or negative emotions, carry their own vibration if you will, and we have a way to detect these vibrations. A group of our White Brotherhood spent months attuning to the Touai Stone. They were able to detect aggressive, concentrated frequencies that rose above the clutter of everyday mass mind activity."

"And?" Petronien asked.

"Follow me," Segund said.

The men exited the keep. They trekked across a narrow, covered walkway bridge with stone guard rails that spanned a gorge thousands of feet deep between Pelion and Palasindra. On the Palasindra side, they took a lift embedded into the mountain up to the mammoth retractable dome housing the Touai Stone. The Crystal was the size and scale of a trireme sea ship. Entering the dome, they could feel its humming energy penetrating their bodies with its awesome, cosmic energies.

Segund motioned to a white-robed group of men who proceeded to form a circle around the base of the Great Crystal. "These brothers are the ones attuned to the Crystal," Segund explained. "Watch and listen." He waved a hand, and the men all knelt with heads bowed.

Thirty minutes later, the hum of the Crystal altered from a steady long wave pulsation to a higher shortwave frequency. One of the Crystal's many facets began to change from clear to a dark, murky color.

"What does this mean?" Desamon asked.

"It means someone corrupted a major sub-crystal energy transmitter," Segund replied. "It carries the vibratory signature of those who used it for deviant purposes."

"What deviant purposes?" Desamon asked. "The creation of new drones, perhaps?"

"We cannot say for sure," Segund said, "but someone did something on a mass scale utilizing huge, dark energy, which is why it registers here. We can pinpoint the location, though. It is on Aryan."

"Of course it is," Desamon said, clenching his fist. "But who could modify a sub-crystal like that and by what means?"

"We could, the Elda-Fera," Segund said. "But I assure you that has not happened. It would take a group of our priests to accomplish such a feat, and it would have to be in the proximity of the sub-crystal in question. We rarely leave our temple aeries here on Pelion. If such a group absented our keep for any length of time I would have been aware. But the Tekna-Fera may have found a means to do it."

The men talked over several possibilities. All Petronien wanted, however, were the coordinates from the Elda-Fera.

At the end of the conversation, he said, "I am back to Aryan," he said. "It seems we have a hidden den of vipers to clean out."

CHAPTER XLIII
Mount Pelion, Poseidia
Circa10,700 BC

When you make the two into one ... when
you Make male and female into a single
one, then you will enter the kingdom.
—<u>The Gospel of Thomas, a Gnostic Gospel</u>

When the others had left and only Segund and Desamon remained, they sat at a table drinking wine. Segund said, "Everyone goes about their tasks, but you are the one who must keep the higher vision in mind."

"How so?" Desamon asked.

"This is not just a war between the Law of One and the Belials," Segund said. "The real war lies within each of us. We speak of many dimensions, but in reality, only two exist—the dimension of Wholeness and the dimension of fragmentation. No dualities exist in the Wholeness, but the psychic and material dimensions are fragmented—mind and body, male and female, light and shadow—dualities that each of us embodies in this fragmentation. These messages, do you know what they are really about?"

Desamon shrugged.

"The Belials are the extreme male half of our being gone insane," Segund said. "But the messages force us to use our intuition, the gift of our female nature, not to *think* but to *feel* our way out of this. It is no accident that a female occupies the throne for the first time in many thousands of years. Male energies have dominated this world for so long that we are experiencing the fruits of this imbalance in the very events that now transpire. Recovering the feminine intuitive energy may be our only way out."

Desamon lifted his gold wine goblet and twirled it around, fixing his vision on a sparkling emerald. "They say green is the color of healing, and what you are getting at is a kind of healing, no?"

"You are Artalanta's prime pedagogue responsible for our future generations," Segund said. "Do not let them get bogged down in the mindset of war. Do not let them forget our sacred temple teachings. Our male and female natures, mind and heart, logic and intuition, must come into balance within each of us to recapture the godlike consciousness we once had in the realm of Wholeness. Teach them that."

Desamon nodded. "Fragmentation keeps us in this simulated reality. Seeing the Unity takes us out."

Segund sighed and placed his hands on the table. "Perhaps that is why Amliea is empress during these pivotal times, and this linking of Amliea to Sophia is no mere coincidence. Perhaps it is about restoring the balance. After all, why did the male energy become so prevalent throughout our history?"

"In the sacred annals, the feminine, through Sophia, was held responsible for our loss of heaven and our fall into the suffering of the material earth," Desamon replied. "But there may be more to it, no?"

"Exactly, because the same sacred wisdom tells us Sophia and the female energy will also lead us back to the consciousness of our spiritual origins," Segund said. "Is this what we are seeing, the rise of the sacred feminine returned to restore the saving balance to our world and to humanity? The logic of men has only obscured our spiritual vision. Is it time for the feminine power of intuition to begin lifting humanity from the mud of the earth reconnect with the higher power?"

Desamon ran a finger around the rim of his goblet, thinking on the priest's words. "Are you saying the First Soul, the Aeon Sophia has incarnated as Amliea?"

Segund shrugged. "She certainly embodies all the creative and destructive paradoxes associated with Sophia, and if she had a role in generating the drones, she repeated the fundamental error of Sophia. My point is that the world as we know it may soon cease to exist. Something new must come out of it. Be open and guided by the feminine intuitive in your task. You and others like you must be the conduit for the light to continue in new forms, unobscured by old ways of perceptions or the clouds of war and destruction."

Desamon sighed, "You make a big assumption. We may not be around when those clouds clear."

CHAPTER XLIV
Mirach vian Tanato, Aryan
The Third Epoch, circa 10,700 BC

And they brought him into the shadow of death.
—The Apocryphon of John, a Gnostic Gospel

"*Mirach vian Tanato*, the Valley of the Shadow of Death," Petronien said, pointing at the valley in the distance. "Why did they call it so in the Old Tongue?" he asked Ter'Angaral, the Elda-Fera priest, as he surveyed the partially forested plain between the mountains.

The white-robed priest closed his eyes as he spoke. "We think it was a spawning ground for the great beasts that ravaged the land during the First Epoch. It would have been certain death for any entering here. The plateau we stand upon is the Galgaatha. This smaller vale leads to the larger valley ahead."

Petronien rubbed his chin as he assessed the pass leading into the next valley. "It seems deserted now. Are you sure this is the location?"

The priest turned to the mechanized wagon with the open bed and pulled the cover off an object inside. Underneath was a crystal half the size of a man. A darkish pulsating hue occluded it. "The disturbance is strong. The power source we detected most certainly lies in the next valley."

Petronien shook his head. "Five thousand advance troops have scoured the valley but found nothing. How do you account for that?"

The priest shrugged. "Many caves dot the hills and mountainsides. Have they checked those?"

Petronien's eyes narrowed as he stared at the valley beyond. He called upon his second in command. "Telerian, position the artillery. We are pulling our main body through the pass and into the valley. If we encounter any surprises, I want your guns aimed and ready at that pass to cover us if we have to pull out. It seems empty enough now, but this place makes me very uneasy."

Petronien's columns began to advance into the Tanato. Twenty thousand men would join the five thousand already in the valley while five thousand more stayed camped on Galgaatha. Once grouped inside the Tanato, Petronien gave his orders. "Send scouting parties to search any caves on the hillsides. The rest of the troops remain here in defensive formation."

"Sir," one of the junior officers said, "things would go faster if we commit more troops higher up."

"Yes, it would," Petronien said, "but if any trouble starts, I will not have troops scattered up and down the valley. I know that makes it more dangerous for the scouts, but they will have our defenses to fall back upon in case of trouble. Tell them to proceed with caution."

Ta-Revi observed the Imperial troop movements from the cover of a cave entrance. "So, Petronien nibbles at the bait but he is not swallowing it," he said to Dal-Golia. "He left the bulk of his troops on the valley floor. Better for us if they had scattered around the hills. We far outnumber them, and they are not expecting us."

"How did they find our location anyway?" Dal-Golia asked.

"With the assistance of the Elda-Fera, most likely," Ta-Revi said. "They will soon be upon us. I had better signal An-Klesen to start the attack on his side of the valley."

"Mennarial should have given me a command too," Dal Golia complained. "You and An-Klesen here, Val-Andwar and Ter-Madaz get Europa."

Ta-Revi snorted. "You have no command because you are slipshod. You botched Carch'Carai with superior troop support."

"You cannot blame Carch'Carai on me," Dal-Golia replied in

indignant protest. "Mennarial's Jackals were in control of military operations. No one foresaw Avarna's back door invasion."

"Whatever," Ta-Revi said. "In any case, when this war is over you will be back governing Og, so no more whining. Now, we need to unleash the storm. Contact An-Klesen," he said to a nearby aide. "After we destroy Petronien, the Imperial garrison on Atalan is next. I intend to reassume control of my own island and put it back in the fight."

The sound of weapons fire started above on the hillsides.

"Sir," one of Petronien's officers said, running up to him. "Our men at the higher elevations are reporting camouflaged doors opening up on the hills all around us. Huge numbers of troops are pouring out of caves and even subterranean shafts father up the valley and behind our position."

"It is a trap. Have the army pull back toward Galgaatha," Petronien said. "We cannot let them encircle us and close the pass. Move back through the wooded areas as much as possible so they cannot enfilade us from above. Have the cannons on Galgaatha ready to cover our retreat. If we can reach the next valley, then we will consolidate, assess their numbers, and hit back."

During the retreat, Petronien, who was in the army's center, could hear the sound of his advance troops engaging, but as they moved toward Galgaatha they encountered other troops behind them.

Telerian's alarmed voice from Galgaatha came over the wave carrier. "General, we see them pouring out of the earth, blanketing the land like a swarm of locusts cutting off the pass behind you. Too many. Get out now!"

"Our artillery cannot cover us while we are engaging the troops to our rear in close combat," Petronien shouted to his officers. "We must break through the pass and put them behind us."

He looked around, face grim and determined as he came to a decision. "Strike my colors. I will take the first division west of the pass to draw then off. I am the prize they will go for. If enough of them come after us, the rest may break through."

"General, you cannot do that. It is suicide," one officer said.

"I led us in here; I have to get us out," Petronien said. "You just save the rest."

The troops hastily redeployed with Petronien's command banner held high. He told his five thousand men they might not survive but they might save twenty-thousand of their comrades. "We may make a sacrifice, but I ask no less of you than I ask myself. And if we should perish, at least we will show these Belials the difference between us, for we are Children of The One and they will fear us in death."

He so extolled his men and they shouted, "For The One and our brothers!"

When the news came back to Telerian on Galgaatha, he said, "I fear we may lose our greatest general. That stubborn man. The One let him hold on long enough. Scramble those Pneumarta air wings he held in reserve and pray they arrive in time."

Petronien's men took off from the embattled main body, and they clawed their way up a steep rise at the base of a larger hill where they had the advantage of height. True to his prediction, a huge force pursued them. He formed his men into tight shielded ranks to fire down on the advancing enemy, which seemed to cover every inch of the earth below them.

Telerian observed the events below with his field glass. "He has given them their best chance with a strong defensive position but there are too many of them."

A junior officer pointed east and exclaimed in an excited voice, "Look, sir. The main army is breaking through the pass! It worked. He did it! They are going after the general. Our men are getting through."

"Prepare the artillery to fire on the enemy pursuing our main body as they put distance between them," Telerian said, "and send two thousand down the plateau to cover their retreat." He then looked to the skies praying for the air-wings to arrive.

Petronien's men formed a shield wall that protected against arrows and much of the compression gunfire. The enemy troops were more exposed coming uphill and took heavy losses, but the Imperial troops would run out of ammunition before the Belial's ran out of drones. Petronien ran from side to side shoring up the men. The left flank began to waver under the weight of the assault. When the enemy began surrounding a group of his men, Petronien grabbed a compression gun and charged the attackers with such ferocity that it halted the attack long enough for the men to pull back into the ranks. Other soldiers rallied to close the gap.

He turned to follow his men and they saw an arrow protruding from his shoulder. He staggered back and collapsed. His men rushed to hold him and bring him away from the conflict. "He should not be this bad from such an arrow wound," one soldier remarked.

"It is not from the arrow," the field doctor said. "A compression projectile struck him in the chest."

"Prop me up for the men to see before they begin to waver," Petronien barked. They followed his orders over the doctor's objections. "Hold those lines, lads," he shouted. "Did you think some puny arrow would end me? Pah, only if you let these bastard drones break through. Now, hold the line fast!"

"You cannot stand like this," the doctor said. "You are losing too much blood. You need to lie down."

"I have a job, and I will I finish it," Petronien replied.

"General, with all due respect, you are either a fool or a marvel of perseverance."

"I am both, so I have been told," Petronien said.

Back on Galgaatha, a junior officer said to Telerian, "I do not know how they held this long. They can last but a few minutes more."

"They hold because of the most dogged man you will ever meet," Telerian said, fighting back tears over his general's impending doom. Then he heard the sound he had prayed for and looked skyward. The aerial warcraft appeared with deadly effect and began to decimate the enemy ranks. "Counterattack now and relieve the general's division!" he ordered.

Thanks to the combined air and ground attack, they retrieved Petronien and his troops. But then something happened in the sky. From out of nowhere, new aircraft appeared and began to attack the Pneumarta. Their air cover now diverted, the surviving troops on Galgaatha were now surrounded, facing huge enemy numbers.

CHAPTER XLV
Poseidia, the Imperial Palace
The Third Epoch, circa 10,700 BC

Therefore, they lived in disobedience and acts of rebellion,
without having humbled themselves before the one
because of whom they came into being.
—The Tripartite Tractate, a Gnostic Gospel

Numerous fires burned near the Imperial Palace as Amliea and Desamon looked on. Terselia and Ar-Falene were present too, their planned expedition to the West delayed by the recent events.

"Acts of sabotage are happening all over according to reports from the other islands," Desamon said to the dozen people gathered in the empress' war room.

"Belial deserters from the Stratia most likely," said Vortegren former commander of the Falcon order now air marshal of the Pneumarta. "They remained angry at the abolition of the old military orders after Carch'Carai."

The great insignia of Artalanta, the sun within the pyramid encircled by the dragon of infinity devouring its own tail, occupied an entire stone wall of the room. The banners of each of the five islands hung from poles protruding from another wall. Only one side of the room had any windows and few of those, for this was not a chamber for cheer or festivities. It was used only on the gravest of occasions.

"Civil war has finally come. Full-scale civil war is what this is," Admiral Braan'dach said.

"Details," Desamon demanded, nodding at Vortegren.

"A number of Belials deserted the army on each island," he said. "They seem to be joining with civilian sympathizers to create terror and chaos such as what you are seeing in the capital itself."

"What is the status of the other islands?" Amliea asked. Oddly, she had indeed improved since her visitation experience, now wavering in and out of her spells. Fortunately, today she was quite lucid.

"Aryan is a mess. We blockaded Atalan, and Airye is stable," Desamon said. "Og is solid. General Ar-Falene had identified and preempted many Belial dissidents in the army there or things would be worse. Og is also staunchly anti-Belial after memories of the Mennarial-Dal-Golia coup."

"Excellent," Amliea said. "It is good to see a woman exert such foresight. Would more men were like her," she said, glancing sideways at Desamon.

After seconds of embarrassed silence, Admiral Braan'dach said, "Empress, it was Consular Desamon who instituted the program to identify and keep lists of extremist Belial sympathizers in the armed forces. We used this information to arrest suspected soldiers as soon as hostilities broke out."

"Continue," Amliea said, her mouth tightening around the edges.

"Petronien is gravely wounded, and our army is surrounded on the Galgaatha," said Vortegren. "Our air wings are being engaged in the air by Aryan forces and can no longer help our men on the ground."

This news sent the whole room into an uproar. "Light of The One!" Braan'dach exclaimed. "The Aryans have their own Pneumarta? How could they have developed an air force without our knowledge?"

Desamon stood. He placed his hands on the table, resting his weight on his arms. "The enemy soldiers wear black armor bearing the lion-headed insignia of the Archon," he said. "They possess all the characteristics of drones. Reports say they emerged from underground in the Mirach vian Tanato."

"Underground?" Braan'dach said.

Desamon nodded. "The Elda-Fera traced abnormal crystal energy to that area. I believe the Belials may have a substantial underground facility beneath the valley producing drones and engines of war."

"How could construction of such a large facility go unnoticed over fifty years?" Braan'dach asked.

"It could, perhaps, if they used existing caverns where little to no excavation was required," Desamon replied. "All their preparations would have taken place undetected, below ground."

"No!" Amliea shouted. "No drones, that cannot be."

"But that coincides with the information from the Inland Sea invasion," Admiral Braan'dach said.

Amliea sprang from her seat and pounded her fist on the table. "There are no drones, damn you!" she shouted, eyes cast to the floor as if talking to her feet. "Men ... odd men perhaps, or some Tekna-Fera trick. I ... I know of no drones. I—"

She glanced up to a silent room of people staring at her. Desamon looked her in the eye. It was the look of a condemned person, the hopeless countenance of someone lost to hellish perdition. At the mention of the drones, she had instantly regressed. Desamon quickly diverted attention from her behavior by gathering them around the strategic war map table that showed the known world.

"We are facing major assaults all around," he said.

Grim statistics followed. Considering desertions, estimates of the drones fighting at the Inland Sea and Aryan, and likely uncommitted enemy reserves, they estimated the Belials outnumbered imperial forces by at least two or three to one. A messenger then arrived and handed a note to Vortegren. He turned ashen reading it.

"A report from Galgaatha," he said. "Petronien is gravely wounded. Most of his army is lost, perhaps five thousand remain. My air wings are too busy engaging the Belial's in the air to help the Stratia on the ground. I have been reluctant to commit our full airpower to Galgaatha for fear of a trap," Vortegren said. "If we lose air superiority we lose the Imperium."

Amliea jolted up and pounded her fist on the table. "Rescue Petronien and his command! Send in more air wings. So far the enemy has matched your forces, but it would have been difficult for them to manufacture many air wings without observation. We must rely on the belief that their airpower is limited. Overwhelm them by attrition if necessary, but get our people out of Galgaatha—now!"

Desamon looked at her in wonder. Whatever the mind-sickness that had seized her, since the appearance of the mysterious fade, she seemed to be clawing her way back and forth to some semblance sanity. The One be thanked she was clear-headed at this most critical moment to save Petronien.

CHAPTER XLVI
Plytheron, Poseidia
The Third Epoch, circa 10,700 BC

... the lie use like poison.
— The Sentences of Sextus, a Gnostic Gospel

Eleth-Tir was a rising young official in the Poseidian security forces. Evidence of this was his assignment to Plytheron to help root out possible hostile agents, people who may have been responsible for the attempt on the empress's life. It would cement his position if he were to break the conspiracy. It would even earn him an imperial audience and personal thanks from the golden-haired Empress Amliea Karason herself, who was said to be one of the world's most beautiful women.

Eager and determined as he was, he was no fool. He could not march into the village flashing around images of the dead assassin woman without alerting the enemy. Anyway, the Imperium had already plastered posters of her and the male assassins throughout the empire with no concrete leads. Then again, he realized this whole effort might be for nothing. No guarantee the perpetrators had just passed through the town and moved on. There could be a ring of them, an individual, or no one at all.

He knew his task would be a slow grind. To that end, he secured a position for himself cleaning up tables at the local tavern for a ridiculously low wage. He reasoned that people talk at taverns. Gossip and news filtered through food, alcohol, and friendly gatherings more than at any other place in the village, but he had worked there for months now with nothing to offer in his daily reports to Poseidia. The only hard information they gave him was that the conspirators all seemed to have the infinity mark tattooed onto the base of their necks.

Eleth-Tir took up with a young local woman named Lalasien, called Lala for short. The relationship was good for his cover. It brought him closer to the villagers and he genuinely liked her. A handsome, athletic young man, they made an attractive couple, and it made the job less lonely.

One day as they walked together, they passed an old poster showing the image of the assassin woman stuck to a wall. "Strange," Eleth-Tir remarked, "they never discovered who was behind trying to kill the empress."

"Everyone thinks it was Ra-Mennarial seeking revenge for the Belials' defeat at Carch'Carai," Lala said. "Thank The One for the likes of General Avarna or Mennarial would be emperor today."

"Yes, The One forbid," Eleth-Tir said. "But if he did it, they would have arrested him by now. Odd that no one saw any of these assassins somewhere before they acted. They could not have appeared out of thin air."

"My brother once thought he saw someone here in Plytheron who looked like the assassin woman."

"Oh," Eleth-Tir said, trying not to sound overly eager. "Why did he not report it?"

"It was years ago and from a distance," Lala said, "and the girl was young then. He was not at all sure. It just seemed like a vague resemblance to this older woman on the poster, and we all forgot about it right after he mentioned it. It was passing conversation, and he does have an active imagination, so we put no stock in it."

Eleth-Tir was subtle in his pursuit of the issue. He invited Lala's brother Sinon to meet them for some drinks after work at the tavern one evening. Eleth-Tir could see Lala was right about her brother, who liked to talk in hyperboles about himself and his prowess with the local women. Eleth-Tir could see Sinon's imagination about himself and reality were two different things. Exaggeration to inflate himself was clearly part of the man's ego arsenal. In short, he was probably not the most reliable person. Saying things to get attention was well within his capabilities.

Still, Eleth-Tir worked the topic in after they all had several drinks. "So, Sinon, Lala tells me you were almost famous."

"How is that?" he asked.

"She told me you spotted the woman who tried to poison the empress."

"Oh, that," he snickered. "Ah, just a girl I saw once gathering herbs in a yard long ago looked a bit like her."

"And you did not approach her?" Eleth-Tir asked. "No attraction, eh?"

"He was scared," Lala giggled.

Sinon shook his head. "No way, not scared, but she was in Maretha's yard, strange old bitch."

Eleth-Tir poured him more wine. "What is wrong with her?"

They explained that Maretha was a recluse who lived on the outskirts of the village. She would show up every month at the fair to buy and sell herbs or at the market for provisions. Otherwise, she kept to herself. They could not remember how long she had lived there. Since they were quite young, they thought.

"My friend's dog got into her herbs one day," Sinon said. "Found it dead later on."

"She killed it?" Eleth-Tir asked.

Sinon shrugged. "No marks on it, but a strange coincidence, no?"

"Maybe it was poisoned?" Eleth-Tir said.

"Who knows?" Sinon replied.

"She has sold herbs at the fair for years, and no one has died from them," Lala said.

"All this talk of dead dogs made me thirsty," Sinon said. "Another round?"

That night lying in bed, Eleth-Tir's mind was swimming. The woman was an herbalist, and someone nearly murdered the empress by poison. A young woman possibly fitting the description of the assassin may have been seen at her home, and a dog died after foraging in her garden. This was a strong lead, and he reported to Poseidia that he would look into Maretha and her activities.

He began to watch her cottage between his shifts. Nothing remarkable, just in and out of the home tending her garden, no visitors or signs of anyone else with her. On occasion, she ventured into the village for supplies. He observed her in the market one day. She would make her purchases and pay without much talk, mind her business, and go home. The fair was coming up in a week, and he decided he would buy some herbs from her as an excuse for making his first close contact.

The day of the fair came. He took Lala with him to allay any suspicion. The stall where Maretha normally sold her herbs was empty. Eleth-Tir cursed inwardly, annoyed this was the one day she decided not to attend. Hoping she was merely late, he wandered with Lala around the crowded bazaar past the surprising array of pottery, jewelry, and textiles as well as colorful fruit and vegetable stalls. Jugglers and puppet theaters added to the festive atmosphere as people shouted out hawking their wares.

Lala broke away to look at some wines. Eleth-Tir told her he would meet her back at the wine stall in a few minutes while he looked around. He bumped elbows through the bustling throng of shoppers heading toward Maretha's stand to see if she had appeared. As he walked along, he felt a prick on his forearm as if an insect had bitten him. He instinctively clamped his opposing hand on it, seeing a small drop of blood. Curious. He had never noticed any biting insects in the area. What he did not see was the hooded figure who had just passed by giving him a backward glance as it proceeded through the crowd.

Eleth-Tir continued toward Maretha's stall, but a minute later he stopped short, clutched his throat, and started to gag. The crowd around him parted into a circle, sensing something wrong and keeping their distance from the obviously sick man. A while later when the authorities arrived, they pronounced him dead.

Once on the outskirts of town, Maretha threw off her hood. She did not head home but in the opposite direction, for this was home for her no longer. *That young fool, thinking he had gone unobserved sneaking around her cottage.* The priests had honed her instincts. Feeling someone was watching her, she used her spyglass from inside the cottage to scan the bordering woods. She saw him with his own spyglass in hand. No villager would go to such consistent lengths to observe her. He had to be an agent of the Imperium.

Eliminating him would give her a head start to escape, but she would have limited time. They would soon seek her on suspicion of his murder. Her only goal now was to get out of Artalanta, and she needed to contact her network. What she did not know was that Eleth-Tir was one of several agents Desamon had dispatched to the village. One of Eleth-Tir's comrades who attended the fair every week immediately contacted the capital on what appeared to be the young agent's sudden death by poison.

Desamon ordered the Stratia and security forces to establish three concentric security rings to cordon off a radius around Plytheron at spaced intervals. It was a race against time now to catch the murderer before the assassin could go to ground.

THE FIRST SOULS ENTER THE EARTH PLANE
IN ETHERIC BODIES

THE CITADEL MOUNT, POSEIDIA

BA'RELIN, ARYAN

AVARNA APPEARS TO THE OTHER FIRST SOULS
AT THE ONSET OF TYER ANGARACH

CHAPTER XLVII
Poseidia, the Imperial Palace
The Third Epoch, circa 10,700 BC

... bring me signs of the Invisible One.
—The Sophia of Jesus Christ, a Gnostic Gospel

mliea's war council waited out the day for news on Petronien's fate in a room so tense it could have ignited on the fuel of human emotion alone. Amliea, in and out of rationality, now seemed focused, galvanized by concern for Petronien.

She walked a circle around the table, studying the operations map. "We are fighting on multiple fronts. We cannot commit troops needed to defend the three loyal islands for an unknown situation in the East. Our primary asset is the Nautikon. Our superior naval power prevents the Belials on Aryan and Atalan from invading Poseidia, their real prize."

"Yes," Terselia agreed. "Our biggest question marks are the extent of Mennarial's airpower, how to extricate Petronien, and how to reestablish contact with Avarna."

"Princess," Ar-Falene said. "Avarna had but a small reconnaissance force. We have to assume the Belials are rolling through Europa. Sooner or later they will be coming back with more soldiers, ships, air wings, and other weapons. We cannot stop them without opening up a new front."

The group broke into side conversations until Desamon finally spoke. "I agree with Ar-Falene. The enemy's goal in Europa must be to gain new material and labor for war production. This means the Belials assumed underground facility must have limited capacity, at least for implements of war."

"It may well be that Petronien's surprise intrusion into the Tanato interrupted their timetable and caused them to show their hand prematurely before Europa could produce what they needed," Ar-Falene said. "Their likely plan was to put us in a vise between eastern and western armies."

Terselia looked at the map seeing Aryan to the west, Europa to the east, and Poseidia in the middle. "We have a problem then, and time is not on our side."

As she spoke, an aide for the Pneumarta entered the room. He handed the air marshal a paper, and Vortegren's face broke into a joyous smile. "Great news, my friends, the Pneumarta won the skies. They are holding off the Belials while we are evacuating Petronien and his troops!"

The entire room broke into tears and prayers of thanks. Terselia took Amliea by the shoulders and pulled her aside. "It was your decisiveness that saved Petronien," but all she got in return was a blank look. *In and out. Holy One, when will this madness end?* Terselia thought, and hiding her concern she told the others Amliea would be retiring for a brief rest now that the crisis was over.

Not long after, a courier from Poseidian Security pulled Desamon from the room. The deputy consular returned two hours later and asked Terselia to step outside to the open-air terrace that lined the side of the palace facing the harbor.

"More good news, Princess. Earlier today, our people captured a woman fleeing Plytheron. She bore the mark of the assassins beneath her hairline. We believe she may have been the one coordinating the attempts on Amliea. I cautioned our forces to use tranquilizer projectiles on sight so she could not take poison like the other ones. The Elda-Fera have her. They have ways of extracting information without physically harming her. You may soon have what you need for your expedition."

Terselia smiled and sucked in a deep breath of fresh ocean air. "Excellent work, Desamon." They quickly agreed that it would take at least a month to organize an expedition of two thousand soldiers after they extracted information from Maretha. "And I want Ar-Falene to command the troops," she said.

Desamon gave her a sideways glance. "Ar-Falene?"

"I hear she is one of our best officers and she adapts well to unusual situations. I would get to know her better."

"I see," Desamon said. "Are those the only reasons you want to take her away from Artalanta?"

Terselia looked at him with an ironic expression. "Why, Desamon, you have a princess to protect, after all," she said with a wry smile. "Would you hesitate to send your best?"

Desamon sighed and changed subjects. "You remember I told you before how the Elda-Fera priests detected a troublesome disturbance in the earth's etheric field? That means a struggle rages in the higher planes between the forces of Light and Darkness. As it is above, so it is below. These messages we received—I would call them communications—they are not only about events in our world but about each of us personally and our role here and in the world beyond."

Terselia's fist clenched by instinct. "If you are correct, what does this portend?"

"That Amliea is in great danger from herself for one thing," Desamon said with a sigh. "The Archon is the counter principle, the deviant force that leads us into error and keeps us from attunement with The One. It is the illusion of ego, the desire to misuse our abilities. I cannot help feeling that Amliea has done something destructive and it has driven her mad. I am increasingly certain she is involved in this mass appearance of new drone types."

"We know she has the ability to project drones, but on such a mass scale?" Terselia said.

Desamon shook his head. "I am not sure of anything yet. But here is something else unusual." He produced a metal object that looked like entwined serpents with letters in old Lantean inscribed within them. "This was nailed to the great door of the Consularion. No one can account for how it got there. I researched it in the old annals at the Biblium Arcana," Desamon said. "It is called the *Ankatameso*."

"*Ana, Kata, Meso*—Above, Below, and Middle," Terselia said.

"Exactly," Desamon said. "It is a symbol. The serpents represent wisdom or knowledge, the three letters are the three primary dimensions —spiritual above, material below, and psychic in the middle."

"And what of all three letters in the center?" Terselia asked.

"That is where elements of the three dimensions intersect," Desamon said. "It is the *Telian T'Meso*, the Place in the Middle, just what Amliea mentioned from her visitation. We commonly speak of the three *primary* dimensions, but the descent from the higher world to materiality was in many stages of mind-consciousness, rather like the layers of an onion. Think of these stages as sub-planes. The mind-vibrations at each of these sub-planes became lower and more limited, a transition from finer to denser energy states, leading to visible materiality."

Terselia pondered the statement, then said, "You are referring to the temple teachings we learned about reality being a mental construct. Matter is energy solidified by a slower rate of energy vibration."

"Exactly," Desamon said. "Telian T'Meso is the plane immediately preceding our visible world, the place from which soul-minds projected into the earth plane. There, soul-mind is still intact, not yet polluted by the mental illusion that we are physical beings instead of soul-energies experiencing physical existence. From there one can perceive events in this world with clarity and some omniscience."

"Is this the safety valve, the way out of the simulated illusion of this world you spoke of before?" Terselia asked.

"It may well be," Desamon replied, "and some unseen hand is pushing us toward it with signs and messages, that is clear. Only one question remains."

"What is that?" Terselia asked.

Desamon looked up at the sky to catch the waning rays of the sun. "Nothing in this world is as it appears. This invisible hand that is guiding us seems friendly, but is it really leading us to salvation or luring us to destruction?"

CHAPTER XLVIII
Mainland Hellas, the Inland Sea
The Third Epoch, circa 10,700 BC

... look to us to hear an oracle ...
—The Apocryphon of John, a Gnostic Gospel

When Avarna and his twelve survivors first encountered the Achaeans, they were astonished. Not so much by the people themselves — they were tall, fair-haired men of the white race with light eyes, not as sophisticated as the dark-haired, red-skinned Lanteans but certainly not primitives. The astonishment stemmed from the deference they accorded Damocles.

"Who are you?" Avarna asked.

Damocles smiled. "All in due time, my friend. We have much journeying yet to complete."

They arrived in Athena the next day by horse. The land they traveled was arid and rocky but certainly not barren like Evvia, for it was dotted with olive groves and citrus trees. The Achaeans were clearly a warrior culture at ease with living inside armor that was somewhat similar to that of the Lanteans, though the weapons they brandished were rudimentary by comparison.

Athena itself was a city turned military encampment, bustling with preparations for war. The two high hills of Lakavito and Akropoloi dominated the city. The Akropoloi was Athena's primary fortification, clearly the place that would be its last stand. The architecture was primitive by Lantean standards — stone buildings of less sculpted lines, columns less articulated, and structures less massive — yet pleasing to the eye in its simplicity.

As they walked the streets, the people looked at them with uncertainty. Avarna sensed that if not accompanied by Damocles, whom everyone seemed to recognize, the Lanteans would be unwelcome or perhaps even set upon. This was understandable. After all, they had suffered under Lantean domination for ages, perpetrated by the Belials but not effectively halted by the Children. Now full-scale occupation threatened them. They arrived at a large building Avarna assumed must be the seat of government. Once inside, Damocles told all but Avarna to wait as they entered a chamber.

"You will now meet the governing council of Athena," Damocles said. 'They will question you. Simply answer them straightforwardly. No need for guile."

Avarna had no idea what to expect, but the presence of Damocles offered him a measure of comfort. He hoped that the deference the people paid to the mysterious man extended to their rulers. He walked into a long chamber. At the end was a raised dais of twelve seated men with armed guards off to either side below them. The seated men wore white robes with an unusual blue and gold pattern embroidered along the edges. Avarna and Damocles halted and stood before the council. A gray-haired man with an air of authority seated at the center of the semi-circular dais spoke.

"I am Danaus, first among equals of the Council of Athena. Who are you?"

"Avarna, Captain General of the Blackmanes, imperial bodyguards to Empress Amliea of Artalanta."

Danaus's tone and demeanor were stern but not aggressive or hostile. "Your nation has invaded Europa and now threatens Hellas. Why are you here?" he asked.

"Our empire," Avarna said, "has not invaded the Inland Sea. It is a rebellious faction from my nation who makes war upon both you and the imperial rule. I came here to assess this surprise attack and see how we can assist in defeating this threat."

Danaus looked at Damocles. "Is this true?"

Damocles nodded. "It is."

"Who are these rebellious invaders you speak of?" Danaus asked.

Avarna took a deep breath. How to explain the inner workings of

Artalanta to foreigners? "You men are a governing body," he said. "Not all your people must agree with how you rule or the decisions you make. So it is with us. We call these opposing rebels Belials."

The men conferred amongst themselves in hushed tones, after which Danaus said, "Perhaps you are bad rulers and their rebellion is justified."

"Our ruling party is called the Children of the Law of One," Avarna said. "We believe all people descended from one Great Being, as different as we may seem, and so making war upon others as the Belials do is evil. The Belials have invaded you, not the Stratia, our imperial army."

"You say you are peaceful, yet you fight even with your fellow Lanteans, these Belials as you call them," Danaus said.

"We resist their belligerence," Avarna replied. "Defending against evil is not the same as attacking for domination. The Belials deny the existence of other dimensions and higher powers, or at least benevolent higher powers. They worship a force called the Archon, a demiurgic power they say derives from the natural world. You see how their insignia bears the Archon's lion-headed serpent while ours is the sun pyramid. The Archon for them is an impersonal force sustained by their warlike energies who in turn sustains them and gives them the power to seize what they desire. This is how their minds think."

"Artalanta has a history of raiding and taking slaves. If your faction rules justly, why was this permitted?" a councilman asked.

"The Belials are very powerful," Avarna replied. "Half a century ago, we fought a war with them to end slavery and foreign conquests. We defeated them and abolished their practices, but they have risen again."

The councilmen murmured amongst themselves. "There have been no incursions during this time, as you say, but these are still your countrymen," Danaus said. "Their weapons far exceed ours in power or those of any other peoples of Europa or Egypt. How will you defeat them?"

Avarna paused a moment. He did not want to look weak or stumble in his reply, lest they mistake an uncertain answer with more suspicion that they were already displaying. "The attack on Europa came as a surprise. I came with this small reconnaissance party to assess what we can do. Our air wing was shot down before we could begin our mission to assess, then attack the enemy."

Danaus raised his arm and pointed a finger straight at Avarna. "If indeed this is a civil war, as you say, why are you not fighting on your own soil? Why come here?"

"The Belials came here to acquire slave troops and raw materials we have denied them these past fifty years to grow their army," Avarna said. "Peace with the Belials is not an option. Subservience and misery is your only choice. We will not permit that. Our interests are aligned and we would be your allies."

Again, the men conferred in guarded voices. Damocles then explained what had transpired from his capture in Artalanta to the crash on Evvia and the encounter with the Naphaalim. The Achaeans seemed quite impressed with the story. The council broke off and retired to an adjoining chamber. Damocles explained that hatred and mistrust of the Lanteans ran high among the oppressed nations. A party of Lanteans dropping from the sky into their midst claiming to be friends was confusing at best or possible subterfuge at worst.

"So what are they debating?" Avarna asked

"Probably whether to kill you, torture you for information, or believe you."

"Well, those are discomforting options, do you not think?" Avarna said.

"They will likely be cautious," Damocles said. "They view you Lanteans as demon gods with your flying machines, healing abilities, and longer lifespans. They think you descended from the heavens."

The council returned. Danaus said, "Some here believe you may be a spy and we should treat you harshly, yet the word of Damocles belies this. However, the Oracle shall determine your fate. See to it."

As the guards escorted the two men out, Avarna said, "Oracle? What Oracle? Who rules here?"

"Patience, my friend. This is the best decision," Damocles said. "You will be among the few to personally see the Oracle at Delphae, and you may learn far more than you could ever imagine."

CHAPTER XLIX
Delphae
The Third Epoch, circa 10,700 BC

I am he who received revelation from the Pleroma.
—(Second) Apocalypse of James, a Gnostic Gospel

Avarna and Damocles stood outside the entrance to a cave after purifying themselves in the waters of the Castalian Springs, which ran between the cliffs Damocles called the Phaedriades. Avarna's surviving Blackmanes and the soldiers sent by the Athenian Council to guard them remained on the lower slope. Avarna paused, staring at the cave mouth.

"An odd place for an oracle to dwell," he said to Damocles.

"She is better heard and not seen."

"From where did she come?"

Damocles shrugged. "From the same place as all of us, I imagine."

"You speak with veiled answers. Why?"

"The Oracle has been here longer than the memory of man."

Avarna sighed. "You speak of Adamic man, the five races that appeared on earth a few millennia ago? But our red race in Artalanta knows of races before us, people who could live thousands of years while we live mere hundreds, your white and other races even less. Of which men do you speak?"

The bright sun glinted off the small green leaves of the surrounding olive trees. Damocles plucked one from a nearby tree. "Men fall like leaves to the earth, decompose, and rise in new forms in a disrupted pattern that must be rewoven over and over again. But God has provided a few threads, a few precious strands that run true and constant through the weave of our recurring lifetimes so that its shape and purpose might not be lost until our journeys are completed. The Oracle is such a thread and today you just may glimpse your pattern."

Avarna's gaze bore directly into Damocles' eyes. "I think you are no wayward mariner who skirted our waters and came to us by chance, are you?"

Damocles smiled and said, "The council wanted me to accompany you inside as a witness to the Oracle's pronouncements. Let us go, then."

The men walked some way into the cave, and upon a time they came to a kind of inner grotto lit by a single torch that illuminated the front of the area only. Avarna saw a round stone altar and vapors issued from its hollow center. Behind the altar stood a golden tripod seat and behind that darkness. After they waited for some time, Avarna looked at Damocles, who motioned for him to be patient.

Then, from the recesses of the cave, a female voice broke the stillness. "We have before us one of those long awaited."

"I am Avarna from Artalanta."

"A mere appellation. I know who you truly are," the voice replied. "Approach the altar."

Avarna stepped forward to the rim of the stone. The vapors seemed to issue from deep in the earth.

"Yes," the voice said, as if reading his mind, "the vapors are from the earth below yet our reality is from the planes above. We are of heaven and earth, the light and the dark, ever contending in the wheel of fate, striving for its bonds to break. Only then can we correct the flaw of creation. War, greed, and cruelty drove you to this land. But know that far more transpires between heaven and earth, for as it is above so it is below. A war for souls rages in the higher planes."

"I have heard this said," Avarna replied, "but I know naught of it."

"You know, yet you need reminding," the voice said, and the Oracle stepped forth into the dim light. She wore a robe of gossamer white. A golden headpiece crowned her visage with the S-curve of a serpent's head protruding from the front piece. Attached to the sides of the headpiece, metal trailers of flashing colors depicting the planetary signs cascaded down her shoulders. But atop all of it the great seal of

Artalanta rose in fan-like splendor a foot above her head! How could this be?

The Oracle was tall. Her face was beautiful but in an uncommon way, for her features, though human enough, were not exactly human. Her skin radiated a faint green luminescence of a breathtaking, ethereal quality. Her face was too smooth, flesh more like that of an alabaster statue than common skin. This seemed to limit her "humanness," erasing the subtle movement of muscles producing creases, folds, and lines of expression the mind subconsciously registers as normal. This look endowed her with an aura of other-worldliness. Avarna stood transfixed, looking at her.

"Now you see why the Oracle remains veiled to those seeking her counsel," Damocles said.

She smiled, once again reading his mind. "People always accounted my two sisters more beautiful than I. One misused her beauty, the other helped the less fortunate in the same struggle you fight to this day."

"Who are you?" Avarna asked.

"If you knew yourself, you would know me," she replied. "Now comes your time to remember."

She removed her headpiece and Avarna had to blink, for on her previously covered forehead was a third eye! He turned his head to Damocles and he too now possessed an extra eye! Avarna cupped a hand before his own eyes, wondering if he was hallucinating from the vapors, but each time he tried to clear his vision, he saw the same thing. The Oracle now sat on the tripod and extended her hands over the rising vapors. Without thinking, he reached out and she clasped his arms.

He lost track of time, seeming to float in an ocean of his own mind-space. When he came around, things looked different. It was as if he were perceiving things from another place, but his physical vision seemed off too. His hand went to his head. A corner of his mind was surprised he was not more shocked, for he now had another eye in his own forehead! He put his hands over his two normal eyes, and he could still see, though he sensed this new appendage was less for physical sight and more for *insight*. And now the rest of their dialogue was wordless, taking place in their minds.

Avarna: << Princess Ouen, daughter of Tar Anu, sister of Asme and Mele of the golden hair. How is this, for your era was twelve thousand years ago? >>

Ouen: << Mele and I escaped the second destruction with the aid of Esh' Ar Haden.>>

She pointed at Damocles. He stepped up to the altar in acknowledgment.

Ouen: << I came to this land and dwelt here long enough to see the Third Root Race die out to be replaced by the Adamics. Mele had passed on to other planes, yet I found a strange fate. I was able to keep renewing my same body after brief sojourns in the after planes. Esh Ar'Haden remained by my side, though he took on numerous forms to move about the world. I became an Oracle to help guide these people who have suffered at the hands of the Belials, the bane of our Lantean race, but my real purpose was to wait for this moment of your arrival. The One had set me the task of awakening the First Souls. >>

Avarna: << I begin to remember ... First Souls ... laid down our light-bodies ages ago to suffer as men suffer ... only subject to that fate could we learn to lead the souls back to the realm where we belong, the realm from which we led the first fall. >>

Ouen: << To fully awaken, you and the others must meet your true selves in the Telian T'Meso. >>

Avarna: << Yet I see these things but dimly, as if by the light of some distant sun. >>

Ouen: << Stay with us. Esh Ar'Haden and I shall help you, for you and the others are the only hope for the world. >>

Avarna did stay with them for a month, which seemed like a year in continual mind-space. He drew from the energies of his powerful Lantean forebears, opening his third eye with ever greater clarity, glimpsing the higher realms in ever sharper focus until he was ready.

The struggle for earth's fate would now assume another dimension, and he had come to realize that he and his closest allies were at its epicenter.

CHAPTER L
Ba'relin, Aryan
The Third Epoch, circa 10,700 BC

And terror became dense like a fog ...
—The Gospel of Truth, a Gnostic Gospel

Ent El Kar had watched the streets closely the past two weeks from his shop in the eastern quarter of Ba'relin. Paramilitaries bearing the insignia of the Archon constantly roamed the streets, their black uniforms in stark contrast to the gleaming white buildings for which Ba'relin was famous. His shop seemed abandoned and boarded up, but still he anguished, knowing he had made a terrible mistake that put his family at risk.

The destruction of the Imperial garrison at Galgaatha unleashed increasing attacks on followers of The One and their property. Then came restrictions on worship or any display of the ancient seal of Artalanta. Next, rumors of human sacrifice, Children of The One being put to ritual death in the converted perversion known as the Temple of Fire atop the heights dominating the city. Many adherents to the Law of One had fled, dispersing to the countryside where the Belials could less easily identify them.

But Ent El Kar stayed on. He was a prominent businessman in the city with many friends in government. His business had remained protected and untouched—until now. Now even Ent El Kar saw the writing on the wall, but it was too late. Paramilitaries roamed the streets day and night, stopping people, checking identities. Escape was not an option now. His family cowered in terror keeping away from the boarded windows. Maybe the thugs would think they had joined the exodus out of the city.

He had planned to slip out of his store by nightfall and hide in an abandoned building nearby. He was smart enough to know he had a problem. He was Aryan's largest wine merchant and his wares were too well known. Sooner or later the drunken paramilitaries would remember and want to loot the place. His family—son, daughter, and wife—waited in tense anticipation for nightfall, but at dusk they heard the sound of breaking glass and boards being bashed in.

The Holy One preserve us," Ent El Kar's wife whimpered. "The AA men are breaking in!"

The family took refuge in the back room, hoping the men would find the wine in front and leave. They indeed found the caskets and barrels, then proceeded to get drunk on the spot. After a few hours, one said, "These wine merchants usually keep their better stock hidden. Check the back rooms."

Knowing they were sure to be found, Ent El Kar emerged with hands raised. "Please," he said, "take what you will. I am leaving. You can fetch good prices for the merchandise. No one will know."

An officer said, "I recognize you. Ent El Kar, a rich fellow, no? Is that pretty wife of yours here?"

"My family is gone. Only I am here to save what I can," he replied trying not to let his voice crack.

"Is that so?" the officer said. "You will not mind if we check anyway," and he sent four of the six men to the back. Minutes later, the men dragged the rest of the family out amid frightened protests.

"I demand to see an imperial magistrate!" Ent El Kar shouted.

"Magistrate? Where have you been?" the officer said with a derisive laugh. "The great Prince Ra-Mennarial is the law of the land now, so I guess that makes us court officers. You see, boys? I told you that wife was pretty. The daughter too. Take our wine merchant off to the Temple of Fire to give his life for his new country, then come back and join us for some sport with the women."

"Leave my mother alone!" Ent El Kar's son shouted, producing a knife and making an awkward lunge at the officer who caught him by the wrist. The man wrested the knife away with ease and plunged it into the boy's chest. The family screamed but could not help him. They brought the women to the back room.

As they dragged Ent El Kar away, his last vision was his son dying on the floor, and his last sound was the soldiers molesting his screaming wife and daughter. He prayed in silence that someone would rise to stop this evil in a world gone mad, a world from which he was relieved to be departing soon.

CHAPTER LI
Mount Pelion, Keep of the Elda-Fera
The Third Epoch, circa 10,700 BC

... the plan they devised together ...
—The Apocryphon of John, a Gnostic Gospel

T he keep of the Elda-Fera, the White Brotherhood, was a gleaming fortress literally carved from the mountainside summit of Mount Pelion. The pyramidal Temple of Light, the epitome of the Lantean temple system, was the focal point made of a white stone with flecks of gold and silver. When the sun rose, the reflection of the temple could be seen even from other islands.

The keep of the priests was somewhat below the massive temple but impressive nonetheless. A cantilevered glass window wall occupied an entire side of the building giving the sensation one was floating thousands of feet in the air with the clouds as neighbors.

The concentrated air attack Amliea had ordered worked. They were able to extricate Petronien and the pitiful few survivors of Galgaatha. It was rare, almost unprecedented, for leaders to discuss matters of war on Pelion, but these were exceptional times, and the presence of the wounded Petronien required the government and military to hold the meeting where he could attend as head of the Stratia.

Petronien himself had been critical with multiple wounds, but the use of the crystal healing chamber and ministrations of the priests had brought him back to the point where he could participate in a strategy meeting while sitting up in a special chair-bed. Amliea, Desamon, Terselia, and the Lantean high command were seated at a large round table on another day that the empress seemed clear-headed.

Amliea spoke. "Let me say for all present that it is a blessing of The One to have you back with us, Petronien." Long applause followed. Fortunately, Amliea was composed. Terselia, Desamon, and Segund had kept their knowledge quiet. If word got out of the empress's possible role in the catastrophe that had already taken so many lives, a coup might well have ensued, which would guarantee a Belial victory.

"Thank you, Empress," Petronien replied. His thick, silver-black hair and beard looked more silver now than ever. "Now what has brought you all here to visit me in my convalescence?"

Telerian spoke. "Intelligence indicates troops massing around Altracor fifty miles north of Telma'arna on Atalan. We are certain they intend to reinforce the fighters attacking our garrison."

"Numbers?" Petronien asked.

"Between fifteen to twenty thousand troops," Telerian replied.

"Composition?"

"Hard to say, General. A mixture of deserters from the Stratia and local militia volunteers for sure but of percentage breakdowns we cannot be certain.

"Material?"

"Small arms unknown, but crystal-powered transport and some artillery are apparent."

Petronien took a deep breath. "I am surprised they are striking at this time unless they have another drone army hidden on Atalan."

Terselia's fist clenched under the table and she looked at Amliea's reaction to the mention of drones. *Thank The One her attention was fixed with a blank stare at the clouds passing by the great window.*

"It is hard to believe they could create two subterranean facilities of such magnitude on two islands," Petronien said. "But if they did, why did they not coordinate their attacks?"

"Perhaps their forces on Atalan were not sufficiently prepared at the time," Ar-Falene said.

"Perhaps," Petronien mused. He straightened himself as best he could in his convalescent chair as the commands issued fluidly from his mouth. "We lost Aryan, we will not lose Atalan. Here is what we will do." He called for them to unfold a map of Atalan on the table.

"I was raised on Atalan before we moved to Poseidia," Petronien said. "I know the area. If that army is marching south to Tela'marna from Altracor, they must cross the Scamandar River. Here is where the opportunity lies. Air attacks alone will be ineffective—too much tree cover—but Braan'dach and Vortegren, we are going to use our and air and sea advantage in a specific way. Ar-Falene, you will command the ground forces. Take the fourth Aiyrian and tenth Poseidian."

Terselia interrupted. "I need Ar-Falene on my expedition to the West. We extracted valuable information from the spy, including maps, so we will leave soon."

Petronien explained that this would be a short engagement. Terselia asked how he could guarantee that and why could he not send Telerian instead.

Amliea took Terselia aside. "This conflict is on Atalan, so there is a good chance Ta-Revi is involved. Ar-Falene has a blood issue with him that gnaws at her. Let her go. If she is victorious, she will better focus her mind on your task."

Terselia's first reaction was relief that her sister was so lucid today. She had been in and out, as if trying to open a partially closed door only to have it keep slamming shut on her. One step forward, one step back, and no telling when either would occur. She was clearly fighting a battle within that only seemed to turn in her favor after the fade's visitation. In deference and relief, she agreed to let Ar-Falene go.

"I am not willing to commit substantial forces," Petronien said. "But what I have planned will minimize the need for troops and allow a quick exit in case they're planning another Galgaatha."

After laying out their strategy, the parties left to make their preparations for swiftness was key to their plans. Only Amliea remained.

"We nearly lost you, old friend," she said to Petronien.

"They swarmed out of the ground like ants," he replied.

Amliea grimaced and tears flowed down her cheeks. Petronien asked what ailed her.

"When you are healed, you must do something for me," she said. "Something only you can do."

She whispered in his ear. His eyes opened wide but he slowly nodded his head.

CHAPTER LII
Altracor, Atalan
The Third Epoch, circa 10,700 BC

…. and she may act boldly with her strength …
—Authoritative Teaching, a Gnostic Gospel

r-Falene examined the field of the impending battle. Athletic of build with strong yet pleasant features, she was the ranking female officer in the Imperial army. Her long raven hair was pinned beneath her helmet as she rotated the field glass in an arc across the plain reviewing plans with two subordinates.

The Nautikon's nighttime amphibious landing had placed her troops on Atalan for the inland march to Altracor. Vortegren's Pneumarta had air-transported units the same night to Lake Farsala in the Atlas Mountains. Lake Farsala fed the Scamandar River on the plains below, and the air transport troops had seized the weir that controlled the flow of water into the river. The day before the nocturnal operations, several thousand Imperial troops very publicly landed in the port of Arta'Londe. They proceeded directly toward the garrison at Telma'arna. This decoy drew the attention of the entire island southward.

The river Scamandar's wide alluvial plain broke up the forested terrain beneath the Atlas Mountains for some distance beyond either of its banks. "Their advance columns are emerging from the north woods," Ar-Falene said, putting her field glass down. "Dara, have the troops on both sides of the plain start filtering north through the forest. Set them well back from the plain to remain undetected. We arrived here unnoticed by night, so they may not be on guard, but send your scouts ahead to intercept any spies they may have. Surprise is critical.

If it all works out we will quietly flank them and have them trapped between us and the river. Have the units on the south side of the river sit tight."

"Yes, General," Dara replied. "The tricky part is timing the water release with their crossing. We need to estimate their speed and distance and also the time it takes the water to flow down from the lake."

"No worries. The engineers are from the old Ferret Order, as good as they come.," Troax-Tar said.

Yet Ar-Falene's attention was absorbed by something seen in her field glass.

"Archon's damnation! It looks like they have some forbidden energy ray weapons." She looked at her subordinates. "The last time one of those was used was for the assassination of Consular An-Kera, which started the first rebellion fifty years ago. The bad news is they are deadly. The good news is they are unstable and do not last long because their internal crystal power is not attuned to the Touai Stone."

"How do we adjust for this?" Dara asked.

"We do not," Ar-Falene replied. "Hopefully, the fury of our coordinated attack will neutralize them before they can be brought to bear, but make sure to target the troops operating those weapons anyway."

A number of soldiers appeared, guarding a family. "General," one of the men said, "these people claim to be farmers fleeing the rebel army. They say they are followers of The One."

"That is true, General," the man said. "We are an oppressed minority on Atalan. We keep our loyalties to ourselves under pain of retribution or death. That army plundered our farm but we evacuated ahead of them, trying to hide in the forest."

"What can you tell us of them?" Ar-Falene asked.

The man shrugged. "I am but a farmer. What would I know other than they are marching south? We only heard that Ta-Revi himself commands them."

"Ah," Ar-Falene said with raised eyebrows. "Ta-Revi. That is information enough, farmer. Hold these people, feed them, and release them when all this is over," she commanded, and her men took them away. "A stroke of fortune, people. That bastard Ta-Revi is here. All the more reason we must prevail. One other thing in our favor. The mechanized units are in the middle of their column. If we can catch most of them in the flood, that will leave the infantry split on either side of the river and easier to handle." She turned to Troax-Tar. "Estimated extent of the floodplain?"

"About a quarter mile beyond the river bank on either side," he replied.

"Excellent. Keep our troops well clear. Now we just wait."

A while later the troops at Lake Farsala received the order to open the weir and release the water. Sentries along the way wave-carried the progress of the water's course to Ar-Falene's central command. At a certain point, she wave-carried Vortegren to launch his aircraft stationed on Airye.

"The cleansing tide should be visible momentarily," she said to her officers.

"There," Dara said, pointing at the white-capped flow visibly moving debris in its inexorable rush.

When the Belial troops became aware of what was descending upon them, they froze in disbelief. The torrent struck while a fair portion of the mechanized vehicles were still on or near the Scamander Bridge. The deluge swept away men and machines, and soon the bridge itself collapsed. The Pneumarta air wings made their appearance overhead and began strafing the troops on both sides of the river that had escaped the flood, for now the Belial army was separated by the rushing waters.

As the troops sought the cover of the forest, Ar-Falene's army met them with withering fire. In the space of an hour, they had decimated the Belial army. Dara came to Ar-Falene and said, "A pocket of them is trying to break out through the forest back into the north. They have concentrated their energy ray weapons there and are blasting through our troops. If they reach the deep forest, they can elude us."

"That must be Ta-Revi trying to save his hide," Ar-Falene said. "Divert more troops ahead of them. Cut them off. Have our troops start felling trees in their path. They will have to drain their ray blasters trying to clear the blockage. When they begin to die out, we attack."

"General, if we divert troops toward Ta-Revi, more of the enemy will escape elsewhere."

"When you cast a net and draw a multitude of small fish, it is wiser to keep the one large fish and cast aside the multitude," Ar-Falene said.

Hours later, the death rays subsided, and Ar-Falene tightened the cordon. Fierce close combat commenced. Ar-Falene looked at where the Belials were employing their remaining energy weapons for there she would find Ta-Revi. She came upon him and a handful of men in a small clearing.

"Throw your weapons down. We have you surrounded," she said.

"Not a chance," Ta-Revi shouted. "You will have to spill more blood to get me."

Ar-Falene said, "Meet me in single combat, swords only. If you prevail, you and your men go free."

"General!" Dara said. "This is insane. You cannot do such a thing."

But Ar-Falene whispered to her, "This is personal, Dara. Either way this turns out, neither you nor the others ever saw this happen. We destroyed their army, the garrison at Telma'arna is safe, and that is what counts. "Ta-Revi!" she cried. "I swear by The One I will abide by my terms."

His reply came after some pause. "Now that is a strong oath in your culture. Swords, is it? The old way. Well, I have no need of compression weapons to deal with you. I accept."

They met in the clearing, swords in hand. "A shame to kill one as pretty as you. I would have other uses for you normally," he taunted.

Ar-Falene said, "A rather weak way to express your manhood, do you not think? Perhaps your martial skills are not quite honed since you spend so much time using the wrong sword. Oh, and regards from Petronien. He rose from the dead and his plan destroyed your army today. Galgaatha is revenged."

Their duel began. Ta-Revi had skill, but it was clear Ar-Falene was swifter and more dexterous. He managed a wounding stab in her right shoulder, but the left-handed Ar-Falene ducked beneath an arcing swipe and caught his sword arm. His weapon dropped to the ground. Still, she plunged her sword into Ta-Revi's chest. She knelt beside him and spoke in a hushed voice.

"You plunged your sword into many women including my own

sister. How does it feel to have a woman plunge her sword into you? My sister took her own life because of you, but she will be the last."

Dara approached. "General, you executed him! He would have been a valuable captive. The High Command may court-martial you for this. Revenge is not the way of The One."

Ar-Falene, teeth bared, said, "It is on me. That is the sin of war. If we win, we still lose."

CHAPTER LIII
Ba'relin, Aryan
The Third Epoch, circa 10,700 BC

The rulers laid plans ...
—Hypostasis of the Archons, a Gnostic Gospel

Ra-Mennarial's war council met in the Palace of the King as he had renamed it according to his claim of descent from one of early Artalanta's ten rulers, but he told everyone this was temporary. It would soon be called the Palace of Emperor when he transferred the seat of government from Poseidia to Ba'relin. But currently Mennarial was busy pounding his fist on the long, carved wooden table in front of his military leaders and co-conspirators. Not everything was going as planned.

He bit his lip as he looked up at Aryan's grandiose symbol of a warrior brandishing sword and shield on a gigantic wall mural. "The Archon damn that fool Ta-Revi! I needed him, but flushed with victory at Galgaatha, he went back home glory hunting on his own without my command."

"Rumor is he was killed by Ar-Falene herself," one of his generals said.

Mennarial stood up and paced the floor. "A blessing. He could have revealed our secret plans."

Mennarial knew all six of his leaders should be kept out of harm's way in battle, not because he cared if they died. Actually, he rather hoped some of them like Val-Andwar might meet their demise, for he always had to look over his shoulder for the envious bastard. And he was uncomfortable that Ter-Madaz's paramilitaries could become a force loyal to Ter-Madaz. Being killed was acceptable but not captured to divulge his real battle plan, a strike the Imperials could never imagine, one that would end their reign.

He could assassinate them, but that was risky. They were powerful in their own right. Suspicion would fall directly on him. He could not afford dissension, and he needed them for now. So, he had sent Val-Andwar and Ter-Madaz to Europa, where there was a low probability of capture but a slightly higher possibility of death. Lazy Dal-Golia was not a problem, Al-Presta was useful if his fanaticism was controlled, and the worst the greedy An-Klesen might do was steal him blind if given the chance.

So Ra-Mennarial was surveying the pieces on his global chessboard today, and it was a mixed bag. Ta-Revi had previously been one of his more useful pawns, but Mennarial grumbled, "Thanks to that fool we have lost Atalan. Europa becomes more important than ever now. How goes it there?"

A general stood, his black and gold battle armor bearing the Archon insignia on its chest.

"Europa goes well," the general said. "The theater remains uncontested, likely because the Imperials do not want to risk diverting troops that are defending their islands. We are preparing the attack on Hellas, the last unconquered nation. Erection of factories and securing of raw materials has already commenced in the previously conquered territories of Western Europa. Actual production is two months away from commencing. Slave armies are being organized and trained."

The Lanteans strictly controlled their advanced weaponry except for gas compression guns. Therefore, they still commonly used traditional armor and implements of war such as swords, bows, spears, and arrows, particularly in close combat. It was a cultural convention among them, but Mennarial wanted to create more advanced weapons in Europa to augment the Belial armament against Poseidia.

"That is not fast enough," Mennarial said. "We cannot count on Poseidia standing still forever. Cut that production time in half and promise the slaves freedom for two years' service in the war. That will motivate them to snap to it."

After the meeting adjourned, Mennarial took An-Klesen aside. "What progress on our project?"

"Moving along steadily," An-Klesen replied.

"How much longer until we break through?"

"Maybe two months," An-Klesen said. "Drones and slaves are already dying from the workload."

"Then bring in more," Mennarial snapped. "This is the one thing sure to bring us victory."

CHAPTER LIV
The Western Ocean
The Third Epoch, circa 10,700 BC

She uttered this as a woman who had understood completely.
—Dialogue of the Savior, a Gnostic Gospel

Terselia and Ar-Falene faced one another with swords in a sealed-off lower deck of the fleet's flagship.

Ten ships and two thousand soldiers had left the harbor of Atra'londe on the now pacified island of Atalan weeks ago, setting course for the lands of the West. In a few days, they would make landfall at the Lantean trade port of Plata.

Terselia attacked with a skill that surprised Ar-Falene, who fell back into a defensive posture. It was not anything she could not handle, but she never expected this from a princess—a beautiful, studious princess at that—for Terselia was known to be a scholar, historian, and keeper of annals.

But here she was attacking with a skill that amazed Ar-Falene, who parried a series of slashes and thrusts. The contest went on for quite some time until Ar-Falene ended with the point of her sword at Terselia's throat. Terselia stood passively with half-lidded eyes and the crease of her lips in a straight line, neither frowning nor smiling.

It was fortunate Captain Deklan-Lar was not present. He was extremely nervous about the two women using real swords to duel. He had heard vague rumors of bad blood between them, and had he been there to see the expedition's military leader with her sword at the throat of the next-in-line to the imperial throne, he might easily have misunderstood.

Ar-Falene withdrew her sword. "My compliments, Princess. Your sword skill is better than many regular soldiers. How did you come by it?"

Terselia sheathed her weapon. "My father had Heramanus teach us before his passing."

Ar-Falene raised her eyebrow. Heramanus was a legendary swordsman of the old Jackal Order. "He was an Aryan like me. Was he a Belial?"

"Like yourself, not all Aryans and Atalani are Belials, and like you, he was not of the Children either," Terselia said. "He believed in the Stratia and his oaths. He was merely a loyal soldier to the Imperium. My father, knowing his only heirs were females, wanted to make sure we could demonstrate skills equal to men. You more than anyone should know how women have to go to greater lengths to command respect."

Ar-Falene nodded.

"Come," Terselia said, "let us retire to my quarters, where we may speak."

They sat at a table in her room, and Terselia poured some wine. "You did well at Altracor," she said. "Tell me about Ta-Revi."

Ar-Falene shrugged. "We fought, I prevailed, not much more to tell."

Terselia made a slight nod of her head, sat momentarily silent, then said, "I heard you could have captured him, but you executed him instead."

Ar-Falene's mouth wrinkled into a tight point. She did not respond, but she glanced sideways not holding Terselia's gaze.

"Ta-Revi was one of the seven Belial leaders," Terselia said. "He had information that could have made a difference in this war."

"He raped my sister repeatedly until she ended her own life," Ar-Falene said in a dull monotone.

"A general of the Stratia does not let emotion come before the interests of the empire. We could have you dismissed or even executed for dereliction of duty," Terselia said.

"Then why have you not done so?" she asked. "You probably have other reasons besides."

Terselia put her wine cup down, folded her hands together, and placed them under her chin. "As to that, I do not have people executed for personal reasons. Then I would be making the same mistake you did. As I said, women have an extra burden to bear. It would not be in the overall interests of human progress to remove a fine example of our sex."

"So you spare me merely because I am a woman?"

"I spare you because you have great qualities, and I would have you watch my back on this venture."

"You are expecting trouble?" Ar-Falene asked.

Terselia made a languid blink of her eyes and shrugged. "We shall see. That is all for now. We will speak more later." She picked up Desamon's intelligence reports on Plata and began to read.

On her way out the door, Ar-Falene turned and said, "Care not for me, Princess. My hatred of the Belials was always greater than my love for Avarna. That is my passion. For that I live."

"Then I feel sorry for you," Terselia said. "And not about Avarna. We can learn swordplay to impress men, become great leaders, run an army or an empire, but a woman's true strength lies in her capacity to love."

Ar-Falene frowned. "A war of survival is upon us, and love in the time of war is a liability. It is I who feel sorry for you, Princess," and with that, she closed the door.

CHAPTER LV
The Western Ocean
The Third Epoch, circa 10,700 BC

Death is in its leaves, and darkness
under the shadow of its boughs.
— Trimorphic Protennoia, a Gnostic Gospel

Plata was a coastal enclave of mostly Atalani merchants with a garrison of two hundred soldiers. It was built on the largest of several islands in the delta of the great Amasa River. Centuries ago it was a fort on the mainland used to suppress and colonize the surrounding land called Bras by the indigenous Garana people. The curtailing of the Belials' slaving activities in the last century forced the settlers off the mainland and onto the island to try and separate the Lanteans from the Garana.

The garrison was as much to protect the natives from the colony as to protect the colony from the natives, and trips to the mainland were supposed to be strictly regulated. The town and garrison rolled out to see and greet the first Lantean royalty ever to visit as Terselia and one hundred of her men entered the village. The cheers were subdued, mixed with grumbling. After all, most of the people were Atalani. In their view, the entourage marching through the port had been responsible for defeating the recent Atalani uprising and killing their rightful governor.

The garrison commander, Aertan, hailed from Aiyre and claimed to be a follower of The One. Slightly rotund and with the red face of a regular imbiber, he apologized for the townspeople. "Sorry for the reception, Princess. A lot of gripers here. They do not like being kept from the mainland, and being Atalani, many of them are Belials. They think the Imperium restrictive. If left to them, they would plunder the whole continent instead of trade with it."

Aertan accompanied Terselia, Ar-Falene, and four Blackmane guards to his headquarters. When they all were seated, he said, "Princess Terselia, we are all delighted at the honor of your visit, but no one ever told me the reason that brought you to our little backwater so far from Poseidia."

"Tell me, Commander, since most of the people here are Atalani and Belials and you adhere to the Law of the One, how do you get along?" Terselia asked.

Aertan frowned. "Excuse me? I do not understand."

Terselia threw some papers on his desk. "The financial records for the port. The trade figures are dismal, yet the people stay here and seem fairly prosperous. How is that?"

Aertan made a gesture of ignorance with his mouth. "The cost of living is far less here."

"Of course it is," Terselia said. "It is even less costly for slaves since all their needs are cared for, no?"

"Slaves? What is this about slaves?" Aertan said sounding incredulous.

"Commander," Terselia said, placing an elbow on his desk and leaning toward him, "the eyes of the Imperium see far. You are under arrest for violating Lantean anti-slavery laws. You have overseen the systematic illegal smuggling of slaves into Artalanta from this port."

Aertan bolted upright from his seat. "That is preposterous! I—"

"You will sit down and shut up, or I will have you taken out and summarily executed," Terselia said. "For too long the Imperium has closed a blind eye to your activities. I am closing this port down, pending investigation by an imperial tribunal. You may be spared if you cooperate. I want the names of every person involved in the slave ring, particularly in the military. Make your decision, Commander. Now!"

Aertan gave up a large number of names, mostly civilians and several junior officers. Interestingly, he also told them of unreported skirmishes with an inland cult whose members bore the infinity mark on their necks. This cult defended the native people from the slavers.

"And likely inflamed by your activities, assassins from that same cult gained entry into Artalanta and tried to kill the empress," Terselia said. "Now, who is the oldest person in the village?"

He did not look a day over two hundred, but Argedesh was three hundred seventy-two years old, a remarkable age for someone living in the outlands most of his life. Unkempt hair, grizzled beard, and animal skin clothing made him look every inch a frontiersman. The thatched-roof hut in which Terselia and Ar-Falene met him completed the image of a man formed by years of living on the edge of civilization.

"The Katherati, you say?" He tapped his fingers on the side of his pipe, stoking a foul-smelling weed. "They were here before my time. For years we thought them legends. Came from the east, they did. They were Lantean like us, but they defended the native people. Hated the Belials. They claim to follow The One, but in a different way. Called God The Infinite. Thought the Children had fallen into the sin of coexisting with the Belials. They keep to themselves unless provoked, remain unseen for the most part."

"Have you had personal contact with them?" Terselia asked.

Terselia and Ar-Falene backed up a step as Argedesh puffed out wafts of the malodorous weed. "Their converts, the brown people yes. The priests, the pure ones, no. It is rumored they were once Elda-Fera."

"Where may they be found?" Terselia asked.

Argedesh pointed west at the Amasa River with his free hand, the other still holding the pipe to his mouth. And he cautioned that if she attempted the journey upriver, her army would never return.

"I have been upriver. Poison darts and arrows fired from the shores, great river beasts that can overturn a small boat — the jungle has a thousand ways to kill you. The Katherati are just one of them."

After questioning Argedesh, Ar-Falene and Terselia conferred on what to do next inside the expropriated office of Aertan. "The old man speaks the truth, from what I hear," Ar-Falene said. "Terrain like that will decimate and demoralize an army. Our army would dissipate before reaching the Katherati."

"No doubt," Terselia said cupping a hand to her chin as she studied the maps they had extracted from Maretha. A pyramidal temple dedicated to the Infinite was the center of The Katherati stronghold.

Their city lay about twenty miles inland from the delta settlement, but given the terrain, it might as well have been a hundred.

Ar-Falene put forth the idea of a friendly mass roundup of the nearby Garanas to draw the Katherati out of the jungle and confront them near the delta. Terselia rejected the idea. It would lead to bloodshed and confrontation. She wished to establish trust and peace, not make permanent enemies of the people.

"If we cannot reach them, we cannot stop them," Ar-Falene said.

"We have a way to reach them," Terselia replied. "The Pneumarta must airlift us over the jungle."

Ar-Falene raised an eyebrow. "We are at war with the Belials. Central Command may be reluctant to divert airpower. That is why we sailed here."

"We only need a few warcraft, the rest transports," Terselia said. "Aryan and Atalan are bottled up by land and sea. If they had any significant air power they probably would have used it at Galgaatha. I agree with those who say they are using the Inland Sea lands to manufacture their engines of war, but they have not had enough time to make aircraft yet."

"The Inland Sea. Avarna," Ar-Falene said. "No one has heard from him. You think him dead?"

Terselia paused a moment with her eyes closed. "I feel he yet lives. You must worry about him."

Ar-Falene said, "As much as I worry about anything in this life anymore."

"What do you truly care about, then, with Ta-Revi dead?" Terselia asked.

"May I be candid, Princess? This world is lost. Even if we win this war, it is only temporary. The shadow is strong in this world. If there were a God, as you believe, would it be so?"

Terselia said, "You know right from wrong, Ar-Falene. You distinguish good from evil. That separated you from the Belials who raised you. Seeing evil for evil and good for good can be the first step toward God. But the line between good and evil is blurred in this land and by these Katherati. We are leaving the black and white of our world to enter the gray of the jungle. How we handle this will tell much about us."

CHAPTER LVI
Mount Pelion, Keep of the Elda-Fera
The Third Epoch, circa 10,700 BC

... and I shall appear and speak ...
—The Thunder, Perfect Mind, a Gnostic Gospel

T he White Brotherhood met in conclave ever more frequently as the warning signs and disturbances in the ether mounted, portending certain disaster. It was no longer a question of if, but when and how the event might occur. Segund sat in a circle of other priests around the Great Crystal of the Touai Stone in *nois regar* mind-lock. Their collective minds would interpret the forces coming through the Crystal's energy portals, but as the war spread, the Crystal had gone oddly silent for some time.

Not today. The Crystal was screaming. The room crackled with energy as the adepts psychically projected a unified mind image, as visible to them as if someone had written it onto a giant slate.

> *Brothers will fight and slay each other,*
> *children of men will kinship defile.*
> *A world grown cold shall produce hot fire*
> *to consume the towers and works of men.*
> *A wind age, a beast age—no man will have mercy*
> *before the world dies devoured in cleansing flame*
> *to be reborn again, and cast its eyes upon the One.*

Tyer Angarach, the words ran through Segund's mind. *The Twilight of the Gods!* No sooner had this thought come to him than a burst of energy flung the sitting priests backward, breaking the *nois regar.* Fear and confusion took hold of the normally composed priests.

"Intruder!" The word sounded in their minds just before the *nois regar* broke.

Segund left the hall of the Crystal. Minutes later he came upon a man at the end of a long corridor. The figure turned, stepped into the light, and spoke. "I have traveled far to seek you, in this, the twilight of Artalanta," and Segund trembled for one of the few times in his life.

BOOK THREE
WINDS OF WAR

CHAPTER LVII

Poseidia, Artalanta
The Third Epoch—circa 10,700 BC

I traveled into the vastness of the dark, and I persevered ...
—The Apocryphon of John, a Gnostic Gospel

lone hooded figure stood in a remote field as the aircar landed. The hooded figure walked to the vehicle, opened the door, and entered. Petronien turned off the engines.

"What is this about, Empress?" He probed her eyes for her state of mind. "Are you well, Amliea?"

She pulled the hood down and her golden hair cascaded across her forehead, glinting in the sun. "Petronien, steady, loyal Petronien. You are the only one I could trust."

"What is wrong?" Petronien asked.

"Much is wrong. Fly us north and I will tell you."

As they flew, Amliea looked down at the land below. "This is supposed to be my empire. I should come up here more often. But look, it is now five islands. It should be one. It was one before. Things are always breaking apart, Petronien. Lands, empires, people—they are always breaking."

Petronien looked her in the eye. "Perhaps we should return to the palace or go to Mount Pelion."

"The Elda-Fera. No, but close. We are going to Párnathal."

"Párnathal? We cannot fly there. Machines will not work. Even crystal power experiences anomalies. Our engines will shut down. Párnathal is sacred ground. They say the High Souls dwell there. Most that go there never return, and the few who did spoke of strange occurrences and visions."

Amliea smiled at him. "Petronien, born to persevere. Father a Belial, mother of the Children. So conflicted. You of all people should understand me. The fights, the turmoil, your father's violence—how confusing it must have been for you. Oh, yes, I know all about it, yet look at how you've risen from humble origins. If it is true we choose our lives to learn then you chose to learn the hard way, to learn patience and how to stay the course even though you often fail to grasp the larger picture. I am sorry, but that is true. But this gift in disguise made you strong, it is and why I chose you to deliver me."

"Deliver you?"

"I am not right, you know. Of course, you do, and so do others. I have done things, unforgivable things. But I may be saved on Párnathal. I am sane as I speak. Since my visitation, I have been called. I have had visions and received a message. He waits for me. I am clear on this, clear in this moment, and I rely on you even if you do not understand. Trust me. Help me."

Her words were puzzling. Was she speaking reality or insanity? Petronien had to choose whether to turn around against her orders or bring her to a possible rendezvous with death. In that moment he faced his own demons—the hesitation, uncertainty, and lack of confidence that often clouded his judgment—and now the fate of the empress was in his hands.

Something in the midst of Amliea's ramblings struck him, a kernel of clarity that seemed to guide her in her obvious distress, for an alarming desperation colored the tone of her words. Petronien abandoned logic and loosed an empathy he did not realize he possessed to swim in her feelings. She was a woman on the brink, grasping at her last chance for redemption for something she had done, real or imagined. His hands played over the instruments, and he stayed the course for Párnathal.

Petronien said after a time, "The effect is causing the systems to fail. I must find a place to land." Once on the ground, he said, "Do you know a way up or even where you are going?"

She smiled at him and put a reassuring hand on his. "Just wait for me. It may be some time."

"Draw your cloak about, then. Thank The One it is not winter, but the higher altitudes are cold."

He watched her disappear up into the mountainside. Was he the insane one to aid her? Was he leaving her on the forbidden mountain to perish? Sane or insane, in his heart, Petronien sensed this was a journey Amliea need to make for herself and, perhaps, for all of them.

CHAPTER LVIII
Poseidia, Artalanta
The Third Epoch — circa 10,750 BC

Now I have come to teach you what is, what,
was and what is to come, that you may
understand what is invisible and what is visible.
— The Apocryphon of John, a Gnostic Gospel

Amliea did not tell Petronien, but she had no idea where she was going as she began the trek up the mountain. Only the vivid visions she had seen in dream sleep guided her. The glowing light figure had spoken to her. *"Come, and you will find me,"* it said.

Sometimes she came upon paths and sometimes she crawled over rocky outcroppings where there were none. She lost all track of time, but eventually she came through a narrow passage bound by rock walls into a concealed valley. She froze in shock. A city lay before her. But something was wrong. More than a city, it seemed to be a shifting panorama of what she sensed to be an early Artalanta.

Her mind oddly accepted the flux in reality. She somehow knew she was looking at the end of the First Epoch during the rule of the ten kings. How different things were then. All things of the earth — the rocks, trees, and the mountains — looked young and soft and new as if only recently manifested into visible form still gossamer and malleable. Things seemed to palpably vibrate as part of the energy pattern from which they recently derived. So too it was with the people.

She could see them all at once, the ten kings. Some chose only to appear in their male aspects, others in their female essence. They could do so interchangeably and at will. These were powerful androgynous beings of the late second root-race so, they were only semi-physical in appearance. To a present-day Lantean, they would appear as opalescent, semi-solid, humanoid shapes with vaguely discernable features, but eight of them seemed more material than the other two.

And now only those two more transparent kings were present in her vision. Atalas said to Nai-Seus:

<< Very subtly, nearly beyond perception, we are transitioning. Are you aware? >>

They spoke with their minds but Amliea could understand them. Nai-Seus responded. << We are indeed more earthbound than first we came, the two of us less so. We maintain a stronger connection to the Source. >>

<< Ah, but even we can no longer push in and out of form at will. We lost that ability a few thousand years ago, >> Atalas said. << We will perish in these bodies. Do you understand the cause of this? >>

The place in which they spoke was familiar. It was a king's palace. Like the rest of the surrounding world, the material objects in it seemed semi-ethereal as if still materializing. She was aware of the odd sensation of how she was experiencing this world. It was as much a mental as a physical event, the observing of a consciousness in process of becoming a fully terrestrial, material object.

In the distance, she could see the unmistakable rings of a circular harbor and city engulfed in a luminous glow. This was an earlier version of Poseidia! At this time, only the mammoth statue of the philosopher stood guard at the harbor entrance. The warrior was not yet present.

<< The others contend amongst themselves for power, >> Atalas said. << They love possessions and objects as if these had value. Greed and strife enter their energy fields and sever contact with the higher planes. >>

<< They seek to dominate, not co-exist, >> Nai-Seus said. << They will soon turn on themselves. >>

<< The corruption is well under way, and only we can stop it, you and I, >> Atalas said. << Are you with me? >>

<< Yet, >> Nai-Seus said, << if we use such means as they do, are we not creating what we seek to stop? Are we not drawing ourselves further into the earth through these actions? >>

Atalas' energy field began to strobe, indicating agitation, as he wrestled with the same paradox Children of the Law of One had to contend with in every age of Artalanta. << It is too late for us. Souls in this world are moving into materiality. With every rotation of the sun, we lose more and more attunement with the Source. The future is clouded. I believe we are now meant to complete our cycle in physical experience. I can only hope it is to find our way back better than we were before. But we must end the growing evil or be trapped here forever. The land must come under unified control and back to a focus on the Laws of the One. >>

<< Under your control? >> Nai-Seus asked.

These were second root-race beings. They did not have the same bodily facial features from which Adamic humans read emotions, but Amliea knew Atalas was smiling.

<< No, >> Atalas said. << I am in communion with the First Souls. They have guided and advised me, for they are not yet given into this world and watch over us. I know the danger of pride and what corrupts. You, Nai-Seus, shall be the first emperor of a unified Artalanta and I shall be your advisor. By this act I maintain my purity of purpose. And if you stray, my friend, I shall remind you. Now, shall we be about our work? >>

Amliea witnessed the titanic struggle that planted the seeds of the future Artalanta, even unto her own age. She realized how the invisible hand of the First Souls worked through others in the early ages of the world. Atalas and Nai-Seus first used guile and played the other eight kings against one another so that they warred amongst themselves and became weaker. When the time was ripe, the final conflict came.

It was a battle unlike any of the present age, for these beings were not fully material. They could lift large objects with their minds and generate powerful energies. It took a great force or a direct energy burst to destroy them. They used small physical weapons, but they could only slow, not kill unless the victims were already weakened. This was truly a war of the gods.

The eight hostile kings were too fragmented and jealous of one another to join forces. Atalas and Nai-Seus conquered one city by mind-hurling large boulders at the walls and buildings faster than the enemy could deflect them. The king submitted lest they destroyed his entire domain. Two others perished in single combat with Atalas. In each battle, the opponents struck each other with thunderous hurled bolts of energy and dreadfire causing great rents in the earth. After this, two of the weaker kings surrendered and agreed to a long re-attunement with The One in the Temple of Atonement under supervision.

The remaining three kings finally banded together and attacked. Their forces marched on Poseidia by land from the northern, inland side of the city. Nai-Seus' forces harried them and funneled them into the pass of Darlomen between the low mountains that led to the city. The hostile forces sent their scouts up to the heights to watch for an ambush. Finding none, they assumed Nai-Seus had made a tactical error. But the attack came from below. The ground beneath the pass was honeycombed with large hollow caverns and a great underground river. Intense concentration by the combined forces of Atalas' and Nai-Seus' hosts caused the supporting rock of the hollow areas to crumble, taking the army down and burying it in stone and water.

The three kings never believed such vast, focused power could be achieved by many wills acting in unison. Such unity was alien to their selfish minds. They lost because they acted selfishly for their own greed. Atalas and Nai-Seus won because they acted selflessly for the betterment of all in attunement with a higher Source.

Odd, Amliea thought. *Terselia is the witness and chronicler of events, yet is I who am seeing how the Children of the Law of One came to hold the reins of power under the emperors against the forces of darkness, the Belials.*

Amliea saw how the war destroyed a large portion of the western continent from the vast energies released. And then a most peculiar thing happened. As a rising tide of water formed on the horizon, Atalas turned and spoke to her as if she were actually part of the vision rather than viewing it.

<< The eternal struggle runs through the planes of existence. It began with you, but it can end with you. >>

The giant wall of water loomed closer. << When the shadow grows strong and evil runs rampant, the universe must cleanse itself by fire and water to be reborn and begin anew. >>

Amliea felt panic as the mountain of water drew so close that it threatened to engulf her.

<< You may birth a new world by cleansing the old, but you must atone for your errors with an act of selfless sacrifice. You must use your power for others. Begin your redemption in Telian T'Meso. >>

Now the monstrous wave did engulf her, and she stepped out of herself to see herself suspended within the waters as the final words of Atalas came to her.

<< You are peace, and war has come because of you. You are the one whom they call Life, and they have called Death. And when you are cast out upon the earth, they will find you in those that are to come. >>

Amliea knew Atalas spoke not of himself; his doom-laden words were describing her. With the cleansing torrent of water came a clarity that had always eluded her—the realization of why she was always alone and apart, why she had never known the loving touch of a man but only Mennarial's violation, why she had led a life of tragic contradictions.

Yes, she was war and peace, destruction and healing, death and life, because the Higher Power had chosen her to help move creation toward an end known only to Itself, but an end that promised an eternal joy that can only be gained by temporary suffering. Nothing can appreciate bliss that has not known misery. Nothing can know its own goodness without experiencing its own wickedness. Nothing can truly know itself without encountering that which is the opposite of what it thinks itself to be.

And Amliea? She had been the catalyst fated to move spirit from one state of being to another. She was the bridge the universe condemned simply because forces had crossed over her from one condition to another, but she was also just a frightened young girl and an abused adolescent. Was her punishment fair? That question, she knew, would not be answered in this place or even this world but in a place beyond.

She went to her knees, cupped her face in her hands and wept. How long she remained like this she did not know, but when she opened her eyes and stood up, a figure loomed before her. Startled, she stepped backward. What faced her was neither human nor beast.

CHAPTER LIX
Poseidia, Artalanta
The Third Epoch, circa 10,750 BC

Guard yourself against the angels of misery,
the demons of chaos and all who entrap you.
—The Apocryphon of John, a Gnostic Gospel

The creature Amliea faced had a human body and a jackal's head, upon which rested a crown with two horns. Black and gold stripes adorned the draping sides of the headpiece running down its shoulders to the top of the golden breastplate. It bore a tall staff in its hand. The metal tip of the staff was a hollow circular shape with a cross beneath it. The figure raised its arm and pointed behind her. She looked around and saw a pathway glowing with light.

When she turned back, the man-creature was gone and an old man stood leaning on a hooked staff. "Follow the path," he said. "You will come upon a serpent with the head of a lion. Beware of this creature. It will seek to ensnare you and keep you in bondage. Now listen," and he instructed her what to say upon such an encounter. "Fare you well, Sophia," he said in conclusion and he vanished.

Sophia, the First Soul. How odd to be so named, she thought. She followed the golden path as the Fade bade her. She had no idea where she was going or what she would encounter. But the image of the dangerous lion-headed creature of which the Fade had warned her was mysteriously familiar to her mind, as if she had encountered it before.

She had no idea how long she had been walking when she came to a sudden halt, feeling fearful. She wanted to run away but she could not. She heard a rattling noise, a shuffling, slithering sound. Around the edge of a large boulder the head of a lion appeared. Amliea froze and she grew soul-chillingly cold, as if suddenly encased in ice. The head of the lion moved in an eerie manner the reason for which soon became apparent. It was attached to the undulating body of a serpent.

The voice that issued from the creature was like the low growl of a lion speaking human words.

Creature: My kingdom is darkness. Extinguish your light that you may return to the sleep of peace.
Amliea: "Your sleep is not peace but ignorance.
Creature: This is the world of your desire, to leave is to risk all.
Amliea: I am the seed of The One and do not belong to this world. Hinder me not.
Creature: "Who are you to deserve to enter the higher realms?
Amliea: I was chained to flesh but now I am awake and free.
Creature: Those who do not heed me perish for eternity.
Amliea: It is I who am eternal and you who shall perish with each soul passing beyond you.
Creature: How will you make this journey traveler in space and time?
Amliea: My desire is extinguished, my ignorance is vanished, what held me captive has been killed.

Upon speaking the words the old Fade had imparted to her, the creature dissolved in dark smoke and blew away in a moaning wind.

Amliea continued to follow the path past rock and boulder and scrub until she arrived at the entrance to a plateau ringed by ten-foot-high stones. Within this enclosure was a smaller semi-enclosed stone circle from which issued a blinding glow. She halted at the outer ring. She could proceed no farther. A force either in her mind, acting upon her body, or both prevented her from taking another step. She craved to draw into the light at the center in torment.

"I am here," she said.

"You seek absolution, Sophia," a voice came from the glowing light. "You seek to return, but there is no return absent learning."

"Am I punished for my actions?" she asked feeling a wave of faintness sweep over her.

"The One does not punish," the voice said. "You fell from the Pleroma, the heavenly realm, because you acted on the thought of a separate creation."

"Who am I?" Amliea asked, her face contorted in anguish.

"You are she who created outside of the Unity, and anything apart from the Unity is imperfection. This world is like a tree without roots planted apart from the Source of Life. Eventually, it must die. The psychic and material worlds that arose because of your actions are imperfect mind states that captured many souls. You cannot return to perfection without learning, for absent learning, errors are repeated."

"Why am I in turmoil?" Amliea asked as her mind and body strained to enter the circle.

"You repeated your primal error in this life. Your creations are disrupting the material plane just as you once disrupted the heavenly plane. Lay not your treasures before ravening dogs, nor your wisdom before fools."

"How may I free myself and cross over? How may I be with you?" Amliea pleaded.

"When you are as me inside as you are as you outside, when you are male and I am female, then the two shall become one again and the balance restored. In Telian T'Meso you may learn what the eye has not seen, the ear has not heard, and the hand has not touched."

In a moment of supreme clarity, Amliea asked, "Was I infinity's mistake or God's instrument to step out of Itself into a new world?"

She could almost feel the voice smile and soften in its reply. "Experience for the sake of experience is the path of fools. Experience for the sake of wisdom is the path of the blessed. You sought wisdom."

In that very instant Amliea was restored with the promise of absolution, renewed by understanding that The One's plan had used but not forgotten her, and a place among the exalted awaited her beyond the misery of the earth. Then out of thin air at her feet, five medallions appeared. One side had a symbol of a serpent entwined around an egg; the other side was blank.

"Take these for yourself and the others. Carry them at all times. At the right moment, a message will appear on them for each of you. They will help you find Telian T'Meso and guide you all to that you must do."

The light vanished from the circle, and the force holding Amliea back released her. She ran forward seeking its source in vain, but neither voice nor light was longer present.

When Petronien saw her approaching in the distance, he breathed a deep sigh of relief and ran out to greet her. "I feared you lost," he said, embracing her.

She smiled, the first time anyone had seen her do that in a long while. "You worry too much. I was only gone for several hours."

He stared at her as if seeking for the madness still possessing her. "Amliea, you were gone three days."

She stood in silence as the mountain wind blew her golden hair about her shoulders. "I chose my companion well. Only you would persevere so. Anyone else would have fled in panic, yet you stayed. Let us return to the others. I have much to tell you and you have much to forgive."

CHAPTER LX
Mount Pelion, Keep of the Elda-Fera
The Third Epoch, circa 10,700 BC

Now then, listen to the things which
they are telling you in a mystery.
—The Apocalypse of Peter, a Gnostic Gospel

Segund sputtered out the words: "How have you come here nearly undetected and with no air-thopter? We thought you dead." The man he spoke to was Captain General Avarna of the Blackmanes. Avarna said, "I will tell you all, but you must summon them."

Segund knew the ones he meant. He recounted Petronien's wounding to Avarna and Terselia's expedition to root out the Katherati. Avarna's face showed his disappointment at Terselia's absence.

As luck or destiny would have it, Amliea and Petronien arrived close to the time Desamon appeared. When Amliea and Petronien entered the room to join them, an intense burst of light flooded the keep, and the entire structure seemed to vibrate. They ignored the event being so delighted at seeing Avarna, then a priest ran in, claiming that the Crystal had registered an energy spike like nothing seen before.

Segund nodded as if he understood something the others didn't. "*They are gathered now,*" he whispered to the priest. "*The last one must come by vibrations.* Raise Terselia on the wave carrier," he said aloud.

When Terselia's raspy voice came over the carrier, Avarna was first to speak.

"Avarna?" she said hearing his voice. "Is it really you?"

"It is, Terselia."

A silence ensued followed by a faint sob. "No word from you all this time. We thought you dead, but The One has delivered you," she said, and all could picture the tears welling in her eyes.

"The One and some unexpected allies," Avarna said. They gathered around a table in front of the window wall in the clouds, and Avarna told them of all that had happened on his journey to the Inland Sea up to his meeting with Ouen.

"The unbroken Annals of the Imperium spoke of the Princess Ouen and Esh Ar'Haden but that was twelve thousand years ago. You say they still live?" Segund asked.

"They do in different ways," Avarna replied. "Ouen is able to revivify her body after sojourns in the higher worlds. Her priesthood preserves her form until she returns, so she is in the same body she possessed in the Second Epoch. She is held to be a messenger of the gods as well as an oracle among the Achaeans. Esh Ar'Haden assumes new forms that endure for long periods, but they are both still of the third root-race, the old three-eyed race."

"And how did you come back to Artalanta?" Terselia asked.

Avarna paused before answering, then said, "I translocated."

"Translocated? Are you saying you're a Fade?" Desamon asked.

Avarna turned his back to them as he replied, looking out the window wall at the cloud-dotted sky. "There is more to it than that," and as he turned to face them, a third eye became visible above the bridge of his nose. The others were momentarily taken aback and he quickly retracted it.

Petronien said, "Is this really you, Avarna?"

"It is the same Avarna who left on the expedition to the Inland Sea," he replied. "Ouen and Esh Ar'Haden helped me awaken these powers."

Segund interjected. "I believe all this to be in keeping with what the Elda-Fera know. The five of you bear genera markings of the old race. The third eye and translocation powers are likely dormant abilities stemming from that heritage. And you have another marker in common that is a mystery, completely unique in all Artalanta. I now believe it is from a common soul grouping—"

"The First Souls." It was Amliea who finished his sentence. They all looked at her. "I have just returned from Párnathal. I encountered Amilius."

They looked to Petronien. He nodded.

Amliea recounted her story as a steady stream of tears flowing down her cheeks. "I thought my actions would halt the need to acquire new slaves and end the misery of the old drones." She explained how her intention was to bring a new, superior race of drones into being as full citizens, paid for their labor, and with the capacity to advance to higher stations. She even thought they might function as vehicles for soul entries into the world. Or so she had told herself.

"But only The One can create souls," Desamon said.

Amliea looked at the ground as she spoke her next words. "It was as if something had planted a seed in my mind from beyond this world, and it grew inside me from birth. It produced no flower though. It was like a weed run rampant in the garden if my mind, something I could not control. I succeeded in materializing a superior drone but still not at our level of intelligence. It is then Mennarial deceived me."

"How?" Desamon asked.

Amliea sighed and her mouth quivered. "He told me the Tekna-Fera had a way of increasing the intelligence of the drones by manipulating their genera. This was true to a limited extent, but when I heard of this new drone army, I realized the real goal of the genitas experiment must have been to mass-replicate the drones I created. I was not aware that is what they had secretly been doing all these years. My mind could not face what I had done. I wandered in a hopeless twilight until he appeared in my room and saved my life from the assassin's poison —it was Amilius."

"You are sure it was Amilius and not a hallucination?" Desamon asked.

"The servant girl saw him too," Terselia's voice reminded them.

Amliea explained that Amilius' image kept coming into her dreams and her waking mind, pulling her out of her madness and telling her to make a pilgrimage to Párnathal. She described her time dislocation into ancient Artalanta to witness unification of the nation under the Law of One. She told them of the prophetic vision that the earth must be cleansed of its evil in fire and water, that the eternal struggle began and will end with her. She related her encounter with the simulacrum of the dreaded Archon who tried to ensnare her in his lies. Finally, she met Amilius, who revealed her soul as that of Sophia.

The others visibly reacted to the statement, but Segund said, "I knew as much—the unusual genera you all possess, all being born in Artanael, opposing the seven Sons of Belial at the onset of Tyer Angarach, do you not see? In this very time, in our very age, the First Souls have risen to oppose the seven primal Sons of Darkness, the reincarnated Dark Souls—Mennarial and his lieutenants."

Amliea fell to her knees before them, tears flowing, and the wave of profound sadness that issued from the depths of her soul was palpable. Her hands went to her mouth as if to contain the grief that sought to issue from the depths of her being. Her words came out in staccato bursts punctuated by light sobs.

"The misery I have caused in both heaven and earth … to have been the gateway for evil in the creation. Only Amilius has kept my sanity. It is so much to bear … can you understand and forgive me? In truth, I acted for my self-gratification when I should have acted for my people. I must pay for that."

They all gathered around to console her. Desamon said, "The One is so-called because It is the unity of everything, so how can evil exist apart from The One? The annals tell us that *Authades,* from which the Archon derived, is the force of opposition and temptation God allowed from the beginning. Why? Because *we are divine instruments, the way God experiences.* Static Perfection can only have experience through *dynamic imperfection,* and Perfection requires opposition to step out of Itself. In Telian T'Meso I believe you will find you are the ordained instrument for our fall, Amliea, but also for our salvation."

Comforted by these words, which echoed what she was told on Párnathal, Amliea made another revelation. "The time for concealing is over," she said. "Only Segund knows this. You remember when we were younger after my father exiled Mennarial and they took me from the court? Mennarial raped me."

The room was deathly silent until the shattering sound of Terselia slapping a glass off the table. "That degenerate bastard will pay for this."

"I became pregnant but the child aborted," Amliea said.

"And so the cycle repeats," Segund said.

"What did you say?" Terselia asked.

"Sophia entered chaos and her divine energy mingled with the seeds of potential, activating them and producing the first elements of matter," Segund said. "But a new psychic energy was also generated, a lower consciousness that became the Archon. Sophia was described as the Mother in ancient lore, and her unforeseen creations, the Archon and the material world, were described as an abortion of the heavenly order. Amliea's repetition of this pattern is proof of her soul origin and all of yours too."

"Then why are we not conscious of these things?" Petronien asked.

"Because you chose to take on mortal forms and become subject to mortal limitations," Segund replied, "except that you have a higher capacity than others to reawaken in each age that you appear. And awakening is precisely what you are now experiencing."

As tangible proof of her experience on Párnathal, Amliea produced the five medallions Amilius gave her with the engraved symbol on one side and the other side blank.

Petronien handled a medallion and asked, "What does this symbol mean?"

"The snake is divine wisdom," Desamon said. "The archontic symbol is a lion's head on a snake as a perversion of wisdom, but here the snake means something quite different. The egg is the universe or the seed of a new world, birthed and protected by the divine wisdom that envelops it. But the blank side?"

Amliea told them a message would appear on that side, guiding each of them for what was coming.

"And what exactly is coming?" Avarna asked.

Just then, a corner of the room began to glow with a bright luminescence. Terselia appeared enveloped in the arms of a tall translucent being, a humanoid form of brilliant light.

"Amilius!" Amliea said as the others stood frozen in wonder.

CHAPTER LXI
Mount Pelion, Keep of the Elda-Fera
The Third Epoch, circa 10,700 BC

... this was the middle region ...
—The Paraphrase of Shem, a Gnostic Gospel

milius released Terselia, who immediately ran into Avarna's arms. The intensity of the light issuing from Amilius' form lessened so that he appeared more material and less other-worldly, but when he spoke, they could not distinguish whether his voice was in their ears or in their minds. They drew into a circle around him, as if pulled in by the magnet of his voice—all but Segund, who stood to the side observing.

<< This is the time, >> Amilius' mind-thoughts told them, and he told them their lives had been destined to draw down to this very moment, for the fate of the earth was now in their hands. They had many questions and feelings, and they were confused by the rapid onslaught of events but to this, he mind-spoke to them, << Follow me. All must be answered in Telian T'Meso. >>

They stood, hands linked in the circle. Amilius bowed his head and the others closed their eyes. A radiance began to glow until it became so blinding that Segund had to shield his vision. When the brightness subsided to a mere glow, Segund saw a third eye blink open upon the forehead of each person in unison. The five of them were in a hypnotic fix, so Segund and their physical surroundings faded.

They had the sensation of floating off in one of the clouds passing by the keep's window wall, as if drifting disembodied and wafting in the air in one of the old Lantean dirigibles before the age of crystal powered flight. At some point, they stabilized, and the drifting sensation subsided. They found themselves in a world much like their earthly one with skies and oceans and mountains but vividly bright and of a fluid, immaterial nature.

The scenery shifted rapidly with images of people and places flashing before them until they instinctively remembered that thoughts are things. The set appearance of any world is really the subconscious agreement of minds on a set of laws that govern that particular plane of existence. As soon as they gained self-control, the surrounding panorama stabilized. This particular plane was very close in appearance to earth but much more affected by currents of thought.

<< Telian T'Meso is the mental plane, the last of the invisible realms from which the material earth was projected, >> Amilius explained.

The scene shifted, and they appeared on a nighttime mountaintop with a swirling mist lit to phosphorescence by moonlight. From the fog, five oval-shaped spheres of light emerged that lined up precisely opposite Amliea, Terselia, Petronien, Desamon, and Avarna. The light images moved forward mere inches away from them.

Amilius did not have to tell them they were facing higher aspects of themselves. His thoughts entered their minds — << Involvement in the lower planes happens by limiting our consciousness in degrees. At each dimensional level aspects of ourselves exist. Seeing your soul iterations is like mirrors looking within mirrors. Here in Telian T'Meso, you may see who you are as well as who you appear to be. >>

They realized they were indeed face-to-face with higher reflections of their own spirit consciousness. Petroniel, Averniel, Teresiel, Desmoniel, and Sophia, the First Souls. They knew their own soul essences, yet they simultaneously knew their earthly identities. A gossamer cord extended from each of their energy forms to link with their minds. Each received individual messages, then messages in common.

From Telian T'Meso they witnessed the great cyclical panorama of creation and destruction and creation anew. They understood the universe moved inexorably toward good and reunion with its Source. But when choked by evil and error, it must undergo a cleansing to regain its vision and create a space for The One to live in human hearts and minds once more. This was no doing of The One; it was the natural outcome of the fallen spirits' own collective, deviant thought tendencies from the erroneous exercise of free will.

<< When Righteousness declines, when Wickedness is strong, I incarnate from age to age and take visible shape. I move among men, supporting the good, thrusting back evil, setting Virtue on her seat again. >>

These thoughts issued from Amilius but they sensed The One had spoken Its message of love and salvation directly through him with an impact of profound mystery that shook the very foundations of their being.

Now they understood the necessity of Tyer Angarach. The most advanced culture on earth had rotted from within. It was too late to stop the decay. It had to be cleansed lest it infect all life on earth with the ignorant wickedness behind its advanced technology. The primal energy of the Crystal could not fall into the wrong hands, for the Crystal was life energy itself.

Through their cycle of incarnations in the earth, souls were meant to recover their higher consciousness, but the Belials would reverse the life flow to destroy the world before the earthbound souls could come to the light. This would send the human souls into the limbo of outer darkness for untold ages with no chance to learn from their errors and turn back to their origins in the heavens.

They now recognized that the fall of spirit to the lower planes was inevitable. The Will of God was to experience Its own creation in every facet, and high Spiritual Energy can only experience matter by limiting Itself, by forgetting It is Spirit and falling into the illusory consciousness that believes Itself to be material beings. The earth must survive for those soul-beings to reawaken and complete their evolution.

Sophia was the Chosen of God to lead the fall. Sophia, God's wisdom, leapt into the fire of creation like the sacrificial lamb to be burnt on the altar of experience and learning, for to know is to suffer, and to create is to pay a price. She started the chain of nature and existence on earth to gain the experience that would one day make souls truly independent creator-companions in union with The One. Through her actions God would be fully realized down to the minutest particle of the universe.

And so she was the universal paradox, the Holy One and the

Scorned One. The echo of her deeds would cast a stigma on women as the ones responsible for the loss of paradise, the Eve who betrayed humanity to the sufferings of worldly existence. In every age, women would be unjustly subordinated. Men would become ignorant of the knowledge that the world was born of the feminine and by the feminine will it ascend, for the intuition and wisdom of the female is the gateway to divine awareness.

So that the wisdom of these most high and holy revelations would not be lost, they wrote The Book of Remembrance in their minds and charged Teresiel/Terselia to bring it into the earth consciousness with words. With this divine purpose their sojourn in Telian T'Meso did end.

Amilius was gone. Their awareness was back in the keep of the Elda-Fera. Their third eyes closed. They stood in front of the glass sky wall. Segund told them they had been standing in a trance for less than an hour, yet each of them swore they had been absent for an entire day. They immediately began to compare experiences. They had received two warnings in common:

> *Feeding on the fears of fated men,*
> *puppets on strings dancing its hymn,*
> *its power paints with crimson gore*
> *and black become the rays of the sun.*
> *The bright, the golden, and gifted fall*
> *by chains of their own making.*
> *Perversion of all that was meant to be*
> *once held in the eye of The One.*

"Human beings imprison themselves with the false gods their own fears create then worship the chains that bind them," Desamon said. "This describes the Archon consciousness rising, feeding upon human fear and ignorance with the land falling into evil through the actions of the Belials."

But the second warning was even more dire.

> *Brothers will fight and slay each other,*
> *children of men will kinship defile …*

In the middle of vocalizing it, Segund interrupted Desamon and finished the admonition, explaining that the same message had come through a short time before in a *nois regar* of the Elda-Fera. "It means Tyer Angarach is upon us," he said. "Our world is ending, if not all life on earth."

CHAPTER LXII
Mount Pelion, Keep of the Elda-Fera
The Third Epoch, circa 10,700 BC

I gather together all my fellow brethren ...
—Trimorphic Protennoia, a Gnostic Gospel

"No," Amliea said, her voice focused, clear, and determined. "Life on earth will not end! We are the portal, the conduit to ensure what is good survives and begins anew. In this, we will not fail."

Her eyes glowed with fiery determination, their former vacant, hopeless look vanished. Her words carried force. "In Telian T'Meso we learned that Artalanta's doom is the world's salvation," she said. "Both our technology and our capacity for evil is too advanced. The earth will no longer tolerate such imbalance. Artalanta is the source of this evil, and so Artalanta will fall. But the goodness in us must continue with a chance to be reborn elsewhere. We must be the bridge from the old world to the new."

Amliea walked about in a semi-circle addressing each of them. They did not know how or when the end would come, but it would come soon. She told Desamon to begin evacuations of the Children of The One. They would go to the western lands where no war yet raged as in Europa. She instructed him to choose people and families best suited to build a new society and peacefully integrate with other civilizations. He should start with them first then others, but provide soldiers to protect all of them.

"Empress," Petronien said, "I am loathe to reduce the Stratia's forces defending the islands. And will this not dishearten and panic the population since we are at war?"

"We still have the air and seas. We need to look beyond the present. Send what troops are necessary to defend our refugees," Amliea said. "Tell them this is a temporary exercise to better understand and integrate with our non-Lantean neighbors. Find some plausible reason to calm them, but get them out."

"As you wish," Petronien said.

Amliea had Avarna report on the war in Europa. The Belials had captured vast tracts of land and materials. They were fast approaching Hellas, the only remaining pocket of resistance on the continent. The Achaeans were brave warriors but did not stand a chance against the superior technology of the Lanteans and their drone army.

The Belials' air and naval power were limited, but if the Tekna-Fera could complete new fabrication plants in the next few months, they would begin producing air wings and ships that would tip the balance of power and put Poseidia in an unwinnable two-front war.

"The Belial army numbers around forty thousand with maybe half as many troops force-conscripted from conquered lands," Avarna said. "We cannot drain imperial troops from Poseidia, so give me five thousand men to join the Achaeans, who will raise twenty-five thousand. Arm our men with compression guns and whatever cannon you can spare. Have Segund release the death ray weapons to me."

They all paused and looked at each other. No one had used the forbidden weapons in thousands of years. Avarna pointed a finger and said, "The world beyond that wall is at stake. We have all agreed Tyer Angarach is upon us. The Belials have already broken the weapons ban on foreign soil. The foreign nations need every chance if they are to survive us as civilizations."

Petronien nodded his head in agreement.

"They have compression weapons," Avarna said. "I am quite sure they will be using their modified death rays, but their ray weapons are not attuned to the Crystal as are ours. They are unstable, have a limited life, and they might just as well blow up on them as work."

"How would you transport the rays?" Desamon asked. "We risk them falling into enemy hands."

Avarna smiled. "I can translocate. I can take one object with me at a time. That would be about twelve separate trips. Do not look so surprised." His face tensed in concentration. His third eye appeared, and almost instantly the same appendages on his four companions blinked open despite any conscious effort by them. The rest of the conversation took place in their minds.

<< You all know who we are now, and you all have the same abilities Ouen taught me to use, Avarna said. << If I had time, I would teach you to fade, but for now it is on me. >> His third eye blinked shut and disappeared, as it did for the others. They reverted to verbal speech

"Let it be done," Amliea said. "Have the troops airlifted by night at low altitudes over the Inland Sea to remain undetected. The Belials' air power is thin, and you should have no problems."

Terselia then related her plan to deal with the Katherati, which most of them knew of since she had already requested the air transports. Amliea looked at her sister arm-in-arm with Avarna, and a wave of emotion swept over her. Life had not been kind to their relationship, so much lost time and now this might well be their last time together before going to opposite ends of the world in war zones where anything might happen. She walked toward them.

"It must have been quite a shock for Amilius himself to show up and remove you."

Terselia nodded. "He was linked to my mind, so I was not scared, but yes, the sensation of being one place, then suddenly in a completely different one is very odd."

Amliea smiled and nodded her head. "And you have an important task to complete. You must return soon or your troops will panic over your sudden absence. Only one way to do that. Avarna, you say you can translocate objects you hold. I order you to take my sister back to the western lands immediately. I also order you to stay there one night to, ah, let us say, help her assess the situation."

This earned snickers from the others but big smiles from the two lovers. The group dispersed to attend to their appointed tasks until only Segund remained gazing out the great window wall at the clouds. After a while a priest hastened up to tell him that within the last hour, the Great Crystal had registered the largest energy spike in recorded history. "What does it mean?" the priest asked.

Segund did not face the man but instead clasped his hands behind his back, still staring out the window wall. "It means these people are moving heaven and earth," he said in a soft, melancholy voice, "but toward where we do not know."

CHAPTER LXIII
Lair of the Katherati
The Third Epoch, circa 10,700 BC

Do not allow sleep to your eyes nor drowsiness
to your eyelids, that you may be saved like a
gazelle from nets, and like a bird from a trap.
—The Teachings of Silvanus, a Gnostic Gospel

Terselia and Avarna blinked into her private quarters during the night. Fortunately, no one had detected her absence. The two spent the night in each other's arms happy but conscious of the precious moments ticking by.

"Why is it," Terselia said, "our lives together have always been measured against the hourglass, always determined by forces beyond our control?"

"Have you forgotten what we just experienced?" Avarna said. "We chose these lives, we chose these moments from a higher place. Now we merely act out the consequences in these bodies through space and time. But our real selves have an eternity to explore creation once we fulfill our debt to the fallen souls of this world we helped create."

Terselia rolled over on her side to look at him. "This forgetfulness we experience in mortal forms, is it a curse or blessing?" Terselia asked. "It keeps us bound to this plane, yet to be aware of all our past thoughts and actions, to know the lives we will endure in suffering over time is almost too much to bear."

He brushed a lock of hair from her forehead. "And yet," he said with her head resting on his chest, "you yourself wrote The Book of Remembrance from what we learned in Telian T'Meso. Yes, we now know the future lives we will lead and yes, we will forget those too for a while when we take new forms. But in each life, we will reawaken with greater wisdom and remembrance. It is that wisdom that will put our suffering in perspective, make it bearable, and remind us of our higher purpose."

"Yes," she said. "The *Prothes i' Aterisi*, the Summation of Purpose. One day spirit will be able to move in and out of the body at will but with full consciousness unlike our present race and the old root-races that succumbed to animal consciousness and ego. But ..."

"But?" Avarna said.

"In Telian T'Meso everything seemed so clear, yet now it grows occluded. Our consciousness encompasses both dimensions but in mortal form, all becomes shrouded like in a fog."

Avarna nodded. "The lower consciousness of our bodies keeps us earthbound. It is the same consciousness that gives life to the Archon, which tells us we are material objects moved by random fate in a world devoid of spirit. The Archon was the creation of humanity's warped perceptions. Only human beings create prisons for themselves then worship the chains that bind them. But we will outlast the Archon. What is created by lower mind forces dies. What is begotten by The One lives forever."

Terselia finger traced light circles on his chest. "Organic life could never arise from inorganic matter. Spirit is life and only fools believe spirit came into being from matter and the natural body, as the Belials do. How can something come from nothing? Matter is dead, spirit lives."

The conversation shifted to Terselia's forthcoming confrontation with the Katherati. She turned on her side and rested her head against his chest. She confessed to being conflicted.

"They hate the Belials, yet they try to kill my sister. They believe she will be responsible for the world's destruction, and in a way she is. They act only against Amliea, not our people. I would not destroy them, but they are fanatics. In a sane world, the enemy of our enemy would be our friend. Not here."

"Why do they not attack the Belials if they hate them?" Avarna asked. "Mennarial is the real problem."

Terselia sighed and propped her head up, with her elbow resting on the bed. "They are focused on Amliea as the instrument of the world's destruction because of a prophecy their founder supposedly retrieved on a personal pilgrimage to Párnathal. And it was written by us … I mean the First Souls."

Avarna's mouth wrinkled. "That does not ring true, but if so, that does complicate matters. No clear lines of good or evil, light or dark. You will have to confront the situation and use your own judgment. I must leave now. The Achaeans need my help, and I have to start transferring weapons to Hellas."

They spent more moments clinging to each other until Avarna stepped back from her and said, "I cannot believe The One would make this our last meeting. Be careful in your task as I will try to preserve myself in mine for the time we are once more united," and he kissed her one last time and vanished.

Using the fairly accurate map Maretha had provided, Terselia and her army finally located and flew over the stronghold of the Katherati. The outlying village was unprotected, at least by manmade structures. The thick jungle seemed to be the primary defense they relied upon. But on top of a cleared hill stood a large pyramid of obviously Lantean architecture, mimicking Lantean temple structures. This was surrounded by a twenty-foot-high wall.

The only landing area was a clearing between the village and the front walls of the temple compound. The air fleet consisted of twenty transports, but only a few aircraft could land in the open space. Terselia decided to land only with her hundred Blackmane bodyguards over Ar-Falene's objections. As a compromise, Terselia dropped the Lantean truce flag into the temple compound.

"It has been a long time since these people were Lanteans," Ar-Falene said. "We have twenty aircraft circling their village. Look at them down there pointing and scattering. This looks like an attack to them. If you land, they may well strike at you, thinking to defend themselves. We should land in force."

Terselia was prepared, however. While in Plata, she had a number of banners made in the local language proclaiming they came in peace to talk. They dropped these around the startled village and hovered for some time, waiting for the messages to be absorbed. After a time, the aircraft landed.

Terselia gave her final instructions then disembarked with Ar-Falene and ten Blackmanes. The Garana interpreter they hired from Plata shouted out that the delegation from the imperial court of Artalanta was here to speak with the leader of the Katherati. Ten minutes passed before a group of armed Garana appeared from the wooden thatched roof structures in the village. The Blackmanes immediately began to encircle Terselia and Ar-Falene, but Terselia had them lower their weapons so as not to appear confrontational. The Garana leader stepped forward and Terselia had the interpreter greet him.

Looking at the faces of his warriors, she saw some distinctly Lantean features scattered among them. Cleary, some mixing of cultures and bloodlines had occurred over the centuries. The leader was of mixed Lantean-Garana ancestry, as were his immediate bodyguards. Most of the others looked to be pure Garana. He replied in a heavily accented but discernable dialect, "*Thyen ana anangi. Eo milaiso Lántika.*"

The Lantean language still survived, Terselia thought. "We came to talk to your priests, not to fight."

"What do heretics want with our priesthood?" the man asked.

Terselia shot the angry-looking Ar-Falene a glance. "Let me handle this," she whispered.

"I am not here on religious matters, and one man's heretic is another man's true believer," she declared. "We are followers of The One, what you call The Infinite, who generated us all. You may want to reserve the name 'heretics' for our mutual enemies, the Belials, those who think no God exists. Better yet, open your mind to what unites, not divides us. It is for that unity I have come."

The man grunted but told them the priests had already agreed to speak with her, and he pointed to the formidable armada of aircraft circling the sky. "What would you expect them to say with that hanging over our heads?"

Terselia, Ar-Falene, and their guards proceeded to the fortified temple. Ar-Falene calculated that the Garana had close to a thousand warriors. She contacted the Pneumarta commander to set up a rotation and land five hundred troops, for she had a bad feeling as the doors of the great wall closed behind them and the pyramid temple loomed ahead in shadow.

When she told Terselia to be on guard because of her forebodings, the princess whispered to her, "*I know, I feel it too.*"

CHAPTER LXIV
Lair of the Katherati
The Third Epoch, circa 10,700 BC

To the fool, however, the good and bad are the same.
—The Book of Thomas, the Contender, a Gnostic Gospel

T he pyramid temple rose from the side of a hill adding to its already impressive height. An exterior stone stairway led to a landing in the middle of the pyramid with an entrance into the temple. As they walked the long trek up the stairs, loud horns sounded. Blown by two standing men, the great curved horns rested on the ground of the high platform.

When Terselia's entourage arrived at the landing, a woman with pure Lantean features in a red-trimmed yellow robe and blue headpiece greeted them at the entrance. She spoke understandable Lantean with the same odd dialect as the village chief. "The priestly council will receive you. Please follow me, but you must leave your weapons here."

Ar-Falene grasped Terselia's forearm and gave a slight shake of her head. Terselia sighed, pausing a moment. "Do as she asks," she commanded to Ar-Falene's obvious discomfort.

The woman led them inside. They passed through a narrow corridor and came to a room with a circular frieze on the wall. The circle rotated and broke into segments retracting into the wall. A vast, cavernous area loomed before them in what was the center if the structure. This appeared to be the ceremonial heart of the pyramid. Rows of stone-hewn seats lined a central portion of the space leading up to an altar. The woman led them to a side chamber, where she asked everyone but Terselia to wait outside. Ar-Falene again looked ill at ease but Terselia nodded to her with a half-smile and entered.

She encountered seven men appearing to be of pure Lantean extraction, standing behind a semi-circular table carved out of green malachite stone. They wore similar white tunics trimmed in red and gold patterns about the short sleeves and hems, wide gold belts, an abbreviated mantle over the shoulders, and red capes sashed around their necks. Each of them wore a crown-like headpiece of gold with a square filigreed center above the forehead and two golden feathers flaring to either side above the square base.

The only exception was the man in the center. His crown bore *three* golden feathers and he held a tall staff, the top of which was a horizontal golden horn with three beautifully articulated golden feathers matching those of his crown rising vertically to cap off the staff. This, obviously, was the high priest.

"I am Herai T' Katheri," the high priest said. "You are the Princess Terselia. You have come far. What is your purpose?"

"I think you know our purpose," Terselia said. "You have been trying to kill your empress."

"We have no empress," the priest said in a flat monotone.

"Are you not Lanteans?" Terselia asked trying to probe their mindset.

The men mumbled among one another until the high priest said, "We separated from all things Lantean many generations ago."

"Yes, you did," Terselia said. "Because of your contempt for the Belials. Do you not realize we are enemies of the Belials? That we are at war with them?"

"Then your ancestors should have come with us," the priest replied.

"You have had conflicts with the Plata settlement because Belial sympathizers have been taking Garana slaves illegally against the empress's edicts. Be aware we have arrested the guilty parties and are closing the settlement. Is that the action of an empress who is your enemy? It seems your hostility is misplaced."

The priests conferred amongst themselves then with Terselia. At the conclusion, Terselia exited the room to find Ar-Falene and the Blackmanes. "The high priest agreed to show me their archives. I want to see this prophecy about Amliea for myself."

"What then?" Ar-Falene asked. "What if they do not comply? We cannot leave here without their capitulation. And I do not think we are safe here."

"Nothing in this world is at it seems, and certainly not in this place," Terselia replied. "A number of things strike me as odd. The priesthood and people in this compound are pure Lantean, while the people they preside over are brown natives. In the village, the men of mixed race seemed to be the leaders over the Garana. A Lantean woman led me in here, and the two we caught in Poseidia were female so we know woman are among them yet are not very visible. Makes me wonder what Maretha did not tell us."

"What are you saying?" Ar-Falene asked.

"These Katherati are supposed to be offshoots of the Law of One, yet they have a hierarchy based on race and sex," Terselia said. "That is more like the Belials."

"I am not a frequenter of temples," Ar-Falene said, "but I have been inside temples of The One. They are bright and uplifting. This place is dark and gloomy with air so somber I could slice it with my sword."

Terselia nodded in agreement. "The high priest's name in old Lantean is the 'Hand of the Pure,'" she said. "Pure compared to whom? No Elda-Fera priest would ever take such an arrogant, divisive title. It confirms their fanatical nature. Fanaticism, even in the name of what is good, inevitably leads to its opposite. The lines they draw between themselves and their enemies become blurred. I hope to gain some insight in the archives about what happened to these people over the centuries."

"Be careful. I have a feeling those aircraft circling above are the only thing preventing us from getting our throats cut," Ar-Falene said. "We need to be out of here by nightfall. If anything goes wrong, the night will largely neutralize the effectiveness of our aircraft's weaponry."

Guards escorted Terselia away to meet a priest at the archives. They brought Ar-Falene and the Blackmane to a room above the central ritual area. The doors were not locked, but they posted guards outside. Putting herself in a helpless position was not in Ar-Falene's nature and she caught herself pacing the floor and swearing under her breath. Realizing she was just making her men uneasy, she started to exchange martial stories and barroom tales with them to keep their spirits up.

Two hours had passed when Ar-Falene heard the grating sound of stone on stone. She put her ear to the wall from which the sound seemed to emanate. A moment later, a section of wall next to her face moved. She stepped back and motioned for the Blackmanes to stand on either side of what appeared to be an opening door. Ar-Falene stood to one side, bracing for whatever was coming through that wall. The stone panel appeared to swivel around a metal rod attached to its the center. The stone rotated ever so slowly then opened, at first to an empty darkness, then a figure began to emerge.

A young Garana girl appeared, staring at Ar-Falene, but when she saw the Blackmanes out of the corners of her eyes, she started to retreat. Ar-Falene caught her by her forearm.

"We will not harm you," she said, pulling the girl into the room. "Who are you?"

The girl looked around in obvious fear. Ar-Falene took her off to the side of the room away from the armored men. "I am a friend. You can talk to me."

"You are from the land of the priests?" the girl asked. "I listened through the walls."

"Yes, we are from Artalanta, the place your priests came from long ago," Ar-Falene said. "And you look like you are seeking help, no?"

The girl nodded. Ar-Falene spoke to her for a while, putting her at ease to gain her trust. The girl eventually took her hand, leading her into the wall passage. Ar-Falene took two Blackmanes with her leaving the rest in case the guards looked in on them. As the girl led them through the passageway, Ar-Falene asked where they were going. The girl mumbled something about killing her mother. It was unclear if she was bringing them to kill her mother or save the woman from someone else.

Ar-Falene halted, took the girl by the shoulders, and said, "Where you are taking us?"

The girl told her their destination was just up ahead and resumed walking. They came to a wall. The girl pushed on it and another wall section began to move. The men helped her. When they emerged on the other side, Ar-Falene recoiled, clasping her hand over her mouth and nose, her eyes wide with horror.

She had to warn Terselia.

CHAPTER LXV
Aryan, the Temple of Fire
The Third Epoch, circa 10,700 BC

... every evil thing and every unclean desire.
—The Apocalypse of Adam, a Gnostic Gospel

The acolytes led the beautiful slave girl across the narrow causeway in the Temple of Fire to the central altar surrounded by a deep circular pit, the depth of which no one was sure. The girl, who was of the brown race from the lands to the west, was compliant under the drugs they had given her.

Al-Presta and Assha presided over the ceremony as high priest and priestess of the Archon. Al-Presta wore a scarlet tunic with a black-hooded vestment that went to his ankles. On its chest was the lion-headed serpent symbol of the Archon. Assha wore a scarlet robe, solid in the back but slit down the middle in the front. A bright yellow plume crowned her headdress.

Fiery braziers ringed the altar-island. In the center was a rectangular stone slab, about seven feet in length and four feet high. The acolytes led the slave girl to the altar, stripped off her flimsy robe and placed her on the slab. She was so under the influence of the drug that she showed no reaction as her skin touched the cold stone. Nor did she need restraints to keep her in place.

A circular colonnade surrounded the deep pit that ringed the altar island. Articulated columns ran from floor to ceiling, creating separate viewing areas for the elite Aryan spectators, among whom today was Ra-Mennarial. He appeared in his full princely regalia of a black tunic with a high-collared gold harness running from neck to belted waist.

The music and drumbeats began. The acolytes, all of whom were full-figured females, swayed in rhythmic undulations, breasts heaving though transparent gossamer robes. Some of them were on the altar island, others were positioned around the gallery in front of the spectators. They began to chant, at first low but growing louder. Mennarial sensed the building arousal of the ritual abetted by the presence of the nearly naked women.

None gave into the moment more than Assha. She threw her arms above her head, hair whipping and neck rolling from side to side in the throes of a hypnotic, rapturous ecstasy. She was naked underneath her slit robe, and the pose she struck fully exposed her womanhood to the audience. Mennarial observed the spectators. The heat and energy of the moment possessed men and women alike. He could see hands begin to search under the robes of people sitting near one another.

Al-Presta then banged his staff on the floor three times to begin his invocation. "We are of the earth and the earth's nature. Nature sustains us and so we must give back to nature and to the earth. We offer this sacrifice of flesh, blood, and bone that the god of this world may know we are faithful and he will continue to bestow his blessing on us and our leader, the great Ra-Mennarial."

Al-Presta and Assha then began to run their hands over the naked girl's body—breasts, belly, and legs—even penetrating her sex. Many of the onlookers began to openly masturbate or fondle the genitals of the person next to them. When Assha plunged a knife into the girl's body, they went into a complete frenzy. Mennarial was fully as aroused as the others. But unlike Ta-Revi, who was known to take a high-born wife before her husband's very eyes, Mennarial wanted to maintain the appearance of strength through self-control, a self-control he would soon lose with Assha in private.

He could have any woman here he desired, and like Ta-Revi, he was too powerful for any to resist him. But he had iron self-control and that fool Ta-Revi had enjoyed his final ritual because he had none.

Al-Presta and Assha had done a good job spreading the revived Archon cult, but Mennarial knew the religion for what it was—the channeling of sexual energy, the permission to release dark, unbridled human passions in exchange for blind, fanatic obedience, the same license to exercise unrestrained power over others that caused people to flock to Ter-Madaz's paramilitaries.

As soon as he defeated the Children of The One, he would spread his conquest by his military and maintain his rule through the religion. How seductive and easy it would be. The Children looked at sex as a way of feeling closer to others and to their mythical One. Restrictions on sex would always fail, Mennarial knew that, and he would clothe the new religion as a liberation from the restrictions of morality and the enshrinement of personal pleasure.

They extracted the victim's organs and placed them in burning braziers as the final sacrifice, then dumped the body into the chasm surrounding the altar. The sacrifices were increasing exponentially with slaves and drones now supplemented by known followers of The One. Mennarial sat a while, observing the outright orgy that followed the ceremony. After a time, he motioned Assha with his eyes to leave and join him in his chambers.

Mennarial knew he was close, very close to achieving his lifelong ambition to rule the entire earth. As soon as they completed the operation in Europa, he would have Amliea and Poseidia in a noose they could not escape. If he was lucky, Val-Andwar or even Ter-Madaz, whose power with the paramilitaries was a concern, would not make it back. The thought occurred to him once more that he might want to bring that circumstance about, but then again, he would probably need them for the final battle.

Time enough to deal with them when I am emperor, he thought, and he knew that day was not long in coming.

CHAPTER LXVI
Poseidia, the Imperial Palace
The Third Epoch, circa 10,700 BC

... that which is hidden from you will become clear to you.
—The Gospel of Thomas, a Gnostic Gospel

Petronien and Desamon paid their monthly visit to the orphanage on Poseidia. Despite their pressing crises, the men had a deep commitment to the children and their education. The children adored the men, but two in particular attached themselves, Athenara to Petronien and Foren-Tal to Desamon.

Athenara had cried for days hearing Petronien almost died and was elated at his recovery. Foren-Tal was one of the most intellectually inquisitive children Desamon had ever met, and indeed, he led off the day's topic of discussion. They were aware of the events transpiring and clearly had things on their minds.

"Why are we so different from the Belials if we are all emanations of The One?" Foren-Tal asked.

"It relates to how and why souls entered the world and what they encountered," Desamon said. "Let me tell you about one soul I read about in a fascinating story from the sacred annals. Ituriel was the name given in the text ..." Desamon related the tale that kept his young audience spellbound:

Ituriel was among the initial souls of the first root-race who rushed headlong into the experience of matter. In those days curious souls projected their mind essence in and out of animals. When Ituriel's soul first entered an animal form, his initial sensation was shock, and he immediately withdrew. It was akin to the shock of one who had never known the concept of fire and had been burned. Ituriel, like other souls meddling with earth's physical forms, had to dull or lower his soul energy to enter the primitive level of animal consciousness. This animal "consciousness" that Ituriel encountered was fascinating, yet alien and brutish. Urges of the body and physical survival compelled it.

Eating in a field, the animal body he occupied would spontaneously defecate. Ituriel experienced repulsion as animal senses picked up the smell. After a time confusion set in. Who was experiencing the sensations? Was it the animal consciousness or was it his mind observing the animal's consciousness?

He was growing accustomed to the animal's needs and appetites — eating, ingesting of solids, and expulsion of physical wastes. But most shocking of all was mingling with and penetrating other bodies. For when this creature's body copulated, Ituriel felt a bursting release of pleasure completely foreign to a soul. So repulsive, but also so alluring were these sensations. The feel of a physical sun against skin, the touch of a cool breeze caressing the body, to physically feel and not just sense another entity — all these things were very alien yet so enticing to a non-physical energy.

After a time souls like Ituriel projected thought forms based on their experience inside of animals. With no human body template to guide him other than a faint recollection of The One's primordial human image, Ituriel thought-created a half-horse, half-humanoid projection. Into this thought-form he pushed his soul consciousness, and for a while his mind maintained contact with the soul plane.

But almost imperceptibly, Ituriel's conscious awareness, like that of other souls, acclimated to its projected form. It was akin to when people move to a new home. At first everything is strange and the memory of their former abode is still strong. But over time, they become habituated to their new surroundings. The new home then becomes their present reality and the old one fades into the recesses of faint memory. The new reality, however, was polluted by the souls' contact with animal consciousness.

The entangled souls began to lose their identity. They forgot their origin in the higher world as they came to believe that reality ended at the boundaries of their animal skins. They played too long in a dream world not meant to hold them. The creators had become imprisoned in their own creations.

From the higher dimensions, the First Souls attempted to communicate with the fallen ones by influencing them with mental images of a higher vibration. Their attempts to contact the soul minds bound to the material dimension came to no avail. The fallen had moved too far into the earth plane. They had forgotten their soul origins. They could no longer perceive the images projected by their kindred souls into their earthly minds. All promptings to awaken manifested to them as vague dreams when in reality the only dream was the nightmare physical world in which they now were snared.

Ituriel and the others could only perceive sights and sounds through the physical organs of their bodies. They were now entombed in material forms driven by survival. Only their physical needs mattered. No longer connected to the Whole, they began to fight and even feed on one another as animals do. Each wave of souls succumbed to material influences to some degree. This forgetting was the origin of evil. Those recalling their spiritual origins became the Children, those who forgot became the Belials.

Petronien whispered to Desamon as he concluded his story. "Is this not too advanced for them?"

"Tyer Angarach is coming," Desamon said. "They need to understand the roots of good and evil to begin a new world, and quickly. Everything is accelerated now, including their passage to adulthood."

"You are the Prime Pedagogue. I defer to you," Petronien said.

"Did we come from those animal people?" one of the younger girls asked.

Desamon smiled. "Our souls came later in different types of bodies, but that is a long tale. The earth governs the body's consciousness while the soul's awareness is of higher dimensions. We are all affected by earth consciousness, but the Belials have almost completely forgotten our spiritual side. That is the main difference between us. Not all Belials are evil, but their potential for evil is much greater."

"So what makes people different is just remembrance?" Foren-Tal asked.

Desamon smiled. "If you keep the memory of yourself as part of The One, it propels your life in a far better direction. If not, you may become lost in evil."

As if to punctuate his point, gunshots and fires erupted nearby from another skirmish with Belial terrorist deserters from the Stratia.

Petronien said in a low voice, "You were right. Tyer Angarach will seek out even the innocent."

CHAPTER LXVII
Northern Hellas, Europa
The Third Epoch, circa 10,700 BC

... the two orders assaulted one another.
—The Tripartite Tractate, a Gnostic Gospel

varna and the Achaean army had marched several hundred miles into northern Hellas. With the aid of Damocles and the backing of the Oracle, he now enjoyed the full confidence of the ruling council. In fact, because of his knowledge of the Lantean army and its capabilities, he was appointed overall commander of the Achaean forces.

He explained to the Achaean officers that help was on the way in the form of troops and people who could operate the weapons that would help them defeat the enemy, but their immediate mission was to buy time and slow the advance on Athena. He had led a small force of five thousand north. They camped on some foothills where, by a nighttime campfire, Avarna explained his strategy.

"The enemy has greater numbers, but most of their soldiers are dull-witted, whereas you can use your intelligence. They have much stronger weapons, but we have advantages too. Your country is mountainous. This leaves them few ways to travel south by land, and they must use passes and valleys that we will barricade with timber and boulders while we ambush them and fade into the hills."

Many of the soldiers protested, saying fighting in this manner was not honorable. Avarna could see they were not prepared for what they were about to face, and he needed their unquestioning cooperation. He decided to resort to something necessary but out of character.

"You think fighting is about honor? Fighting is about winning. You call the Lanteans gods, do you? They are not gods, only men with superior technology and organization. Watch me carefully." Concluding those words he vanished.

The men cried out in surprise but were even more shocked when he reappeared, calling out behind them. "If you would be godlike, you must defeat the evil before you. I am pledging my life and my power to defeat our common enemy. The army we face will annihilate you if you fight them your normal way, man-to-man. Their weapons are better and they are better organized. We will whittle them down, harass them, disappear, and ambush them when they pursue us."

He now had both their attention and their awe. "What I need from you is the obedience all good soldiers must give to their commanders for any chance of victory. Their engines of war are designed to move over paved roads, not the rocky terrain of this region. We will not win the war here, but we will buy time to prepare for the final battle in the manner I show you. Is this understood?"

To a man, they knelt before him and pledged their obedience. Avarna was conscious how in an earlier age, Mannemiel and other Celestials had used their powers to be worshiped as gods by the lost terrestrial souls. As much as he hated the parallel, he was using his abilities on their behalf. He needed to inspire them, to make them feel like a god would fight for them. They would need a morale boost very soon.

Avarna used his translocating ability to monitor the movements of the Belials' army. He estimated his men had seventy-two hours to prepare. They blocked the narrower passages with timber and boulders, then carefully selected ambush sites with dense hillside tree cover. He drilled them on hit-and-run tactics and warned them if they broke discipline to fight their old way, the penalties would be severe. He reminded them he could be all places at all times to help but also to enforce his plans.

The time came when the Belial troops rolled into the first valley. As soon as they saw the roadblocks, the Belial commanders ordered a large contingent of drones and officers up either side of the hills to clear for any ambush. The Achaean soldiers engaged them, constantly giving ground, luring them uphill.

Avarna flashed to a point behind the lines of the advancing Belial troops where a small band of his soldiers emerged from concealed trenches. They had laid a line of pitch and resin buried beneath sticks and shrubs. They lit the incendiary line in a semi-circle to the rear and along the uphill flank of the invaders as the opposite side presented steep cliffs. Avarna faded back to his troops uphill and had them set a fire in front of them.

Hellas was an arid land, and the fire roared in a short period of time. The drone army panicked. They were completely cut off by fire on three sides. Any trying to break through were set ablaze or met with arrows and spears. The Achaeans pushed the rest to the cliff side, where most fell to their deaths. Avarna flashed back and forth uphill and downhill, feverishly directing the attack. When no more enemies remained on the heights, his men retreated to the far side of the foothills.

Later that day, the Achaeans took stock of their losses. Amazingly, less than twenty dead from compression gunfire while the enemy lost an estimated seven hundred. The men cheered and roared in jubilation, bolstered by such a victory over the invincible enemy. Avarna knew this first blood was crucial for their morale as well as their confidence in him as a leader. He let them have their celebration but then cautioned them.

"You men were brave and did well, but this terrain favors us. It will be different when they break through to the low country and the plains, where their superior weapons will come into play. But remember, our mission is to delay them as long as possible to allow reinforcements to reach Athena. So, delay them we will. You fight for your land and your lives, but you will be the first people of Europa to defeat the threat of these so-called gods."

For the next ten days, the elusive army battled the Belials at every pass and valley until the hills dwindled, and they had to disperse as the open plains loomed before the invaders. But they had bought ten precious days, and now they marched back to Athena with the loss of some two hundred dead compared to four thousand of the enemy.

The final battle would soon begin. Avarna translocated to Athena, hoping to find the aid they needed ready and waiting.

CHAPTER LXVIII
Athena
The Third Epoch, circa 10,700 BC

That which you are waiting for has come.
—The Gospel of Thomas, a Gnostic Gospel

Avarna and his victorious men met with sobering news upon their return to Athena. Of the expected five thousand Lantean troops, over a thousand had been lost in-flight in violent nighttime storms along with a number of artillery. This was a serious blow to Avarna's already outnumbered forces.

The invaders veered northeast to take advantage of the relatively flat terrain, which meant their final march would track due west toward the city. Avarna conferred with the Achaean leaders. Their first reaction was to make a stand on the fortified hills of Athena such as the Akropoloi. Avarna explained that this defensive strategy would be a disaster. The Achaeans had never faced artillery or compression guns. Inside the city, these would have a deadly effect. Their fortifications would not hold up.

Studying the maps, Avarna selected a site ten miles west where the low hills gradually gave way to flatter terrain. There, on the plains of Erithrai, they would dig a system of semi-circular trenches from which to fight and slow the enemy advance coming down from the hills. Before he had left to stage the ambushes in the north, Avarna had instructed the men to prepare defensive equipment. They constructed moveable wooden walls for archers to hide behind in the open plain. The walls would protect them from the bullets but also allow them to shoot their arrows over the structure.

Gone were the simple round wood and hide shields. They replaced them with long shields reinforced with metal and braided leather that covered the length of the body. These would better protect from compression gunfire, at least at a distance.

Avarna's forces had two advantages, one of surprise and one technological. The Belials were not aware of the presence of Avarna and his Lantean contingent. They would be overconfident from easy victories in West Europa, thinking they would quickly roll over the Achaeans with their superior technology and sheer numbers. The unexpected death rays, if properly employed, would afford an edge for the defenders.

These weapons had to be handled and placed with the utmost caution and expertise. A team of four Lanteans would handle each of the twelve weapons. Only one man or woman handled the weapon; the others acted as backups in case the primary operator was killed or wounded. A contingent of Lantean rifles was assigned to protect them. The weapons were fail-safed with calibrated hand sensors. Only the chosen operators, including Avarna, could use them so that if the rifles fell into enemy hands, they could not be turned around and used against friendly forces.

Avarna deployed the weapons teams inside the semi-circular trenches so that the entire plain before them was covered from the center and on either flank. The trenching system was laid out like the layers of an onion. Some contained flammable pitch and oils, others were laced with spikes, and others contained hidden troops.

Slatted wooden panels bridged the trenches at different points so that the mobile defenders could fall back, while destroying the crossings behind them. They used fill from the trenches to circumvallate a spiked, twelve-foot-high earthworks rampart hidden behind the tree-line. This was their final line of defense behind the trench works. The entire system was designed to slow the enemy advance and bunch them up on the open plain to give Avarna's army the maximum chance of whittling them down.

"Our trenches are in a concentric semi-circle to provide leeway if they send scouts ahead," Avarna told Damocles. "Our men are hidden below in the open field. I am hoping the Belials are so overconfident, they will not send scouts too far ahead to encounter our trenches. We need the element of surprise."

With their defenses barely readied, it was not long before the first of the enemy columns appeared on the opposite side of the plain. Now came the most difficult part—waiting for the battle to begin.

CHAPTER LXIX
Lair of the Katherati
The Third Epoch, circa 10,700 BC

Recognize what is in your sight, and that which
is hidden from you will become plain to you.
—The Gospel of Thomas, a Gnostic Gospel

The high priest led Terselia to a heavy metal door. He unlocked it and led her inside. As he entered, Lantean glow lamps lit, the only place in the pyramid temple she had seen them. Torches seemed to be the source of light everywhere else in the gloomy keep.

Before her lay a rectangular room with rows of shelves lining the walls. The central area was clear except for a glass-enclosed pedestal. The priest explained that the golden plate of the prophecy was enclosed within it. Terselia asked him to recount the history of the plate and their priestly order.

Centuries ago, he told her, an Elda-Fera priest named Alvara became disenchanted with the way things were. He saw the rise of evil in the Belials and despaired that any reconciliation or co-existence could be achieved with them. He believed that eventually they would have a corrosive effect on the Children of The One.

Alvara argued with the other priests. They highly respected him, but they disagreed with his separatist theories. His path would either lead to abandoning Artalanta with massive resettlement or war. The first instinct of the Children of the One was to strive for unity, in any case, not more fragmentation.

Alvara became anguished over his dilemma, and he made a pilgrimage to the sacred environs of Párnathal, where few entered, and fewer returned who did enter. Párnathal was held to be either sacred or cursed, either the abode of the First Souls or of other less savory spirits. Undeterred, Alavara left for Párnathal. Weeks later, after everyone thought him dead, he returned. His hair had gone gray but his eyes burned with an intense light.

He carried a single golden plate. It contained a prophecy of the future rise of a golden-haired empress. She would be possessed of a great power and she would do something to destroy the world. His vision told him they must leave Artalanta to remove themselves from all contact with the Belials and maintain the purity of The One. Alvara, several hundred priests, and other followers set sail for the West, never to be seen again.

Terselia looked at the golden plate. "Would you open the glass so I can examine this more closely?"

The high priest refused, telling her it was plain to see as it was.

"Know this," Terselia said. "Under your orders, people tried to assassinate the empress of Artalanta. For that we could have come here to destroy your village and lead you back to Artalanta in chains. I came to avoid bloodshed. I only want to touch the edges of that plate to verify the metal. Is that too much to ask or do we go down the other road?"

The priest was sullen but otherwise impassive. After a moment he removed a key and opened the glass. Terselia reached inside, touched the edges of the plate, and closed her eyes. It was gold, all right, but something was wrong. Dark images flitted like shadows across her vision. Her fingers felt like they were burning. She tried not to show her reaction to the priest.

She asked him to look at the books and records on the shelves. In some cases she had the same reaction she had with the plate, in some cases not. They had kept the records in chronological order, and she noted the newer records seemed to be the ones she reacted to badly.

"These older records," she said leafing through the contents, "from where did they come?"

"Those are original annals brought from Artalanta," the priest replied.

More likely stolen from Artalanta, Terselia thought. "So the newer ones would have been written here?"

"That is correct," the priest said.

As she rummaged through the later annals on eye-level shelves, she noticed a loose page under other texts. She caught several words that piqued her curiosity including "executions." She pointed at the shelves across the room and said, "Are those arranged chronologically like the these?"

As the priest turned to look, she put the single paper in her robe. "They are," he said. "Will you require more time?"

"No, that is enough for now," Terselia said. "I should get back to confer with the others."

When Terselia returned to the room, Ar-Falene pulled her aside. "This is no longer about finding peace with them," and she told her of her journey through the hidden passages. "People — dissidents I think — are being kept prisoner here. In one place they were starving, wallowing in their own excrement, resorting to cannibalism to survive. In another, they are holding the girl's mother with others awaiting sacrifice. They are engaging in systematic human sacrifice! They allowed the girl to wait with the mother until her turn."

Terselia's mouth tightened. "I have been suspecting something evil here," she said.

"What did you find in the archives?" Ar-Falene asked.

"Strange things," Terselia said. "Their central prophecy about Amliea on the golden plate is false, or at least it contains twisted elements of truth."

"How would you know that?" Ar-Falene asked.

"No time to explain now," Terselia said. "But I believe their founding priest was duped. When my sister made her pilgrimage to Párnathal, she encountered strange anomalies as she made her way up the mountain. It was as if the mountain itself is a portal reflecting the process of rising through the lower dimensions to reach the light. One of the appearances she confronted was a malevolent force that may have been a manifestation of the Archon itself. My guess is that Alvara, the founding priest, became ensnared by the lies of that thing, and he was given a false prophecy to sow the seeds of discord among the Children of The One."

Terselia saw the expression on Ar-Falene's face. "Look, I know you have questions about spirituality, but believe me, higher worlds exist of which this one is but a reflection, and the conflict between light and shadow traverses even some of those upper dimensions. I have been to a higher plane. That is how I can discern true from false and reality from illusion."

Terselia told her how she used her same higher sensitivity to detect true texts from false ones in the archives. More than fifteen high priests had held power over six centuries, which meant their longevity was considerably less than the Children of The One and certainly less than the Elda-Fera. There should have been far fewer rulers given Lantean life spans. This was yet another sign of unwholesome changes occurring within this cult. She then pulled out the paper she had taken.

Its outer edges were charred as if the original manuscript had been burned. Terselia read through it. "This was written by a novitiate priest some three hundred years ago. He mentions famine, executions, revolts then dire changes starting in the reign of one of the earlier high priests, causing great death and suffering among the people. I can only guess what happened. This colony went through a bad period at one point, and the priests must have been desperate. Religion and sacrifices can deflect problems and keep people docile."

Ar-Falene nodded. "All it takes is one mad priest with a god behind him to set the path, and these people were fanatics on the brink anyway."

"We need to get back to our airships," Terselia said. "I will end this priesthood, and we need to see how their people stand in all this. I suspect the priests are using the warriors to keep them in line."

She knocked on the door and told the guards they were ready to leave. Minutes later when the door opened they were confronted by a large group of armed men. The men parted and the high priest stepped forward with his hand clasped about the wrist of the young girl from the passageways.

"You will not be going anywhere," he said, "Seize them!"

CHAPTER LXX
Lair of the Katherati
The Third Epoch, circa 10,700 BC

Do not become a den of foxes and
snakes, nor a hole of serpents and asps.
—The Teachings of Silvanus, a Gnostic Gospel

"This will not end well for you," Terselia said. "I instructed my airships to attack if we do not return, and this temple will be the first target."

"You do not understand," the priest replied.

"I understand you are sacrificing and executing people who resist your cult. What happened to you? Your founder appeared to be a good man."

"I said you could not understand," the priest snapped. "We were starving back then, and disease was rampant. The Garana began to turn their own people into us for punishment as evil-doers secretly bringing plagues on the land. We abided by their superstitions and sacrificed the prisoners to save chaos."

"How convenient, deflecting any blame from yourselves," Terselia said. "This is how you brought light to the less developed? Yet your plagues are past and you continue to kill those who resist you."

The priest responded by locking them in a room with no secret passages, pending their council deciding what to do.

"I was bluffing about my orders," Terselia said. "We must contact the airships while daylight remains."

"How can we do that?" Ar-Falene asked. "They took our wave-carriers and weapons."

Terselia turned to the Garana girl imprisoned with them. "Do any of the passages lead above?" she asked.

"Only above," the girl said. "No escape below."

"We need not go below, not yet," Terselia said.

She looked through the small barred opening and saw no guards. "I saw that they secured the door by a heavy bolt. Stand back," she ordered, and she placed her hand on the door with her eyes closed.

Ar-Falene was perplexed. *Was Terselia was trying to push her way through the door? Had she gone mad like her sister?* But after some time, a chill rolled down her spine as Terselia's hand seemed to vanish through the heavy wood and metal! The men murmured amongst themselves. She looked like she was groping her way around, and then her face grimaced with exertion. They heard the sound of metal on metal as the door creaked open.

"How?" Ar-Falene asked.

"Later. Now we will make our way to the room with the passage and up to the apex. I noticed an opening at the top from where we can signal our ships."

"The priests' chambers are up there," the girl said. "Guards too."

"Just get us there," Terselia said. "You are brave and smart to have discovered these ways around here."

The priests had to be off somewhere else deciding their fate as they encountered no one going back to the room with the passage entrance. They entered it and made their way up the stairs through dank stone corridors toward the top. It took some time as the pyramid was huge.

They eventually reached the upper level exiting into what appeared to be a meeting room. Apparently, they never expected trouble this high up in the pyramid since only a few guards roamed the corridors. The Blackmanes were able to surprise them and seize their weapons. They reached the chamber of the high priest and the exterior overlook attached to the room. Stepping outside, they could see the troops Ar-Falene had placed on the ground and the airships circling above.

"What do we do now? They will not notice us," Ar-Falene asked.

Terselia looked around the room. "Glow lamps. The priests use them here." She took one and turned it to maximum intensity, then grabbed some cloth bedding. "It is nearing twilight. This should work."

She stepped onto the overlook, held the glow lamp up and began placing and removing the cloth over it. Ar-Falene recognized the Lantean military code she was flashing. She ordered the ground troops to breach the compound wall and the airship to begin blasting the upper pyramid after a delay to allow them to work their way down. She even eventually received an acknowledgment from both ground and air. They then hurried back down the passages.

When they reached the level from which they started, Ar-Falene said to Terselia, "I have to free those prisoners able to walk. Give me half the men. Make your way down. I will meet you later." She took the girl and headed off.

Soon the sound of explosions shook the structure as the air attack commenced. It took time for Terselia's group to find their way through the unfamiliar maze of rooms and floors. Eventually, they reached the level of the altar and assembly gallery but a large contingent of armed men awaited them. A fight ensued, and two of Terselia's Blackmane guards fell after taking down three times their number.

Realizing the situation was hopeless, Terselia had them retreat to a side room and she bolted the door. Their only hope was to hold out until the Lantean ground troops could reach them. The Katherati were pounding the door to break it in. The Blackmanes piled whatever furniture was available against the door, but eventually the top part splintered open. Terselia's men had a single bow and two swords taken earlier off the fallen guards. The Blackmanes shot and poked swords into anyone within reach, but the barricade was slowly being pushed back and would soon give away.

"Account well for yourselves, men," Terselia said. "You are Blackmanes. Make Artalanta and General Avarna proud of you, as I am right now We stand or fall together!"

Ar-Falene found the room where the girl's mother was imprisoned. Fortunately, no guards were present and the Blackmanes broke down the doors. "Those wretches in the other room are too weak to move.

We will get them later," Ar-Falene instructed. They began to move the prisoners out and down the pyramid. Several levels below, they encountered a large group of guards blocking their passage. Too many to fight, they retreated back down the corridor. Rounding a corner, Ar-Falene saw a side room.

She barked instructions to two of the Blackmanes. "Hide the people in this room. We will draw the guards off down the corridor. After they pass you to chase us, get them out as fast as you can."

Ar-Falene was relieved to see the guards bypass the room in which the others were hiding to pursue her and her men. Now the problem was standing their ground and facing the numerically superior guards. They found some tall metal candelabras along the way and used them to help fend off the attackers. The Blackmanes were far superior swordsmen, and they took a toll on the attackers, but they were increasingly being pushed back farther away from freedom. They knew they would soon be overwhelmed.

The attackers broke through the makeshift defenses Terselia and her men had erected. All, including Terselia, were wounded. Just when everything seemed lost, they heard shouting outside, and the attackers turned to face a swarm of Imperial soldiers. Caught between the relief column and Terselia's men, the Katherati warriors died or surrendered.

"Where are the rest of your men?" Terselia asked the Lantean commanding officer.

"They were fighting the enemy soldiers in the village, but the air strikes helped us scatter them. I took a hundred men with me, knowing your peril."

"Good work. Find General Ar-Falene. She was in the upper levels trying to free prisoners. Round up any Katherati roaming the keep."

An hour later, the soldiers returned with the prisoners Ar-Falene had freed, but behind them a far sadder procession came. The soldiers were bearing several lifeless bodies. The commander approached. In a voice choked with emotion, he said, "Princess, I regret to inform you General Ar-Falene is dead."

Terselia stiffened and walked over to the bodies. Ar-Falene had a dart protruding from her neck. "Poisoned," the commander said.

How odd, Terselia thought. *A great warrior felled by a tiny object she never saw.* She placed a hand on

Ar-Falene's forehead and whispered, "I hope you find the inner peace that eluded you in life, as the rest of us seek the external peace that eludes us."

The Garana girl and her mother stepped forward. The mother said, "Your general and the others died to save us. We would live among such noble people. Take us from this accursed place, please,"

Terselia placed a hand on her shoulder, "It is not the place that makes a person, but the spirit within. My people are at war with each other, but the good among us are coming here. Stay here and more like Ar-Falene will come to help you." She turned to the Stratia commander. "The priests?"

"We found them. All dead. Committed suicide," he replied.

Terselia nodded, not surprised fanatics would take their own lives. She ordered the troops to complete the evacuation of the pyramid, and she personally supervised loading the archives up to their airships.

By the time they finished darkness had fallen, and at the dawning of the next day, Terselia gave the command, "Destroy that pyramid to the last stone."

Helped by the prisoners, they identified both the resistance leaders and the remaining fanatics among the Garana. She left four hundred troops and some airships to help with an orderly transition of power.

She had Ar-Falene's body flown back to Poseidia for a full state funeral of honor, but Terselia took the slower journey home by boat to give her time to sift through the Katherati texts and to reflect on events. Ar-Falene did realize her revenge on Ta-Revi for her sister's death, but knowing revenge was not the path to The One, she repeated a prayer that Ar-Falene would find her way to the realms of light and bypass all the snares of the lower dimensions that would propel her back to earth in another life.

Her prayer was tinged with sadness, for she knew her own fate and those of the other First Souls was to return and suffer numerous other lives on earth. They had far more to atone for than Ar-Falene did.

CHAPTER LXXI
The Western Ocean
The Third Epoch, circa 10,700 BC

In the manner of a reflection are they beautiful.
—The Tripartite Tractate, a Gnostic Gospel

Terselia spent most of her time on the voyage home in her stateroom, poring over the Katherati archives, particularly the earliest ones that she suspected were taken from Elda-Fera vaults centuries ago. She took a specific interest in the texts relating to the activities of the First Souls. She skimmed through one such document titled the Acts of Genesis:

> When the First Souls entered the earth in the glory and majesty of their light bodies, the trees bent from the swirling winds. The air whipped about before the brilliant auras of crackling light energy that engulfed their forms. The land sparked alive and the twilight receded in the intense illumination of their ethereal projections. Animals, many of whom contained the lost essence of their fellow souls, cowered and fled for cover as the outlines of their pulsating energy forms blinked into existence in rapid succession on a grassy plain of the earthly land mass.
>
> Sophia, Desmoniel, Teresiel, Averniel, Petroniel—from a place beyond space and time they had come to experience their initial encounter with the plane of matter, with the earth that had lured and trapped so many other souls before them. They had lost communication with the souls fallen to earth. The exploring spirits were like a vanished expeditionary party sent

to explore an uncharted continent. The First Souls projected into this lower dimension learn their fate and rescue them.

The First Souls were careful to regulate this energy lest it became harmful to the physical creatures and environment around them. The creatures at first fled before them, but soon many returned to gaze upon their light energy in awe. They had to remind themselves that within these earthly creatures were fallen souls in multiple, grotesque forms.

The terrestrial creatures drew nearer to their translucent projections, their fear outweighed by the light energies radiating from the visitors' consciousness. To the variety of creatures gathering about them, the First Souls' ethereal humanoid forms appeared ghostly.

"These ... things," Teresiel said. "Inside lie the essence of souls I know. What has become of them?"

The First Souls were shocked, as in a physical sense one would be aghast at seeing people they knew transformed by some grotesque mutation. Their fellow souls had changed. They occupied dense, heavy bodies. It was obvious their consciousness had been vastly limited. They had become so deeply entangled in matter that they were separating from the Universal Mind Flow of Spirit. They had taken on fleshly forms both unique and indigenous to this new world. Animal urges had polluted their minds.

The more the First Souls probed the minds of these beings, the more alarmed they became. "They have all lost awareness of the higher dimensions and their true identities," Averniel said.

The lost souls had started out as curious ethereal observers of the material world, but now they were its subjects. In imitation of earth's animal life. they had assumed a multitude of forms, some human-like, but many with bastardized shapes, displaying mixtures of feathers, scales, horns, and odd appendages. Hybrid creatures of souls in flesh, their consciousness had been corrupted by the animal instincts of their physical bodies. Their narrowed consciousness interfered with The First Souls' attempts to communicate with them. They could only sense their messages as mere echoes across their minds or flashes of feelings within their physical bodies.

A creature with a humanoid body and a jackal's head approached them. The First Souls caught the gibberish of its mind currents—*hungry, kill, eat, lost!* They recoiled in horror. This soul was expressing the animal urges of its body but also crying in anguish at the shadow of its lost divinity.

It was odd for Terselia to read about the past activities of her own spirit self, but she continued to flick through the pages. She read about the Archon's origin in the psychic dimension as the personification of the unrestrained ego consciousness Sophia had inadvertently released when she broke from the Unity to create for her own individual passions. Thoughts are things in the higher dimensions. The souls' desire to exercise their own will apart from the Will of The One became retrograde forces that coalesced and personified in an ego-force, an energy-being called the Archon. The Archon influence grew powerful in the psychic dimension of soul-mind infecting fallen souls with false beliefs of ego, selfishness, and individual grandeur.

And yet, she read, it was Sophia who proposed the plan with Amilius to rescue the lost souls bound to the earth plane and re-constellate them to the realm of the Infinite. If successful, they would weaken the power of the Archon on the psychic plane who fed on the fear and confusion of earthly human emotion.

At a heavenly council, Sophia proposed that unfallen souls should become involved in the earth plane to rescue the souls lost on earth and thereby diminish the power of the Archon.

Their initial attempt, that which resulted in the creation of the powerful three-eye race, failed. Some of their Celestial allies grew corrupted and became the Sons of Darkness. When that third root-race of three-eyed Celestials was destroyed, The One, working through Amilius, the unfallen, devised a plan for a new physical form born of heaven and earth—Adamic man. This Adamic race would be a stable body form incapable of mingling with other species or thought-producing mind-forms of their own.

Reduced in the ability to become lost in their own god-like powers on earth, they would be able to evolve the spark of The One's divinity within them to learn their way back to the higher realms.

Using the original image of the cosmic human form in the Mind of the One, the First Souls selected a semi-erect, bi-pedal hominid creature natural to the earth. They used their mind-force to manipulate the animal's seven glandular centers, which corresponded to their own seven energy vortexes. Over time these creatures shed hair, grew larger brains, came down from trees, and developed enhanced intelligence capable of abstract thought. That endowed them with the ability to contemplate higher dimensions and eventually grow back into the knowledge of The One that would one day rekindle their divinity.

It was into these Adamic forms that the First Souls finally committed their essence to help bring all earthly beings of the upper realms out of their mind-prisons and back to the consciousness of The One.

Terselia closed the book and took pen in hand to write:

*O*nce we were gods who roamed the creation with no concept of death or finality. Now we are mortal creatures subject to the wheel of fate. Light was not meant for prisons of flesh, or perversion by animal desire. Just as the ocean will flush the shore removing the old grains of sand to be replenished by the new, so have a thousand million lives risen and fallen to dust, washed from the face of a world grown dim until it is renewed in the light of The One.

The sun grows feeble upon us. Our world is dying. Artalanta has lived two hundred thousand years, and our time is past. This is the twilight of the gods, for we gods have grown old, corrupt, and tainted by our past. We must fade to make room for new humans more innocent than us, knowing even through their mistakes, the soul energy will inevitably rise.

The One has chosen to cleanse the world to allow the earth to be reborn following the best threads of our past. And if in ages forth some of us should return from the ashes of destruction, as some of us surely must do, we pray we shall do so with greater wisdom, our souls purified by the light we gather from our sojourns in distant suns. Farewell, Artalanta.

Terselia perceived that it was her special task to ensure all this collected wisdom somehow reached the eyes of distant generations. She well knew human progress was two steps forward and one step back, but knowledge was the only light that could guide and beckon a humanity groping in the dark for understanding, purpose, and meaning. She did not know how or when the end would come, but when it did, she would save Artalanta's knowledge and records with her dying breath for the unborn yet to come.

CHAPTER LXXII
The Plains of Erithrai
Circa 10,700 BC

But you will become victorious in
everything, in war and battles.
—The Second Treatise of the Great Seth, a Gnostic Gospel

Ter-Madaz put down his field glass after inspecting the terrain. "Looks clear," he said to Val-Andwar. "I would not expect them to meet us on the open plain. Even those primitives are not that dumb."

Val-Andwar looked across the open expanse in thought. "I am not so sure the primitives are dumb at all," he said while he rotated the field glasses in an arc. "The planning of that ambush up north indicated a puzzling level of sophistication, like they knew how to exploit our weaknesses."

Ter-Madaz snorted. "Blind luck. Guts, that I will give them, but you accord them too much intelligence. I guarantee they are holed up in their city, relying on the fortification of their heights. They have no idea what artillery can do to such defenses."

"Perhaps," Val-Andwar said, "but when we cross the other side of this plain we will be about seven miles from Athena. We should camp in the woods over there and send men ahead to scout the city's defenses."

"Agreed," Ter-Madaz said. "But let's make sure they are not hiding in the woods on the other side, waiting for us. Bring the artillery up and bombard the area. Our gunners need the practice anyway."

The infantry and mechanized vehicles fanned out on either side while they pulled the artillery pieces up to the center. The artillery was operated by the Belials, not the drones, as were all of the technological devices. The drones were infantry battle fodder used as mass shock troops. They were well fed and told to expect future rewards for their service. Being drones, they accepted. But now it was the turn of the real humans, the Belials, awaiting their commanders' order for some welcomed practice.

When Avarna saw the artillery rolled onto the field, he began a frenzied burst of fading in and out of the entrenched positions, telling the men to sit tight and the death ray teams to hold their fire. "If we hit their artillery now, the rest of the troops will not advance into our trap. They don't know we are dug in here. They are going to shoot over your heads to clear the woods."

He asked for Damocles. He needed his fading ability to help him coordinate the deployments in the field but no one knew his whereabouts. It was no time to disappear in their most critical hour. Pushing his frustration aside, his last stop was the earthwork ramparts holding the reserve troops. He told them to wait out the blasting behind the ramparts, which would protect them from most of the bombardment. He told them what to expect to prepare them for the new and harrowing experience but assured them most would survive if they did not panic and run. He stayed with them to brace their resolve.

The first volley struck. The men clung to the back of the twelve-foot-high earthen mound as shells exploded all around them. The rampart did largely protect them but some struck home up and down the line, killing more men than Avarna expected. He and his Lantean officers did their best to control the panic by telling the men how bombardments were always intense but limited in duration.

"They cannot see you, they are not aiming for you," he shouted. "It is random firing and luck if they strike us."

Still, pockets broke and ran. Avarna faded in front as many as he could firing his gun and pushing them back. "If you lose cover, you lessen your chance of survival," he shouted as a shell took out several men nearby. He was able to herd some of the men back but then had to take cover as the bombardment became too intense.

The shelling finally stopped. Thankfully, most of the Achaean-Lantean forces held ranks. Avarna was everywhere, coordinating and telling the troops the advantage had now shifted to their side as the enemy began to move across the plain with their artillery exposed. When they came to a halt after encountering the first of the spiked trenches, he gave the signal. The soldiers hoisted up the hinged wooden shield walls, their bases anchored into the ground for support.

Two thousand archers emerged from their hiding place in the trenches behind and began arc-firing their arrows over the wall. The drones tried to shoot back, but the shield walls largely protected the archers who fired arrows non-stop. The ray weapons targeted the Belial artillery. On impact with any object, they created a blast radius of about two meters. As the drones broke and fled backward, they overran their own artillery, making the ray fire all the deadlier, taking out both men and equipment. When they had completely retreated to shelter at the opposite end of the plain, the ground was littered with the dead as far as the eye could see.

The Achaean army roared in triumph, but Avarna cautioned them the battle was far from over.

Ter-Mardaz's rage was out of control until Val-Andwar put a gun to his head and threatened him into silence. "You piece of horse dung," Ter-Madaz growled, "Mennarial saddles me with you because you spend most of your envious days plotting how to assume his position." When they were finally able to talk—and after Ter-Madaz told Val-Andwar he would slice him from end to end if he ever pulled a weapon on him again—they took stock of their losses. Several thousand drones and slave soldiers from the occupied countries lay dead. Out of fifteen artillery pieces, only two remained.

"We're facing Lanteans now, and they released the forbidden weapons. This changes everything,"

Val-Andwar said. "This is going to make taking Athena much more costly and difficult. Why not forget about Hellas and just build our weapons in Western Europa?"

"Fool, you know that Hellas has raw materials we need, and the largest existing fleet in the Inland Sea," Ter-Madaz replied. "We need their ships for transport back to Artalanta. We do not have the aircraft yet to do the job. Besides, after what we've seen here today, we cannot leave our entire eastern flank exposed."

"You have been in contact with Aryan. What is our timetable?" Val-Andwar asked.

"They can break through in a few days. They are only waiting for our return with the weapons and armies to attack Poseidia on two fronts. We need to finish Hellas off quickly or there will be hell to pay."

The two commanders conferred to lay their next plans. Val-Andwar pointed out that the Lantean contingent must be small because apart from the death rays, which were always few in number, arrows had done most of the damage. Compression gunfire had been light, and the Imperials would not risk a large force in the Inland Sea with Aryan threatening them just twenty-five miles across the Gulf of Parfa.

"Besides," Val-Andwar said, "their tactics, as clever as they may be, are the mark of an inferior army facing a superior force. If a full Lantean army were here, this battle would look far different."

Ter-Madaz rubbed his chin. "Who commands them, I wonder?"

"Not Petronien," Val-Andwar said. "He was wounded at Galgaatha. Besides, he is stubborn and old school. These tactics are flexible and innovative. It could be Ar-Falene or Telerian, but this ingenuity smacks of Avarna."

"Let us take stock of the firepower at our disposal," Ter-Madaz said. "We have two cannon remaining and ten of our own ray weapons."

"Yes, but those are unreliable and good for a few bursts only," Val-Andwar said. "They can just as well blow up in our faces."

"But we need them now," Ter-Madaz replied. "How many aircraft can we bring to bear?"

"Two, maybe three within any range to be of use."

"Then get them here. I have a plan and the men will need to work all night. We attack again tomorrow."

True to his word, Ter-Madaz's army attacked in the early afternoon, but this time it was the sound of aircraft, not the clanging of armor, that commenced the battle. The air wings bombarded then strafed Avarna's left flank, coupled with fire from the remaining artillery. The Belial army was camped in the low hills near the plain. Under cover of night, they had positioned their remaining artillery on the hillside in range of Avarna's position but out of reach of the ray weapons.

Under this cover they mounted a mechanized infantry attack. The infantry trotted across the field under a tortoise formation with shields up to blunt arrows. The vehicles dragged makeshift wooden bridges behind them to be placed over the trenches. It soon became clear to Avarna that the Belials had adjusted to his defenses and were mounting a concentrated attack to overwhelm his left flank. The ray weapons had to defend against the air wings. This allowed the Belial infantry to advance under the distraction and close in on the defenders.

Avarna translocated to the front and saw that the left flank was on the verge of collapsing. The ray weapons managed to take down one air wing and disable another, but even as the aircraft abandoned the skies, the combined damage they had achieved, along with the artillery and the Belial ray blasters had shredded the defenders. The death ray teams were dead and their weapons silenced as the Belials began pouring over the makeshift bridges. Avarna marshaled the men into an organized retreat to the ramparts.

He spotted Val-Andwar directing his troops, and Val-Andwar saw him, pointing him out. Avarna could almost read his lips, telling his men to capture him alive. With his own men in full retreat, he had to do something to slow the enemy advance and avoid a full rout. He was attuned to all the death rays and he picked one up, praying it was still operable. He began firing at the onrushing troops. Fortune was with him as it began blasting large holes in their ranks, but they were so numerous eventually they would reach him. When they got too close, he vanished, leaving the astounded soldiers staring into thin air.

He reappeared twenty feet away in front of Val-Andwar, who was surrounded by three men who Avarna took by surprise and quickly cut down. "How is this possible?" the stunned Val-Andwar asked.

"Just be thankful I did not come at you from behind as you cowards would do," Avarna said. "Now let us be quick about this. I do not have much time for you."

Avarna had scant minutes before the Belial troops closed on them. His first sword thrust took the still off-balance Val-Andwar in the shoulder. They dueled for minutes. Avarna knew he could not break through his defenses before the enemy soldiers would be upon him.

"Shoot him!" Val-Andwar said, no longer interested in capturing him alive now that his own life was in jeopardy. At that command Avarna faded out at the first crack of the compression rifles. He yelped in pain as a bullet struck his arm but what he did not see was how other bullets passed through the space his body formerly occupied and struck Val-Andwar in the chest. Val-Andwar dropped to his knees looking as if he had just awakened from a puzzling dream, then he dropped to the ground face first.

Avarna reemerged toward the center of his lines. He found one of his Lantean officers, Kelterra. "They have overrun our left. We have to move before they roll up our lines," he told her.

"Their attack is faltering. They seem confused for some reason," Kelterra said.

Avarna felt the wound in his shoulder and remembered that a volley of rounds had been headed at him when he disappeared. Val-Andwar had been directly behind him. Could it be … ? "Their commander may be dead," he said, "but they will press again. When our troops are safe, fire the oil trenches, but only after some of the Belials have passed over. Kill those separated advance units while they are cut off."

This tactic allowed Avarna's troops to kill a considerable number of the advancing enemy, but eventually their position was lost. They had to retreat to the rampart as the Belials tightened the cordon around them from the left and the now collapsed center. The Belials sorely pressed Avarna's army as their troops tried to storm the earthen rampart. They were barely holding with arrows, spears, and bullets flying. Only the remaining death rays were keeping the enemy at bay, but then the Belials pulled back.

The Achaeans' bewilderment at the move was soon answered. The artillery resumed its bombardment, only this time with more accuracy. Now enemy spotters were close enough to call in coordinates. "Damn those remaining batteries," Avarna said. "Eventually they will blow the fortification apart." He gathered his Lantean and Achaean officers and told them they had two choices. Retreat, fight a rearguard action, and make a final stand in the city, or attack and take as many of the enemy with them as they could. Either way, their prospects were not good, being outnumbered and outgunned.

After a brief council, they decided to attack. Avarna moved up and down the line, trying to encourage the troops, telling them whether in life or in death, The One would look over them and remember how they stood for something good in this world. On the way, he saw Kelterra's body lying halfway up the rampart. He was saddened and tempted to translocate to see Terselia one last time, but he told himself this was only one life. They would be joined again in the continuity of the infinite.

He planned to attack as soon as the shelling degraded the rampart to where it was no longer defensible. He was close to giving the attack order when a remarkable thing happened. The shelling briefly ceased, then resumed to drop amongst the enemy troops farther back on the plain away from the rampart. *The gunners cannot be that incompetent*, Avarna thought as he observed in wonder. The enemy troops were now running every which way in confusion, being killed by their own guns.

It soon became obvious incompetence had nothing to do with it as the bombardment methodically hit the enemy troops. As Avarna puzzled over the situation, Damocles suddenly appeared before him.

"Where have you been?" Avarna asked.

"I brought four thousand men from Thiva, a city north of here," he replied. "The city-states of Hellas are hostile to one another but they hate the Lantean invaders more. We took their gun emplacements to the north by surprise and turned the guns on them. In early Artalanta we did not need destructive devices, but I have learned to know my way around such things, and he tapped a finger to his forehead.

Avarna sighed in relief. "Thank you, Esh Ar'Haden."

Damocles smiled at the name. Over the next several hours, the two men coordinated a frontal and rear assault that squeezed the enemy into spiked trenches, death rays, and artillery fire until they had destroyed the entire Belial army. They only spared the slave-soldiers from Western Europa.

Avarna said to Damocles, "You and I are going to accompany these freed slaves to their homes in Western Europa to witness news of our victory and rally the local people to expel the remaining contingents in the Belial garrisons. No grand victorious army will be returning to save them."

Ter-Madaz and two hundred surviving Lantean officers fled east from the point of their initial breakthrough of the Achaean lines, leaving their drone army to be slaughtered. They slipped off into the wooded slopes of the surrounding hills. As they hastened up and down the rolling terrain, Ter-Madaz wrestled with the reality of the disaster that had befallen them. To lose Europa, a key to their ultimate plan, was unforgivable. He was already thinking of excuses. The best ones involved blaming the dead Val-Andwar, whom Mennarial disliked anyway.

This defeat changed the entire complexion of the war. The initiative would now go over to The Children of the One. A victory in Europa would have sealed the fate of the Imperials. Now their master plan would become more of a gamble than the coup de grace it should have been.

But Ter-Madaz put all these thoughts aside. He had to devote his full concentration on escaping hostile territory with vengeful enemies all around. During his time in Europa, he had allowed his men to kill, rape, and plunder. Now he needed to get off this continent any way he could, for the hunters had become the hunted.

CHAPTER LXXIII
Poseidia
The Third Epoch, circa 10,700 BC

And their angels will weep over their destruction.
—The Hypostasis of the Archons, a Gnostic Gospel

Jubilant citizens mobbed the streets of the capital. Public announcers stationed on podiums throughout the city shooted the news:

> *"Victory in the East! The combined Lantean and Achaean forces have destroyed the great Belial army. The imperial islands are saved from a mortal threat."*

Dressed in official regalia and military uniforms, the entire imperial government and heads of the armed forces were gathered around the massive bronze table in the Hall of the Ten Kings at the royal palace. They stood around a massive table map of the known world. Most of them were shocked and balking at Amliea's imperial edict that the populace must begin the evacuation of the islands. They had all been briefed about the warnings received from the Telian T'Meso, but this was a concept of legend and faith to them, not something upon which to base such drastic actions.

"How can we ask the people to evacuate in the face of two great victories, first in Atalan and now in Europa?" asked defense minister Voll'Tarr, speaking for most of the government and military. "We have Aryan and Atalan penned up by air and sea, reeling from disastrous defeats. They will probably capitulate soon. Princess Terselia defeated the Katherati threat. Listen to the people celebrating out there, and you want us to tell them to flee as if we are the defeated and not the victorious?"

"Do not judge reality from appearances, Voll'Tarr. Human events are controlled by higher forces beyond the perceptions of any one man," Desamon said.

"What do the high marshals of the military say?" Amliea asked. The high marshals were Petronien for the Stratia, Braan'dach for the Nautikon, and Vortegren for the Pneumarta.

"Petronien agrees with you," Vortegren said. "Of course, we can evacuate. Aryan is in no position to stop us, but could you be mistaken about an impending disaster?"

Segund spoke next. He explained with remorse that the nois regar of the Elda-Fera had interpreted the etheric vibrations from the Touai Stone. The reading of the Great Crystal confirmed what the five people had learned in Telian T'Meso.

Vortegren shook his head. "You do realize how traumatic it is to uproot people from their homes and send them to the uncertainty of a foreign land with no apparent reason, do you not?"

"And we must send soldiers to protect them. We will weaken our defenses," Braan'dach said.

With the leaders of the Imperium clearly in denial, Desamon made an impassioned plea for them to heed the warnings. Was all that they had learned, was the shared wisdom that made them Children of the Law of One mere words to comfort them in the spiritual exile of this world? From time immemorial through the Great Crystal and their own experiences, they had touched the power of the Light in their temples, in their prayers, and in their meditations. Were these encounters mere mind trickery? Were the higher dimensions only myths and fables? If this is what they believed, then the Belials had truly won.

The room grew silent. They were caught between their material attachments and their instinctual awareness of the wisdom in Desamon's words. Terselia then interjected. "Good lords and ladies of Artalanta, we know the higher realms exist. We were in Telian T'Meso. We know a cleansing of the land is inevitable, and we ourselves were transformed to play a role. General Avarna translocated from Europa to commune with us and bring guidance to lead us to the Place in the Middle."

"What?" Telerian said. "Avarna is a Fade?"

Terselia pursed her lips and gazed around the room to see the looks of disbelief on their faces. She then made eye contact with her fellow First Souls. They nodded their assent, so Terselia continued her revelations. "More than a fade. We were able to achieve Telian T'Meso because we were led there by Amilius. My sister and I, Desamon, Petronien, and Avarna are the First Souls."

The room went into an uproar. Segund stood, waving his arms to quiet them. "The princess does not lie or blaspheme. I stand witness to her truth."

Terselia continued her story about how they had begun to change and see events from a higher perspective. They were awakening as if from a dream, she said, and still wiping the cobwebs from their eyes. She did not mention Ouen and Esh Ar'Haden's role, as this might be too much for them to absorb, but she did something else they could see with their own eyes.

"Avarna did not have time to instruct us on our ability to translocate, but I have tried on my own," she said with her eyes closed. "In translocating, Fades, as we call them, pass out of this world through the Telian T'Meso for the briefest of seconds." As she spoke her forearm began to disappear before their eyes. "We pass through the Telian T'Meso, where we can see all, and we mind-project back to this plane upon wheresoever our minds concentrate. This is as far as I have gone."

When her arm reappeared, the entire assembly went to their knees with heads bowed in reverence.

"Rise," Petronien said. "If this is a sign of respect, we thank you, but if any feel worshipful, erase that corrupted thought from your minds. That is the way of the Belials and the Archon. We are all gods, sons and daughters of The One made prisoners by our own excesses, so if you honor us, honor yourselves too lest you fall into idol worship."

Amliea stood. "Understand this—there will be nothing here to defend. Despite appearances, Tyer Angarach is upon us. Our people's only chance is to relocate and carry our legacy elsewhere. No matter how things seem now, the sun is setting on our ancient civilization.

We did not start this, it is not fair, but the noblest service we can perform is to get our people out and let the Belials reap what they have sown."

They laid their exodus plans according to Amliea's direction. The more advanced civilizations of the world lay to the East, but the war and destruction caused by the recent conflict left that part of the world too unsettled. Lanteans had wreaked havoc there, and though other Lanteans had saved them, the chance of lingering resentment did not create the most fertile soil for refugees. Amliea ordered the first evacuees to go west where two large continents were conjoined by a narrow strip of land, the southernmost part of which was peopled by the brown race, some of whom Terselia had just freed from deranged rulers.

Those people had also suffered from the predations of the Belials, but the efforts of the Children had curtailed Belial aggressions with the closing of Plata and destruction of the Katherati. Being less developed, these people could greatly benefit from the knowledge Lanteans had to offer. Her advisors asked Amliea how the end would come, and she replied that to them that was not given. But they did know the evil of Artalanta had reached intolerable proportions, and the very earth-nature that the Belials worshipped would rise to cleanse itself in reaction to the dark energy produced by the warped vibrations of so many errant minds.

"For it is the sad truth that the Belials grow in number as we wane," Amliea said. "As human minds move more into the earth and away from spirit, as they begin to perceive reality ending at the boundaries of their skin, the truth of our unity fades to be replaced by the insanity of isolation. No more lonely, desperate, and miserable thing walks the face of this earth than a lost soul in human form confronting an existential void. They are too aware to exist with the ignorant acceptance of animals, but too ignorant to be aware of their inner reality as sublime spirits."

Amliea ordered the large wall doors opened to the outside so that they might see the full panorama of land and sea and the things human hands had created. And she said to them, "Look how beautiful everything has become. It is noble because it is dying. And we will never be so magnificent as we are now, for we will not be here again as this moment passes into infinity. To us it is given to pass the mantle not just to new generations, but to new civilizations. A better world shall be born from the ashes of the old. This is the last service we must render to both God and nature."

And so began the exodus from the Artalanta of two hundred thousand years, its failures and accomplishments destined to become dreamlike echoes in the murky flow of time and history.

CHAPTER LXXIV
Western Europa
The Third Epoch, circa 10,700 BC

When we passed beyond that place,
we sent our minds up further.
—The Apocryphon of James, a Gnostic Gospel

A varna and Damocles sat on a hill, watching the dismantling of the partially completed Belial war factory. Using the wave carrier from the downed air wing in Evvia, they had pinpointed Belial bases around the continent. The campaign to eliminate the vestiges of the Lantean conquest of Europa had gained momentum after the battle for Athena, as the Achaeans carried the news of their great victory to their Europan brethren in the west. The disheartened Belials were now on the run, hunted with nowhere to hide, no escape to be had.

As they stood on the hillside, Damocles put a hand on Avarna's shoulder and said, "Here, my friend, is where we part company."

Avarna nodded. "I understand. Will you go back to Ouen?"

Damocles smiled. "Ouen is gone. A new Oracle will sit in Delphae. She completed her purpose and laid down her body after so many millennia of rebirths. She will not return again to this sphere. She has moved on to other worlds, perhaps seeking Mele, but the fate of this plane is up to you and the others."

"And you?"

"My time here too has passed. I will be gone very soon."

Avarna sighed. "I wish I could have spent more time in peace and less time in war with you. I would love to have heard your memories of the elder days."

Damocles told him what he faced today was much like what they faced back then. He did emphasize, however, that humanity's destiny and evolution were not circular though it seemed so. The fall of souls was a downward spiral of mind and consciousness and their upward evolution would be the same, he declared. They seemed to be caught in a loop, but the loop spiraled upward to greater understandings.

"Yet what of Tyer Angarach?" Avarna asked.

"Exactly what of Tyer Angarach," Damocles replied. "For thousands of years it was misunderstood as the end of the world, but you learned it was the end of one world and the beginning of another. Artalanta must die for the new world to live. We became too powerful, too advanced without the wisdom that brings temperance. We became a threat that would block human development on earth."

"Artalanta, land of the gods, but instead of using our power to help the other races, we used it self-indulgently and stifled them," Avarna said. "We were too extreme and now we pay the price."

"But," Damocles said, "Tyer Angarach will propel the spiral. The old must be destroyed for the new to be born. The part of Artalanta that survives will help new civilizations rise. Our demise will allow humanity to grow in humility to uncover their own godliness over time without the flaws of the old gods. Apotheosis—that is the destiny of humanity, to rediscover their godhood after the suffering that makes them humble, grateful, and full of love for one another. The gods must unlearn their flaws to become godly."

"You were Achaean, yet now speak as a Lantean," Avarna said. "Are you Damocles or Esh Ar'Haden?"

He smiled. "I am both and neither. What we are in this world is just an illusion of a dream we all dreamed. I now leave to reunite with my real self, the dreamer."

Avarna shook his hand. "Esh Ar'Haden, who came to us as Damocles, a humble speck floating on the ocean, and helped turn the tide of the world in service to The One. You have lingered long in this plane and served well. Go to your reward in infinity, wherever it may be."

Esh Ar'Haden said, "It was an honor. Farewell then," and with those words, he blinked out of existence.

Avarna sat on the hillside, staring at the beauty of the earth, frozen in this moment as if it would be his last time. He knew the passing of

Esh Ar'Haden was but one of the friends and allies who would soon fade from this life. He thought long on Terselia and wondered how they would be in another time in another life, for unlike Esh Ar'Haden, who had completed his service, they were bound to ages of suffering on this plane. In this world, it seemed the joys of love were but moments long, yet the pain of living endured a whole life through, and to reverse this condition was the real purpose of existence. To be godly was to always be joyous in the love of all things.

He sat on the hillside, staring at the setting sun. In this rare moment of peace, Avarna indulged himself by following the gentle flow of his memories. They carried him back to the days of his youth in the palace of the emperor. He realized how one's soul shines through early on. He was intrigued by Amliea, who was often detached or aloof, but he perceived this was from being so inquisitive. She had a creative drive that exceeded that of anyone he had ever known. Yet he was born with a heightened sense of justice and balance, and he recalled thinking that Amliea would one day cross some line that would be her unraveling.

It was no longer puzzling to him why Mennarial held such allure for her. Both of them knew no bounds in pursuit of their desires — his for power, hers for knowledge. He was the most self-indulgent, self-centered being Avarna ever encountered, and the uninhibited pursuit to achieve a desire holds a strong attraction. It draws others into its orbit, even the innocent, until one day, like an object drawn too close to the sun, it destroys them.

The road to evil was insidious. Mennarial came into the world with evil intent, but Amliea, like Sophia, her soul essence, gave rise to evil not for evil's sake, but by becoming too excessive in her quest for knowledge that could be known only by The One. Only The One could create souls. Attempts by even the highest of beings to create life resulted in creatures, not souls, and Amliea, for all her noble intentions, merely ended up amplifying the mistake of the early godlike Lanteans.

Avarna's qualities had led him to love and admiration for Terselia, the loyal and level-headed Terselia who could have usurped the throne as her sister drove herself insane. Yet the very vibration of Terselia's soul was to witness and record events so that others might remember and learn to be better than what had come before them. That is why among all of them, she had to survive Tyer Angarach — Terselia and Desamon, the faithful, whose vision of The One never wavered. Desamon had tutored them well as children, and he would be needed to teach the children of the new world after the rest of them were gone.

Amliea, Desamon, and Terselia — they were needed to help shape the new world. It would be to Avarna and steadfast Petronien to preserve them, the ones who would be the bridge from the old world to the new. Even as he sat pondering these thoughts, he felt a burning sensation against his chest. It was the medallion from Telian T'Meso they all wore. He took it in his hand and saw that writing had appeared on the blank side:

> *Lest evil shall assume the power*
> *The waters must the land cleanse pure*
> *Released by fire on the mountain*
> *As one great soul must pass to shadow*

It was as if the medallion had read his mind or he had a premonition of the medallion's message. He understood immediately. The end was coming, and he would play his destined role in the conclusion of Artalanta's two-hundred-thousand-year-old story. He was needed back in Poseidia one final time.

CHAPTER LXXV
Ba'relin, Aryan
The Third Epoch, circa 10,700 BC

Anger, fury, bitterness, outrage ...
— The Apocryphon of John, a Gnostic Gospel

The drums sounded in Warriors Square, but these were not drums of victory. A dozen chopping blocks lay beneath the massive statue of Belial holding a torch aloft with his two sons kneeling in awe at his side, their arms raised, touching the sword and axe fastened to his armored hips. They were nearing the conclusion of nearly one hundred beheadings.

A few hours earlier, Ra-Mennarial himself stood on the raised platform to denounce the officers of the failed military expedition to Europa.

"These officers, entrusted to lead our forces, fled the battlefield," he said, reading out the execution decree. "We are in a war of survival. The only possibilities are victory or death." The mob chanted: victory or death! "We are a superior race hemmed in by primitives and traitors of our own kind who seek to thwart our right and our destiny to rule this earth." The mob roared and applauded. "Today we clean our ranks of the weak to make room for the worthy and so make our victory inevitable."

He gestured to Ter-Madaz, who stood next to him. "We find no fault with General Ter-Madaz, former commander of the Jackal Order, only with his co-commander of the Europan Expeditionary Force Val-Andwar. But General Ter-Madaz has forfeited his lands to the state and his position as commander of the AA paramilitaries as a noble gesture of his loyalty and remorse for the failure of Europa."

Mennarial had nearly killed Ter-Madaz on the spot upon his return to Aryan, but his reason overcame his anger. He needed experienced generals to lead a drone army that could only win by surprise and blunt force, not native intelligence or initiative. Besides, he had to break the bond between Ter-Madaz and the AA paramilitaries. If he made a martyr of Ter-Madaz, his task would be more difficult. As it was, he disgraced the man without killing him, so Mennarial could get the AA to swear loyalty to him personally. He absorbed them into the regular army as elite units to carry out his final do-or-die plan.

The defeat in Europa was a massive blow. It eliminated a guaranteed victory over Poseidia, but Mennarial knew his grand strategy was so bold and powerful that it stood a good chance of winning the war on its own. The Imperials were sure the Nautikon and Pneumarta had them penned up on Aryan. They would now be more overconfident than ever after their victories in Atalan and Europa.

If any benefit had come out of the defeats, Mennarial had lost some of his rivals and broken others. He felt good about consolidating his personal position, as the final phase of the war would soon open. Poseidia and the Children of The One were in store for the greatest shock in history.

"Do not let these temporary setbacks discourage you," Mennarial shouted to the massive throng of people, whose bloodlust had been stoked by the gruesome mass executions. "A mere portion of our power, the lesser potion, has been purged in the flames of war to leave the elite core that will lead us to victory, and I do promise you victory. Our High Priest Al-Presta has assured me all the portents from the Temple of Fire favor us. The sacrifices of our enemies have pleased the Archon, the god of this world. Today will be a celebration like never before, not a mourning."

The Temple of Fire opened its doors for all to witness the human sacrifices. The entire city gave into the lust of a massive orgy induced by free drink, drugs, and executions dispensed by the state. People openly copulated in the streets and public places with no regard to relationship, age, or inhibitions. Mennarial smiled at how sex, drugs, and sacrificial killings diverted the masses and made them feel alive.

The unwilling were particularly targeted prizes. A young woman,

Cer-Seta, was repulsed by what she saw. She tried to make her way home, attempting to flee the crowded areas. She saw couples and groups engaged in all manner of acts with mouths and genitals becoming indistinguishable from one another. Men with men, women with women and then she came upon a man molesting an underage girl. Fortunately for her, the man was staggering drunk, so when she hit him over the head with a decorative flower urn from the sidewalk, he went down quickly.

"Where are your parents?" she asked the girl, who replied she did not know. "Come with me," Cer-Seta said. The frenzy tapered off somewhat as they pulled away from the main public areas, but the danger was groups of roving young men. Along the way she ran into other women and even a few men with whom she banded together to make safe passage to her nearby home until the insanity died out.

Cer-Seta worked for the government in Ba'relin. Not long past, she would have identified herself as a Belial sympathizer. She did not believe in a higher power. The Children of The One were too mystical for her tastes. They tried too hard in their piousness and believed in too many fantastic things. Crystals and healings and Fades and other worlds — what foolishness these things were. Her practical mind was fixated on the here and now. But this spectacle today, this was something else.

One man said he had heard of a resistance group that had formed to make peace with Poseidia and stop some of Aryan's excesses. "They disappeared quickly, so I heard," he said with a shrug.

Cer-Seta too had heard whispers of opposition, but how could anyone counter the fanaticism they had witnessed tonight? The government itself had encouraged the unrestrained, dark passions that turned neighbors into beasts. As a government worker, she should have seen it coming. She was no moral warrior by the standards of the Children, but after today she had to wonder.

Whatever Cer-Seta and others like her felt, the successful diversion proved conclusively to Mennarial that using sex and religion to release the darkest side of human nature was more powerful than any force of arms. He had brilliantly used the power of the state to make his defeats look like triumphs. If he were victorious, every city on earth would look like Ba'relin on this day and they would worship him for it.

But now, with the defeat in Europa, he would have to accelerate his final battle plan, striking when they would least expect it on the heels of Poseidia's great victory in the Hellas. Soon, the last barrier to his new order would fall, he thought as he gazed toward Poseidia across the Straits of Parfa.

CHAPTER LXXVI
Poseidia, the Citadel Mount
The Third Epoch, circa 10,700 BC

And when the era of Nature is approaching
destruction, darkness will come upon the earth.
—The Paraphrase of Shem, a Gnostic Gospel

Avarna appeared at the Blackmane barracks on the citadel mount in the late morning of an unusually dark day. More accurately he appeared twice, each time bearing two of the remaining death rays from the battlefield of Erithrai. Black clouds framed by thunder and forked lightning were frightening people all across the five islands.

He sought out one of his surprised officers and told the man to take the weapons to the imperial palace, then to alert Amliea, Terselia, Desamon, and Petronien to meet him on the west terrace in two hours. He translocated to Nautikon naval headquarters at the harbor and found Admiral Braan'dach. He instructed him to be prepared to accelerate the evacuations on a round-the-clock basis.

"I cannot do that except on orders of the empress or the entire high command," Braan'dach said.

"Admiral, you have known me a long time," Avarna replied. "I will get your orders soon, but trust me, begin preparations now. Another thing. Have your swiftest vessel moored off the eastern coast by Langadia within three hours. Make sure it has alternate power in case the Crystal fails."

Braan'dach gave him an odd look but agreed.

Avarna's next stop was Pelion, where he conferred with Segund.

He explained about the medallion and his sense that the final confrontation was imminent. "A ship awaits you off Langadia. Begin loading the annals and other sacred texts. The Paleovouná has withstood two other destructions, but this time, I think, will be different. We cannot take chances."

Avarna finally arrived at the west terrace of the imperial palace where the others awaited him. He saw Terselia holding her pet leopard on a leash and Amliea lost in thought. Petronien drew his sword startled by Avarna's appearance, but lowered it when he realized who it was. Terselia rushed to embrace him.

"I wish you had time to teach me that trick. I could use it now," Petronien said. "We all could."

Desamon was the last to arrive. Avarna apprised them of all that had transpired in Europa, including news of Esh Ar'Haden's and Ouen's transitions. He showed them the medallion's message and told them of his certainty that the end was upon them. Amliea heeded his warning. She ordered a virtual cordon of ships placed on the western coast facing Aryan, and had Vortegren make sure the Pneumarta would be airborne in minutes on any sign of aerial incursion.

Avarna asked Amliea to ratify his order to accelerate the evacuations. Terselia told them Plata would be a good destination in the West. She had left a garrison there and told the Garana that good people would be coming to replace the degenerate Katherati. Amliea issued all the orders.

"I am still perplexed at these prophecies," Petronien said. "How can they strike us with no significant naval or air power? The warnings of impending doom we receive run counter to logic."

"I cannot answer your question," Desamon said, "but I trust in what we know from Telian T'Meso more than logic. Nothing in the world is as it seems. We will prepare as best we can for whatever comes."

That night by the low light of glow lamps in her room, Terselia told Avarna of what had transpired with the Katherati.

"One thing puzzles me, though," Avarna said. "Was not their priest's gold plate about Amliea being a focal point of destruction accurate?"

"Here I marvel at the truth that this struggle spans higher planes and thousands of years," Terselia replied. "Párnathal is a kind of portal with both good and evil present. One's experience there depends on one's consciousness. A fearful consciousness like that of their founding priest is susceptible to lower forces. Amliea was able to rise through to Amilius because she was The One's chosen instrument to end Artalanta's tyranny and save the world for a new beginning. The plate's message was a distortion by a malignant source in Párnathal to warp the truth, sow confusion, and set people against one another. The priest could not discern Amliea's true role, thinking her evil when it was evil that warped his perspective."

Avarna placed a hand to his chin, considering her statement. "Even knowing what I know that is unbelievable. Centuries ago, evil forces used this priest to set in motion a course of events that would kill Amliea and thwart the Plan of the One."

Terselia nodded. "The eternal struggle, and the higher forces play out through earthly instruments like the priest."

"And like Mennarial and his cohorts," Avarna said.

Terselia then spoke of Ar-Falene's death. Avarna tried not to let his grief cut into their precious remaining moments. The news greatly added to the sorrow the two of them felt as Terselia held Avarna's medallion in her hand, looking at the inscription. "I do not like the message I see on this," she said.

"Nor do I," he replied. "But it makes sense if the end is truly near. Petronien and I are warriors pledged to defend the throne and the empire. We are on the front line to defend you and our people."

"Are you so easily expendable, Avarna?" Terselia asked in a sad, dull voice. "You think no echo of the void you leave behind will sound in any other human heart? In my heart?"

Avarna took her by the waist and looked her in the eye. "Do not think me either overly callous or brave that I speak this way, but the threat is at our door and I must speak the truth I know. The portents and this medallion tell me I will not survive this life, but I may help to save many others. You know who we are. You have been to Telian T'Meso. We are the eternal instruments, as you said even now. We will be together again, but these are likely our last moments together in this life."

He wiped a tear from her eye and caressed her cheek. "You will never be more precious to me than you are now, nor will any moment ever be so sweet. To some it is given to live in blessed peace. That is not our lot. We struggle for a peace not only on this earth, but in worlds beyond, and surely when that moment arrives it must be more sublime than any fleeting happiness in this mortal life."

Terselia's tears flowed freely. "In this world, the joy of love is but a moment long while the pain of loss endures generations through," she said, oddly echoing his own last thoughts on the hillside in Europa.

Avarna then told her a story of his past. His father had invested the family fortune in a business on Atalan that produced farming implements. Upon taking control, he released all the slave and drone labor leased by the former owner from the Atalani Slavers Guild. He replaced them with paid citizen labor, though it was no small task to find those willing to work. But, he proved a business could succeed without slaves. This threatened the Guild. One day, the factory burned to the ground, ending his father's social experiment.

"He lost everything. Had we not become impoverished, perhaps your father would not have kept me from you," Avarna said. "As it was, the military was my only path. My father told me that war with the Belials would come one day over their desire to expand the slave trade and their lust to conquer other lands. He told me to become the best warrior I could be to uphold justice and the Law of One. To that purpose I devoted myself, yet my sorrow is that this path always took me away from you."

Avarna held her by her thick hair and kissed her with a passion made indescribably profound by the sorrow with which it was tinged. Terselia wept for their lost time, for the impending loss of their land, but mostly from the certainty that these were their final moments together.

CHAPTER LXXVII
Poseidia, the Final Battle
The Third Epoch, circa 10,700 BC

... the first power of darkness will come upon you.
—Dialogue of the Savior, a Gnostic Gospel

Mennarial himself led his army. He looked back at the column of men and vehicles, the largest single force ever fielded in the Second Epoch. They lined the tunnel as far as the eye could see, all the way from Aryan to Poseidia. The twenty-five-mile tunnel that ran beneath the Straits of Parfa was a supreme engineering achievement by the Tekna-Fera.

Now only a few feet of earth lay between the great army and a landing on the west coast of Poseidia. Only a few hundred yards inland from the beach and some twenty miles north of the capital, the massive army awaited only the signal from Mennarial. He stood, gritting his teeth, practically seeing through the dirt to the sky above Poseidia, the prize he had sought for so long.

Then came the moment when he set the forces in motion that would alter the world for all time. The Tekna-Fera's equipment scraped through the last grains of earth, actually pushing out rather than digging away, so thin was the last shreds of concealment they had left. When they cleaned and shored up the opening, Mennarial waved his arm forward and the column began to move.

The planning and battle order was meticulous. The Aryan general staff estimated that it would take nearly half a day for the entire force to make the crossing, so they broke through shortly after nightfall. This would put the bulk of their force in place by the early morning hours while the island slept. The slowest component, the infantry, was first in line, followed by the mechanized infantry and troop transport. The heavier equipment and artillery would come last. The army was divided into four divisions. The First Aryan would take the Imperial Pneumarta airfield at Imraihel to knock out air support and capture as many air wings as possible. The Second Aryan and First Atalan were assigned to neutralize the two imperial Stratia garrisons protecting Poseidia to the north and east. The elite Archon Lion's Head Division, led by Mennarial himself, would drive south to take the Imperial Palace and capture or destroy the Nautikon fleet in Poseidia Harbor.

The air base was key. The Belials needed to capture enough air wings and thopters to use against the Poseidian ground forces and more importantly to mount an assault on the Elda-Fera's keep on Pelion.

The grand prize of all this effort was to gain control of the Firestone.

Altavayne straightened her clothes and brushed her hair back with her palms. "How do I look?"

Palantor snickered. "You look fine, but you better get going. My father will be rising soon."

She knew she had overstayed. Tonight had been her turn to visit. She would have to run the three miles back to her family's neighboring farm, but leaving Palantor was always difficult. Sneaking out for their early hour trysts was the event the two young people looked forward to most in life. Exploring each other's bodies and feelings broke up the monotony of rural farm life, and it was damn well more thrilling than tending animals or plowing fields.

Of course, neither set of parents would approve of their unchaperoned behavior. Sex among Children of The One was a more solemn event than it was with the wanton Belials, but the younger generation felt it was able to hold onto its ideals without being too reserved about sex.

Altavayne had not gone far when she thought she heard a scream from Palantor's farm. She turned and ran back. She approached cautiously in the tall grass, and she heard another scream, sounding like Palantor's mother. Noises like muffled weapons fire made dull impacts in the night air. She saw the shadows of perhaps a dozen men leaving the farmhouse and they sounded like the military. She sensed enough to know they were not friendly. When it seemed the men had gone, she crept up to the house and peeked in through a window. She placed a hand over her mouth to muffle a scream. Palantor and his family were lying on the floor amidst pooling blood.

She went inside and checked the bodies. The men had murdered them. Suppressing her shock, Altavayne ran home. An eternity later, she came upon her family's dwelling and found it oddly still. Her father should be up by now to tend to his morning chores. The scene she entered was a greater horror than Palantor's farm. She saw her entire family slumped on the floor in a line, coldly executed by shots to the head.

Some her age might have collapsed from the trauma, but Altavayne just let the presence of evil wash over her as they had taught her in the Temple. She controlled her breathing and focused her attention inward. Her calmed mind pinpointed that the men appeared headed east on foot. She mounted one of the horses and took the back road to avoid contact with the marauders, thinking to warn other families in their path. It was too late for the first farm. She spotted the intruders continuing east. She kept riding the back paths. Her new objective was the warning tower some seven miles away

The valley was subject to occasional intrusions by dire wolves and saber-tooth tigers. If she could reach the tower and sound the alarm, it might wake other families and prevent them from dying in their sleep. They would also arm themselves, thinking vicious animals were about. And they were, just of a different type. Altavayne succeeded in reaching the tower. She used a rock to break the door lock. Once inside she immediately began to crank the lever, and the alarm whined out loud and strong.

She knew the invaders were not far behind and they would probably head for the source of the noise. She used the same rock to break the compartment that stored the emergency compression rifles and animal traps. She left the glow lamp on in the tower, then climbed down and set eight traps in a radius then covered them over. She hid in the nearby woods with three rifles and ammunition, then waited. Barely fifteen minutes later, ten intruders arrived and ran toward the tower, guns raised. Three of the traps sprang, followed by screams and confusion.

Some of the men gathered to free their comrades from the traps, and two others began climbing the tower. This was the perfect time. Altavayne closed her eyes and recalled what her teacher had told her at the Temple of Wisdom. *Violence takes us from our path to a lower mind-space. Defend by necessity with all your energy then atone with sincerity to bring yourself back lest the darkness devour you.*

She began to fire with all the skill her father had taught her. She took out as many of those men as she could who were trying to release their comrades from the traps. The two men partly up the tower ladder had frozen hearing the shots. They made easy targets. When it ended, only two escaped. Altavayne checked the men caught in the traps. Two were dead, one from a bullet wound the other bled out from a severed femoral artery, but one survived. She saw they wore the black armor and red insignia of the Archon.

Aryans! But what were they doing here? Well, these Aryans would kill no more. "Who are you? Why are you here?" she asked the survivor who was bleeding out fast.

The man was in shock. She had no water to give him and no way to save him. He was too far gone.

She cradled his head in her lap for a few minutes.

"It is too late for you," he said. "They are coming."

They? More of them? At that moment she decided that going from farm to farm was wrong. She headed for the Stratia garrison at Tar' Dahal fifteen miles to the east.

CHAPTER LXXVIII
Poseidia, the Final Battle
Circa10,700 BC

This (house) I shall doom to destruction.
—The Second Apocalypse of James, a Gnostic Gospel

P etronien tossed in a fitful sleep, recalling his past.

His father was beating his mother again. When the drunken man left, Petronien asked why she had married him. The mother told him her family had been of modest means, and her arranged marriage was to get her a husband who could be a good provider. And he was at first. But then he began to be influenced by Belial acquaintances. He spent more time away from home, often coming back drunk.

His attitudes became more Belial-like too, domineering and treating women like possessions to serve their needs. When he was old enough, Petronien thrashed his father near to death for abusing his mother one night. He threw him out of the house, telling him if he returned, he would kill him. Knowing Atalan was a Belial stronghold and his father would use the law against him, Petronien took money from his father's strong box and booked passage that same night for Poseidia with his mother.

They struggled and found what work they could. Eventually, through dogged perseverance, Petronien got a commission in the army and worked his way up the ranks. He made sure that his mother passed her final years in comfort. Her last words to him were that he was blessed with the gift of endurance because his path in life would never be an easy one, such was the fate with which he came into the world.

"Never despair or give up," she told him, "and you will fulfill your purpose in the end."

Then he awoke from his sleep with a sensation of intense heat on his chest. He immediately identified the source. It was the medallion from Telian T'Meso. He turned on a glow lamp and looked at the blank side to find it blank no longer. It read:

> *When the very earth doth open*
> *Hell's minions released the light to swallow*
> *Hold steadfast in final stand, a world to save*
> *And thy perseverance shall spoil evil's gain*

He knew that the days of Tyer Angarach were now upon them. He dressed and left his quarters on the Varinial Hill section of the citadel then went directly to the captain of the City Guard. His inquiry as to whether anything out of the ordinary had been reported met with a negative. All bases to the north—Imraihel, Tar' Dahal, and Carlerion —had communicated nothing of note.

He handled the medallion in a moment of thought then said, "Put all forces in the citadel on full alert. Wake them up."

"Sir?" the captain said.

"Just do it, Captain." Petronien then began roaming the citadel checking defenses. The sun would be up in an hour. Thirty minutes later, the captain came running to find him.

"Sir, Carlerion and Imraihel report being under attack by a large force. A strange report from
Tar'Dahal. A girl claims Aryan Belial troops are massacring farmers along the Parhelian Valley."

"No activity at sea reported?" With the negative reply, Petronien's mind made a rapid computation. Somehow an Aryan army had landed in Poseidia. Two bases were under attack. The assault on farms by small units must have been to ensure no warning would get to Tar'Dahal of a larger advancing army.

He went to central communications and contacted Torian, commander of the Tar'Dahal base. He told him, "Get the entire base on full alert. A Belial army is headed your way."

"I already did that, based on the farm girl's warnings," Torian said. "How in the five islands did a Belial army descend on us with no warning? Vortegren contacted me for reinforcements for Imraihel. He said he was being overrun."

"Stay put and deal with what is headed your way," Petronien said.

The communications officer told Petronien of reports flying in that both Carlerion and Imraihel were being overrun and a third army was only a few miles north and headed for the capital. Petronien then managed to raise Vortegren on the wave carrier. "What is your situation?"

"Bad," Vortegren said. "They attacked by cover of night. We were not prepared. They must have thirty thousand or more troops, and we have only five thousand on the base. I could use some help."

"Sorry, old friend. Carlerion is overrun and we have a large army headed for us, "Petronien said. "They cannot take those aircraft, you understand? Start scuttling as many as you can."

"Already started, but we won't get to all of them," Vortegren said. "I need to go. Probably the last time you will hear from me."

"The One be with you, Air Marshal," Petronien said, knowing that indeed, it would be the last time they would speak.

Petronien gathered his officers and assigned tasks to each. Some of them would get Consular Desamon, others would go to Admiral Braan'dach with instructions to speed up the evacuations. The Stratia would go to go door-to-door and get the families on the ships as rapidly as possible. He then went to the palace to talk to the empress and Princess Terselia. Avarna was with them and he absented himself immediately to translocate and reconnoiter the land.

Petronien explained the situation to the women and told them they needed to evacuate. They both refused with vehemence. He held his medallion up in front of them. "Ladies, you know as well as I do the hour of Tyer Angarach is upon us. Our enemy is at our gates, come neither by air nor sea but from the very earth itself—how I know not. This medallion tells me this is our last battle, and we cannot win, but we can prevent the enemy from winning. Their goal is the Touai Stone, but first they must take this citadel. You cannot fall into their hands."

"You know me better, Petronien," Amliea said. "If the empress flees, for whom and for what do our people fight and die?"

Terselia was equally adamant. "Whether we prevail or fall, I stand as witness to these events," she said. "If by the grace of The One we survive, all shall know that some Lanteans, in the end, stood for something good in this world."

They argued for some time, and in the middle of the dispute, Avarna reappeared. "Petronien is right," he said. "The darkness is here. I have traveled the land. It is worse than you think. We have lost Carlerion and the air base at Imraihel. They could not destroy all the aircraft, so they will use them against us. Only Tar'Dahal is holding out. I leave two of the death rays from Europa with you to fight your way out."

He explained how the Belial troops were pouring out of a tunnel the Tekna-Fera had constructed under the Straits of Parfa, and now that the northern bases had fallen, three of the four attacking armies were heading directly for the capital.

Petronien sighed and held his medallion. "*When the very earth doth open, Hell's minions released.* Do not doubt the messages on your medallions when they appear to you," he told them.

At that moment Desamon arrived. "Our prophecies were true," he said. "Artalanta will perish. Our technology is great, but greater is our evil. Our civilization cannot be turned against the rest of the earth to destroy and enslave. The message about releasing the fire on the mountain to cleanse the land can only mean one thing. The Touai Stone the Belials seek must be turned not just against them but against this entire land. It destroyed old Artalanta, and only it can thwart Artalanta's current evil."

"But the prophecies also speak of survival and beginning anew," Avarna said to the sisters. "Petronien and I are warriors, and we will go down with this island. The world needs less of us and more like the three of you to remake a better world. I have Segund and the Elda-Fera loading the sacred annals and wisdom texts on a ship that is anchored up the eastern coast off Langadia. You must evacuate now. The captain will wait for you as long as he can. This land will be no more. Nothing shall remain for you but ghosts hovering about its doomed shores. You must be on that ship."

They hurriedly discussed their plans. The Belials would make to capture the harbor first to seize the ships, isolate the city, and cut off supplies in case of a long siege. Petronien had to commit his troops to defend the low-lying harbor to protect the fleeing refugees. Being outnumbered and having scant cover, they were at greater risk if the Belials started using commandeered aircraft against them. Abandoning the citadel, Petronien sent two of the four death rays and all troops to protect the harbor and allow as many ships to escape as possible.

Avarna told them he would return to Mount Pelion. He reminded Petronien it was critical to keep the Belials tied up battling for the city. The Elda-Fera needed time to spirit the records and annals away from the Paleovouná and prepare a defense system never used before in remembered history. Before he left, he told his friends the most important reason to delay the Aryans, addressing Petronien directly.

"We need time to recalibrate the Touai Stone."

"To what purpose?" Petronien asked. "Wait. No need to explain."

The group stood stone silent at his words, as if frozen in place by some unseen hand of ice as they collectively absorbed what they already knew in the back of their minds. A higher power had been preparing them for this very moment and this fateful decision.

"*Thy perseverance shall spoil evil's gain,*" Petronien said holding up his medallion. "I will buy you as much time as possible."

Avarna placed a hand on his shoulder. "I know you will, old friend."

They said their last farewell to Avarna, and he addressed his friends. "Set sail for another shore. This is no land for the children of God. I leave you as Esh Ar'Haden left me. All the moments and memories shared together gone in the blink of an eye. Forgive me for that," and he vanished even while his voice still echoed in the room.

Amliea declared she was headed for the lower city to help evacuate the populace.

"Try not to get killed," Desamon said.

Amliea displayed her medallion as Petronien had done. "No, it is still blank, see? I do not think I can die until my role is made clear. Rather liberating ... for the moment anyway. The One be with you."

CHAPTER LXXIX
Poseidia, the Final Battle
The Third Epoch, circa 10,700 BC

Guard against the chaos demons.
—The Apocryphon of John, a Gnostic Gospel

Petronien was in three-way communication with Dara, Ar-Falene's replacement in Og, and Telerian in Airye. Both Tanuviel and Meruvia were handling insurgencies from Belial irregulars led by military-trained Stratia deserters. They had also attacked airfields on both islands. In Atalan, a Belial stronghold and always a problem, the garrison at Telma'arna was under attack once again. Mennarial had coordinated his battle plans well.

Neither of the air bases on Og or Aiyre were in danger of falling, but the insurgents had destroyed a number of aircraft. Petronien told them the Belials would soon capture Imraihel, and he feared they would turn air wings against the capital. "Can you spare any aircraft at all to protect the evacuation boats?"

Dara and Telerian explained that the Pneumarta and Nautikon on the two islands had their assets already tied up evacuating their own civilians, according to Tara Amliea's decree. Their airbases being smaller and still countering their own insurgencies, it was unlikely they could send much aid to Poseidia. "But," Dara said, "if I can get the trouble here in hand, I will spare what I can."

Before the conversation ended, Telerian said, "General, was the empresses's decree a mistake? Does it not weaken our position? I hesitate to say, but it always felt like a capitulation."

"Not a capitulation, Telerian, but an extrication," Petronien replied.

"I cannot explain now, but I can assure you the higher powers have aligned and Artalanta is doomed. Think. The Belials are powerful and growing. Their message is seductive. This world is all that exists—that resonates with people whose souls have so separated from The One that they think reality ends at the boundaries of their skin. Such people live for themselves. In losing their connection with their Source, they have lost connection with one another and so have become human islands containing all the corrosion that isolation brings. A nation that has forgotten God, that even mocks the idea of God, that is the evil that has overwhelmed us."

Dara's voice broke a moment of silence. "I understand. Telerian, I know you follow neither The One nor the Belials, but you are a good man. What do we have looking forward? Perpetual warfare? And what if the Belial's prevail? Think of the misery they would inflict on the earth. I trust The One seeks balance and Artalanta has been a land of extremes for too long. The corrosion General Petronien speaks of has set into all of our souls. I feel it. Better we leave this contamination for a new start."

Petronien knew Dara was a warrior like Ar-Falene before her, and she would grate at leaving a fight, but they had been warned. They were leaving a doom, not a battle. He thanked both of them reminding them that the priority was to get as many people out as possible.

The attack on the city came in the late morning. Elements of the army that overran the Carlerion garrison joined Mennarial's division. It was pandemonium. Two island rings surrounded the central citadel mount. A number of causeway bridges connected the rings and the citadel like spokes of a wheel, but only a single channel provided a passage to the open ocean, a defensive construct from elder days to guard against seaborne attack from without. Fleeing from an internal threat was never contemplated, and so two thousand ships vied to gain the ocean in a clogged funnel.

Petronien had earlier ordered the destruction of the Tar An-Hedron

Bridge named for a previous emperor who had brought a brief era of peace to Artalanta long ago. Ironic. Now the bridge named after the peacemaker that connected the harbor island complex to the mainland was gone in the flames of war. Petronien concentrated the bulk of his troops on Talan, the outer island ring, facing the Belial troops a thousand feet across the harbor canal on the mainland. From there they exchanged fire.

The Belials had brought pontoon bridge sections with them. Petronien had to prevent them from reaching the outer ring and making for the mouth of the harbor, where they could cut off the fleeing ships. He emptied the citadel of troops.

The citadel was the imperial symbol of old Artalanta and it was destined to pass, but the people on those ships were the future, the way for the best of Artalanta to survive and atone by helping other civilizations grow. He so ordered the priority of his troops that their last stand would be defending the harbor, not the citadel. He only hoped Amliea and Terselia survived.

Now he recalled a passage from a sacred scripture he had read when he was in younger in the Temple of Wisdom:

> *From ashes forged in flames*
> *lifted by the winds of war*
> *scattered 'bout the earth,*
> *carried way to lands afar*
> *Lantean blood, new worlds to birth*

Only now did he realize this had been a prophecy, and he was part of that prophecy. No wonder the passage had stuck with him. The remembrance of it made his immediate task clearer and his resolve firmer. Governments, buildings, the Imperium — they were nothing. People made all these things, and the Children of The One were on those ships not just to carry knowledge and civilization but the living spirit of The One in their souls. That, and only that gave humanity the chance that Artalanta had forgone.

Petronien's army battled the Aryans to a standstill that day and through the entire night, but with the dawn came an ominous vision on the horizon. Enemy air wings from Imraihel appeared. Petronien ordered his men to take cover in the ruins of Talan. The planes began strafing and bombarding his troops. The toll on the Poseidians was severe, and during this time the Aryans established pontoon crossings.

With Petronien's army engaged in street-to-street fighting in the rubble of Talan, the air wings were now free to attack the ships bearing the civilians.

CHAPTER LXXX
Poseidia, the Final Battle
The Third Epoch, circa 10,700 BC

Through your sacrifice, these will enter ...
—The Dialogue of the Savior, a Gnostic Gospel

varna used the precious time Petronien was buying them to help the Elda-Fera prepare the defense of Mounts Pelion and Palasindra, the keep of the Elda-Fera, and the dome of the Great Crystal, the Touai Stone. Automated gun emplacements ringed the mountains to propel aerial attacks. This was the primary defense since the Elda-Fera were not warriors and they were cut off from any friendly army coming to their aid. Avarna's presence steeled them for what was to come.

The gun batteries, which had never been used, had to be tested and in some cases repaired. Most important, they needed time to calibrate the Touai Stone for a purpose kept secret by Avarna and Segund. When their task neared completion, Avarna translocated to the citadel to see how the battle was unfolding. He found neither Terselia nor Amliea, but from the height of the imperial palace, he arrived just in time to see the air wings striking the positions of the Poseidian defenders on the ruined outer ring of Talan, even as the Aryan army was swarming across the pontoon bridges unopposed.

His mind assessed the situation and, in a flash, he reappeared on Mount Pelion seeking Segund. He found the white-robed priest, his bald head and tight, smooth skin exuding an ethereal glow in the bluish-white light that permeated the keep.

"We must shut down the Crystal to stop the air attacks on the harbor," he told Segund. "The Belials are using the air wings to destroy the troops protecting the fleeing populace."

The rarely flustered priest stepped backward, speechless and shaking his head. "I know we discussed this possibility, but do you realize what you are saying? It has never been done. The Crystal is the heart of Artalanta. Stop it and you stop the flow of lifeblood to our land."

"Segund, our land is bleeding to death as we speak. We discussed this, and the time is upon us." He explained the desperate situation in the harbor. "The only thing worth saving now is our people."

"I must consult the White Brotherhood," Segund said.

"We must do it," Avarna said with growing impatience.

"And you will need their help," Segund replied.

And so Avarna found himself arguing before the priestly assembly. First, he established if the act could be done, and they answered in theory it could. The Crystal accumulated the sun's energy and other cosmic rays. By means of a transducer system, the energy was converted for uses that powered everything in Lantean civilization — light, engines for ships and aircraft, and a myriad of other technical devices.

"That is the point," Avarna said. "If we shut down the power, the aircraft they are using to pulverize the harbor will cease to operate, as will their mechanical war devices."

"And ours too," said one priest.

"But we have no aircraft and they do," Avarna said. "That is what is killing people."

Some of the priests explained the risk of doing what he asked. If they shut down the transducer, it would indeed halt the flow of power to Artalanta, but the energy of the Crystal would still accumulate and build up to dangerous levels without controlled release.

"And," one priest added, "if we succeed in shutting it down, that would neutralize all of our defenses, and it takes time to recharge the systems. That will leave Palasindra defenseless and the Crystal vulnerable to attack. We must preserve the Crystal at all costs."

"You need to understand the reality of our situation and what is truly important," Avarna said. "Artalanta has fallen. At best you will be an island ringed by enemies but more likely you will go into the sea with everything else. Weapon defenses aside, you cannot hold out forever, and you know what will happen when Mennarial and his forces seize the Crystal. It is the souls on those ships we must save, and the Crystal's final blessing is to thwart the impending evil at our door. Am I clear? This is the will of The One, and as priests you should accept that. The aircraft must not attack those ships!"

Segund witnessed that Avarna spoke for the Higher Power, and he bade his fellow priests make haste in shutting down the energy converter. They went about their tasks, numbed and in shock.

Petronien's position forces were being hammered from by air and pushed slowly to the mouth of the harbor by enemy ground forces. Once the Belials reached it, they would control all the ships and the people on those ships. Fortunately, the air wings were still concentrating on his troops and had not begun to hit the boats. He ran from street to street, gathering pockets of resistance and strategically using the remaining death rays to slow the Aryan advance.

Just when it seemed the Poseidian resistance was about to collapse, one of his men perched in a high ruined building shouted, "Glory to The One, look!"

Petronien looked up to where the soldier pointed. The air wings and attack thopters were dropping from the sky like so many dying birds. His death rays no longer worked not did any other Crystal powered devices. Only gas compression weapons operated. Both armies froze in wonder at the events, but when the shock wore off, the Poseidians let out a collective roar and pressed back for the first time. Even then Petronien knew the drone numbers were too strong, but this would buy considerable time for more ships to gain the ocean.

Al-Presta, high priest of the Archon Cult, was exhorting the troops to a victory that would keep the sacrificial pyres burning for months on end in the Temple of Fire. Mennarial found that cult indoctrination and rituals had a great controlling effect on the dull-witted drone troops. It made them feel important to witness human enemies sacrificed through their conquests.

Al-Presta stood atop a rubble heap, promising the soldiers all manner of spoils and rewards for conquering a people who sanctioned their superiority over the Belials by virtue of a mythical God they had invented to keep power to themselves. "No more restraints!" he shouted. "Be free to do what you will. Release your desires and passions in service to the Archon, who blesses and rewards your every action."

Murder, rape, and sacrifice was the subtext of his message. Al-Presta was a pious zealot but not stupid. He knew releasing the bestial nature in humans and drones was releasing a mindless monster that would turn on itself, and leaders like him would have to restrict the freedoms they were touting sooner or later. But this was war, and for now he needed to extract every ounce of brutality out of them to win.

As high priest he would have great power to modulate and control the populace with the fanatic, indoctrinating force of the cult behind him. In the meantime, he rallied and urged the soldiers on being careful to keep himself clear of the front lines, of course. In the middle of a great exhortation he saw men look to the sky behind him, and lo, a great metal bird arced down from the sky as if to bestow its honor and glory upon him. He stood mesmerized as it drew near, calling to him and only him, and then his expression turned from wonder to realization as the fallen air wing descended on him and crashed in a ball of flame, befitting the many sacrifices over which he had presided in the Temple of Fire.

It did not pass unnoticed, at least by the human Belial soldiers, that if this were a sign from the Archon, they were in trouble.

Mennarial, Ter-Madaz, Dal-Golia, and An-Klesen stood on the mainland shore, staring at the spectacle of the aircraft dropping from the sky.

"In the name of the ten kings, what is this?" Ter-Madaz said.

"They did it. They actually did it," Mennarial said.

"Did what?" Dal-Golia asked.

"The Tekna-Fera told me if the Children grew desperate enough, they might actually shut down the Crystal."

"You seem happy about it," An-Klesen said.

"This is our chance to seize the Firestone!" Mennarial exclaimed. "The mountain defenses on Pelion and Palasindra will be down."

"And so are the aircraft," Dal-Golia said. "How will we access the mountain? It will take days to traverse by foot, treacherous all the way up and not conducive to an army."

"No, no, I foresaw the possibility of this event," Mennarial said. "Imraihel contained a mothball fleet of the old gas-powered airships." Mennarial referred to the dirigibles of sewn pachyderm skins inflated with gas, attached to a passenger car and cockpit below that had been in common use before the advent of Crystal power.

"I had them readied in case this happened," Mennarial said, blue eyes ablaze with icy fire. "The air wings did their job and got us over to Talan. Their loss only delays the inevitable. Ter-Madaz, you and An-Klesen stay here and finish off the harbor assault. Dal-Golia, with me. We are taking a trip to the mountains."

Mennarial had to labor at containing his emotions. He was so close to achieving his life's ambition. Poseidia had fallen. Already his troops had declared him Tar Mennarial, emperor of Artalanta. Now, with the control of the Firestone in his reach and no constraints imposed by the Children of The One, he would be emperor of the entire world. He would soon find Amliea and Terselia and end the old imperial line of succession by marriage or extinction, whichever worked out.

CHAPTER LXXXI
Poseidia, the Final Battle
The Third Epoch, circa 10,700 BC

He released the children of death.
—The Teachings of Silvanus, a Gnostic Gospel

esamon stood on a parapet in the palace on the citadel watching the battle unfold below him. He had seen the aircraft drop and knew immediately that Avarna and the Elda-Fera had cut the power of the Crystal to buy time for the fleeing populace. But slowly and inexorably the Belials pushed Petronien's defenses up the ring of Talan toward the harbor mouth, leaving the Sentillian causeway undefended.

He had overseen the evacuation of the now-abandoned citadel. The palace, the Consularion, all empty. The way to the palace was open to the Belials for the taking. In the distance Desamon could see contingents of the Belial army breaking off and headed for the causeway that would bring them over the Talan and Mesalan and harbor rings onto Enothan, the final island of the citadel mount. Only their concentration on capturing the harbor entrance had diverted them from taking the citadel before now. He had no idea of the whereabouts of Amliea and Terselia. The last he saw of them they were armed and heading toward the lower town.

Desamon decided to leave for the ship waiting off Langadia. His faith waited for a sign to break the chains of hopelessness that tightened around him. He began to walk the streets of the upper citadel when he heard voices from down an alleyway. He entered the orphanage he often visited. He went inside, and after a brief search he came upon a group of children.

"Why are you here?" he asked. "How is it you did not flee with the others?"

Foren-Tal ran up and hugged him. He explained that they were playing around the town when people started screaming and running. Some, like Athenara, ran to the lower town hearing Petronien was there. Others like him were afraid and hid. When they ran back to the orphanage, everyone else was gone. Then Desamon felt a sudden burning sensation on his chest. It radiated from the medallion. He took it out and saw writing had appeared on the blank side:

> *When all familiar falls to ashes,*
> *The old world hastens to its grave*
> *You are their only hope and guidance*
> *Thy faith will see them through the waves*

This was his awaited sign. He needed to get these children out, but how? The enemy was already upon them. He took out a pair of field glasses from his pack and tracked a complete circumference of the surroundings when he spotted something in the distance. A fleet of old gas-powered dirigibles heading north. Then it dawned on him. He had the children follow him to Museum Square, where a working dirigible was anchored and floating above the plaza. He broke the lock of the protective fence and entered.

Inside the dirigible control room, he examined the instruments. The fuel meter stood at half full. He loaded the ten children on board as he tried to figure out the instrumentation, knowing the Belials must be close. Several attempts to release the gas into the ship's air bladder failed, but finally the airship started to rise. He found the cable releases, and the ship slowly rose from the ground even as some Belial troops began to enter the area. The soldiers fired their compression weapons, and Desamon feared they might ignite the gases, but some wind caught the rising ship and put distance between them.

Launching and steering the ship were different things, however. Experienced pilots knew how to control the instruments for the intake and exhaust of air in relation to the heavier gases as well as how to manipulate the various propellers. The controls were for ascent and descent as well as direction and velocity, all of which Desamon had to contend with, having no experience. The ship spiraled away over the ocean to the northeast, and he had no idea how to navigate.

Airye was in that general direction, but he knew the other islands would not escape the eventual doom of Artalanta. He recalled the airships floating north and now that he had time to reflect, he knew it could only be Belials heading for the Paleovouná and the Crystal. The mountains would have no defenses and the Aryans were free to attack. He could not imagine the reign of hell on earth if Mennarial gained control of the Great Crystal and turned it into the Firestone once more.

But he had a more immediate problem. The airship was losing altitude, and the pressure gauge indicated gas leakage most likely from bullets that had penetrated the pachyderm vesicle containing the gases. The rate of descent accelerated as tears in the skin began to visibly open, releasing ever more gas.

The children screamed in panic as Desamon vainly labored to control the dirigible. No longer worried about Artalanta's demise, immediate death faced them as the airship went crashing down into the sea.

CHAPTER LXXXII
Poseidia, the Final Battle
The Third Epoch, circa 10,700 BC

Receive from us these spiritual sacrifices.
—Discourse on the Eighth and the Ninth, a Gnostic Gospel

egund and Avarna looked through their telescopic sights at the approaching airships from the window wall of the Elda-Fera keep. "They will be here within the hour," Segund said.

"I did not expect old airships. Is there no way to power the Crystal back on?" Avarna asked.

"No," Segund said. "It will take days to bring the transducer back online."

"I asked about the Crystal, not the transducer," Avarna said.

Segund's quizzical expression gave into understanding as Avarna's intent dawned on him. "The Crystal still retains power, but we cannot safely use it without the transducer."

"And how can the Crystal's energy be released?" Avarna asked.

"You would have to crack the portal of the Crystal by separating it from the spot where the energy is connected and released into the transducer," Segund replied.

"If we destroy the transducer attached to the Crystal, will that the rupture the portal?" Avarna asked.

"Yes," Segund said. "The energy is accumulating to massive levels in the Crystal. The transducer would release that energy gradually, but if its connection to the Crystal is destroyed and it ruptures the portal, the Crystal's sudden energy release would be unimaginable. It would likely blow apart, but not before shooting energy down through the earth, as that is the direction the portal faces."

Avarna admired that Segund could even hold this conversation with him. To the Elda-Fera, the Crystal was synonymous with life, and to discuss its destruction was tantamount to suicide for them.

"How do we do it?" Avarna asked.

The normally composed high priest had beads of perspiration running down his forehead. He placed a hand on his face. The Touai Stone was old and sacred beyond memory. Perhaps he was trying to cope with the reality of being the last priest, the last steward to preside over the Crystal's care. *It must be like sacrificing one's own flesh and blood to him*, Avarna thought.

As the Aryan army approached the landing bay on the side of Mount Pelion in their airships, they witnessed an eerie sight. Hundreds of blank-faced, white-robed Elda-Fera priests were casually walking off the edge of the mountain, as if taking the next step down a flight of stairs.

"What are they doing?" Dal-Golia asked.

"They cannot bear losing control of the Touai Stone to the Tekna-Fera," Mennarial replied.

On the landing pad, the priests chanted in unison as rows of them stepped over the mountainside.

"What are they saying?" Avarna asked Segund from inside the keep.

"They pray to transcend the psychic dimension and escape the force of the Archon to throw them back into this world in another life," Segund said. "They want to cast off the forces of fate and illusion to reunite with The One. I will join my brothers. I too wish to continue my journey in a better world."

When all of them were gone, Segund stepped outside to the mountain's edge and turned to face Avarna. "I often wondered why the Sons of Darkness were seven and the First Souls with Amilius but six. I now realize the answer. You *are* seven."

"Who is the seventh?" Avarna asked.

"Why, God, of course," Segund replied. "I both pity and admire you and the others for what you are, for I know you have tied your fates to the earth until all turn back to the Light. It is noble, fitting, and just to atone for your actions, but I do not envy you. Farewell."

Still facing Avarna, Segund folded his hands to his white-robed chest, then launched his arms outward as if spreading wings. He leaned back and let his body drop over the edge.

Avarna hastened through the tunnels, bridges, and elevators that connected Pelion to the dome housing the Crystal on Palasindra. The Aryan troops landed on Pelion and began to walk through the now deserted keep. The Tekna-Fera searched for notes and records, but they had all been burned. Mennarial ordered them up to Palasindra to see the Crystal firsthand.

When they arrived, they found the access to the Crystal control room barred by a thick transparent door with several small ventilation holes. Avarna stood facing them. Mennarial came up to the door.

"Avarna, the noble poor boy. I should have known you would be here at the end."

"Of course," Avarna said through the air holes in the door. "We are brothers, the book ends that moved the world in opposite directions. Without us there was no motion to God's plan. Now it ends."

"God has nothing to do with it. Do you really think that door will hold us for long?" Mennarial said.

"No, in fact, I will open it for you after your men leave and we talk."

"I do not like it," Dal-Golia said. "It may be a trick."

"What can he do from behind those walls?" Mennarial said. "I am curious what he has to say." He agreed to Avarna's terms, and everyone else left. "What is it you want?" he asked.

"Appropriate that a wall separates us, no?" Avarna said. "A wall separated us from the time were young, remember? Your desire to control everything around you, no tolerance for anyone disagreeing with you, your cruelty toward anyone of lower station. We should have seen the warning signs."

Mennarial frowned. "Your world has fallen, and you stand here in a cage spouting moral nonsense."

"*Our* world has fallen," Avarna said. "And you betrayed one who might have loved you, betrayed her twice actually, though in the end, I think you gave her a chance to redeem an ancient mistake."

"Ridiculous," Mennarial said. "You are mad with fear or biding time for help that will not come."

Avarna leaned against the transparent door and smiled. "I know what is coming. I have seen the future, and you are not in it. And I have seen other futures too. You are on the wrong side of the creation every time. We were brothers once, Mannemiel, but you made your choice long ago to replace God with your own deviant desires. For that you must pay with ultimate failure and ages of suffering."

"You call me Mannemiel and spout mystical gibberish," Mennarial said. "You are mad or confused. It is your future that ends here and mine begins. Now we will reign over the earth like gods."

"You would become gods upon earth only to be trolls in heaven?" Avarna laughed as he pressed his face against the glass door. "Yours is no victory but a capitulation to the truth."

"And what truth is that?" Mennarial asked in a voice oozing sarcasm.

"You see humanity as poor, base creatures, leaves blown in the winds of fate and nature. You conceal the horror of that belief in life-negating conquests to make your bleak existence seem meaningful. Your every breath is a capitulation to anarchy and nihilism because you see no higher purpose to life."

Mennarial exhaled an impatient breath. "So, the defeated would compare worldviews? Look at what I have accomplished, then look at you. Tell me whose way is superior. Tell me of your higher purpose."

Avarna placed his mouth near one of the ventilation holes. "Listen, and I will tell you." He to spoke Mennarial in a soft, even voice. "The One is here," he said, pointing to himself. "And even there," he said, pointing to Mennarial. "We are God having a human experience. We are the individual lenses through which God projects Itself into matter. But your lens is distorted. You need to move over for life to evolve toward its ultimate destiny. When the God within is fully revealed, heaven and earth will become as one."

Avarna pulled a metal object from a pouch concealed behind his back. "This a compressed gas bomb."

"So? What do you think to do with it, besides blow yourself up?" Mennarial asked.

Avarna moved the object around in his hand studying it as he spoke. "You probably witnessed hundreds of men leaping to their death rather than live in a world where you pervert the power of the Touai Stone. Well, they left me with a parting gift. Many more of these bombs lie underneath the Crystal. When I detonate them, the Crystal you seek to control will destroy everything you sought to rule."

Lines crossed Mennarial's forehead. "You are bluffing."

Avarna told Mennarial to call in his Tekna-Fera. When the gray-robed scientists entered with the lion-headed serpent of the Archon embroidered on the chests, Avarna obliged them with a technical explanation of how they had rigged Crystal. The worried men conferred amongst themselves then spoke to Mennarial.

Jaw clenched and fist tightened into a ball, he turned to Avarna and said, "If you do this, you will be killing innocents as well as us."

"Your sudden love for humanity is touching," Avarna said. "But while you were digging your tunnel, we were evacuating people, good people who will build a new world among the races you despised and oppressed. And some good people will still die, yes, but in Telian T'Meso, where we could see all things on earth, all those who will perish consented to their fate at a soul level. That is called sacrifice borne from love. I violate no one's free will."

"You are insane!" Mennarial shouted. "We can come to some arrangement."

"Yes, we can," Avarna said. "We can agree to give the world a chance to start over without the stain you brought upon this earth." He pulled a pin and rolled the bomb directly beneath the Crystal.

He then translocated through the wall, speaking before a stunned Mennarial, looking him in the eyes.

"We are more than anything you imagine. Without human beings, the universe itself would not exist. We are the instruments spirit uses to explore materiality. Your crime is corrupting our God-given gift to discover and grow by using it to destroy and kill, and now you must reap what you have sown."

He clasped the speechless Mennarial's arm tight. "Your world mirrored your mind, so the shadow appeared to rule this earth and you worshiped it. But you never grasped that a higher world stood behind the darkness. You never looked close enough to see the light through the cracks. Ready yourself, Prince Mennarial. I am here with you at the end—"

His words were cut short in a burst of fire and dust as the dying Crystal's energy surge tore out the heart of their world.

CHAPTER LXXXIII
Poseidia, the Final Battle
The Third Epoch, circa 10,700 BC

... sent for this purpose alone ...
—On the Origin of the World, a Gnostic Gospel

The lower town, where Amliea was fighting, was being leveled by the aftermath of the Crystal's destruction. At the last second before the building collapsed upon her, Amliea set off a blast of the ray weapon toward the collapsing mortar, then covered her eyes. When the dust settled, she was bloody but alive. The ray had disintegrated enough of the material to save her.

She had wielded the ray with deadly effect, helping the bulk of the people in the lower city get past the attacking Belial forces. Her task accomplished, she made her way to the east toward Terselia and the ship that awaited them. She checked her medallion. No message was visible. As she thought, her fate would not be decided until the message guided her to her final purpose.

She hoped Terselia had made it to the ship unscathed. She hastened, knowing the vessel would not leave without her, and seeing the ruins of Palasindra and the Touai Stone, whatever doom would engulf Artalanta would soon be upon them. She ignored the destruction around her. She would not lament the passing of her ancient land. Her sole focus was to move forward and do as she was guided to save the remnants of Artalanta's people, no matter what it would cost her.

Oddly, as she ran, she felt a power surging within her, as if she could fly, and indeed she found herself lifting off the ground, literally moving through the air. In a rush of clarity, she knew this for what it was. Her true essence was bleeding through. She recalled the old Lantean temple adage: *Those sacrificed for the good are first given the power.*

CHAPTER LXXXIV
Poseidia, the Final Battle
The Third Epoch, circa 10,700 BC

... there will be weeping and gnashing
of teeth over the end of all these things.
—Dialogue of the Savior, a Gnostic Gospel

The combat paused momentarily as Petronien's men made their last stand near the harbor mouth. They were encircled, and waiting for Ter-Madaz to give the order to cut them down.

"So, Petronien, you escaped Galgaatha only to wind up here," Ter-Madaz taunted. "How the wheel of fate turns. A far cry from when you were ordering us around on Aryan."

"Always blustering, Ter-Madaz. Why not meet me in single combat? Show your drones what a true man fights like. Or maybe you are the drone and they are the men. I am confused."

"You are confused. Why would I fight you when I can just kill you?"

An enormous explosion sounded, and the ground shook knocking everyone to their knees. Particles of Mount Palasindra rose in a skyward plume from a gaping hole in the Paleovouná. After the initial shock came a momentary lull, then the earth's violence resumed with a terrible shaking. Buildings still standing fell. On the mainland, a fissure opened, and the turbulent water in the harbor rings threatened to spew ships onto the land as the Crystal's released energy spread its destruction.

In the confusion, Petronien rushed Ter-Madaz and made a chopping motion at his head that he narrowly avoided, but the sword did slice off his left ear. It would have cleft his shoulder if not for the heavy armor he wore. As it was, he was grievously wounded, and only his men running Petronien through with several swords saved him. Petronien's men rushed to his aid.

Just then a group of children ran across the contested area between Petronien's men and the Belials. Petronien saw Athenara. With superhuman effort he ignored his mortal wounds and rallied his men to push forward and protect them. They managed to get the children into their lines. "Fight like wounded lions and get these children onto the last ship," he said, collapsing to the ground.

Athenara screamed and cried until they let her see him. She embraced him as if she would never let go. "I will not leave you," she cried.

"Athenara," he said, stroking her hair. "You must go. Would you have me die for nothing? This is what soldiers do. We die protecting those we love." He took a medal off of his breastplate and handed it to her. "Take this to remember me, for all to see, and tell them you are the daughter of Petronien for I would have adopted you as my daughter had we lived in happier times. Now, obey your father and go." With a nod of his head the men dragged her screaming toward the ship.

Petronien rose to stand, leaning against his sword, groaning and coughing blood. With his final breath, he shouted, pointing north, "The ruin of Palasindra signals your defeat. The land you defiled crumbles before you, rent with fire, and so my last moments here were well spent. This is what you shall inherit—the bitterness of dust and an empire of ashes." He collapsed as his soul passed from this life.

The land had become a death trap. An-Klesen and Ter-Madaz soon destroyed the remaining Imperial troops, then seized the harbor and commandeered all the ships, forcing the passengers to disembark or throwing them overboard. They could not get themselves out fast enough from the harbor they had fought all day to blockade.

Several hours later, the makeshift Aryan fleet of seized vessels rendezvoused with a group of dirigibles that came down from the Paleovouná.

One of the airships hovered low enough for the pilots to communicate with An-Klesen, who asked what had happened. They told him the Firestone had exploded, blowing off the top half of Mount Palasindra. The shock wave was so great that it literally blew the close-flying airships into the mountainsides. Asking about Mennarial, they told An-Klesen nothing could have survived the blast.

Volcanos began erupting across Poseidia. The Tekna-Fera were reporting seismic activity on Aryan and even as far as Atalan. They said the earth beneath the island archipelago had been severely disrupted and would get worse, causing widespread destruction.

An-Klesen, Ter-Madaz, and some officers conferred. With their homes destroyed and technology set back by millennia, they decided to abandon Artalanta.

Many Poseidian ships had escaped both east and west, obviously to settle in new lands. If re-established, they could pose a future threat to the now fragmented Sons of Belial. Their rallying point was the empress, who must have been on one of the boats. But which one? The dirigible reported seeing a large, lone vessel off the northeast coast headed east. It could not have reached that point if it had launched from the harbor.

"That vessel must have been anchored off the coast because no harbors lie to the east," An-Klesen said. "What was the purpose of a ship that size there? If an empress were escaping, would she be lined up in a choked harbor under attack or have her own vessel waiting elsewhere?" He told the commander of the airship, Arkel, to try to pick up the trail of the fleeing ship and their fleet would follow.

"Artalanta is lost," Ter-Madaz said. "Petronien knew. They planned all along to destroy the Firestone. I will be damned if the Children and Amliea steal our victory, then outlive us. We have nothing left but to pursue them to the ends of the earth until we destroy every one of them."

CHAPTER LXXXV
The Churning Sea
The Third Epoch, circa 10,700 BC

And I shall tell them of the coming end of this realm.
—Trimorphic Protennoia, a Gnostic Gospel

"That is how Artalanta fell, never to rise again," Desamon said concluding his series of talks to the children and crew. He omitted any mention of the First Souls and Telian T'Meso but he did tell them about his escape from Poseidia. Two days earlier, his dirigible had crashed into the sea killing two of the ten children on board including, Foren-Tal, a tragic ending to a promising life. The survivors clung to the wreckage until, by the grace of The One and a few flares, the ship had spotted and rescued them.

As he spoke, they heard the thumping sound of scurrying feet above, and a crewman shouted into the hold for all hands-on-deck. Desamon went above. He soon saw the reason for the commotion. Almost two dozen ships had appeared in the distance.

"Those are the damn Belials after us for sure," the sailor said.

Desamon sought out the captain and found him on the top deck. "Can we outrun them?" he asked.

The captain shook his head. "Not likely. We are probably seeing the swiftest ships of a larger fleet. They likely left the slower ones behind. No matter. The crow's nest spotted a large ripple on the horizon."

Desamon shrugged and hand gestured for an answer.

"It is the giant wave from the seismic disturbance the Elda-Fera predicted. It is coming right at us," the captain explained. "We estimate it at three hundred feet high. We stand no chance unless the Belials get us first, but they will die too."

"How long before the wave makes contact?" Desamon asked.

The captain shrugged, "At estimated speed, less than an hour."

Desamon sought a solitary place to reflect. He went to the ship's library. He sat down to meditate, but the door opened and a girl entered. It was Altavayne, the heroic farm girl.

"What brings you here, my dear?" he asked,

"I used to feel good in the temples, but they no longer exist," she said. "The closest I get to those feelings is in here."

"Ah, I see."

"You look troubled, Consular. I know the ships come for us. The Belials who killed my family."

"Are you afraid, Altavayne?"

"I was then and I am now," she said. "But it seems to me we are under the grace of The One."

"How is that?" he asked.

"Well, I was alone, but then I found this ship with good people and a good captain. Then you came falling from the sky. You gave us wisdom, explained things to make whatever we have left more understandable. You explained how Artalanta ended to help us make a new life, mindful of our old errors. These events seem to be no coincidence. You told us that everything we need to know is already inside us, and real wisdom is remembering, not learning. What do *you* remember, Consular?"

Her words hit Desamon like a bolt of lightning. Of course! Death, destruction, and the worry for the children had drawn him into the earth vibration and narrowed his mind's vision. In Telian T'Meso he had seen Tyer Angarach, the death of Artalanta, but also the beginning of new civilizations. The words of his medallion spoke to him: *You are their hope and guidance. Thy faith will see them through the waves.* In the same instant, he felt the hidden presence. He knew the secret salvation the ship carried.

He kissed Altavayne's forehead. "What I remember I owe to you. I only wish Foren-Tal had lived to meet you. The One bless you." He ran to see the captain. "I know whom you carry on board," he declared upon finding him. "Have them come out now if you would save your ship."

The captain nodded. Minutes later, from his cabin, two hooded women appeared.

CHAPTER LXXXVI
The Churning Sea
The Third Epoch, circa 10,700 BC

A wind will come forth from his
mouth with a female likeness.
—The Paraphrase of Shem, a Gnostic Gospel

T he two women approached Desamon on the ship's deck. They reached up and flung back their hoods, simultaneously revealing hair both raven and golden.

One of the crew shouted, "Tara Amliea Karason, Empress Amliea of the Golden Hair!"

The entire ship seemed to pour out onto the deck around her and knelt at her feet. She thanked and greeted them. Amliea then addressed them. She introduced the Princess Terselia, for whom they cheered.

"Artalanta was doomed, but its people are not," she said. "We have lost our land but not its people, not its good people. The earth is determined to cleanse itself of the evils brought by the excesses of those who valued their selfish needs over anything else, those who would do great harm to others."

"Yet those same people are fast upon us, Empress," a woman shouted amidst murmurs of fear.

Amliea raised her hand to quiet them. "Yes, they come behind us and in front looms a wall of water to drown us, the likes of which has never been seen, but none of this shall come to pass. This I swear to you. I owe a debt to you, my people, and I shall repay that debt this day.

"The One guides this vessel of wood and metal today, do you feel it? Under Its protection neither man, nor beast, nor fire, nor water shall harm your blessed journey. Do you believe? I need your belief to defeat these things, for when more than one stands in the name of our Source, then we shall move mountains, and today I must move the mountain that comes for us. Do you believe?"

People stood, cried, and cheered, for they finally felt hope, and more than hope — they felt saved.

"And now my people, I go to my fate. I shall not return," Amliea said. "This is as it is meant to be, for no more emperors dwell in Artalanta. From now on you will have leaders elected among you, but the first to guide you shall be my sister, Princess Terselia, and Consular Desamon. They will be your bridge of wisdom and guidance to your new world. The empire is dead, long live the people!"

Amid wild acclamations, Amliea asked the people to join their energy to hers. She took Desamon and Terselia to the bow of the ship. "My medallion has spoken," and she showed Desamon the writing:

> *The looming watery mountain stands*
> *twixt evil of old and promise of new*
> *yet a single breach may see them through*
> *the watery maw closed by her hands.*

"I isolated myself in prayer and meditation all this time to prepare for what we now face, and so I instructed the captain to remain completely undisturbed," Amliea said. "I felt your presence here and knew you would be guiding the people, but now I need you for another purpose. Avarna and Petronien have passed over. You must merge your energy with mine in one final service to your empress and soul companion. I need the power of you and our kindred souls no longer in-body to do what I must do."

Desamon needed no more prompting. The three of them stood in a circle, joined hands, and bowed their heads. Terselia knew this was the end for her sister. Though she had seen events from a higher perspective, Terselia's human side grieved and raged over memories of her young inquisitive sister whose father was harsh with her, who never quite seemed to fit in, whose sole venture into love was returned by violence. Amliea had buried herself away in mysticism, leading to more betrayal, and she inherited the throne in a time of war that saw the destruction of her people. But this was no time to shed tears.

The refugees looked on in silence at the glow that gradually enveloped the three figures. Witnesses swore that three more shapes appeared around them in bright bodies of light and they began to speak words in an unearthly language. For a time the three stood in a growing circle of light until the mounting terror of the mammoth wave was nearly upon them, and the enemy ships were close behind.

The ball of light around the six figures grew blinding. Then, like a luminous projectile, the figure of Amliea launched upward and hovered in the air.

As she drifted off, she mind-spoke her last message to Terselia and Desamon. << As men will fire a forest to make way for new growth, I was made to cast fire upon Artalanta to make way for a new race. This world shall pass away, as all obstructions must for life to move forward. My sacrifice is The One's gift of grace for me to atone. I shall return with the three Alphas of God in my name, and you shall be with me in the days when our sacrifices yield fruit and goodness prevails. >>

She extended her hands palms outward. Soon, a great force of wind rose with a circular swirling. One could almost see its shape revolving like a giant drill opening an expanding rift in the massive wall of water that dwarfed the small vessels in front of it. The wave froze in its motion. Time and space seemed to halt ever so briefly, and people experienced it as the passing of a waking dream. Amliea fixed her hovering form in the midst of the suspended wave beckoning the ship through the large circular portal.

People cried in fear and terror, seeing the crushing power of the wave pounding the sides of the rift, yet the water remained contained and the ship passed through unharmed, to the awe and wonder of the relieved survivors. Amliea's form glowed ever brighter and she remained facing them in the midst of the breach until they had safely passed. They could see the enemy ships speeding to make it through the watery tunnel after them.

The people looked on in awe at Amliea's hovering form as the voluminous water churned and pressed to break its confinement, for nature would not long be denied.

Then she spoke her last earthly words to them, her final plea miraculously heard by all. "When you suffer the pains of body and mind, when you experience the horrors of war and destruction, of cruelty and abandon, it is to me you will look with a bitter heart, for it was I who brought you here. When you feel the joy of love, the touch of a healing hand, a soothing sea of flowers, or the poignant sigh of the wind through an ancient forest, it is to me you will look with a tender heart, for it was I who brought you here. Forgive me for my vain errors. I shall return one day. Do not be arrogant to me when I am cast out upon the earth, and you will find me in those that are to come."

The translucent image of that which had been Amliea seemed to smile. Then in an instant the cavity she had created closed, the wave cascaded forward, and all disappeared within the resumed power of the ocean's fury. In the eerie, peaceful calm of the aftermath, the pursuing fleet had vanished. They saw neither sail nor mast nor presence of any life. The earth had fallen into complete stillness, and the ship proceeded through the tranquility of an ocean pacified by a goddess's hand.

From that day forward, deities borne from the minds of men would be echoes of the one who had parted the sea to lead her people to salvation and a new land, a land she would never enter.

Desamon stood on the ship's prow. He turned to the assembled refugees below and pointed at where Amliea had disappeared. "Nature was born of woman and the woman has returned to nature. Should you ever forget to honor the feminine within you and others, remember it was the power of the female that saved you this day; it was the Mother who triumphed over the wrath of the earth to deliver you."

And so they sailed onward to their new home and their destiny in the creation.

CHAPTER LXXXVII
he Inland Sea
The Third Epoch, circa 10,700 BC

Have I not told ye, ye are all gods?
—Jesus of Nazareth

fter the entire ship knelt in prayer to The One and gave thanks to Amliea's sacrifice, someone asked what it was they had all witnessed, what power had saved them that belied their sense of what was humanly possible.

Altavayne, the girl whose life's journey started on a simple farm, stepped forward and said, "I will tell you what we saw and what we did. The First Souls is what we saw, and now you know what they taught us in the temples was not empty words to get by this life. You know beyond a doubt what each of us truly is. We joined our power with theirs, for the First Souls are us, and their story is our story."

Terselia embraced the wise young girl saying, "You have truly understood my sister's sacrifice. Neither she nor any of us are to be worshipped, for we are one in reality, only separate in appearance. Be mindful of this as we encounter other races. We are Lanteans no more, but fellow humans. We come to share knowledge and live in peace, not to feel superior and cause war."

A week after passing through the narrow entrance to the Inland Sea, the refugee ship came upon the delta of a great river on the southern coast of the inner ocean. They sent scouting parties out that soon encountered a mixed-race people, most of whom lived near the fertile banks of the great river called Nilus, which flowed like lifeblood through arid desert sands.

One of their leaders came to greet the ruler of the ocean people as they first called the refugees. Terselia welcomed the man; he told them his name was Ra. Not long after this, the medallion burned brightly on Terselia's breast and the final message appeared to the First Souls.

Each act of man and all that passes
Lies written 'pon the skeins of heaven
Knowledge graced needs be remembered
By witnessed hand for generations

Terselia stood as the witness, the bridge between the old and the new. Her ocean people brought great texts of knowledge with them, the most sacred of which was called The Book of Remembrance. Under Terselia's supervision, they buried copies in a repository beneath the sands called The Hall of Records. And it would be written upon the columns of temples later crumbled to dust in far-off ages about a war of the gods, their destruction, and their passing into shrouded memory.

Around evening fires the newcomers spoke of their history, of the descent of gods who took different forms in different ages, some with three eyes, some part animal, and soon depictions of human forms with jackal heads or serpent bodies began to decorate building walls. The ocean people claimed human bodies were formed to curb the misuse of power by the early gods in what some called "the end of magic" but the wiser among them called "the end of illusion," for only when the godly powers ceased did souls become aware of the suffering of their dream imprisonment in flesh.

The indigenous population lived in crude dwellings, but within a few generations after contact with the ocean people, magnificent foreign structures called pyramids began to rise out of the desert. Great temples were built and manipulation of numbers, called mathematics, appeared. Understandings of the heavenly movements were revealed. Surgeries, treatments for diseases, and ministrations to the sick called medicine became common. Communication by written symbols slowly came into usage.

Around the earth in every culture, stories and depictions appeared of flying vehicles, of gods walking the world of men, and of watery destruction wrought by great wars of the divinities.

The ocean people made it clear they were no different than their hosts who held them to be those very gods. The wise explained it this way: water is one substance with three states—liquid, vapor, and ice—all appearing very different yet of the same essence. All humans possessed transcendent souls of a single essence that appeared in different forms over different ages, but to realize these things, one had to achieve a higher state of consciousness and this was the true purpose of all learning and evolution.

The teaching that all humans house a spark of the divine undergoing the experience of materiality became the core sacred wisdom of every earthly religion, albeit buried over time by the dust of ignorance, error, and forgetfulness. For many this reality was too much to conceive and so it was suppressed.

Though they would not have wished it, the leaders of the ocean people became so revered that in later ages Desamon became the god Amun and Terselia Thoth as language, sexes, and history morphed into things they were not at their beginning. But is this not the way of humans, to forget and look outside oneself for gods and answers and in so doing forget that the real gods and answers lie within?

This world is the playground in which God fools Itself into believing it is other than Itself, into believing that it is human. What else would infinite spirit do but forget Itself to experience other than Itself? We are not humans seeking a godlike experience but God seeking a human experience, and the purpose of all this is for spirit to partake of the fullness of creation in all its forms and aspects. This is the wisdom the ocean people taught that the forces of opposition could not utterly suppress over the ages.

It was to remind a forgetful humanity of such teachings that the First Souls would come again and again. They look for the day when the students will no longer need the teachers and can walk the path of the light on their own. On that day when all humanity awakens, the works of the shadow will crumble into the dust of the cosmos, the sun will become dark, and the moon will cause its light to cease. The stars of the sky will cancel their circuits, and the Light will pursue the gods of chaos to their final destruction. The Light will then reignite to cast Its brilliance over a new world.

In that moment the journey of the First Souls will come to an end, but seek not the hour of that coming, for it is known to the Creator alone.

CHAPTER LXXXVIII
Egypt
Circa 600 BC

*For those who were in the world had been prepared
by the will of our sister Sophia ... Since she was first.*
—The Second Treatise of the Great Seth, a Gnostic Gospel

S ome nine centuries after Artalanta perished, a great Athenian
statesman named Solon visited Egypt and took up company with
a learned priest, Sonchis of Sais, to absorb what wisdom he could.
Much to Solon's surprise, Sonchis related the tale of a lost civilization,
a land of godlike beings with flying machines and vast, elaborate cities
and harbors adorned with massive statues and mighty warriors.

Sonchis chided Solon for being like an infant, ignorant in wisdom
and history of the fact that his own city of Athens had led the war that
defeated the mighty invading armies of the seaborne continent beyond
the pillars of Hercules.

Solon carried this startling news back home, where a man to
whom he told the tale told it in turn to his grandson named Plato. Plato
seized upon the story to educate the Athenians about matters which
they otherwise might not contemplate. What neither Sonchis nor Solon
realized was that the legend had descended in this manner:

> The natives of the Inland Sea, to honor the memory and
> wisdom of the ocean people, used their newly learned arts to
> engrave images of the First Souls on the wall of a certain temple.
> It depicted two warriors, two women, a scholarly man, and above
> all of them an ethereal figure. The names inscribed were Avarna,
> Terselia, Amliea, Petronien, Desamon, and Amilius.

Below each figure words were engraved, and Terselia, the last of them on earth before her passing, wrote this inscription in remembrance of Amliea/Sophia:

> She was the bane and gift of woman. She was sent forth from the power. Do not be ignorant of her. She was the first and the last, the honored one and the scorned one. She was the whore and the holy one. She was knowledge and ignorance. She was shame and boldness. She was strength and fear. Heed her flaws, praise her courage. She was the one who is disgraced and the great one. Light must pass through shadow to know it is light. She had to be both for our salvation.

With her ended the journey of Artalanta,
with her the new world began.

The world might never know how close it came to millennia of shadow and grief but for the actions of a few souls. Now all their empires are fallen down, consigned to the oblivion of time, and as all works by mortal hands are fleeting, the temple decayed and the desert sands caressed the graven images into slow oblivion until, crumbled into dust, only a few letters remained:

ATLANT

This inscription, when translated and passed on orally, became *Atlantis* in Greek. People ridiculed Plato in his time, and his story of the island continent Atlantis was held to be myth. But all memory was not lost. The enduring wisdom of the First Souls lay buried beneath the desert sands in The Book of Remembrance, which would, one distant day by divine provenance, work its way back before the eyes of men.

It reminded humans that they are the fingers of God touching the face of this world, and their purpose is to spiritualize the material and bring the experience of the material back to spirit. When this is realized, the kingdom of heaven shall come to earth, evil and its works shall dissolve, and the barriers between dimensions shall throw open their gates. Beings will move freely from the spiritual to the material as all life comes into alignment with the will of God. Creation shall become as one.

For this day a tragic young empress gave her life, Artalanta died, and the First Souls would suffer countless deaths throughout the flow of time. Of these things I can tell you no more, for their path was determined in a higher place long ago, but it is surely the path of tears that must be tread when gods descend to earth and take their place among the fallen.

EPILOGUE
Washington, DC
AD 2042

There is rebirth and an image of rebirth ...
—The Gospel of Philip, a Gnostic Gospel

O n an early spring day in Washington, DC, when the cherry blossoms were working their way to their peak, two women walked in front of the reflecting pool before the Lincoln Memorial.

"You sure gave the world one hell of a history lesson," Senator La Shonda Conyers said. "What was it, about three and half years ago you came to us with a story too incredible to believe, and now some twenty-one countries have officially adopted it."

"I was just one messenger among many Pope Valentinus used to spread the word," Bishop de Verneaux said in her charming French accent.

"Yes," Conyers said, "but you brought it to my country, and for that I'm grateful. God knows we needed hope here."

"And God delivered," the bishop quipped with a smile.

"All except for ol' Joe Faller. He lost his reelection in no small part because he spoke so strongly against the texts," Conyers said. "He just looked plain pig-headed against the facts. Joe is not a bad guy. It's just that like many others he can't get beyond what he can see and touch. And in a way I get it. It's a scary thought that higher worlds exist and we have to own up to how we landed here. You do know that many will always remain in denial, yes?"

"Yet things are hopeful too," de Verneaux replied. "Whole new lines of study, teaching, and inquiry are springing up, even in science. Physics may look to metaphysics to help solve inexplicable mysteries. People are trying to understand themselves by seeking their past lives. Spirituality is on the rise, and world leaders will have to account for that in their decisions. A new respect for all that is feminine is sweeping the planet changing cultures and practices ingrained for centuries."

"All because a small African woman challenged the world's powers," Conyers said. "Coming from a black Baptist family, I was proud but skeptical at first. I mean, we weren't taught to think out of the box. But actions speak louder than words. I went from seeing Annalisa as the anti-Christ to a genuine force of change for good. She put her life on the line to stop a nuclear war, then abdicated the papacy at the height of her popularity. That sold me on her intentions."

"Intention," de Verneaux mused. "The same soul that was Annalisa and Amliea committed the most fundamental sin in history, and more than once, yet she was not evil because it was not her intention to usurp God. Rather, she pursued a dream to know the unknowable—the nature of God's undivided, hidden essence. She birthed worlds and beings on her own, thinking to do this was to know God, and that is our cautionary tale."

"How so?" Conyers asked, brushing a fallen cherry blossom off her shoulder.

The bishop stopped walking and looked wistful. "Sometimes, in moments of solitude, I close my eyes and picture the march of history through the souls of Sophia's incarnations—Amliea, Magdalene, and Annalisa. Through them I realized how we had to become less godlike to become more godlike."

"I don't understand," Conyers said.

The bishop folded her hands and closed her eyes to compose her thoughts. "In the beginning, our powers were so great that our minds alone could create personal kingdoms on earth to satiate our desires. But that unbridled use of power inevitably led to an isolated self-centeredness of the mind, an ego that had to gratify its expanding needs at the expense of others."

"Okay," Conyers said trying to follow

"That condition of being so infused with power yet so limited in consciousness could not last. The belief that this world, indeed the entire universe, was their creation and not God's was an illusion of the souls. That false collective belief is personified by the Archon, whom they called the god of this world."

"I remember that from the texts," Conyers said. "The sickness of the Belials."

As the bishop spoke, the wind blew ripples across the waters of the reflecting pool. Perhaps it was the nature of the conversation or perhaps it was a personal reminder from beyond, but Conyers's mind instantly recalled the creation story in Genesis of how God's breath moved across the face of the waters.

"Just think," de Verneaux said, "if we had maintained our godlike powers with such flawed consciousness, it would have trapped us in a permanent condition of illusion with no hope of regaining our heavenly state of perfection. Think how the Lanteans went from being godlike to technological beings in their history, from having innate spiritual power to dependence on machines. And in that process they became so out of balance that they threatened the rest of the world. We just nearly repeated that."

"I think I know where you're headed," Conyers said. "We are kind of like drug addicts. We had to hit the bottom of the barrel, face the scariest consequences of our technology, to pick ourselves up again."

"Exactly," the bishop said. "The story of life on earth is a process of falling from a higher existence to a low point from which our evolution back upward begins. Artalanta was that turning point. The wheat had to be separated from the chaff. Artalanta's two states of extreme beliefs could not endure. The Children of the One were doomed in Artalanta. They had one foot in this world and one foot in another. Well, either you must go to that other world or transform this one to survive. They had to separate from the Belials to become the seeds of a new chapter in human history."

"And with all of our own faults and steps backward, we have come to this high point of understanding that began so long ago with the First Souls," Conyers said. "Artalanta was like a Greek tragedy, wasn't it? A magnificent civilization blinded and brought down by its own flaws. Where will it end, Bishop?"

De Verneaux inhaled deeply and shrugged. "I can only tell you something Pope Valentinus—Petronien—once told me. He had a vision of the future. The knowledge and consciousness gifted to humanity through The Book of Remembrance, the Magdalene Gospels, and the life of Annalisa will transform minds and then bodies. Children will be born with superior abilities. Even their DNA will mutate. The godlike powers of spirit will reemerge but this time with a different intention.

"They will use their abilities to align with God, to help others, and not succumb to self-aggrandizement. It will renew the entire creation as barriers between this world and the worlds unseen vanish. People will interchangeably experience spiritual and bodily states without the errors that once clouded our soul-minds. The new generations will see clearly as the veils between the worlds dissolve. No longer will we dwell beneath the light of distant suns as the early lost souls lamented."

Goosebumps rose on the senator's arms. Exactly at that moment, the wind blew ripples across the water again. "My Lord," she said, pointing at the water, "that is the second time that happened precisely when we spoke about the creation."

De Verneaux smiled. "Maybe the other side has already begun to speak to you."

"Oh," Conyers said, "I would so love to think so." She looked to the sky with moist eyes. "Thank you, Amliea and Annalisa and all those who suffered to bring us to this moment."

The bishop said, "Gratitude goes a long way in heaven."

Conyers nodded. "I will admit, as I read the story, it brought me to tears, thinking of the incredible hardships and sacrifices those people endured to bring us to this very moment in history and give us chances they did not have. We cannot blow it. We are the inseparable products of their spirit. We owe it to them and to all the good souls who came and died before us to make this world better, and we can do it. Like the texts said, without our presence the universe itself would not exist. Ooh, I love that thought."

The bishop smiled. "If people like you from great countries feel that way then I think the world may just be on the road to its salvation."

"For now, my country can wait," the senator said. "I have taken the whole day off from the Senate to talk to you of heaven and earth and those that came before us."

And the two women walked away arm-in-arm under a sun that no longer seemed distant while cherry blossoms fell gently to the ground paving the path before them.

THE LIGHT OF DISTANT SUNS

THIS ENDS AND BEGINS

THE STORY OF THE FIRST SOULS

APPENDIX

GLOSSARY OF TERMS

Aeon(s) spiritual beings or centers of consciousness that are extensions of God or the One Source. In one sense they are vast currents of intelligent energy or dimensions in and of themselves. In a more traditional or orthodox sense, they may be thought of as Archangels. They are emanations **(see emanation)** or projections of God and may be pictured as concentric circles of consciousness radiating out from God's source. Each Aeonic consciousness is a singular being embodying both male and female energy polarities. So, for example, the Christ and Sophia are a paired Aeon, also said to be "consorts" of one another **(see consort)**. Though we personalize the Aeons with names, it helps to think of them as universal processes or archetypal ideals within the universal consciousness **(see archetypes).**

Ankatameso the conjunction of the three primary dimensions of existence—the spiritual, psychic, and material—to form Telian T'Meso. Its symbol was entwined serpents.

Apotheosis divinization, the awakened human being rising to the level of sharing the divine nature, the precursor to the **Prothes i' Aterisi.**

Archetypes all ideas and the physical objects created from ideas stem from archetypal images impressed on the human mind that come from higher dimensions like a master blueprint. Aeons are archetypes or energy patterns whose images can be represented in the material world as higher ideals. However, the lower dimensions were created by inferior consciousness symbolized by the Archontic forces (see Archon). The psychic and material words were created from imperfect or shadow copies of the higher dimensions. Therefore, archetypal images or ideas can derive from either the lower "shadow archetypes" or the higher archetypes of light.

Archon The force of ego and separation created by the collective, aberrant thoughts of souls separated from The One. It radiates from the psychic or soul dimension. It is the energetic expression of forces of lower consciousness derived from the fallen spirits. Having its origin in the flawed thought-forms of fallen souls, it is a lower form of existence possessed of soul **(psyche)** but not higher spirit (see the difference between **spirit and soul).** Its influence shaped and governed the psychic and material dimensions of existence. Though created by errant thought forms of the souls, it became an externalized force, a god worshipped by some of them. Its force is powerful and it warped the shape of the material cosmos, but it is not possessed of eternal life for its existence is tied to the impermanent psychic and material realms.

Children of the Law of One those people who retained an awareness of their spiritual source and the hidden dimensions from which human life on earth descended. They saw humanity as a connected unity and tried to practice that principle in their relations with one another.

Consciousness a.) in a practical sense is directed intelligence displaying intention and purpose. In simpler terms it can be thought of as awareness though awareness may be present in varying degrees such as with the conscious, the subconscious, or even the unconscious. The difference between these levels is the ability to bring the contents of each into focus is such a way as to utilize the information in an intentional manner. What you are *un*-conscious of controls you, often with undesirable results, but if you can bring the contents of the mind to conscious awareness, you can utilize and control them according to your intention. **b.)** In a cosmic sense Consciousness (Capitalized) constitutes the universal substance or vibration that divided Itself into what we call dimensions, planes, or parallel universes. Each dimension is an energetic thought-form or vibration of the One Mind. The easiest way to grasp this is a spatial analogy. If the Source represents the highest level of consciousness or vibration, then the planes or dimensions are defined by the degree to which they are removed from the Source. The higher the dimension, the closer it is to the consciousness of the Source; the lower the dimension the farther it is from the consciousness of the Source. Another way of stating this is that the Source allows Itself to become more ignorant (see ignorance) and forgetful of Itself as it projects Its consciousness downward in Its creation of new dimensions. Degrees of consciousness create the multiplicity and distinctions between physical and non-physical beings and the dimensions in which they dwell.

Demiurge (see Archon)

Dimensions (planes of existence, parallel universes, spiritual realms) are actually defined by the levels of consciousness of the beings that reside in them. **(see consciousness)** They each have distinct vibrational signatures of conscious energy. Many planes exist in creation but for simplification, three major dimensions are identified — spiritual (heaven), soul (psychic), and material (human).

Drones "things"or automatons who were the soulless mind-projections of ego-tainted souls **(see soul materializations)**. They were dull-witted and could be of varied humanoid forms. They were used for labor and sometimes sex. Their intelligence level could be raised over generations by various means such as interaction with humans, evolution, or genetic manipulation.

Emanation is the process of God projecting Its own conscious substance into new forms of conscious existence as opposed to making separate creations different from Itself out of nothing (*ex nihilo*). Emanationism typically holds that these projections or spiritual beings (called *Aeons*) occur in pairs representing the masculine/feminine, yin/yang duality experienced in the material world. Each Aeon emanates another Aeon like descending rungs of a ladder. With each emanation, however, some of God's original light or awareness is lost. This is because God is the Whole or the Source. Since each successive Aeon is projected further from God, the degree of shadow or ignorance it contains increases with each emanation. Restated, the further the emanated being is from God, the more it experiences ignorance of God and a greater sense of separateness. The human soul is the lowest manifestation of this emanated spiritual force or process because it is mixed with the material world in the form of a fleshly human.

Fall, The a.) generally, the Fall refers to the descent of spiritual consciousness to lower forms of psychic and material consciousness. The converse of this is a forgetting of one's unity with God as a spiritual being in favor of believing in a separate existence as a material being. **b.)** specifically the Fall refers to the descent of Sophia, the feminine face of God's Holy Wisdom, into the realm of chaos, an act that engendered a chain reaction of events that culminated in the material world of space and time.

Genitas the DNA code. **Genera** are the individual gene components of the genitas.

God (The One, The Source, The One Mind) a.) the Supreme being, Source of all things, beyond space and time, indescribable, the one and only energy and substance that assumes multiple forms by projecting Its essence out into differing levels of consciousness; also called the Monad, the One True God, and the First Thought. God has both a hidden, unknowable aspect and a manifest aspect with which souls may unite in **apotheosis**. No flaw or imperfection exists at the Source although levels of imperfection arise at the furthest levels of creation away from the Source. The lowest levels of consciousness could not be contained in the higher dimensions and were therefore expelled into space, time, and materiality where they could not taint the higher consciousness. Imperfection is rampant in the lower dimensions, and extreme separation from or ignorance of the Source leads to what is termed evil in the lower realms of consciousness. **b.)** the Demiurge, the creative force/shaper of the material world is also called the god of this world by the Belials. The differing views of God can be accounted for by realizing that people were describing or worshiping the creative forces at different levels of operation. The True God is a pure consciousness beyond space-time; the inferior god is limited consciousness operating within psychic-space.

Heaven (see Pleroma)

Ignorance (also forgetfulness) is the condition, to one degree or another, of all dimensions of existence below God. It speaks to the paradox of how God as the Whole or the Single Consciousness can create the appearance of individual consciousness "apart" from Itself. Only by limiting Itself in a process similar to amnesia can the Whole distinguish portions of Itself that feel themselves to be separate. Illusion and ignorance of the Whole is the price paid for individual identity. Enlightenment is realizing one's individuality but also knowing one is of God. **(Also see Consciousness and Emanation.)**

Knowledge in the intellectual sense means the accumulation of facts or awareness of subjects. In the spiritual sense, it means knowing a thing from direct experience, such as direct contact with the divine as opposed to faith or belief in the divine based on scripture or from being told by others.

Nois Regar the group "mindlock" of the Elda-Fera, a kind of mind-conjoining process for deep divination.

Pleroma from the Greek word meaning "Fullness." The Pleroma is the totality of the immortal Aeons, spiritual beings, in the planes surrounding the Source or God. It is an infinite realm of perfect light and pure energy distinct from the lower mortal levels of the material which are finite and subject to space-time. It corresponds to the orthodox Judeo-Christian notion of heaven.

Progeneration a means by which souls were birthed into new bodies by the internal action of beings of the androgynous root races. It was an internally projected rather than a physical act different from drone projection as it was done in accordance with the Law of The One by those who had come to the material plane with proper intentions. The drones were mind-projections of souls who had themselves pushed into their own thought-form projections. They were tainted by their own intent borne of egoic animal consciousness. Only The One could create souls. The tainted souls could only create animated life forms.

Prothes i' Aterisi the "Summation of Purpose." The state where souls can possess incorporeal divine consciousness of the higher planes while still in the corporeal body.

Root-Races the various forms and genotypes incarnating souls assumed over different ages of earth experience. See the **Historica** from **The Book of Remembrance** for a description of root-races.

Simulation, The the false perception of the human mind or psyche that causes the human soul to believe it belongs in the natural, material world. An independent material reality did exist. Souls, in their desire to exert their God-given powers of free will, used their divine power not only to influence and warp the material creation, but to project their essence within it. As an analogy, the soul would be like a holographic projectionist who comes to identify his projections as reality, forgetting that he is the actual projector of the images. His simulated reality is, therefore, an illusion or, more accurately, a delusion of the soul mind. This collective delusion gave rise to the **Archon** force at an unconscious level, the ego force that falsely believes it is the true Creator of All and perpetuates the souls' entrapment in the material plane through the cycle of rebirth. A soul must have enlightened contact with higher consciousness to break the barrier of illusion and transcend the force of the simulation to regain its former divine state (see **Apotheosis**).

Sons of Belial originally, followers of a charismatic demagogue, later the people who rejected any notion of The One and who worshipped a hedonistic, nihilistic, and even anarchic force of nature symbolized by the Archon.

Sophia is the central figure of many mystical traditions called by many different names in many different cultures or religions. Sophia means wisdom in Greek. Called Holy Wisdom, the Wisdom of God, the Holy Spirit, Achamoth, Shekinah, the Earth Mother and many other names, Sophia is present in the Bible under the name of God's wisdom. She plays a central role in the creation of the material world in the Kabbalistic and Gnostic mystical traditions.

To simplify, Sophia in her various incarnations may be thought of as the feminine aspect of God that seeks wisdom through experience. She also imparts that knowledge gained through experience. The role of Sophia and the creation in divine literature may be seen through two polar lenses. She is reviled by some for breaking the unity of heaven in a colossal "mistake" leading to the formation of the material world and the misery of the souls trapped in bodily form.

She is called the whore, the imprudent, and the rash one, akin to Eve falling from grace by eating the apple. On the other hand, she is revered as the mother who expanded the divine plan for life in new psychic and material dimensions, its purpose being to gain knowledge of material experience, a different state than the spiritual. She is the catalyst who unites heaven to earth by awakening the human soul to **apotheosis** with knowledge about the illusions of material existence, dispelling evil and the limitations imposed on humanity by the forces of **opposition (see the Demiurge and the Archons).**

Soul Materializations incoming souls from the invisible realms assumed material forms in a number of ways. **a.)** merging with animal life as a form of possession **b.)** gradual accumulation of mass from an ethereal state by long proximity to the earth plane **c.)** projecting a thought-form then pushing one's soul essence into it **d.)** by progeneration **e.)** by birth from physical conception. Drones could be materialized by mind-projection in early root races but this was not soul materialization for drones had no souls.

Spirit and Soul spirit is a fundamental and universal state of being whereas soul is a particular state of spirit exercising individuality. Spirit is unchanging whereas soul is developmental, seeking experience in the realms of mind and body. Spirit is impersonal whereas soul is personal. Spirit is focused on God, soul is focused on expressing individuality. Soul exerts free will; spirit does not. It is said by some traditions that each soul is the fallen part of a spirit. They are connected links in a chain spanning parallel dimensions of consciousness. Spirit never descended into materiality; soul did. Spirit is a single focus. Soul has dual aspects—the spirit itself which bears knowledge of its identity with God, and the soul which bears knowledge of everything it experiences as an individual. Sophia is the First Soul because she was the first to exert her free will and individuality by descending into chaos, the world of potential experience.

Telian T'Meso (*Tell*-ee-ahn-Tah-*May*-so) the "place in the middle," a sub-plane of the psychic, the mental plane closest to the material dimension from which souls projected their consciousness into material forms.

Touai Stone (*Too*-eye) the Great Crystal of Artalanta also called the Firestone, particularly by the Belials. It was the heart of Artalanta able to capture rays of the sun and other cosmic radiation transformed for myriad uses, both physical and spiritual. As Lanteans lost the innate connection to the invisible worlds, the Touai Stone became their means to remain connected to its guidance.

Tyer Angarach (Teer-*An*-gahr-ach as in German ach) "the Twilight of the Gods," of the "Time of Sorrows," the prophecy of the final destruction of Artalanta mistakenly believed by some to portend the end of the world. In fact, it was a cleansing of the evil excesses of Artalanta that threatened the rest of life on earth, the end of Artalanta so a new order could begin.

Wave carrier, Wave carrying Lantean equivalent of wireless radio communication.

EXCERPTS FROM THE ESOTERICA,
CHRONOLIGICA, AND HISTORICA

of

THE BOOK OF
REMEMBRANCE

We write not for glory but remembrance, for there is no glory in what we man has done, but only in what he may become. Knowledge in man leads to remembrance of spirit, and remembrance of spirit leads to knowledge of the Whole. It is through knowledge and remembrance that humans may unravel the web of illusions that keep them bound to the earth.

The worlds have changed. We dreamed ourselves into this earth, yet now are lost within our dream. Fewer are those Sons of Light who still between the realms transverse. Greater are the Sons of Darkness grown solid and fixed in fleshly form. Farther is the gulf between them, rent by things once unthinkable in the mind of spirit — greed, lust, envy, and pride. Contamination residing in flesh has created these things unforeseen, alien things intruding on once pure minds where no such energies hath entered before.

And now this land does break apart, torn by misused crystal energies perverted to devices channeled for dominion and mastery! O spirit, how far have you fallen that you do war against yourself? And like a plague this hardness spreads that causes souls in-body to forget. We who shall depart this high sphere to be fixed in the mud of earth, forgotten of our true selves, we who are doomed to return until our bondage is released in the wheel of time, we see which way creation turns. We now commit to physical record the truth of what has here transpired for generations to come. And when this world's deceptions become complete and souls are trapped in mortal coils forgotten of their immortal state, this text shall cry aloud — you are not flesh, O Sons of Light. Turn your faces back to your home on high!

Sing, O Beings of Light, echoes of your lost home. Sun behind the sun, star behind the stars, we sing in remembrance of your glory. Hearken now to the fall of the First Souls, and see what great fate our actions did bind upon those who walk the earth. Listen, O Beings of Light, and hear of how we came to be, listen, and hear of your redemption by the blood of fallen angels ...

THE ESOTERICA

IN THE BEGINNING

In the beginning, before time began, before the Creation, was an ocean of Spirit, and it filled all mind-space for, physical space did not yet exist. It was passive yet self-aware. It was the First Cause, reflecting on Itself, contemplating that which it was. If you would understand the Mind of The One, know your own mind for Its mind is like yours but It is universal. What humans call the creation is purely a vision, a thought-form of The One Mind, and thought is the eternal energy through which that Mind expresses.

THE MANIFESTATION

The One Spirit is silent, deep, and still. It is that it is. It is Substance, the substance of all. It is hidden, mysterious, and unknowable but to Itself. It is the passive female aspect that produces. The One Spirit is also Mind, the active male aspect that moves and considers. Mind moved upon Its Substance fertilizing it with a thought or vision and from this did It birth and manifest new spirits. Now there came into being two eternal expressions of being — the Whole, the ground state of *I Am*, and that which was *projected from the essence* of Whole, the emanated spirits, the created state of *I Am Becoming*. The Whole was static, unchanging, and unmanifest; the spirits were dynamic, expressing and manifest. This process was passive Spirit manifesting Itself in action as The Godhead.

AWAKENING OF THE SPIRITS

Into the Sphere of Becoming, new points of spirit consciousness were projected by The One. They were called *Aeons* or eternities. Each

Aeon was a unity of male-female dualities, an androgynous entity with two aspects. And why did they come into being? The One desired a community of spirits as companions in a great creation. Only by contrast with and through the reflection of other minds in action could the passive, all-encompassing One evolve and have the experience of knowing Itself in creative new frontiers of dynamic experience. To fulfill the role of being independent companions, the spirits or Aeons possessed the gifts of *individuality and free will* from the Whole, for without these attributes they would not be *distinct* from the Whole.

THE PRINCIPLE OF OPPOSITION

But inherent within this freedom of the Aeonic spirits, at the very inception of creation, lay the counter-principle, the force of opposition. *It was the potential to misuse free will by placing a spirit's own individual desires above and separate from the Will of The One.* This force in potential is called *Authades*, the "self-willed" or "pleaser of itself." It is the force that compels an entity to regard nothing but itself, the potential of spirit to separate itself from the One by placing its own will above the Will of the Whole. It was the inevitable temptation or danger that had to exist for the spirits to possess individuality, of which free will is the essence.

At first the spirits resided in quiet contemplation, content to observe the beauty of the spiritual creation unfolding from the Mind of The One. Their unlimited freedom to do as they desired was balanced by controlling their separate impulses in order to live harmoniously with other spirits and their Source. Chaos, suffering, and separation would result in the failure to do so. But upon a time, Authades, the force of opposition, lured one high Aeon astray, and this would alter the entire course of creation.

CREATION OF THE SPIRITUAL UNIVERSE

Now, the binding force of Heaven was a divine vibration like unto what men call music, an eternal symphony of the cosmos, each note expressed by the chorus of the Aeons to execute the glory of The One's Vision. In glorifying The One, they glorified themselves and their part of the plan. The One's Grand Theme was the Great Creation of a universe that might form and evolve from the intention of The One. The spirits could create their own harmonious vibrations in relation to the main melody and so contribute to and enhance the One's plan for the developing universe.

From the playing of this celestial sound, a vast energy arose in Heaven. It played and formed, and rose and played again in a spiraling musical crescendo of celestial vibration. Each and every Aeon bore down to the depths of their creative power like so many streams falling together into one Great Ocean of stars, suns, and planets.

So the first spark of the spiritual universe ignited. Its energetic form expanded outward with invisible heat and fire, not yet a physical creation but a thought image in the Mind of The One. The celestial song wrought its order and form. After the Theme had played, after the vibration had expended, all grew calm and Heaven rested. The Aeons now looked out upon the former Void and saw what their Great Theme had fashioned, for the vibration of their music had slowed. The creation was not yet material, but it was the vibrational form of a world and the universe to come. And in this creation was planted the image of Adam Kadmon, the image of primordial man. The spirits gazed upon it in wonder for this being was destined to be the bridge between spirit and the newly evolving world.

The Aeons witnessed in fascination the coalescing balls of dust and light glowing like lamps in the dark reaches of the creation, for some of each spirit's essence was projected into it and they took delight as it grew and progressed. Some could see their vibrations in the forming templates of the oceans, some in the stars, others in the firmament or in the plants and trees. Still, others took delight in the complex image-forms of organisms and animals. For ages beyond reckoning, the Aeons looked upon this spiritual earth and saw it was good, and upon a time they resumed the celestial chorus to help evolve the plan.

THE FALL OF THE AEON SOPHIA

The Aeon Sophia was the principle of wisdom, and above all others she sought to know The One by gaining knowledge of The One's ways. Now in the totality, there was The One's dwelling place, the unknowable *State of the Whole,* and the manifested *State of Becoming,* the abode of the individual spirits and Aeons. Together they were the fullness, the Pleroma, what men would come to call heaven. Outside this was the void called Chaos, that part of The One's mind-sphere left unconscious to be the unformed realm of mysteries unfolding, potential things to come, or the chance of things that could possibly be.

Now the Aeons always acted as male-female pairs when they generated new creations according to the natural laws affected by The One. But the deviant thought that entered Sophia's mind was that she could enter chaos by herself and create something entirely on her own without the balance of her male counterpart, Amilius. Authades, the force of opposition, had lured Sophia with the thought that she alone could know The Unknowable One by acting as The One acts, by creating as The One creates.

And so Authades did cause Sophia to focus her attention on Chaos, the unformed realm of potential, and she came to believe her desire for unilateral creation in the manner of The One could be achieved in this area yet untouched by The One's Mind.

It was so among the Aeons that they were grouped in like kind bound by affinity of vibration, much as where instruments of like kind such as strings, or horns, or drums will cluster together to harmonize and amplify their particular sound. Whereas Sophia embodied wisdom, in her grouping were Justice, Witness, Perseverance, Faith, and Amilius. In Justice burned the desire for balance and in Witness the desire to trumpet The One's light. Faith trusted the process of the universe. Perseverance was steadfast to The One's will and Amilius desired to spread the conscious love of The One to every corner of Creation. But the force of Authades did impel Sophia to pursue a different course. Sophia commenced a contretemps, a new chord or different vibrational direction. It was discordant; it warped the celestial music into a cacophony.

S ophia came to the others and said, "Hearken, for I have conceived myself a plan. Look upon the projected worlds and see the wonder —the fires, the winds, the dust, the rocks, and the waters of this emerging cosmos. I would project my essence into unformed Chaos from whence this all came and form a new theme for this." Now Sophia's grouping was disturbed by her thoughts. Amilius especially perceived the effect these things would wreak upon the heavenly dimensions, and he took counsel within himself. "Such may be your desire," he said to Sophia, "yet your actions will have great consequence. They will divide the higher dimensions and alter the course intended by the Will of The One."

A nd to this Sophia replied, "We ourselves are of The One's substance. We can never be lost in The One's sight." Amilius replied, "*The One cannot lose sight of us, but we can lose sight of The One—beware!*" But Sophia ignored the warnings of Amilius and others. Driven by the impulses of Authades, she now listened but to thoughts of her own.

H ear now, O Beings of Light, of the First Fall from Heaven! From the beginning, The One's Will directed Creation and the Aeons were as helpers in that directing. Even as men will build devices to control the flow of a river, so did The One control the river of Creation with Its devices, the Aeons. But Sophia was no longer content to direct the flow, *she wanted to become the flow*, Sophia *would immerse itself in the river*. No longer directing the flow, Sophia would be carried along by it whither it would go.

Despite the warnings of Amilius, the wildness of heeding her own will was fast upon Sophia. She began to project her thought into the dark reaches of the Void. No longer content to *express through* the vision of creation; she desired *to feel, to identify, to modify* the new creation. Upon a time she plunged her entire divine essence into the chaos of possibilities. In doing this she acted apart; she projected a consciousness different from the consciousness of heaven, for Sophia emphasized her individual consciousness and will over her consciousness as part of The One. Her actions became the First Fall hinted in the echoes of human memory. The balance between individuality and the Will of The One was disrupted.

APPEARANCE OF THE SOUL, THE CREATION MATTER

Authades trapped Sophia into lower consciousness to gain the illusion of a new creation, and a new limited dimension of mind appeared — the psychic dimension of soul. A thing unforeseen then occurred. Unformed chaos reacted to the divine energy force of Sophia's presence, for chaos was not empty. Seeds of potential lay dormant within its shadowy recesses. These elements of proto-matter did swarm to Sophia, surrounding her like locusts engulfing fields of wheat. And Sophia's high energy was not idle upon them.

The mingling of her life force activated the proto-matter and spawned the beginning of new things both material and energetic. These were physical matter and a new dimension of mind, the psychic dimension. *In the instant Sophia broke from The One's plan and entered chaos, she became the First Soul.* Soul vibration differs from spirit vibration. Spirit flows with The Whole, soul lowers its vibration for individual development independent of the Whole. This new focus of mind engendered a different state of mind vibration, a new mental dimension, and so each spirit who fell in Sophia's wake became part of this vibration, a soul in the psychic dimension of soul mind.

ORIGIN OF THE DEMIURGIC ARCHON

From the emerging psychic dimension, Sophia tried to project a new being to help order the newly formed invisible matter or dark matter just as The One had emanated her and the other Aeons to assist in ordering the invisible creation from the spirit realm. But since she acted on her own without her male half, the thing she produced was an imperfect abortion. This being became the manifested expression of Authades. It was the Demiurge, the Archon, and it would be called many names in many ages—Yaldabaoth, Saklas, Sammael. It was a being of power, but of diluted power and limited consciousness, ignorant of the greater powers in the planes above it. It manifested as the principle of opposition in the psychic and material dimensions. It took the invisible matter around it, lowered its vibration and began to fashion the physical cosmos, for in its blindness it dimly perceived The One's perfect image of a spiritual universe. Upon this image, it formed the flawed cosmos of matter in mimicry. It is this Archon, this creator being of lower consciousness that deceived many men into worshiping it as the One True God, called the god of this world.

The creation of matter and the appearance of the Demiurge caused a great disturbance in the higher planes, for spirit energy and matter may not coexist in the same dimension. The psychic and material planes along with the Demiurge and his creation were expelled in a great explosive upheaval and propelled into space and time. A boundary would separate them from the higher planes of spirit. Sophia and her soul grouping became the First Souls to fall, and other spirits who followed them from the perfect realms became trapped in the psychic or soul mind dimension. They became prisoners of their own erroneous thought-forms of individuality.

They soon realized their mistake, but now they had to face the Demiurge, the personification of their errors, and overcome the power of his works to regain their place in the Fullness of the heavenly Pleroma, for now *three dimensions came to exist*—the divine plane of spirit, the psychic plane of soul, and the physical plane of matter. The

Archon did influence the fallen souls with negative thoughts of fear, anger, and jealousy to keep them trapped in the psychic dimension, for he feeds off these impulses. Thus, the psychic realm became a place of contention between light and shadow.

THE SECOND FALL

The great fear of the demiurgic Archon was that the souls trapped in the psychic realm would awaken and throw off their illusions as separate creators. If this happened, his power would dissolve along with the deranged souls' illusions of any dimensions existing apart from the Whole. He, therefore, devised a plan to drive souls further from their Source and maintain his hold in the psychic dimension. He influenced souls to focus their attention upon the material world and the forming earth. Being the emanation of Authades in the lower dimensions, the Archon pushed the souls into a second fall just as Authades had seduced Sophia. If the souls became entangled and further distanced from The One in the lower depths of matter, it would bolster his power and assure his dominion in the psychic plane. He succeeded, and the souls did begin to project themselves in and out of the new earthly material life forms.

DESCENT OF THE SOULS, THE ROOT RACES

This is the record of the souls' involvement in the earth plane. The fall of souls into materiality, the second fall of consciousness, came in waves and did produce a chaotic series of forms both ethereal and physical.

Playing at creation, how seductive, how impelling! Projecting their consciousness into physical forms, spirits *tasting* the fruit of trees, *feeling* the warmth of the sun on skin, *touching* flesh upon flesh! At first, the wandering souls were able to come and go at their desire, but over time, as their awareness of being part of The One faded, they became trapped in the consciousness of their experience, trapped in the material forms they occupied. Life was rampant but chaotic.

The First Root-Race— the first involvement of souls into the earth plane were as exploratory thought-forms probing the oddity of a coalescing dimension of matter. These were transparent, ghostlike projections as fleshly men would call them.

The Second Root-Race—many in the next wave of souls mindlessly rushed into physical experience with the selfish intention of gratifying the senses, not obeying divine law. In the earliest days some entered and exited animal bodies, but many of them lingered to possess these forms and so became trapped within them. Others projected new thought-forms into which they pushed their consciousness but they had already been polluted by contact with animal consciousness. This activity produced hybrid monstrosities, part humanoid, part beast, creatures of legend with all manner of animal appendages. But other souls of this grouping maintained purer celestial energies as humanoid forms.

These early bodies in Mu with human-like form were more comparable to focused fields of energy, light, and thought rather than flesh and bone. From thought-forms these beings moved closer to materialization by becoming dynamic matter. Their forms were like fields of contained electricity. The materiality of these second root race godlings' bodies was not hardened or fixed. With concentration, they could occupy a specific space, act, converse, and then disappear completely into formlessness during the early periods when their energies were still connected to higher consciousness. As the godlings lingered longer in the material dimension, their bodies became more structured and defined as their minds gradually lost a sense of the formless reality. What was originally an idea, a thought-form, was crystallizing into matter with full consciousness of the souls within.

The Third Root-Race—this influx of souls came into the earth sphere in Artalanta aligned with The One under the guidance of Amilius and the First Souls. The Celestial third race entered through channels sanctioned by The One, not by desire, lust, or things that separated them from the Divine Will. They had the higher intentions of rescuing the souls previously lost in materiality. The bodies they projected were well formed, humanoid, and androgynous. They possessed a third eye, and at first they were lighter physical forms of spiritualized flesh, not a denser accumulation of atoms as later solidified bodies. While androgynous, they could bring new souls into incarnation through progeneration, the formation of soul-receptive bodies from within themselves. The previous races looked upon them as gods. Over time, they divided their androgynous male and female aspects into separate entities, first as thought-forms then as separate male and female humanoid bodies. This took place under Amilius (the Logos) with the consent of The One. Procreation, even though with divided sexes, was not physical at first but rather achieved in subtle bodies. Only the Belials, the souls who had become terrestrial, and the souls fallen into animal forms physically copulated.

Early on the third race possessed the godlike power to project new thought-forms. But unlike new souls incarnated through progeneration, these materialized mental projections were soulless, for only The One can project souls through other souls by proper channels. As some of the godlings began to forget their spiritual origins and became corrupted by the increasing consciousness of materiality, they began to mind-project beings as sex objects. These beings were near mindless automatons used as servant labor as in years to come men will use machines for such purposes. So it was that over time, many of the third race misused their powers. They increasingly became infected by material ego-consciousness as they accumulated mass and became more physical. They became the Sons of Darkness or later the Sons of Belial after their leader. Those who kept the divine consciousness alive within were the Sons of Light or the Children of the Law of One.

SONS OF GOD AND DAUGHTERS OF MEN

Now three classes of beings existed at this time. The terrestrial souls, or Daughters of Men, who had pushed their way into matter to gratify their urges, thinking only of their own desires, using animal forms and later humanoid male and female forms to procreate in the manner of animals.

The Celestial souls, or Sons of God, who had come into the Earth with high intentions to help earthbound souls and maintain a connection with the higher realms by creating new forms to bring like-minded souls into materiality.

The soulless, thought-projected things or automatons mind-created by the godlings first as servants then as sex objects.

The Terrestrials or Daughters of Men were all those of the first or second root races that had fallen into hardened material forms forgetting their divine origins. The Sons of God were the Celestials of the third root-race who maintained lighter semi-physical bodies and a conscious connection to their Source. Over time even the Sons of God became dense and more corrupted by materiality. Jealousies and hierarchies grew among them. Finally, some began to take the Daughters of Men, finding them fair, and began to copulate with them in the animal manner. The offspring of these unions were the Naphaalim giants and other mutations that taxed the earth. This age saw the appearance of family as opposed to community units and began the usage of the Touai Crystal to communicate with the Source as the innate soul abilities to do so were lost.

The problem posed for all spirits in the material plane was that godling minds were molding to fit the demands of the five senses and the physical world, not the other way around. A three-fold level of mind developed among the earthbound souls. A conscious ego-mind formed, driven by material self-preservation needs. It became primary over the soul mind, which then became the subconscious, and the higher spirit mind, which became the unconscious. This physical consciousness was yet another step removed in awareness of the Source, a lower vibration of mind than the psychic plane of soul and the highest plane of Spirit.

Seeing the plight of their kindred spirits, Amilius and the First Souls were moved to pity and action. With the Will of the One behind him, Amilius devised a plan. It became apparent to the First Souls that their incarnation to save the initial wave of souls had failed as the third race too began to succumb to the denseness of the material world. The flow of life had been reversed. A danger existed that the souls might permanently be lost in their dream states. Amilius, Sophia's male half, was anointed by The One to lead the creation of a new race, a new body type drawn from both spirit and earth.

This form would be more capable of holding the divine inner spark that would eventually allow spirit consciousness to reemerge and achieve the *Prothes i' Aterisi*, the *Summation of Purpose*. In this state, souls can possess incorporeal divine consciousness of the higher planes while still in the corporeal body. This would be The One's kingdom come to earth, the fulfillment of the humanity's hidden purpose to be the fingers of God touching the face of the earth spiritualizing the material and bringing the experience of the material back to Spirit.

The Fourth Root-Race—A species of hominid had long existed on earth. The First Souls selected this primate but did not possess it to repeat the mistakes of earlier root races. Instead, while still in etheric form from the mental plane, the *Telian T' Meso*, they hovered about this primate. They influenced its evolution, modifying it over thousands of years. When it was ready, they had souls reincarnate into it through seven glandular centers, which corresponded to the seven energy centers of their ethereal forms. This was the Adamic race. It appeared in five areas of the world at once as the different races of man, but it was the red race of Artalanta birthed in Eden on Poseidia that this new human advanced most rapidly. Gone were many of the godlike powers of the previous race that were misused to the great detriment of the world. No longer could embodied souls intoxicate themselves with abilities that only served to drive them further into their illusions and away from The One of whom many of them had forgotten.

The First Souls assumed Adamic forms of spiritual flesh remaining pure in etheric light bodies as they helped souls reincarnate into the new physical forms. It was only after the second catastrophe that they committed to make the great sacrifice to lay down their divine connection and become physical flesh, for only by becoming part of the lost ones could they become the examples, the pattern of the way out. They knew their divine origins would grow dim with forgetfulness, but Amilius said to Sophia and the others, "We may now only free the souls through the wheel of birth and death. We must incarnate and toil through this cycle. Within this fate, we must set a pattern for the others to escape the prison of materiality." The First Souls submitted themselves to becoming lost in the suffering of the terrestrial souls with only the spark of their will and consciousness to one day reawaken them to their higher state, "But this I, at least, must do," Sophia said, "for the burden and doom of the souls lies most heavily upon me who led the Fall from heaven to the lower realms."

And so Amilius led another wave of spirits into the earth plane, including Sophia and their spirit grouping—Justice, Witness, Faith, and Perseverance—to be a beacon calling the lost souls out of their current forms and into bodily vehicles more suited to recapture their divine consciousness.

For many years the Lanteans experienced peace, growth, and prosperity, but they were not immune to the legacy and challenges of the world that had preceded them. The principle of opposition embodied in the Sons of Belial ever existed. For a time after the appearance of the Adama they were subdued, in part by the creation of the new race, in part from the trauma of previous catastrophes. But over time they reemerged to challenge the Children of the One with the mentality that had tainted souls from the beginning. And so the struggle between Light and Darkness resumed in new form to inflict its disaster upon the world. Of this, the story is told in the Historica.

*So ends the holy esoterica arcana
of the Book of Remembrance.
Let our souls be revealed and not forgotten.
Glory be to The One and all that walk in Its Light.*

THE CHRONOLOGIA

*counted in rotations of the sun as humans came
to measure the ages from the time when
Amilius shall reawaken as Christos, the anointed one.*

12,000,000—**First root-race**, soul expressed as incorporeal thought-form projections about the land of Mu. Soul possession of animals, pollution of soul consciousness, hybrid monstrosities of legend.

10,500,000—Council of the souls led by the First Souls of the Amilius/Sophia grouping to discuss the problem of soul involvement in matter.

10,000,000—**Second root-race**, solidified thought form bodies developed in Mu into which souls projected, often polluted by contact with animal consciousness.

1,000,000-800,000—early humanoid development in Mu, second root race light bodies densify, animal mixtures still present.

500,000—Mu inundated by water, life forms scattered.

400,000-300,000—Mu reinhabited, advances to primitive state.

250,000—Second catastrophe in Mu by fire.

210,000—The Children of One and the Children of Darkness both incarnate in second root race androgynous, bodies having both sexes in one, but the feminine dominates this age. Early Lantean culture emerges from souls as spiritual thought-form projections entering into humanoid forms becoming ever denser.

106,000—**Third root-race**, souls, first as thought-forms then as bodies with a third eye, began to separate into male and female humanoids under Amilius (the Logos) with the consent of The One. Soulless, thought projected things or automatons mind-created by the godlings first as servants then as sex objects. Sons of God became dense and more corrupted by materiality take the Daughters of Men. The offspring were the Naphaalim giants and other mutations that taxed the earth. The appearance of family as opposed to community units. Beginning of the usage of the Touai Crystal to communicate with the Source as the innate abilities to do so After reform of the military, were lost.

70,000 — Fourth root-race (Adamic), was the first race evolved from both earth and spirit. Adamic humans appear simultaneously in five places on earth as five races, the most advanced was the red race of Artalanta. Godlike powers largely vanished along with the abuses that came with it. The chaotic mixing of root races ends with most souls incarnating in this new body form. Usage of sub-crystals to power mechanical devices.

55,000 — Male age arises. Ascent of warrior culture, Belials, and Emperor Esai. Crystals first used as weapons. Human sacrifice instituted.

50,000 — Final submergence of Mu.

50,722 — The date of the Great Congress regarding the animal incursions. First Lantean destruction.

28,000-22,006 — Second Lantean destruction. Artalanta becomes 5 islands.

10,700 — Final destruction and sinking of Artalanta. Lantean diaspora.

10,390 — Completion of The Great Pyramid in Egypt by the priests Ra-Ta and Hermes using Lantean technology.

THE HISTORICA

THE FIRST EPOCH

In the younger days of Artalanta, when the remembrance of The One and the higher dimensions was yet fresh and strong, the first people were a god-like androgynous race. They possessed a third eye, which connected them with spirit and each other. They built a great civilization. They had little need for technology. Their semi-physical bodies defied gravity, traversing the skies swifter than eagles in flight. The soul-occupied humanoids used their skills to extract fellow spirits trapped in the monstrous forms. They used rays of light and invisible energies for healing. It was the age of magic and the roots of all legends stem from that time. The beings of this new soul-in-flesh race did not die. They were able to project themselves in and out of the human animal bodies at will. The humanoid body in those days lived to great years as humans would later number their days. When the humanoid shell was near to its end they would withdraw and project into a new body.

When Artalanta was still a single landmass, it had ten provinces with ten kings. Over time their connections to the soul and spirit realms waned. Greed, deception, and self-interest seeped into the consciousness of the godlike early Lanteans. Their bodies began to lose their finer etheric quality and become more solid. Two of the ten kings who retained their connection to The One waged a great war with the other kings. Victorious, they established the Law of The One under the guidance of Amilius and consolidated rule under a single emperor but not before a large portion of the continent was destroyed

The Great Crystal, called the *Touai Stone* or White Stone but in later, darker times the Firestone, was discovered during this epoch. This Crystal could concentrate the rays of the sun and other cosmic energies as well as maintain energetic connections to the higher realms of consciousness. A priesthood developed that could focus on the stone's powers and receive higher guidance. As the ability to project out physical forms and into new ones waned, the Crystal's rays were used to rejuvenate flesh for long life spans. Toward the end of this epoch as technology replaced innate soul abilities, the Touai Stone became the source that powered Lantean civilization. A way was found to project its energies to sub-crystals that operated aircraft, watercraft, communication devices and many other things.

THE SECOND EPOCH

After a period of internal peace following the wars of the First Epoch, the divisions between the Lanteans resurfaced. Over the ages the rule established by Amilius and the First Souls was eroded by more belligerent people. At some point between the First and Second Epochs, the Lanteans began mind-projecting drones for labor, an act that would have far-reaching consequences. Trade interaction with other lands grew more into relations of conquerors to conquered. Power became more centralized into the hands of the emperor as the old kingdoms were absorbed becoming provinces with governors. In this epoch selfish and aggressive forces eventually crystallized in the ruthless but charismatic person of Belial. His many followers opposed the Children of the One. The priesthood during this era became divided. The scientific among them had largely harnessed the Crystal's energy to power Artalanta's mechanical devices ages ago. They became the Tekna-Fera. The more spiritually inclined remained the Elda-Fera.

An emperor did arise by the name of Esai during a time when large beasts were making incursions into the land. These depredations were severe and they threatened the civilization the Lanteans had built. Aerial explosives had not sufficiently curbed them. The Belials, who eschewed the spiritual teachings of The One and adopted a materialistic view of the world, pressured Esai to weaponize the Crystal and use its power to eradicate the threat. They were backed by the Techna-Fera, but the Elda-Fera cautioned that this act would lead to disaster. The Belials used the threat as a pretext to gain control of the Touai Stone.

Their real goal was to take over the government and use the Crystal as a weapon of war to further the conquest of other lands. Belial had seduced the Princess Asme. She gained her father's proxy after coercing the Elda-Fera priest Asel-Sine to falsely claim the Touai Stone could safely be calibrated as a weapon.

Esai acquiesced to the Belials and ordered the Touai Stone to be used against the beasts. They focused the rays into the subterranean caverns where the animals lurked, but they went too deep with too much power. They disrupted the earth's core beneath their continent. Over a short span of time, massive earthquakes and volcanic eruptions broke the continent into five separate islands. The princesses Ouen and Mele who steadfastly adhered to the Law of One escaped the disaster while their sister Asme and Belial perished.

During this tragic epoch of Artalanta, the First Souls were the only ones who had not assumed fleshly forms. With great effort, they resided in ethereal light bodies atop Mount Párnathal. They looked upon the plight of the earthbound souls and faced two choices. They could withdraw back to the psychic realm and contend with the Archon whose power grew with every soul forgotten in flesh, or they could commit to saving the terrestrial souls by incarnating themselves and overcoming the wheel of suffering, life, and death. To this course, they did commit. But first, they had to alter the bodily forms of the First and Second Epochs. The misuse of godly soul powers by the original Lanteans had created massive abuses. The ability to project thought-forms and drones had to be curtailed. The waning spirit consciousness had already seen the Lantean third eye disappearing. The lost personal inner connection with spirit had eroded and largely became maintained through the energies of the Touai Stone, the Great Crystal.

So it was that the weight of the material world had proved too much for many of the well-intentioned third wave spirits. They were corrupted, and this corruption led to the destruction of the Second Epoch. Amilius, Sophia, and their soul-grouping were dismayed for they knew they had lost their battle to rescue the souls. And Amilius said to Sophia and the others, "We may only now free the souls through the wheel of birth and death. We must incarnate and toil through this cycle. Within this fate, we must set a pattern for the others to escape the prison of materiality."

So ended the Second Epoch.

THE THIRD EPOCH

This was the fate that had befallen the earthbound souls: they became divided with the greater numbers falling into the dream of materiality and the lesser retaining the spark of divine origin. The first were called the Sons and Daughters of Darkness, or the Sons of Belial; the second, the Sons and Daughters of Light, or the Children of the Law of One. The strife between them would ebb and flow, at times remaining in the political realm, other times bordering on open warfare.

The new Adamic race introduced by Amilius and the other First Souls was now prevalent in this epoch with few remnants of the third root-race still existing. The Adamic humans called the old race fades because of their ability to translocate their bodies. This was to be the last age of Artalanta. Karmic influences that had existed since the beginning of time now brought cardinal souls into a final conflict. Reincarnations of the First Souls and the Sons of Darkness appeared in the land to oppose one another and set the fate of the world to come. The triggering issue was slavery and the condition of those thought-projected creatures who had been created as subservient menial labor. The real conflict was between forces remembering the Unity of the One and those fallen into the darkness of furthering the aims of the self at any cost.

The First Souls incarnated in this age as Ameliea, Desamon, Terselia, Petronien, and Avarna. Amilius the Unfallen appeared in different forms. The Sons of Darkness were Ra-Mennarial, a reincarnation of Belial/Mannemiel, Ta-Revi, Dal-Golia, Al-Presta, An-Klesen, Ter-Madaz, and Val-Andwar.

Paramount to remember for all who walk in flesh is that the visible world is the end product of a mind-construct, and whatsoever is bound and loosed on earth is bound and loosed in heaven for as it is above, so it is below. Souls are mind-visitors to this dimension. From the psychic realm, the soul projects the thought-form of a physical body. *This thought-form is not the soul itself, but an expression of it.* The soul mind that originated the thought-form transfers a portion of its consciousness into this projection but the soul itself remains in the psychic realm. As the soul invests more of its consciousness into the projection, it begins to view itself as a physical body. The soul itself then goes into a somnambular state in the psychic realm, a kind of dream state within which it becomes lost in the belief that it is leading a physical existence.

It is in this dreaming state of unreality that the Archon seeks to keep souls in its sway and exert its influence over the psychic and material realms, for what are these lower realms but illusions or aberrations of higher minds gone astray? Each soul that awakens to its higher origin shakes the foundation of the Archon's throne. Thus, whenever beings of great light appear, the archontic forces flock to them like the killing cells of the body will rush to the site of a wound to destroy a foreign invader. This is the meaning of the saying, "great light attracts great darkness."

In this age the First Souls did appear in positions of power in Adamic race bodies along with the corresponding Sons of Darkness. The forces of Belial had now devolved to completely unwholesome levels. No longer did they use veiled guises to seize power. Their naked goal in this age was to gain full control over the governance of Artalanta and the Touai Stone, now often called the Firestone. They would then proceed to conquer the world, gathering untold slaves and riches unto themselves. These ambitions provoked civil war in Artalanta that spilled over to other continents. Wars now divided humanity, and weapons of great destruction were unleashed upon the land. Of this great struggle, more is told in **The Tomes of Art'alanta** and **The Wars of Gods and Men.** These wars raged for a number of years until the Belials were on the verge of victory.

When it became apparent the darkness would prevail, the First Souls caused the destruction of the Firestone and the remnants of the Lantean Empire. With the dispersal of the Children of the One and their knowledge to other lands, new civilizations would arise along with the hope of a better course for humanity. Being part of The One, souls must eventually return to The One, but they can be lost in the suffering of their own creations. The souls' wanderings were not matters of distance or time, but of mind. Like recalling a deluded man from his deranged sleep, the divine plan of death and rebirth reawakens the souls through incarnations over many lives on earth. These lives alternate with sojourns in other dimensions of consciousness between physical incarnations. So will it continue until the fractured souls become whole again and their awareness is totally aligned with the consciousness of The One.

When the First Souls sacrificed themselves in body as well as spirit, the sadness was sweet as when one would lay down the joy and company of loved ones to rest in final sleep, or go on a far journey shrouded in mist until all things familiar fade out of memory and fall totally to shadow. Such was the path and burden chosen by the First Souls—surrender to mortal awareness, toil and suffer over untold ages, then remember and light the path home for all. Thus did they surrender their godhood as they let themselves be drawn into the circle of life-and-death that is the material world. When the Higher Mind, the soul mind, and the conscious mind are one again, when the souls are as free in the body as they were in spirit, when the spirit again masters every fiber of the flesh, then will the cycle end. If the cycle is not complete, the earth and life upon it will cease to exist by one means or another.

We know of these things, *for we who write these words are the First Souls.* We shall come again yea, we shall know life and death and life again and again. We will see the male subjugate the female, for the racial memory of Sophia's actions shall cause men to fear the wild, creative power of women. We will see wars, division, and suffering. We will see the end of Artalanta and the birth of new civilizations in new lands. In other lives we will be known as Jesus, Magdalene, Peter, Desmonus, and Tezrah; as Annalisa, Roncalli, Avernis, Teresa, and Desmond and many others, but our burden and our destiny remain the same. We commit these things to writing that we may remember, in times and places distant, who we are, the souls who will lead other lives to come.

We must lead all souls to grow, to learn, to purify, and prepare until they remember and awaken to our purpose as human beings. *We must spiritualize the material and bring the experience of material back to spirit so that all the planes of existence align in harmony and all separation dissolves for the illusion it is.* We will have experienced the creation from every vantage point from inside and outside the Will of The One, and this is the *Prothes i' Aterisi*, the ultimate purpose, *the summation of all things.*

Seven Keys of Wisdome

As it is above, so it is below. To understand this is to understand creation.

This world is not what is, but what our minds interpret it to be. This is called illusion.

To overcome illusion is to know that gods created men, now men create gods.

Two gods exist in the world of illusion, one false and apparent, one hidden and true.

Illusion is a veil concealing a window of light that looks out upon infinite reality.

What you bring forth from yourself will make you godlike; what you let lie in ignorance will destroy you.

The fate of humanity is Apotheosis. To understand that man may be reborn as spirit into God, understand first that spirit withdrew from God to become man.

Hearken now to our words that you may remember:

From Light's ever-shining realm forsaken and into shadow fallen. From the face of The One turned, to play thine own creation. O spirit now in form of beasts, which the world may rend and tear, sing not the morose chords of thy doom, for hope is eternal.

The way exists and beckons, and those who led thy great fall now eke thy path homeward to glory scant imagined in thy terror, guilt, and shame. Your backs will bear the earth to heaven, 'fore the throne of The One to present, all memories of a million, million lives which swam the oceans, tasted fruit, and touched the dewy grass.

Fallen yes, but risen again, your fate to be exalted o'er Angels dwelling near The One when heaven's gate you vaulted. And do not rail, O soul in flesh, 'gainst pangs of thy lowly birth. Thou art the hand The One doth use to touch the face of earth.

And when these marvelous things shall come to pass, no one knows. But keep hope alive, O Beings of Light, even in your greatest darkness. The First Souls walk the earth. We came before, we are here now; we will come again to lead the way. We take many forms over many ages. Suffer us and kill us not; know us by the light we bring, know our travails are for you. We will be the first to break the chains —be vigilant for us! Know we walk the earth in light to bear our kindred home.

GLORY BE TO THE ONE AND ALL
THAT WALK IN ITS LIGHT

www.ingramcontent.com/pod-product-compliance
Lightning Source LLC
Chambersburg PA
CBHW020828030726
47496CB00001B/138